24 Hour Telephone Renewals 0845 071 4343
HARINGEY LIBRARIES
THIS BOOK MUST BE RETURNED ON OR BEFORE
THE LAST DATE MARKED BELOW

STROUD GREEN 020 8489 8776

Roddy Doyle is the author... collection of stories, and *Rory & Ita*, a memoir of his parents. He won the Booker Prize in 1993 for *Paddy Clarke Ha Ha Ha*. He lives and works in Dublin.

ALSO BY RODDY DOYLE

Fiction

The Commitments

The Snapper

The Van

Paddy Clarke Ha Ha Ha

The Woman Who Walked Into Doors

A Star Called Henry

Oh, Play That Thing

Paula Spencer

The Deportees

Non-fiction

Rory & Ita

Plays

Brownbread

War

Guess Who's Coming for Dinner

The Woman Who Walked Into Doors

No Messin' With the Monkeys

For Children

The Giggler Treatment

Rover Saves Christmas

The Meanwhile Adventures

RODDY DOYLE

The Dead Republic

Volume Three of
THE LAST ROUNDUP

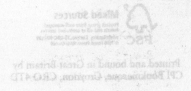

Printed and bound in Great Britain by
CPI Bookmarque, Croydon, CRO 4TD

VINTAGE BOOKS
London

Published by Vintage 2011

2 4 6 8 10 9 7 5 3 1

Copyright © Roddy Doyle 2010

Roddy Doyle has asserted his right under the Copyright, Designs
and Patents Act 1988 to be identified as the author of this work

This book is sold subject to the condition that it shall not,
by way of trade or otherwise, be lent, resold, hired out,
or otherwise circulated without the publisher's prior
consent in any form of binding or cover other than that
in which it is published and without a similar condition,
including this condition, being imposed on the
subsequent purchaser

First published in Great Britain by Jonathan Cape in 2010

Vintage
Random House, 20 Vauxhall Bridge Road,
London SW1V 2SA

www.vintage-books.co.uk

Addresses for companies within The Random House Group Limited
can be found at: www.randomhouse.co.uk/offices.htm

The Random House Group Limited Reg. No. 954009

A CIP catalogue record for this book
is available from the British Library

ISBN 9780099546894

The Random House Group Limited supports The Forest Stewardship
Council (FSC), the leading international forest certification
organisation. All our titles that are printed on Greenpeace approved
FSC certified paper carry the FSC logo. Our paper procurement
policy can be found at www.rbooks.co.uk/environment

Haringey Libraries	
SS	
Askews & Holts	11-May-2011
AF	
	HAOL27/4/2011

This book is dedicated to
Belinda

If you're trapped in the dream of the other, you're fucked.

Gilles Deleuze

PART ONE

1

It looked the same. There was a break in the clouds, and the sea was gone. There was green land down there. A solid-looking cloud got in the way – the plane went right in. It was suddenly colder. I stopped looking for a while and when I looked again it was back down there. The green thing. Ireland.

I'd left in 1922. I was flying back in, in 1951. It was twenty-nine years since I'd left, and five since I'd made up my mind to come back.

The plane dropped a bit more. It shook and rattled. The ground was getting nearer; there were no more clouds. I looked down at my country and felt nothing.

It landed – there were the jumps on the tarmac, and the burst of clapping from passengers in front and behind me, cast at the front, crew at the back. Me, in the middle. I didn't clap. The engine died. The propellers became visible, and stopped. I watched two big-faced lads push the steps towards the plane. I heard the door open, and the rush of real air, and gasps of excitement. There was sea in the air.

My face hit the wind. I went down the steps. Ford was surrounded by the Company and the hangers-on.

—Welcome home, Mister Ford.

—A hundred thousand welcomes.

—You brought the weather with you, Mister Ford.

The red faces on them, wet grins for the Yanks with the heavy pockets. They had him standing on the Pan American steps, with John Wayne on one side, a few steps down, and Barry Fitzgerald above, the three of them waving and smiling. Wayne's wife and brats were beside me, cold and waiting.

I walked.

I heard the voice.

—Where's Henry?

I kept walking. I didn't wait for my bag.

—Where's Henry?

He wanted me standing beside him, with his hand on my shoulder. He was the man who'd brought me home. The man who'd pulled me out of the desert. The last of the rebels, with the last of the rebels.

—Where's Henry?

He'd paid for my suit and for one of my legs. I was his I.R.A. consultant, my wages paid into my hand by Republic Pictures.

I got into the back of a taxi.

—Welcome to Ireland, sir.

—Don't fuckin' talk, I said.—Just drive.

To the nearest bed for rent in Limerick, and I fell face down on top of it. I lay there and felt the country crawl into my lungs. I felt it bubble and turn. I'd been living too long in dry air and deserts. I coughed.

—For fuck sake.

It was an Irish cough – I'd forgotten – the big hack, the rattle. The sheets, the mattress, the wall to my left – they were fat with old breath, and soaking. I coughed again, and heard a voice through several walls.

—Ah, God love you.

I lay on the bed. I felt the rejection and let it slide over me. I felt it rub and pull at my skin.

I slept.

The wooden leg creaked and whispered. I pulled up my trouser leg and looked. It was fatter, expanding – I could see the wood grow as I watched. The wet air was seeping into it. The varnish was already giving up. It was peeling away, and the shin was getting pale and blotched.

I stepped out into rain. It was already adding weight to my suit. It all came back, the slant of its fall, the touch of each drop on my skin, its dance on the black stone around my feet. I fuckin' hated it.

I held up the sagging brim of my fedora and saw the black car crawl out of the lightless rain. I couldn't hear the engine but it was getting slowly nearer. The approaching car and its low hiss over the water brought back pictures that had never gone away.

4

Model Ts prowling the country, men in trenchcoats moving in to kill me. But the Civil War was three decades gone, and it was just a Limerick taxi. I stayed still and waited for it.

—Good morning, sir.

—I'm not American.

—Where d'you want me to take you?

—Roscommon, I said.

—You're joking.

—No.

—Is it not wet enough for you here?

I looked at him.

—Will you take me or won't you?

—We'll need a map.

—We won't, I said.—I know the way.

He still hadn't moved.

—The old homestead, is it?

—No, I told him.—Someone else's. Will you take me?

—Right, he said.—I will. I'm curious.

He was young, half my age.

—But you're the navigator, he said.

—Fair enough, I said.—Let's go.

—Will I be bringing you back?

—No.

—You've no bag or nothing.

—No.

—And you've got the money?

—Yeah.

—Right.

He leaned forward, like he was giving the car the first push. We began to crawl into the rain.

I should have been going to Cong, in County Mayo. I should have been there already. That was why I was in Ireland. I was the I.R.A. consultant, come home to watch the filming of my life. But first I was going to Roscommon, to the house my wife had come from. I had to see the house.

It wasn't there. The house was gone. It had been burnt out when I'd seen it last, just before I'd left Ireland for good. My wife's mother, Old Missis O'Shea, had moved into the long barn, and I'd slept in the kitchen, under a tarpaulin roof. But the wall that

5

had held up the tarpaulin, and the other walls – *all* the walls – were gone. And the barn – it was gone too. I was standing in the right place, but there was nothing. I wasn't there to find anyone; I wasn't that thick. But it felt like another death.

My bearings were exact. The few bits of trees, the yellow furze, even the cows had stayed more or less put, where I'd left them in 1922. But it was as if the house and the outhouses had never been there, or the well, or the low stone walls that had kept the cows out of the bog.

I walked to where the door had been. I knew exactly where I was going, where there'd once been a stone step. I could feel it in my muscles; I could feel the knowledge sing through me.

I stopped. There was no hint that there'd once been a door there, not a thing. I stamped my foot. I felt nothing under the grass. I walked around, to the wall we'd been put against, myself and my new wife, Miss O'Shea, with her cousin Ivan and the other cousin, as we were photographed on our wedding day, in September 1919. I could feel that day's heat and shine as I turned the corner. I knew exactly where Ivan had placed his lads, to guard our normality for that one afternoon in the middle of the war. But there was no wall, no hint of dry clay where the wall had fallen, or hardness in the ground where it had stood. My trousers were wringing. It wasn't raining but it must have been just before I'd paid the taxi driver and got out. I was in the middle of a field, in good wet grass. Not the edge of the field, where there'd once been a wall surrounding the kitchen garden. I could have coped with that, the walls knocked and covered, topsoil thrown over the map of the house. That would have made sense; it had been a long time. But this was just weird. My angles were perfect. I'd walked exactly here, trying to feel running water, with my father's wooden leg held in front of me, and I'd heard her voice – *Two and two?* – and I'd seen her boots and the laces made fat by the muck. But there wasn't even muck here.

I walked back now through the field. My own wooden leg was groaning, protesting, biting into the folded flesh. I could feel no water under me, and the well I'd found that day was gone. But I grabbed the gate and the top rung was there, exactly as cold as it should have been. I'd held that gate before, even if the path from the gate to the house was gone. The gate was real; it felt like sanity.

I walked out onto the road. I left the gate open. They weren't my cows. They were Ivan's cows, probably. If Ivan Reynolds was still around and living. On the drive from Limerick I'd passed dozens of abandoned farmhouses, falling in on themselves, left standing beside the newer, brighter houses. But this was different. There was no new house, and no ruin. Ivan had razed the house, then he'd buried it too deep to be remembered.

I'd paid the taxi driver and sent him back to Limerick. I was alone on the road. The heat was picking up the morning's rainfall. The rest of the day was going to be hot.

They were all dead – my wife, Miss O'Shea, and my children, Saoirse and Rifle. All three were dead. I'd never thought that they were going to come running to find out who the man was, getting out the taxi. I never thought I'd see my wife or daughter looking out the window, over the window box, as I marched up to the door. My son wasn't going to be mending an outhouse roof or gelding a fuckin' greyhound in the yard. They were dead, somewhere. They'd been dead for years.

I'd come to see the wall, maybe put my hand against it, break off a piece of whitewash, put it in my mouth and taste it. But just to see it – that would have been enough. To find its foundation in the grass, to feel it in the sole of my good foot.

Proof.

I had sat in front of the wall. I had held my new wife's hand. I could have started from there and worked my way forward, to the old man standing in front of the fallen wall, or squatting in the grass, picking up pieces of clay. That was me, what I'd come to this place to be. I was the old man. I was only forty-nine, but not many would have believed it. I wasn't sure, myself, what I believed – if I believed. The wall would have helped.

I sat down beside the gate.

I'd cycled every inch of every lane of this county. I'd lobbed bombs from most of the ditches. Bullets had slowed me down, but nothing had ever stopped me. Thirty years ago. *Only* thirty years. It wasn't a lifetime. I looked at my hand, at yellow, knuckled bone. The hand had once held guns and women. I closed my fingers and felt nothing.

I used to be heard. My eyes used to kill.

There was no white wall.

I was once a man called Henry Smart. I was born in Dublin, in 1901, and I fought for the freedom of Ireland. I married a beautiful woman and we tried to save Ireland together. There was a baby, a girl called Saoirse, born when I was hiding. I went into exile when my comrades decided that they needed me dead. My wife was in jail. I went alone to England, then to the United States, with a false passport and a wedding photograph. I hid again, for years. I changed my name and cities. I found my wife again – she found me – in Chicago, when I broke into a house with Louis Armstrong. But I had to run again. My old comrades – a man who might have been called Kellet – had caught up with me. They put me against a wall. But my wife shot the men who were going to shoot me. I ran and, this time, we ran together. I had a family, and it grew. We had a boy we called Séamus Louis, and I called Rifle. We rode the boxcars through the years that became the Great Depression. We never stayed still for long. We were rebels again and we were happy. But I lost them. We were boarding a moving train. Rifle slipped. I caught him, saved him and fell. The train moved on, taking my family and my leg. I recovered. I learned to walk with a wooden leg. But I never found them. I searched for years. I heard stories about them and I followed the stories. The stories stopped, and I stopped searching. I crawled into the desert to die. I lay down and let the sun burn me to nothing. I died. I came back from the dead when Henry Fonda pissed on me. He was acting in a film called *My Darling Clementine*, emptying his bladder between takes. I was brought back to life, and I met John Ford, the man who was directing the film.

This had happened five years before, in 1946.

Ford knew me – I didn't know how. He knew all about me. He knew my scars and how I'd got them. He looked across the darkness, straight at me.

—You're the story, he'd said.

He was going to make the film of my life. That was why I was there now, in Ireland, sitting against the stone wall. I remembered it like quick pain, like the anger that was my real blood. I remembered the decision: I'd go home. I'd go home and tell my story. I was an old man – the bullets and grief had caught up with me – but I felt bright and new. We shook hands. Ford was an old man too; he understood. I looked up at the black-blue sky, at all the dead and wandering stars, and I shouted.

—My name's Henry Smart!

I stood up now. I got up, away from the wall. I knew where I was going, and I knew what I was going to do.

I was going to kill John Ford.

8

2

The sound was a surprise.

—I didn't know you could do that, I said.

—Do what? said Ford.

—The voices, I said.—The music and that.

It was three months after I'd met him. We were out of the desert, and in Los Angeles, somewhere, in a dark room. There was a movie projector clacking behind our heads, and we were watching one of his old ones, a thing called *The Informer*.

—Well Christ, he said.—What was the last picture you saw?

—*The Gaucho*, I told him.

I'd seen it with my daughter in Oak Park, just after her mother had found me.

He was staring at me. He had to shout; the projector was right behind him.

—That was, when? he said.—1927, '28. You like it?

—Yeah.

—See any of my pictures back then?

—I don't know, I said.—Was your man, Douglas Fairbanks, in any of them?

—Nope.

—Then probably not.

—*The Iron Horse*, he said.—I made that picture.

—No.

—You didn't see that one?

—No, I said.—Or if I did I don't remember.

—Fairbanks is dead, he said.—They're called talkies.

—What are?

—Pictures with sound. The worst thing ever happened to the picture business – fucking sound. Watch.

It was supposed to be Dublin, in 1920. A thick-looking lad

9

called Gypo had been turfed out of the Organisation, which I guessed was the I.R.A. I didn't catch the reason why he'd been expelled. Then he informed on his pal, Frankie, for twenty quid. He went on the batter and spent it. And that was it, till they caught him. It was Dublin, but there wasn't much that brought me back. None of the corners or accents were real. And some of it was just ridiculous. There was a bit at the start, a flashback, where Gypo and Frankie, old comrades and pals, stood at a bar, singing and drinking, with rifles on their backs. All through the film the lads in the trenchcoats were afraid that the informer would point them out. But they still brought their rifles when they went out for a few pints. It was full of things that made no sense at all.

But it sucked me in. I watched and I cared. Gypo's girl reminded me of Piano Annie, the woman who'd taken me in after I'd escaped from Richmond Barracks, in 1916. She didn't look like Annie, but there was something that was right. Her voice wasn't Annie's, but she looked at a poster in a window, *£10 to America*, and the eyes, just then, were Annie's. I wanted to go back there and hold her, to send my hand through the projector light. I wouldn't have wasted the money like Gypo, I wanted to tell her. I'd have got her the ticket to America.

The lads in the trenchcoats weren't the real thing, the ones who spoke, but the faces around them in the shadows were good, all the certainty and fear. I liked the fog and the blind man who came tap-tapping out of it. I kept telling Gypo to keep the money in his pocket, to go easy on the juice, to rescue himself and Annie. But I loved the way he threw it around, bought drinks and chips for everyone, and left a trail that, back in Dublin in 1920, would have had him dead in five minutes. I loved his face, and the question he asked that stunned me – *Isn't there a man here who can tell me why I did it?* – the question so real I thought I'd asked it myself. I liked how he smiled and grimaced, and tried desperately not to be stupid. And I liked how he died, how he carried the bullets across the street and into the church, to Frankie's ma – *Frankie, Frankie, your mother forgives me!* For fuck sake. He held out his arms, like your man on the cross, and dropped dead. I knew it was over, but I was hoping he'd get up.

I knew what it was that had shaken me. The music. The songs. *The Rising of the Moon* and *The Minstrel Boy* – they were rippling right through the film. I'd always hated them; I thought I had –

but I was all set to die for Ireland. The film was over, the music gone with it, but I needed a minute to become an old man again.

It was still dark, and darker now that the projector was off. Ford sat, waiting. He'd lit a cigar; I could hear him sucking away. He sat low, well back in his chair. I heard him creak.

—Well? he said.—It's a good one.

—Yeah.

—Hell of a story.

—Yeah.

—You liked it.

—Yeah.

There was silence then. (I'd learn; there'd be a lot of silence.)

—You didn't like it, he said.

—I did, I said.

—No.

I knew the tactics. I'd just seen them done badly in the film. I'd been interrogated before, many times, so I knew what was happening now.

—I don't think so, he said.

I didn't answer.

—What did you like? he said.

—Ah, fuck it, I said.—Most of it. The story and Gypo, and —

He slapped his leg with his hat, like Gypo would have done in the film.

—I got it right, he said.

—Got what right? I asked.

—Well, the time and the place, you fucking rebel.

—No, you didn't.

There was more silence. I could see something white – a handkerchief. He was chewing a corner of it.

He stopped.

—But you liked it? he said.

—Loved it.

—Jesus. Why?

—Well, I said.—I haven't seen a film in years.

He laughed, and the light went on – both exploded at the same time. I could suddenly see him slouched there, his chin inside his collar, and he was laughing. The woman who'd turned on the light sat down on a folding chair behind him. The projector was between me and her, but I saw paper on her lap and she held a fat pen over it. Her name was Meta Sterne.

—Great, he said.—Great. So, where did I get it wrong? With me, Meta?

He didn't turn as he spoke to her. The hankie was gone, back in his pocket.

—With you, Pappy, she said.

—Great. Take it down as he says it.

I was still being interrogated.

—Great, he said, again.

I couldn't see his eyes behind the dark lenses. I wondered how he'd even managed to see the film.

—I got it wrong, he said.

—It's good.

—Fuck good, he said.—Fuck great. I know it's good. I got a goddamn Academy Award for that picture. It's a good picture. But I didn't get it right. You were there, in 1920. Right?

I nodded.

—You were one of those guys.

I nodded.

—You were the leading man.

—I was never a fuckin' informer.

—But you were there. In the fucking thick of it. I'm right?

—Yeah.

—So, what's wrong – what's not accurate about my picture?

—Most of it, I said.

—Get that, Meta? he said.

He lifted his head slightly and spoke to a high corner of the room.

—I got that, she said.

—Most of it, he said.—That's a son of a bitch. Too late now. I made that picture in – when did I make that picture, Meta?

—1935.

—1935. Thank you. So, Henry. Let's approach this differently. What's right about it?

—The trenchcoats.

—Got that, Meta?

—Got it.

—We'll bring in the trenchcoats, he said.—Hundreds of 'em. This is great. What else?

—The doorways.

—They took you back.

—Yeah, I said.

12

—Trenchcoats and doorways. Guys in the doorways, collars up. Great.

He sat up, a bit.

—I'm being serious, Henry, he said.—We got to get this right. What else?

—Well, I said.—That time near the end, when they're all picking matches to see who'll have to shoot Gypo, and your man picks the short match.

—That was good.

—Not at all, I said.—It was shite.

—Get that, Meta? Shite. Do not omit the *e*.

—Don't worry.

—I mean, it was good, I said.—The story. The look on his face. The fear there. It was spot on. Because most of them were amateurs. They were terrified.

—Not you, though.

—Collins had a name for it. When you were going out to put a bullet in someone.

—I knew him, he said.

—He called it a no-come-back job. And that was good, in the film. Your man's face.

—The face, Meta.

—Got that.

—Yeah, he said.—I knew Mick Collins. I was there, you know, in '21. On the boat, when he came back to Dublin with that Treaty. I was on that goddamn boat.

I said nothing to that.

—Picking the matches, he said.—What was wrong with that?

—The choice, I said.—There was never a choice.

—How did it happen?

—It was a fuckin' army. You were given the order, not a box of matches.

—Right.

—I'd be given a name, I said.—On a piece of paper. And that was it, you just did it.

—Shot the guy.

—Yeah.

—Paper, he said.—Slid across a desk, right?

—Sometimes.

I was doing more talking than I'd done in years.

—See there? he said.—What do we need the fucking talkies

13

for? That says everything there. Piece of paper sliding across a dark-wood desk. Upside-down?

—Sometimes.

—A death sentence, he said.—A no-come-back job.

He creaked again. He was sitting up.

—I love it.

He was assembling the story, starting the job. I understood that then.

—What about the paper? he said.—After you read the name. Burn it?

—No.

—What did you do with it?

I knew he'd like this.

—I slid it back across the desk.

—Beautiful, he said.—The eyes. The fingers.

He lifted his glasses. He leaned out of his chair. He looked at me properly. He let me look at him. The eyes were gentle blue, a kind man's eyes, much younger than the surrounding skin and creases. But he couldn't see me. Without the glasses, he was blind.

—I knew it, he said.—Two fucking rebels.

His grin was huge and brown; it threatened to demolish his face.

—We've got a picture here, Henry, he said.—There's one more in the old man. It's a hell of a good story.

That was the start of it. And it went on for years.

3

I had a new leg one day. It just arrived, at the end of my stump; I'd no memory of buying or being given it. I left the room and went right out, to give it a go. The leg was light; the straps were soft and soundless. I could move without hauling it after me, leaning out to drag it ahead, waiting till it landed clean and I could go on and take the next step.

I was the only man on the street. There was life behind the walls and windows but the street itself was deserted. I didn't know where I was. I'd no street or hotel name – I knew I'd just been in some sort of hotel. I'd walked straight out, into white sunlight; I was crossing the same street into shade. I stepped onto the sidewalk, no bother, no real determination needed. I looked out from the shade, back the way I'd just come, into the glare and shimmering air. I saw, far off, where the hotel was, a figure, someone on the street. Male or female – I couldn't tell. But I thought – I hoped – it was a woman. And that hope was a feeling that just opened its eyes and stretched. I kept looking. I liked being in the shade. I liked the feeling on my back, like reassuring hands. The figure got no bigger; no shape or colour was added. I stood there for a while, until the figure had faded to nothing, and no other figure replaced it. I could stand there; I had the strength to do that. The leg was already my own. I knew what I was doing.

Then there was fuck-all.

I was in a car. I was sitting in the back. The driver was talking to me. I saw his eyes in the rear-view mirror. I'd been in this car before. I'd seen the eyes.

—It took a while, he said.

His name was Bill. I knew that.

Another of those long streets. There were no real corners in this place.

He was Ford's driver.

I was in Ford's station wagon.

—Where are we going? I asked.

—Mister Ford's place, said Bill.

—Where's that? I asked.

—It's at Odin Street.

It meant nothing.

—Have I been there before? I asked.

—Think so, said Bill.

—Did you bring me there?

—I think so, he said.—Yes, sir.

His eyes were on me again.

—Three, four days ago, maybe, he said.—It took me a while to find you this time.

—Where was I?

—Where we just came from.

—Where was that?

—Well, Christ – excuse me – that was your new hotel. The Elsinore.

—New hotel, I said.—New?

It had happened before. I'd gone missing, more than once. And this guy finding me; there was a routine. But the curiosity was new. The collapse of proper time was getting on my wick and I didn't like the stupid man it made me.

—That's right, he said.—New. I'd never looked for you in that particular establishment before.

I saw his eyes. He didn't look surprised or spooked.

—Like I said, said Bill.—It took a while to find you. To figure out what happened.

—Tell me.

—Well, he said.—They wouldn't let you back into your hotel. Remember?

—No.

—Far as I can make out, you went out for a stroll.

—Yeah.

—You remember?

—Yeah. When was that?

—Two, three days ago. They weren't sure. You remember coming back?

—No.

—You had a few under your belt, I guess.

16

—No.

I saw him nod.

—They wouldn't let you back in, he said.—The hotel people there.

—Why not?

—Said you didn't look like the type that would be a paying guest in their establishment.

—But I'd already been there.

—That's right.

—The fuckers.

—That's about the size of it, said Bill.

—Did they not see me going out?

—Well, said Bill.—That's Los Angeles, I guess.

I could still see his eyes. He wasn't smiling.

—There's a world of difference between getting in and going out, he said.—Going out is something you can do for yourself. But getting in?

—I'm with you, I said.—It's the same everywhere.

I knew what I was talking about. My life was there to back me up.

The room was dark. The cigar glowed, and faded. I heard him shift the butt across his mouth. But he didn't speak.

I'd been there before. I knew it when Bill the driver brought the station wagon up the drive. And in here – I'd been in this dark room before. This time the smell reminded me of something, a jail cell. The old breath, and the leaks of a man who'd been locked up for a long while.

The cigar was red again, and faded.

I didn't move. He was blind but he'd be watching. He wasn't going to get the better of me.

The cigar was red again. He muttered words too dry and broken to catch.

I heard legs crossed, but not in front – beside me. They weren't Ford's legs.

Meta Sterne's glasses caught a fragment of the light that tore at the edges of the window blinds.

—Good afternoon, she said.—Pappy's glad you're here.

Pappy could go and fuck himself.

—That's great, I said.

17

—There's a chair beside you, she said.

—Grand.

I was rusty. She'd been there all that time. I hadn't even considered the possibility that there might be someone else, besides myself and Ford. Thirty years before I'd have been dead for that, or she'd have been.

A click – she'd turned on the light beside her.

I didn't blink. I sat in front of Ford. His head was hanging. There was white cake on the corners of his lips. He was wearing one of those bathrobes. It was manky, and his bare legs were yellow and shining.

He muttered. His tongue went out, and in.

The Sterne woman held her pen ready.

He'd been that way the last time I'd been there, sitting in the same chair, with the woman to my left. I'd done this before; he'd been drunk for weeks. But her presence beside me had still been a surprise.

I locked my eyes on the black lenses and the eyes behind them. I watched his tongue wetting his lips, again and again. I remembered what I'd told him the last time I'd been there. About my wedding and the photograph and the few guarded hours in the middle of the war. He'd loved it; he'd forgotten he was drunk.

I waited.

Meta Sterne leaned out of her chair. She spoke quietly.

—Pappy says Thank you.

There was no hint of sadness on her face, or malice. She was simply giving me the message.

I stood up and walked out.

There was a hat on the table beside the front door. It was one of the slouch hats Ford liked wearing. It would do till I found something better.

I walked past the station wagon.

—Mister Smart?

It was Bill the driver.

—Mister Smart?

I kept going.

Pappy says Thank you. There was an evil little fucker hiding inside Pappy. But I was grateful to him, and not because he'd hauled me out of the desert. He was making me angry; he was making me think.

18

I was out on the street now. Somewhere. Under palm trees and a high sun.

The anger felt like fingers, straightening me, pulling and prodding me into shape. Ford could find me if he wanted. I wasn't on the payroll.

I didn't even know if that was true. I hadn't thought about it, until now. I had the new leg. I had a room, in a place called the Elsinore. I checked my pockets. I had six paper dollars and some change. I hadn't a clue where I'd got it. I was on a street with no sidewalk, wearing another man's hat.

I sat on the bed. The room was hot. I could feel the hat, a band around my head. I took it off. It was a fedora, brand new. It wasn't pearl-grey. But it was mine. I was sure of it.

I looked around the room. There was no one else there, and nowhere to hide. It was the bed and a chair, a window and the door.

The knock didn't surprise me.

—Mister Smart.

—This is the Elsinore.

—Sure is, he said.—Nice hat.

—Thanks.

—Ready?

—Lead the way.

—Eaten?

—Not in years, I said.

—You don't eat?

—No.

He left it at that.

I felt it as I walked across the empty lobby; I knew where I was. I knew that Bill would have to pull the door, not push.

The station wagon was right outside.

—Well, sir, said Bill.—Mister Ford is looking forward to talking with you.

—Yeah.

He got us moving.

I looked at Bill there behind the wheel and I knew what he was doing. Louis Armstrong had taught me how to drive. *Stop when you see the cotton, Pops.* But I hadn't driven since I'd lost the leg. I didn't know if it could be done with wood. I hadn't really wondered, until now.

19

Now.

I let that sink. I'd map the trip. I'd remember the street names and distances. I'd no idea where I was. It was just more fuckin' palm trees.

—What time is it? I asked.

—Ten-abouts, said Bill.

I felt the car turn. Another avenue of trees.

—Where are we going? I said.

—Studio.

I saw the sign now. I was on Washington Boulevard, in Culver City. This was the start. I'd keep jabbing at that all day, keeping it awake.

—Were you there that time? I asked him.

—That time?

—The time in the desert, when your boss found me.

—No, he said.—No, sir, I wasn't.

—But you heard about it.

—Yes, sir.

—How long ago was that?

—Must be a year.

—Yeah.

—More than a year.

—It's hard to keep track, I said.

—You been busy.

—There you go.

We turned off the street. We stopped for a guy in a uniform, under some kind of an arch. He wasn't a real cop but he had a Webley in his holster. I lifted my fedora so he'd see I wasn't hiding.

The toy cop nodded and we moved again, slowly. We went between two high warehouses. People on the narrow street got out of the way, as if they knew the car. I took it all in. We turned another corner, into thick shade and, suddenly, there wasn't a sinner.

They'd brought me here to shoot me – memory poked me in the back.

I didn't get out of the car.

Bill opened his door.

—You okay, Mister Smart?

I listened for the slap of shoe leather, metal sliding over metal.

—Mister Smart?

—Okay, I said.

I got out of the car. The heat, even in the shade, pulled at my face and shirt.

No one was going to whack me; I was fine. I followed Bill to a black metal door. There were two caged lightbulbs right above, green and red. The green one was lit. Bill grabbed the door and pulled it back. He waited – he wanted me to go in first.

I grabbed him – I got a hold of his jacket. He was my shield and I was tucked in right behind him. I pushed him in ahead, through a black heavy curtain.

I was back in the fuckin' desert.

I let go of Bill and made my way through a loose gang of men in blue uniforms. I stopped. I was standing on sand but there was solid ground beneath it. There was a cactus and tumbleweed, not tumbling, and some scrawny-looking sage and creosote brush. It was a little square of the desert, under a high roof and heavy lights.

A lad with a cap picked up a cactus and moved it a foot to the left. He bent down and hid its base with handfuls of sand. There were men and girls rushing about, over the sand and around it. There were more men way up at the overhead lights. There was coffee somewhere; I could smell it. There were rifles and guns all over the shop, leaning against a flimsy-looking wall, or lying on the floor beyond the sand. But no one there was going to shoot me.

There was another guy in front of me.

—The hat's wrong, he said.

—What?

He looked up at the lights, and at me again.

—Wrong century, my friend, he said.—We did not conquer the West a-wearing felt fedoras. The gangsters are on Stage 11.

His hands came up, and he pushed my chest. I grabbed his wrists.

His life was saved by an accordion. Someone was playing *The Minstrel Boy*.

Some men picked up a horse trough and carried it away. And I saw Ford. The black lenses were staring at me. He was sitting well back in a canvas chair; the bottom half of his face was hidden by one of his knees. His chair was on the sand, and the Sterne woman had a chair beside his. I couldn't see his eyes, but he was sober. He was wearing the slouch hat I'd taken from his house.

I let go of the twerp and walked towards Ford, over the shallow sand. He broke the gaze; he said something – he threw words over his shoulder. The lad I'd seen with the cactus came running from behind a dusty black drape, with another canvas chair. He put it beside Ford's, made sure it sat nicely in the desert. The accordion still played *The Minstrel Boy*. Then it changed, and I was listening to a song that had never been written.

—The bold Henry Smart, said Ford.—Sit down.

I didn't have a choice; I thought I was going to fall over. The accordion played on. And Ford joined in.

—THE HEART OF A FENIAN —
HAD THE BOLD HENRY SMART.

He nodded, once, and it stopped. I saw the accordion player, another small guy sitting on the back of some kind of a wagon, off the sand. He smiled across at me.

Jack Dalton had sung that song, the night we met and he brought me into the Irish Republican Brotherhood. That was in 1917, and five years later I found out that there'd never been a song. (—You wrote it yourself, you fuckin' eejit. It was only ever a couple of lines.)

—Where did you hear that? I asked Ford.

—I told you once, he said.—I was *there*.

—It wasn't a real song, I said.—Only a few lines.

—Great lines, he said.—The heart of a fucking Fenian. We'll be using it. This is going to be your picture.

I nodded at the little desert in front of us.

—This?

—No, he said.—Fuck this. This is just a job of work. A Western. What's it called again, Meta?

—*Fort Apache*.

—*Fort Apache*. That's it. And I'm almost done with it. A few more bits of business and it's someone else's. The wedding.

I remembered. I'd told him about the wedding, and the photograph.

—Tell me a bit about the gal.

—My wife?

—That's the one. The Miss O'Shea.

—She's dead, I said.

—Get past that, he said.

He was looking straight at me. There was no brutality in what he'd said.

22

—She was a looker?

—Yeah.

—Great, he said.—That helps. Hair red?

—Brown.

—Close, he said.—And maybe it won't matter. Brown is red in black and white. What she do?

—She was a teacher.

—The schoolmarm, he said.—Goddamn. There's no escape. He laughed quietly.

—And she was a rebel.

I nodded.

—Handy with a gun.

—Yeah, I said.—She wore —

I stopped. I knew he'd like this. I suddenly knew: I was writing my own story.

—Two bandoleers, I said.—Across her chest.

—Got that, Meta?

—Bandoleers.

—Schoolmarm with a chest, he said.—This helps.

He kicked the sand at his feet. It filled the air, drifted and fell slowly.

—All this shit costs money, he said.—We'll have to deal with the goddamn producers. But they'll know it. Chests and bullets will make 'em a buck. You don't mind me talking this way?

I shrugged.

—No.

I couldn't help it; I'd sunk back in the canvas chair, so my head was level with his.

—She was older than me, I told him.

—She cook?

—We had a bike, I said.

—You ate a fucking bicycle?

—No, I said.—Listen.

But he obeyed a different voice.

—We're ready, Coach.

I didn't see who spoke but Ford stood up.

—We'll talk, he said.—Stick around a while. Write *bicycle*, Meta. And give Henry the story.

He looked at me again.

—Read the story, he said.—See what you think.

He stepped onto the sand, and the lad with the button accordion

23

started playing *Bringing in the Sheaves*. He followed Ford as he walked to the far side of the desert.

A magazine fell into my lap. The *Saturday Evening Post*. It looked old; it was dry around the edges. The cover was a painting of a sailor, some sort of an officer, with white gloves and binoculars. He was a coastguard; the badge was in a bottom corner. He held onto the rail of a boat and there was an iceberg right behind his head.

I looked at Meta Sterne.

—You'll love it, she said.

She looked at her notes.

—Your wife's first name, she said.—I didn't catch it.

—She didn't have one, I told her.

—No?

—No.

Ford shouted.

—Give me the wind!

I heard a motor to my right, and a giant propeller I hadn't noticed turned reluctantly, then became one noise, and sand rushed across more sand, and men with cloths across their faces pushed against the wind, pushed the sand back onto the desert with wide brushes.

I put my weight on the leg; I gripped both arms of the canvas chair and stood up.

There was another man in front of me. He was tall, and thin, in another of those blue uniforms. He had a careful moustache and a tiny piece of beard right under his bottom lip. He wasn't smiling but there was something relaxed and honest about the way he stood. His eyes – I'd seen them before. They reminded me of someone I'd once known.

—How are you? he said.

He had to shout.

—Grand, I shouted back.

—Good, he said.—I'm glad to hear that.

He held out his hand. It took me a while to cop on: he wanted me to shake it. It was a long time since I'd done that. His hand was the size of my own, dry and strong.

He let go.

—We never got a chance to do that the last time we met, he said.

—No.

I heard Ford roar.

—Where's Hank?

—Good to see you looking so well, said the man in front of me. He turned, and walked back across the sand.

—Who's that? I asked Meta Sterne.

—That's Henry Fonda, she said.—Hank.

—He's the fella that found me.

—That's right.

He'd been Wyatt Earp in *My Darling Clementine*. He'd walked off the set for a slash and found me dead in the heart of Monument Valley.

But that wasn't why I knew him.

I looked in the mirror. The *Saturday Evening Post* was on the bed, with the coastguard and his iceberg. *TRIAL BY WATER*. I still hadn't opened it. The window shade was down; the sun was a dull square patch behind me.

I looked back at the old man. I made him move his mouth. I pushed the face closer to the glass. The skin was dry; the old lad's white beard was breaking through. I closed one eye. I could see the skin clearly. The holes, and grey creases.

It was the 7th of November, 1948. I was forty-seven. But the date on the *Saturday Evening Post* was the 11th of February, 1933. That made me thirty-one.

No, it fuckin' didn't. The pages were dry and cracking, like my skin.

I looked at my face again. The 7th of November, 1948. The next day would be the 8th. I'd look in the mirror and I'd see the same face. I'd know who I was looking at.

I stood back and looked again.

The eyes. I knew where I'd seen them before. On Henry Fonda. His eyes had reminded me of someone I once knew. Henry Smart. I went back into the glass. I stared. The eyes were old and worn. But they were still blue. Still killers.

—Did you read that story yet?

—No.

—You can read.

—I know I can read.

We were in a room with a big desk and three chairs. Layers of cigar smoke had been drifting under the ceiling for years. There were pictures, big photographs from films – horses and hats. Henry Fonda and other people I hadn't seen.

It was the 27th of November.

Ford was behind the desk. There was no doubting that. My side looked exactly like his but he was the man behind it, facing the door. There was a third chair, and a man sitting in it. He had a handful of paper, and a pen that was too big for the hand holding it. Ford didn't introduce us and I didn't introduce myself.

Meta Sterne was in another room, behind me. The door was open and I knew she'd be listening and taking her own notes.

—So, said Ford.—Why haven't you read the story?

I stared into the black lenses. I could see blacker eyes behind them.

The story frightened me. But I wasn't going to tell Ford that. I hadn't written it, so it had nothing to do with me. There was an ambush hidden inside that *Saturday Evening Post*. I wasn't going to touch it.

But the meetings were different. I came to his meetings and felt myself being put together.

The other man coughed.

—That a real cough? said Ford.

—Yes.

—I doubt that, said Ford.

He looked away from me.

—But it worked, he said.

He looked back at me.

—Read the story, he said.

I said nothing; I might have nodded.

—I gotta see this bicycle, he said.

I'd been telling him about the bike I'd commandeered and made my own, and me and Miss O'Shea up on it, cycling towards the post office.

—Well, there's me, I said.

—Right.

—And there's her.

—Great.

I opened my arms, to accommodate the woman on the crossbar. The man beside me was scribbling fast.

26

—She'd made a frame for the Thompson gun, I said.—On the handlebars.

—She sing? said Ford.

—On the bike?

—On the bike, on the john. It doesn't matter. Did she ever sing?

I didn't know.

—I think so, I said.

I couldn't remember if Miss O'Shea sang, if she'd ever sung. I couldn't hear her. It was a sudden hole, a pain that had been there all the time. I could see her. For the first time in years. I could see her eyes. I could see her laughing when I was a child sitting at a desk, and years later, when I was a man, three minutes before I fell beneath the crawling train. I was watching my own broken film, and Ford was watching me.

But I couldn't hear her.

My children were there too. Saoirse and Rifle. Their big grins and tears. The frowns and voices, snot and singing.

It was there now – I could hear it, getting louder.

—We're in the money, I said.

—What? said Ford.

—She sang that one, I said. —*We're in the Money*.

Rifle pulled his head back and roared it up to the sky, and Saoirse and Miss O'Shea sang along beside him. I could only hear two voices. But she'd sung as well. I could see her now, striding along, swinging her arms, between my daughter and my son.

—*We're in the Money*, said Ford. —It was one of those Depression tunes, right? '33, '34?

—Round about then, said the man beside me.

Ford's elbows came off the desk. I saw him sit back and sink.

—So, he said eventually.—You're on the bike. Henry?

—Yeah.

—You're on the bike.

His voice was soft now.

—Yeah, I said.

I couldn't hear her voice.

—She sang that one, I said.—*We're in the Money*.

—But not in the war, said Ford.—Not in 1920, back home in Ireland.

—No.

—Later.

—Yeah.

—We'll get there, he said.—You're on the bike. You're flying.

—Yeah.

—Downhill.

I didn't know, but I made it feel like that. I could feel the pedals under my feet – two feet. I could feel the effort in my legs. I could smell her hair and her jacket and the smoke and damp from her mother's house, and the sods she'd slept on the night before.

—She's, what? said Ford.—Gripping the tommy?

—No, I said.—The handlebars.

—As you cycle into town.

I could feel her there. I rested my chin on her shoulder. We were riding into Ballintubber on market day, to rob the post office. She held the handlebars. I held the Thompson gun and pedalled.

—What are you going past? said Ford.—You're going faster than anything else on the road, right?

—A couple of jaunting cars.

—Great.

—And a cart, I said.—With those churns. Going to the creamery. The creamery's important. They burnt it down later – the Black and Tans.

—Later, said Ford.—Night time.

—Yeah.

—They doused it, he said.—Sent it up in flames.

—Because of us, I told him.—They burnt it down because of what we'd done earlier.

—Right, he said.—How was she dressed?

—We shot a cop.

—Irish?

—Yeah, I said.—The police were Irish – the normal ones.

—We'll make him English, said Ford.—Keep it simple.

—We wanted them to do it, I said.

—What?

—Burn the creamery, I said.—The reprisal came after what we'd done. That was the whole point of it. We knew they'd run amok.

—The Black and Tans.

—That's right, I said.

—The Tans were Limeys.

—And Scottish and Welsh.

—We'll stay with English.

28

—We hit them, I said.—And they came back later ai
out on the town.

—You're on the bike, he said.—Dust.

I shrugged.

—There must have been, I suppose. It wasn't paved or tarred
or anything.

—Dirt track.

—Not dirt, I said.—Not like here. There was grass down the
middle.

—Got that? said Ford.

—I grew up in Wyoming, said the guy.—I've seen some grass.

He looked up and smiled.

—They got rebels like Henry in Wyoming? said Ford.—The
Wyoming Republican Army?

—No, said the guy.—But I haven't been back in a long time.
Who knows what's brewing there right now.

—Nothing much, is my guess, said Ford.

I could hear the anger, just behind his teeth. He sank further
into his chair. He was angry with me; I was sure of it. But he
was staring at the man with the pen.

I looked at the pen. DUST! It took up half the page.

Ford stood up. His teeth were fighting. He held his side of the
desk. He was going to upend it. He already had it an inch off his
side of the floor.

Meta Sterne was there now, going past me. She handed Ford
a note.

—What's this?

—Read it, she said.

He read. He looked at her.

—Okay, he said.—Okay.

He sat down. He nodded. She turned and left. Ford still glared
at the other guy.

—Henry, he said.

—What?

—Cheer me up, said Ford.—One rebel to another.

—What? I said.

—You're on the bike.

—Okay.

—With the Miss O'Shea.

—Yeah.

—She'll need a name, he told the other guy.

29

—Alright.

—Mary, said Ford.—Or Kate. I like that one. Something Irish.

He looked at me again.

—Don't worry, he said.—It's your story. We just need to call her something, for the script.

He pushed his hat up off his forehead.

—Now, he said.—Make the old man happy. What's she wearing?

I was wearing my riding britches; she'd made me wear them. She wore her Cumann na mBan uniform.

—I can't remember, I said.

I looked back at him.

He knew what I was doing: I was reclaiming my life. And I knew what he was doing. He was making me up. There were two stories being dragged out of me.

—Does she sing? he said.

I gave him that one.

—Yeah, I said.—She sings.

I lay back on the bed. I enjoyed the certainty and softness of the mattress. I unstrapped the leg. It came off without a whinge. I took it away, and there was nothing there in its place. I'd never felt the ghost of the real leg. And that was grand. There were enough ghosts in my life. I needed a rest.

I leaned over the bed and lowered the leg to the floor. I saw the *Saturday Evening Post*, where I'd thrown it. I saw the coastguard. I poked the cover with a big wooden toe. I lifted it slightly, then more. The paper came with the foot. I swung the foot out and the paper dropped open.

Two flat pages, four tight columns. And the name of the story. *The Quiet Man.*

I didn't read it.

I asked Meta Sterne what she'd written on the piece of paper she'd handed to Ford as he got ready to throw his desk. This was four days later, the 1st of December. I was standing in the little office in front of Ford's.

This was new – or it felt new. Starting a conversation. Being interested. Remembering. One day followed the last one.

—I didn't write anything, she said.

30

—Was it blank?

—No, she said.—It wasn't. He wrote it.

—You gave him his own note.

—Yes, I did.

—For fuck sake.

—Don't lose your temper, she said.

—I'm not, I said.—I'm grand.

—That was the note, she said.—*Don't lose your temper*. And look.

She slid open a desk drawer. There was a large stapler, some envelopes and a stack of small sheets of paper just like the one she'd handed to him.

—How many?

—Ninety-eight, she said.

—You've given him two.

—That's right.

She didn't smile; there was nothing conspiratorial about this. It was amusing but it wasn't ridiculous or mad.

I was learning other things about Ford. He'd been in the war; he'd earned himself medals. Bill, the driver, told me. But I knew nothing about the Second World War; I'd missed it.

—Battle of Midway, said Bill.

I nodded, like I knew the one he meant.

—Filmed the whole thing, said Bill.—Took a bullet and got an Oscar.

—That sounds fair, I said.

—I guess you're right, Mister Smart, he said.

—What's an Oscar? I asked.

—You don't know what an Oscar is?

—No.

I didn't care what an Oscar was. But I didn't want to ask him about the war, to let him know I knew nothing.

(—Watch and listen, Victor. And the answers will come strolling up to you. What do you do?

—Watch and listen.

—Good man.)

Now, I was waiting for Ford. I didn't like his other names. Pappy, Jack, the Old Man. They masked a lot; the old prick hid behind them. He wanted me to call him Seán. But I wouldn't.

—What is this place? I asked.

—Well, said Meta Sterne.—This is Pappy's studio office.

31

—And the other ones?

Outside the door, left and right, was a line of bungalows exactly like it.

—Other directors, she said.

—What about over there?

I pointed at the doors, across good grass and a buckled-looking tree.

—The writers, she said.

—Is that fella in one of them? I asked.—The guy who was here the last time.

—I don't think so, she said.

—Will he be here today?

—I don't think so.

She was spot on there. I never saw him again.

I heard the accordion. Then I saw it. It filled the open door. I saw four fingers pressing buttons, and the other hand flat against the front of the squeezebox. It was like the song was gasping for air, then the accordion popped into the office. Elbows shot out at each side, like ears, and it had legs and a head as well.

Ford was right behind it. Singing.

—OH, THE DAYS OF THE KERRY DANCING —
OH, THE RING OF THE PIPER'S TUNE —

The guy squeezing the box kept going, into Ford's office.

—OH, FOR ONE OF THOSE HOURS OF GLADNESS —
GONE, ALAS, LIKE OUR YOUTH —
TOO SOON —

I'd told him, when he'd asked me what Miss O'Shea sang.

—That one, I'd said.—*The Kerry Dances*.

I didn't know why. If he'd asked me to hum it, I wouldn't have been able to. But she must have sung it, some time. It came out of my mouth; I didn't even make it up.

—OH —
TO THINK OF IT —
OH —
TO DREAM OF IT —
FILLS MY HEART WITH TEARS —
OH, THE DAYS OF THE KERRY DANCING —

He stopped in front of me. He wiped his mouth.

—That the one? he said.

—Yeah, I said.—That's it.

He shouted.

—Okay, Danny.

The playing stopped, and the small man came out of Ford's office.

—We got it, Danny, said Ford.—We got our song.

—I like it, said the small man.

This was Danny Borzage. He was part of the Company, on the set of every film Ford made. There was a song for each of the actors, when they came to work. It was good for morale, Meta Sterne told me. Everyone loved it; the songs made them special. I believed her.

Danny Borzage went sideways out the door.

—We got our song, Meta, said Ford.

—It's a hit.

—It's a big day, Henry, said Ford.—*Agus conas atá tú inniú?**

—What?

—It's fucking Gaelic, he said.

—I know that, I told him.—But I don't know what it means.

—Hear that, Meta? he said.—It's fucking tragic.

He walked into his office, the old man's shuffle. The lenses weren't enough for him. He hid behind his ancientness as well. But he wasn't much older than me.

I sat down in the usual chair. I sat right back.

—What's so important about the song? I asked.

I was taking things in. I was listening to the language.

—A girl walks in here and straight back out, said Ford.—Got that?

I nodded.

—But I miss her, he said.—Because I'm pulling up my sock, down here.

He disappeared under his desk, and came back up.

—I straighten up and I see her ass going out the door. And I ask you, who was that? But you don't know, so I ask you what she looked like. She's, say, thirty-three and it took her thirty-three years to get to the point where she walks in here. I'll have known her some of those years, and you'll say, She had a dimple here on her cheek. And I'll say, Yeah, I know her. I'll know the dimple and I'll have seen the rest of her face getting older while the dimple stayed put and started to look a mite out of place on that face.

* And how are you today?

33

He stopped. I could see him thinking. He took his white handkerchief from a pocket.

—Now, he said.—In our picture, the woman walks in but we don't know her. She's thirty-three but the picture's only four minutes old and two hours is how long it's going to last. This new girl is fictional. Even if she's based on a woman we know. Miss O'Shea. That's a ready-made woman pretending it's her. Say, Maureen O'Hara. You know Maureen?

I shook my head.

—No.

—You'll like Maureen, he said.—She's Irish. Born there, bred there. Big ass. The real spud. Anyways, we need shortcuts to get all those years up there on the silver screen. We need the audience to think it's taken thirty-three years for her to get there, when they see her the first time. Understand?

I nodded.

—Great, said Ford.—That's where the music comes in. You read that story yet?

—*The Quiet Man*, I said.

—Great, he said.—You read it.

—No.

—Why not?

—Fuck this, I said.—It's my story, right?

His answer came out from behind the hankie.

—It's your fucking story.

—So why should I read someone else's fuckin' story? I said.—Who's Maurice Walsh?

That was the name right under the title in the *Saturday Evening Post*.

—He's a good guy, said Ford.

—I never met him, I told him.—And there's nothing in his story that's about me. So why do you want me to read it?

—Who's making this picture? he said.

—It's my fuckin' story.

—Fuck you, he yelled.

Meta Sterne stood up.

—Don't bother your arse, I told her.—She's going to get you a piece of paper with Don't Lose Your Temper on it, I told Ford.

—Bring two of 'em, Meta, he said.—And give one to this thick son of a bitch.

—Well, she said.—Can we take them as read?

—Did you hear that? said Ford.

—What?

—I called you a *thick* son of a bitch.

—So?

—I got it right, he said.—Didn't I? The Irish way for saying *dumb*.

He smiled.

—I *know*, he said.—You don't have to worry. I'll tell it right. You'll see.

I looked back at him. Under the peak of his cap, right in behind the lenses.

—What's so important about the other story?

—Hank Fonda, he said.

—What?

—You're Henry Fonda, he said.

—Oh, yes, said Meta Sterne.

—I'm right, Meta? said Ford.

—You're right, said Meta Sterne.

He stood up. He was gone. I felt his hand on my shoulder minutes after he'd left.

MELODY NASH.

GRANNY NASH.

THE OTHER HENRY – A STAR.

I found a notebook with a pebbled cover in the room, in a drawer that had no handle. There was a pencil in there with it. It was a hotel but the sign on the wall outside had been turned off years before. You got the room and you got the fighting all around you, the radio music and comedy shows, the riding and crying, and the stink of bad soup and ageing.

DOLLY OBLONG.

ALFIE GANDON.

I knew that none of the names I wrote into the notebook would be in the story inside the *Saturday Evening Post*. I took it off the bed and threw it on the floor every night, and it was back on the bed every time I came back into the room. But the room was never cleaned.

I changed dives. All I packed went into my pockets. I went out the back way, through unused kitchens and hollow corridors, and I walked down the street to the next dead hotel. I made them come after me; I kept doing it. I left *The Quiet Man* behind me on the floor. But the fuckin' thing found me every time. And once, it got there before me. It was waiting on the bed when I unlocked the new door and walked in.

I burnt it. Bits of paper broke away from the cover and rose in the heat. I grabbed a piece and opened my hand – a fragment of the coastguard's red scarf. I remembered being on College Green, years before, watching as flames ate the Union Jack. (The wind picked up tiny flakes of charred cloth and scattered them over us.

—You're in right trouble now, yeh Fenian bastards.

I grabbed a piece and expected to be burnt. But I felt no pain. I wondered had I missed it and opened my fist. It was there, a tiny island of red left in the middle of a burnt-black triangle.)

I let go of the burnt paper. I held the magazine over the trash bin until the flames were bigger than what was left and I felt the magazine lose weight. I dropped it into the bin.

That was that; I even washed my hands. I looked at my face in the mirror and saw Henry Smart, not Fonda. I threw water on my face. I lifted the window blind. It was a different room; the sun was well behind the block. I hoisted the window – I felt the weight in my arms – to get rid of the smell of burnt paper. I looked down at an alley, a broken corner of it. I picked up the bin. It was warm, although the fire was out. I brought it to the window. I held it out, upended it and watched the magazine's ashes drop and sail away. I let go of the bin and waited till I heard it hit the alley. I went across to the bed. I picked up the pencil. I wrote, DAVID CLIMANIS, MARIA CLIMANIS. I decided to sleep, lie back and listen to the voices in the other rooms around me. This was the day I set fire to *The Quiet Man* and threw it out the window.

But it was back on the bed the next day. I didn't notice until I remembered what I'd done the day before – it *was* the day before. The coastguard was on the bed, still with his back to the iceberg.

I looked for the bin. There wasn't one. I'd thrown it out the window.

The yellowing paper. The broken, frayed edges – it looked like the same copy.

I didn't touch it.

I opened the window. I looked out at the alley. I couldn't see much; I couldn't see the bin. I looked back at the bed.

The coastguard lifted slightly, held up by the breeze the open window had let in.

Could I trust my own head? I'd been falling in and out of the years, for years; I'd even forgotten who I was. I was only getting the hang of living day to day. I'd already lost track; I didn't know the date.

I'd burnt it.

But it was on the bed. Waiting to be burnt again.

I'd burnt it.

I grabbed it and threw it away. I heard it smack against the wall.

I opened the notebook. DAVID CLIMANIS. MARIA CLIMANIS. They were the names I'd written after I'd dropped the ashes into the alley. There was solid memory, the evidence of my eyes.

But what was the thing lying on the floor against the wall?

I could burn it again. But it would never end. I'd have to do it every day.

I hadn't burnt it, or it was a different copy of the same *Saturday Evening Post*.

I picked it up. It was the same magazine, the exact same weight. I'd held it before; I'd held it the day before. I put it back down on the floor.

It hadn't happened.

I'd wanted it to happen. I'd wanted to burn it. But I hadn't. I breathed deep. I took it in. I accepted it.

I sat on the bed. It was quiet around me. The hoor above wasn't snoring or working. The oul' lad in the next room wasn't dying.

I took off the leg. I lay back.

I saw it.

Right beside me, on the pillow.

Red.

I didn't move, I didn't breathe. I didn't want to blow it away. The coastguard's red scarf, the little bit of paper that I'd caught as it rose in the heat – the day before. It was on the pillow, three inches from my nose.

—The cunt.

He wasn't in any of the beds. There was a woman fast asleep in one of them, in the room I'd guessed would be his. Mary, the wife. She was alone, and lying straight down the middle. She hadn't had company in years.

I was in Ford's house, 6860 Odin Street. It was three in the morning.

He had two kids, he'd told me, but they were grown up and gone. I didn't think there were servants. But it was a strange house. It wasn't huge, but it had been added to; it went off in three different directions.

It was years since I'd been in a house at night. But it was coming back. I'd remembered the address. I'd found a handy window. I'd climbed up to the ledge and got in without grunting. The wife would wake up in the morning and walk across the space where I was standing, and she'd never know that I'd been watching her. I was older and slower, with a leg that announced itself when the wood hit wood. But I still knew what I was doing.

I went back downstairs. I found the room I'd been in before, where Meta Sterne had surprised me. It was hidden away, a den, behind a bigger room. I stayed away from the windows and got to the door of the hidden room. I held the handle tight, like I was going to kill it. The door made no sound as I slowly turned the handle and pushed.

Thousands of books, the desk, old smoke. No bed, and no Ford.

I closed the door.

I went into the other downstairs room. A long table at the centre; I didn't count the chairs. The curtains were open. There was a steep hill rising, right behind the house. I got under the table and sat there.

I looked along the walls.

I hadn't seen him in weeks but I knew he wasn't off making one of the films. I didn't know why I knew but I trusted the knowledge. The smoke in the air was old but it wasn't ancient. He was near me.

There was one hidden room in the house. So there'd be more – there might be. But I could hear nothing new; nothing slid in beside the usual hum. I looked along the wall, where it met the floor. And I saw it. A thin line that might have been nothing. My arse – I'd found the fucker.

I crawled – I didn't grunt – along the length of the table, to the wall. I was sweating. I stood up. I needed the table now, to help me.

I was right in front of where I'd seen the line, in front of a wood-panelled wall. The only wall in the house not covered in pictures from the films. I pushed; it was solid. I shifted quietly, one step nearer the window. I pushed the wood. It gave, very slightly. There was something behind it. I pushed again and sent my hands towards the window, an inch – another. The panel went with them; I was opening a sliding door. I stepped away from the doorway and the block of light that fell into the room.

I could hear him. Asleep and fighting.

The booze came with the light, and the smell of piss and vomit, and his cigar.

I went in.

He was sunk back in an armchair. His eyes were shut. His neck looked broken and useless. His cap had come off; it was stuck between his head and the back of the chair. His bottom half, to his gut, was inside some kind of sleeping bag. One hand held a bottle of bourbon – the label was turned in towards him. There were empties on the floor, on the table beside him.

I took the *Saturday Evening Post* from my pocket. I unfolded it and put it down his sleeping bag.

4

They found me. I recognised Bill, Ford's driver – he was the shadow across my legs – and then I knew.

—How long this time?

—Don't know, Mister Smart.

—How come? I asked.

—Don't know how long you was gone before Mister Ford told me to come get you.

I was sitting on a bench.

It wasn't a bench. It was a low cement wall, at the edge of a dry dirt park.

It was hot.

—How long have you been looking?

—Six days, he said.—Maybe seven.

—That must be a record.

—I don't think this one counts, Mister Smart, he said.

—Why not?

—Well, he said.—Here's what I think. This time you weren't hiding. This time you were lost.

—You might be right, I said.

But he wasn't. Granted, I didn't know where I was or the last time I'd known the day and the date. I felt my chin. There was a beard there; I couldn't get through to the skin. I'd been gone but I hadn't been lost. I'd been on the step, beside my mother. I'd been looking up at the stars, at my dead brother and the other ones. I'd been running barefoot through the streets of Dublin. I'd been running away from Granny Nash.

I opened my shirt. It was filthy, and I stank. I looked down at my chest. I looked through the grey hair for the bruise Granny Nash's finger must have left when she'd poked at me. I couldn't see it. But I could still feel her stab.

I felt Bill's hand under my arm, and I stood up for him.

—Come on, Mister Smart.—Time to go.

—Where?

—Back to your roots.

—Ah, fuckin' hell, I said.—Dublin?

—No, sir. Monument Valley.

I knew where that was. It was where I'd been found the first time, in the dirt, by Henry Fonda.

—I want a wash, I said.—I want a shave.

—Sure.

I'd been running through Dublin. I'd been under the ground, in the rivers and sewers, with my father, and alone. I looked down at the leg and the shoe. They were both dirty but undamaged. There were no water-stains in the leather or on the wood. But my ears were still full of the words trapped under the city.

I pulled my hand over my scalp and across the back of my neck. The skin was rough and baked; I felt it come away on my fingers.

I looked around but there was no sign of my fedora.

—Do I still have the room? I asked.

—I guess so, said Bill.

—The rent?

—Taken care of.

I'd been home. While my beard grew and my head crusted, I'd gone back to Dublin. I'd sat with my mother on the step, and all the steps. I'd crawled all over her; I'd tried to find my place on her lap, in among my brothers and sisters.

I stopped.

Bill waited for me; he didn't pull at my sleeve.

I tried to remember the names of the brothers and sisters. And the dead ones too, the ones who'd gone up to join the first real Henry in the sky. There were girls and boys, one a year, for years – but I couldn't see any. I could only remember one name.

—Victor, I said.

—Mister Smart?

—Victor, I said.—Remember that for me.

—Sure, said Bill.—Just Victor?

—That's it, I said.—If I ask you again, will you tell me?

—Sure.

—Grand.

He drove me back to the dive. He parked right outside.

—I'll wait here, he said.

I wasn't his prisoner.

—What room am I in?

—Thirty-seven.

—Give me half an hour.

—Sure, he said.—Take your time.

The pebbled notebook was still on the table, with the pencil. My hat was on the bed, but there was no *Saturday Evening Post*. I picked up the notebook. I read the names. VICTOR. It was there already.

Gracie.

—I had a sister called Grace, I told Bill.

I was sitting beside him as he took us through the desert, into more serious desert.

—That right? he said.

—Yeah.

—Back home in Ireland.

—Yeah.

—What was she like?

—I don't know, I said.

I'd a feeling Gracie had died before I was born. I seemed to know that – I wasn't sure. But I knew the name, and I'd always known it.

We'd been driving a long time, in and out of darkness and into settled daytime. We'd gone past towns and the signs for towns before I remembered that I'd wanted to know their names. Barstow, Ludlow, and Bagdad. We crossed the Colorado River at Bullhead City. I'd been in that water before. I'd washed myself at the bend I looked down at as Bill drove us past. But I didn't recognise the name, Bullhead.

—New city, said Bill.—Built to support the Davis Dam construction. Got a new name too.

—What was the old one? I asked.

—When I came out this way with Mister Ford before the war, I seem to recall it being called Hardyville.

That name meant nothing either. But I'd been there.

I took the notebook from my jacket pocket. I opened the page I wanted.

—And Victor? said Bill.

—My brother.

—Remember him?

—Yeah, I said.—I do.

I looked at the burnt rubber lines, left where the cars had gone off the road. We kept rolling over them. There were hundreds of the lines, but none of the cars.

—And yourself? I said.

—Brothers and sisters?

—Yeah.

—I don't know, he said.

His eyes were on the road. He was bringing us north now and the colour of the land ahead was changing, becoming red.

—I grew up in an orphanage, he said.

—How was that?

—I knew nothing else.

I printed the name. GRACIE. I closed the notebook.

—What date is it, Bill? I asked.

—December 16th.

—Still 1948?

—Yes.

We kept going; he didn't stop. I could see the red towers from twenty miles away, the buttes and mesas of the valley. The buttes got higher. They must have been a thousand feet, but they got no nearer. It was like I was watching a raw, new place pushing up through old ground. There was still no valley, just the towers. Then the engine's hum changed and we were going down, into Monument Valley, back to where I'd died.

—What's this one called? I asked.

—*She Wore a Yellow Ribbon*, said Ford.

—Any good?

—It's a Western, he said.—They're what I do. It'll be a masterpiece.

He was looking a lot better than the last time I'd seen him, soaked inside his sleeping bag. He sat with his back to the set, staring out at the strange red land and the red sky that joined it, far away.

There was a canvas chair beside him. I sat down.

He pointed.

—Over there, remember?

—Is that where you found me?

—Yep.

I looked at the huge land in front of us; I moved my eyes slowly, from left to right.

—How can you tell it's the place? I asked.—It's all the fuckin' same.

—I guess you didn't read that story before you left it back at my house.

—No, I didn't.

—Okay.

—Where's the town? I said.

—What town?

—There was a town here when you found me, I said.—Where's it gone?

—That was Tombstone, he said.—It got taken down after we were finished with it. My friends, the Navajo here, they used it during the winter months. Kept them warm, I hope. The real Tombstone is south of here, at the other end of the state of Arizona. Matter of fact —

He looked at me.

—The real Tombstone doesn't exist, he said.

—What has *The Kerry Dances* got to do with Miss O'Shea? I said.

—What?

—That stuff you said – I don't remember – about the song letting people think they know her.

—That's right, he said.

—What?

—They see her the first time and they hear it, like it's going around her head, like a breeze. It seems to be her tune. And it is her tune, her theme. She goes off the screen. Walks out of the frame. Five minutes, and they see her again. And this time they expect it. Her tune. And they get it. So they know her. It's all in the notes, her whole life. It's one of the tricks. There's something you've got to understand.

He waited, made sure I was with him.

—I've got this whole valley here —

It was vast, all in front of us. The whole world was this red valley.

—But I end up using the same spot, he said.—I guess four or five times now.

I heard him chew his cigar, shift it from one side of his mouth to the other.

—I come out here to get far away from the goddamn producers, he said.—I love it.

He put his hand on my arm.

—But my point is —

There was no show or big drama; we were alone.

—I want to tell your story, he said.—But I'll have two hours, if I'm lucky. So, I have to condense your story. You're what? Forty-seven?

—I think so.

—Well, there ain't that much film stock. We have to pick and choose. Understand?

I nodded.

—Just like the stories your mother told you when you were a kid, back in Dublin.

I looked at him.

—No? he said.

—No.

—Well, Jesus, you got kids of your own, right? You told them stories.

I nodded.

—All done in a couple of minutes, he said.—Between Once upon a time and Happily ever after. We'll have two hours, max. But it's plenty. If we do it right. We already have the story. But I need the tools. Pictures. Music. The shortcuts. *The Kerry Dances*.

—It wasn't her song.

—We make it her fucking song.

He wasn't angry.

—I'm having to fight, he said.—I'm making this one here —

He nodded back at the fort.

—so Herb Yates – he's the fucking producer – so he'll give me the finance to make ours. I'm the most bankable director in Hollywood, every one a sure-fire hit. I've won fucking Oscars. But our picture's set in Ireland. It's too far way. They don't think it'll make them money.

He sighed.

—We're nearly there, he said.—We'll make it. How'd you meet her?

—School, I said.

—Sat beside each other, he said.—On the first day. It's a bit corny, but it could work.

—No.

45

—Why not? he said.—What?

—She was my teacher, I said.

—That's right, he said.—You told me she was the schoolmarm.

—Yeah.

—But you didn't tell me she was *your* fucking schoolmarm. Jesus. You were, what? Ten, eleven?

—Eight.

—She was what, twenty-five?

I shrugged.

—Well, listen, he said.—Here goes.

He sounded like he was getting ready to sit up. But he didn't.

—We won't get that past the censor, he said.—They just won't allow that.

—I met her again in the GPO, I told him.—Years later.

—There now, he said.—You're thinking like a writer. The place is burning down, right?

—Yeah.

—Bullets in the air.

—Yeah. And —

—Go on, he said.

—The glass dome above us, I said.—It started to melt.

—Great, he said.—Drops of molten glass.

—Yeah.

—See? he said.—This is one of the shortcuts. Love and liberty in ten, fifteen seconds. Miss O'Shea —

—I rode her in the basement on a bed made of stamps.

—I'm right there with you, Henry, he said.—But we won't shoot the fucking.

—Fair enough.

—You understand.

—Yeah, no; you're grand. I understand.

—But what we'll do is, he said,—we shoot two good faces. Whoever's you, probably Hank, and whoever's playing your schoolmarm, probably Maureen or maybe Joanne Dru. You'll like Joanne. She's here, somewhere.

He nodded back, at the fort.

—Two faces, he said.—Two pairs of those Irish eyes. And the eyes are saying it all. And the glass drips and the bullets fly. And cut. You can see that?

—Yeah, I said.

—This is great, he said.

46

I agreed with him; I believed him.

—Great, he said.—Bed of stamps, right?

—Right.

He started singing, quietly.

—OH, THE DAYS OF THE KERRY —

DANCES – What was her name?

—I don't know, I said.

—Meta told me you'd keep saying that.

—I never knew her name.

—We'll have to give her a name.

—No.

—We'll see.

—No.

—We'll fucking see. How do we get that across? The woman has no name.

—She had a name, I said.

—But you don't know it.

I nodded.

—You didn't want to know it.

—That's right.

—Was it a secret agent thing or a better-fuck thing?

—Better-fuck.

—How do we tell that in a picture? Without the guy explaining, putting us to fucking sleep?

—He could put his finger in his ears just when she's going to tell him.

—Your pal, Douglas Fairbanks.

—What about him?

—You ever see him put his fingers in his ears? Or Valentino? Or Hank Fonda?

—Okay.

—I don't think I could even make Duke Wayne stick his fingers in his fucking ears.

He turned his chair to face the set again and he was suddenly surrounded by busy men, and he was up and gone, into the phoney fort. I turned my own chair. I heard the accordion – *Bringing in the Sheaves*. There were horses – I was suddenly hearing them – kicking up the red dust, and men in blue uniforms trying to stay in their saddles. I could see dirt settle and sink into the sweat on the horses and men. There were other men rushing around, off to the sides. And voices, above and through

47

the chaos of the horses. And the louder voice of a man I couldn't see.

—Hold those fucking horses!

There was a dog asleep, in front of the horses' angry feet. I waited for the big voice – *Move that fucking dog!* But it didn't come. And I realised something: the dog was supposed to be there. The dog was part of the story. The dog was a cavalry dog and someone owned the dog and probably loved the dog. Ford had put the dog there, and I thought that was fuckin' brilliant. I laughed. The little touch, the bit extra; the horses and men weren't enough. They were the story but I'd always remember the dog. Because the dog made them human. I knew now why Ford kept digging at me, and I knew I'd come up with my own dogs.

Ford walked up to the lines of horses. He was looking at their feet. He stepped over the dog and kept going. He stopped and patted one of the horses.

—This one, he said.

A lad with a brush and a tin of paint got down on one knee and painted the horse's feet. They suddenly looked blacker, too black, even from where I sat, through a screen of rolling dust. Ford examined the feet.

—Great, he said.

I couldn't see him now. I could see no one who wasn't in uniform. But I heard him.

—This will be picture.

Even the horses were waiting.

—Everybody ready? We are rolling.

It was simple and fast. I heard the accordion under the hooves and voices. The dust was now deliberate.

—AROUND HER NECK —

SHE WORE A YELLOW RIBBON —

The men on the horses were singing, going past me, with the dog trotting along beside them.

—SHE WORE IT IN THE SPRINGTIME —

AND IN THE MONTH OF MAY —

There were other voices. Everyone, in front of the camera and hidden, was singing.

—AND IF YOU ASKED HER —

WHY THE HECK SHE WORE IT —

SHE'D SAY IT'S FOR MY LOVER —

WHO'S IN THE CAVALRY —

The dust blew over me. I could still hear the horses. They hadn't gone far. The filming was over. The hidden men were back, shifting the lights, painting, sweeping, making it all new again. And the dog was still lying there.

Ford walked towards me. I picked up my chair, so we both had our backs to the fort.

—The dog on the ground, I said.

—What about him?

—I saw him going off with the horses.

—Different dog. You killed men, right?

I nodded.

—Yeah.

—Tell me about one of them. Ready, Meta?

She was behind us, sitting on an Indian blanket, under her huge hat. I couldn't see her eyes.

—Ready, she said.

—I shot him in the back of the head, I said.

—Provoked.

—No.

—You had to have a reason for killing the guy.

—I did, I said.—I was told to.

I slept that night in a tepee. There were two of them outside the perimeter fence of the fort. The tepees were real, but just there for background. I crawled into one, with a thin grey blanket I'd found in the back of a truck – it had been folded around a case full of lightbulbs. It was dark now, hours since the last of the film people had gone to their rooms at the trading post, somewhere off on the other side of the dust.

I lay down.

I wasn't alone. I knew it like I used to know it, with the fast, smooth certainty that had often kept me alive.

I saw eyes. I waited for them to shift or blink. They didn't. I held my leg beside me, ready.

I whispered.

—Navajo?

—Yes.

—Irish.

—Okay.

I must have slept.

There was a thin pillar of light coming from the hole above me where the prop-sticks met and leaned into each other. My Navajo pal was gone but there was someone else there, sitting back on his blanket.

—You shot the poor fuck in the head, said Ford.

—He wasn't a poor fuck. He was a cop.

The light missed his canvas fedora by inches. He was sitting right beside it.

—Got his just deserts, right?

—Yeah, I said.—Probably.

He watched me strap the leg on.

—We can do that, he said.—We can show him doing some of the bad things that earn him his bullet. That's doable.

I folded my blanket. I pushed it in under the deerskin wall of the tepee.

—I've an oul' lad's bladder, I said.—I'll be back in a minute.

—Your turn to piss on a dead man.

—If I see one.

—Plenty of 'em out there, he said.

I didn't go far. But Ford was gone when I got back. The day was well on. The sun was up and biting, and the ground looked like the horses had been across and back across it.

—What date is it? I asked a guy who was passing.

I'd seen him before – I remembered – in the little studio desert, carrying a cactus, when they were making *Fort Apache*.

—Date?

—Yeah, I said.

—Well, he said.—I'm not sure. Say, Duke?

A big guy —

I was big – I suddenly remembered that. I pulled back my shoulders and tried not to let the pain get loud.

This big guy was some kind of an officer. His hat was different, his moustache was well looked after. He'd been made up to look older than he was. The grey in his hair wasn't real. I wasn't sure the hair was even real.

—What can I do for you? he said.

He was huge but it looked like he'd been cut in half; a bigger top was balanced on the legs and arse of a smaller man.

—What date is it? asked the cactus guy.

—Ah Jesus, said Duke.—I don't have to know things like that. That's someone else's job.

I watched Duke step over the dog.

—Is that Duke Wayne? I asked.

I remembered the name. Ford had said it, often.

—Sure is, said Cactus.

I watched Wayne go up some steps. There was a swagger but he got up the steps like a lighter, careful man. He'd have done well in a flying column in 1920.

Now I saw someone I did know.

—How's it going, Gypo?

It was the guy I'd seen in *The Informer*. Gypo Nolan. He was older and wider, but it was him. He was hung-over, still half-pissed. He stared at me like he was trying to see through deep water.

—Say, Vic, said Cactus.—What's the date?

—Fuck off now, said Gypo.

He sounded Irish. But he didn't – he was pretending to be Irish. It was the accent he'd had in *The Informer*. He kept going, kicking dust, up the same steps Wayne had danced up. But Gypo tried to smash them as he went. He followed Wayne through an open plank door. There was nothing behind it, only more of the desert.

—What's Gypo's name? I asked.

—Vic, said Cactus.—Victor McLaglen.

—He's not Irish.

—No, said Cactus.—But he thinks he is. Pappy told him he was and Vic believed him. He's English, in actual fact. I think.

I heard the accordion behind me. There was a young-looking skinny lad coming across the dirt and Danny Borzage was walking ahead of him, squeezing out *The Streets of Laredo*. Ford came through the door to the desert and it was as if the accordion had been shot dead and brought back to very quick life; *The Streets of Laredo* became *Bringing in the Sheaves*. Danny went to meet his master coming down the steps. Ford stopped in front of the skinny kid. He pushed the kid's cap up an inch, looked at it and left it like that. The kid's forehead was burnt and his red hair matched it.

—Ready? said Ford.

—Yes, Uncle Jack, said the kid.

—Got your lines?

—Yes.

—That's the idea, said Ford.

The accordion was sucking in and shaping the dust. The red air danced around Ford. The noise, the sudden space in front of the camera, the blast of white light, the concentration on all the wet, dirty faces – they were ready to roll, just waiting for the go-ahead from Ford.

He stopped in front of me.

—It can't be in the head, he said.

—That was how it was.

—Fuck how it was. It's a story, not the Gospel according to fucking Luke.

Then he shouted, straight into my face.

—I've changed my mind!

But he wasn't talking to me. The lights went quickly out, and hidden men appeared from behind walls and fences.

—Come on, said Ford.

He was quick on the feet; I hadn't seen him move like this before. He charged out the front gate of the fort, past my tepee. I couldn't keep up; my leg didn't like the broken ground. Danny still played but the song, the rhythm, was breaking up the further Ford strode from the fort. He was on the small hills now, marching over them. I was passed by the crew and stuntmen, the horses and, now, the trucks pulling generators and huge propellers – the wind machines – and men clinging, hanging from the backs and sides of the trucks. I could feel the dirt, between the wood and the meat of my leg, scouring, cutting.

I knew he'd stopped because the music became music again. Dust settled; so did the noise. I could see Ford, over the heads and hats of the men who'd gone in front of me.

I stopped, and I was angry. But I watched. The resolve, whatever it was I'd pulled together, had blown away. Ford had me where he wanted me, in the middle of red nowhere. I didn't even have an accordion to squeeze and hide behind.

The music stopped.

He didn't shout, but I heard him.

—Here.

Another voice took the word.

—Here!

Ford turned, a half-circle. He pointed.

—And here.

—Here! Let's go!

Ford marched off the chosen hill. This time I waited. I didn't want to move.

—I think Pappy would like a word with you.

Meta Sterne was beside me.

—Are you quite alright? she asked.

She took off her big-brimmed hat, so she could look up at all of me.

—I'll be grand, I told her.

—The heat?

—Yeah.

Ford stopped at the bottom of the hill. The cactus guy unfolded two canvas chairs and put them side by side, backs to the hill. I saw Ford speak to Danny Borzage, and Danny turned and walked towards me. I saw his fingers, and heard that poxy bit of a song, *The Bold Henry Smart*.

And now I moved. I met him halfway, keeping an eye on the ground I'd have to cover. I went straight for him, through him; I made him and his squeezebox get out of my way.

Ford didn't turn. But I saw his fury in the stiffness of his shoulders and neck. As I came up behind him I could see his white handkerchief. He was chewing it, sucking it up like a piece of very white spaghetti. I sat beside him. Most of the hankie was in his mouth. A corner of it, a fat rat's tail, sat on his chin.

Meta Sterne was beside him now and, for a while – a few long seconds – I wasn't there. It was her and him. Her wide hat brim made shade for both of them as she stood beside him, and slowly pulled the handkerchief from his mouth. It began to dry in the heat; I could see the steam lift from it. She picked up her blanket, flicked it open, and was sitting on it before it had properly settled, just beside Ford's feet.

—Ready, Meta? he said.

—All set, she answered.

Her hat darkened the paper on her lap. It was like she was putting her hand into a cave to write.

—Lil, I said.

—What?

The name had just dropped in front of me.

—I had a sister called Lil.

I wasn't really talking to them. I just needed to hear it.

—She in the story? said Ford.

—She was my sister.

53

I searched for the pebbled notebook. Trousers, jacket – I had more pockets than I'd ever owned. I found it, inside my jacket. The words were there, the names. They were all there. I looked at the last one I'd written. GRACIE. I waited till my hand, my arm, stopped shaking. Then I wrote the new name. LIL.

I tried to see her. I tried to see all of them. But I couldn't. I could feel them and – I thought I did – I heard them. Their cries and whines. But no more names dropped for me. GRACIE. LIL. Just the two. There'd been others – lots of them. I could make up a number – ten, eleven, seventeen. Any big number would have been right, and useless. I was the only one who'd lived.

I didn't know that. It only hit me then. Lil and all the crawling brothers and sisters – they'd died because I'd stopped looking at them. I'd taken Victor from the last damp cellar. He'd followed me, less than a year old; he'd pulled at my trousers, all the way. It was just me and Victor then. We'd go back sometimes, and they'd be there, and new ones, on top of my mother, crawling over her, as their weight pushed her slowly into the ooze. I went back one day, and they were gone. They were dead – my mother too. Because I didn't see them.

I was forty-seven. Lil and Gracie, they were younger; they'd be women in their forties. (But Gracie *had* died; memory kept telling me that.) They might have been in Dublin, Liverpool or New York, any of the places I'd lived in. In among the Paddies or out on their own. They might have been married, mothers, grand-mothers. The boys too; they'd been there as well. I didn't even know their names. Just the surname, Smart, and nothing else.

Lil and Gracie. Two names; solid, remembered. Two shapes, two wails.

I waited until dark. Then I found a rock, a slab of a thing that looked like it had been put there by the film people. It was still warm from the day that was now dead. I sat back on it; I lay right down. I could feel the cold air sit hard on my chest. I let myself get used to the cold. I shivered my way into it.

I looked up at the stars. There were so many of them – all that death and none of it hidden. Every dead infant and toddler; they were all up there – the starving, milkless, tortured. There were millions of them, more than millions. They looked down at me and waited.

—I'm sorry.

I tried to see them, the brothers and sisters who were waiting for me. But all I could see was stars.

It was still dark when I gave up. But I was stuck to the slab – I couldn't move. I couldn't feel my hands. I couldn't move my head, or shut my eyes. I had to keep looking. I couldn't budge. I had no choice.

There was one star. It seemed to grow; it got brighter, yellow – then white. And I knew who it was.

Henry.

The other Henry. The first and the real. He glowed proud and angry. He stared at me. He'd pinned me to the slab. He could have killed me – he was going to. A sudden shaft would slice and burn me up to nothing. I'd be a shadow left on the rock. I tried to stare, tried to match him. But it was hopeless.

He came no nearer. He got no brighter. He waited too. Until I understood: they were behind him. The other stars, our brothers and sisters. They were tucked in there, behind the other Henry. He was hiding them from me, behind the white glare, and he was hiding me from them.

The stars faded. I saw them drowned by dawn light that slowly bleached the sky. The shadow of one of the massive buttes cut its way over me. It grabbed my legs and pulled me to its freezing hold. And, as it took my face and eyes, the dawn glare was gone and I saw the other Henry, still up there, still guarding what was his.

—Gracie!

I could yell again. I could move.

—I only want to see her! Lil!

The shadow raced over me, like a gravel current.

—Gracie!

The stars were gone. The sun was already eating at the long shadows.

He was still up there.

It was night when I woke. He was sitting beside me. He'd brought a canvas chair.

—Susie, I said.

—Susie O'Shea?

—No, I said.—I told you about that. I didn't know her fuckin' name.

55

—Who's Susie?

—My sister, I told him—One of my sisters.

The name was breaking up, becoming another. But I got it down – there was enough light – below the others. GRACIE, LIL, SUSIE.

—It's all coming back, he said.

There was no sneer in the words.

—Tell me about the wedding, he said.

I kept looking at the names on the page. But the light was climbing out the hole at the top of the tepee. I'd woken up with other names around me, but I'd only managed to grab the one. I could feel the others; they were still in the air, breaking.

His foot tapped my knee.

—The wedding, he said.

They'd gone. But I'd caught one of them. A real name, not a hidden star.

—We did that, I said.

—What about the dowry?

—What dowry?

—You should have read the fucking story, said Ford.—There's always a dowry.

—What's a dowry?

He leaned out of the chair, and then pulled himself back in. He'd taken a piece of paper from a back pocket. He brought the page right up to his face; he lifted his specs. There was less than an inch between his eyes and the paper.

—Can't make out Meta's scrawl here.

He coughed. He read.

—Dowry. Noun. An amount of property or money brought by a bride to her husband on their marriage. Origin. Middle English.

He stopped reading.

—That clear? he said.

—Yeah.

—Great, he said.—Middle English, my ass. It's an Irish tradition. So, what did she bring?

—Nothing.

—Nothing?

—Just herself.

I could see her now. I could feel her – no, I couldn't – but I could remember her skin, and her heat and breath. I could put her together. I had my words and pictures. I was there – in the tepee, not in Dublin or Roscommon. And I wanted to stay there, in the fuckin' tepee. I wanted to put my life together, to tell my story. But I didn't want to crawl back into it, or even think that I could do that. I wanted to live properly. I wanted to keep going.

He was waiting, looking at me.

—*Macushla*, I said.

—The tune? John McCormack?

—She liked that one.

—Great, he said.

He hummed it a bit, and stopped.

—It'll fit, he said.—It's a song about fucking a corpse, but we can use it.

—Good.

—No dowry?

—No.

—See, we need that tension. The brother won't hand over the dowry. So she won't let the guy fuck her until she gets the dowry. The legs stayed crossed, and these are *legs*. So he fights the brother. Fights the fucker right across the country. Bam, bam. For twenty minutes. Gets the dowry and throws it in the fire.

He sat up.

—She needs the dowry, he said.—We have to see that fight. We have to see her angry, you know, red-haired and fucking furious.

—She was in the I.R.A., for fuck sake. How much more anger do you want?

—Mary Kate, he said.

—Who?

—I told you. This woman has to have a name.

I looked at him. He looked at me.

—Okay, I said.

—Okay?

I nodded, once. I could give the man the name. That way, the story would stay mine.

—Great, he said.

He was happy. He loved the name; I could see that. He was rolling it around.

—Yeah, he said.—Mary Kate. Two names. Enough for two fine women. That's what we call them in Ireland, right? Fine women.

I said nothing.

—We'll still go with the Miss O'Shea thing, he said.—But

57

then he finds out her name is Mary Kate. Right after she becomes Mary Kate Smart and her brother won't hand over the dowry.

—She didn't have a brother, I said.

—What did she have? Her dad's dead – has to be. Who gives her away – at the wedding?

—Her cousin.

—He can be her brother.

—No.

—The man of the house. A big guy. Colludes with the British. Makes sense. We can shoot *him* in the head.

—Hang on a minute, I said, and I took out the notebook.

I wrote the name. IVAN REYNOLDS. Her cousin. I went back some pages. I found it. MISS O'SHEA. I wrote below it. NOT MARY KATE.

He nodded at the notebook.

—You're writing stuff down there.

—Yeah.

—Remember what I said? We got to get it all into two hours, less. We got to take shortcuts.

He held his hand out. He wanted the notebook.

—Go on, he said.—I already ate. I just want to see it.

I let him take it from my hand. He opened it and brought it to his face. He lifted his glasses.

—This is great, he said.

He mumbled. I saw him turning pages.

—Names, he said.—Names. Tell me about Victor.

—My brother.

—Yeah.

—He died.

—He dies, you take up arms. It's good.

—There were dogs, I told him.

—Christ. They ate him?

—No, I said.—No.

I was remembering; I was going further. I could hear the rats, I could feel them slide under my fingers. I made sure I was still in the tepee. Then I told him about the fighting dogs, and the rats myself and Victor had caught to drive the dogs mad before they were set at each other. I told him how we'd boil the babies, how we'd rub the soup onto our hands and arms, to drive their mothers wild and careless, so we could more easily catch them.

58

I told him how we'd bring the rats to the secret places on the edge of the city, where men would bet on the dogs, and how I'd lower my hand deep into the sack and keep it there longer than I needed to as Victor went among the men with a hat held out for their guilt money, and how I'd pull out a frantic rat and hold it over my head, the claws scratching the air just over my scalp, and I'd drop the rat into the pit for the dogs, and I'd make sure that Victor's hands and arms were washed clean of the rats before we'd lie down and sleep, in whatever corner we found and made our own each night.

I finished. The story had its dogs.

He said nothing. He sat still, looking at me. And I knew: Victor wasn't going to make it. Mary Kate would have a brother but Henry Smart wouldn't. Henry had to be a loner. I was a writer then, and I'd killed my second brother. I'd blame Ford later but I knew exactly what was happening.

He stood up.

—This was good, he said.

His hand was on my shoulder.

—You need to get out more, he said.—A wigwam's no place for a rebel. We have to get at this. Because this is going to be my next picture.

He stooped to avoid the deerskin wall. And he was gone. I stayed there. I made sure I did. I wasn't in Dublin, running with Victor, or holding Victor as his last cough faded to nothing – I'd killed him.

That was stupid, sentimental shite – I knew it and I pushed it away.

I got back to work.

I wasn't running from the cattle drovers, or lying on top of Piano Annie —

I picked up the notebook.

I'd tell Ford about Annie. She'd make it into the story.

The moonlight – it was yellow – crawled slowly across the blanket. I looked back through the notebook. Her name wasn't there. I wrote it now. PIANO ANNIE.

There'd be two stories. There'd be Ford's, *The Quiet Man*, or whatever it was going to be. Ford called it *ours*, but he wasn't hiding anything. He'd pick the pieces he wanted and needed.

PIANO ANNIE, ANNIE'S DEAD HUSBAND. The names would be my story. I didn't want Annie on top of me; I couldn't

59

have coped with her. I just wanted to remember Annie, and her
dead husband, and where'd they'd lived and I'd lived, and when
she'd got me the start on the docks, and when I'd met Jack Dalton,
when he'd sung a song he'd composed himself and turned me
back into the Irish rebel that Ford was going to make his own.
Ford was going to love Annie. Piano Annie rubbed her arse against
me and I became the Quiet Man.

—Can't use her.
  —What?
  —Can't use her.
  —Annie?
  —Great name, said Ford.—Put her in the book.
  —What book?
  —Your notebook there, said Ford.—Now *that's* a good idea. Meta?
  —Right here.
  —Mary Kate's brother has a book. Black. The names go into
it. Guys he needs to settle scores with.
  —But —
  —Better still. He has someone else who holds the book for
him. Puts in the names. Puts lines through the names. He barks
the name, the other guy writes it in.
  —Like me, said Meta.
  —Like you, said Ford.
  He turned back to me.
  —Annie's part of the story, I said.
  I'd fight for Annie. (I hadn't fought for Victor.) I could see
Annie in the picture, up on the screen, leaning out over the open-
mouthed young fellas in the front seats.
  —Okay, he said.
  —She's in?
  —No, he said.—She isn't. We can't have two women.
  —Why not?
  —Who's he meet first? Mary Kate or the Piano piece?
  I said it; I gave her the name.
  —Mary Kate, I said.
  —The love of your life. Right?
  I shrugged.
  —I'm right? he said.
  I nodded.

—So Piano Annie comes along, he said.—We forget about Mary Kate?

—No.

—Out of nowhere, you come up with Piano Annie, a woman you've never mentioned before. Right, Meta?

—I think so.

—Right, he said.—I think so too.

—She's one of the reasons I became a rebel.

—You were already the rebel. You were in the post office there – your G.P.O.

—She sent me down to the docks to work and —

—She's some kind of whore, right?

—No.

—No?

I stared at him; I wasn't sure why.

—No.

—So, explain.

—She got me the work on the docks. It'll look great. The cranes, the river.

—I've seen that river. The Liffey, right?

—She got me the job. And that's how I met Jack Dalton.

—We don't need that. He'll meet you anyway.

He stood out of his chair and turned.

—Look, he said.—See over there?

He nodded across to the set, to a horse and cart.

—The girl sitting up there, he said.—That's Joanne Dru. See her?

—I see her.

—She's Annie, said Ford.

—She wouldn't be right for Annie.

—She's Annie. For now. We're looking at her here and we're not complaining. Are we?

—No.

—She's Annie.

—Okay.

—And Maureen is Mary Kate, he said. —Maureen O'Hara. You'll have to meet Maureen. The best-looking woman on this earth. From Dublin too. She's Mary Kate.

—Okay.

—So, there you are, with Mary Kate. In the G.P.O. You're made for each other, it'll be in the eyes. She's the love of your life. You can see that?

—Yeah.

—You can.

—Yeah.

—So, then we have Joanne.

—She wouldn't —

—Some other Joanne. It's not going to make sense.

—It's the way it happened.

—People will hate her.

—They won't.

—Yes, they will.

—So what?

—It's a picture, Henry. You keep forgetting. You're a writer now. You make decisions. Imagine it – picture it. Your Annie comes between you and your wife.

—She wasn't my wife then —

—The love of your life, he said.—Maureen O'Hara. Jesus. And you leave her.

—I didn't —

—Shut the fuck up, goddamn it. It'll never make sense. Because Maureen is the love of your life. That's the story. And very few women can stand beside Maureen. It's a picture, Henry. There are no other loves. You're not Don Juan or Casanova. You're an Irishman. And you're not going to fuck every riverside whore you meet. Not in my picture. In my pictures you fall in love once and you don't fuck at all.

5

The communists in Hungary had jailed a cardinal. There were more communists taking over China. There was a new place called Israel and another new place, the Republic of Ireland.

I grabbed the man's paper. I was sitting in a diner and he was sitting at the other side of my table. The paper was on the table, folded, beside his plate and eggs. I'd been reading it upside-down. *REPUBLIC*, and then *IRELAND*.

I read it the way I ate, my face right over the table and the page. A hand tried to grab it back. I growled.

The Free State had become the Republic. There'd been no civil war, not even a scrap. A man called Costello, the Irish Prime Minister, had just changed the name and then announced the change. There was no picture, just the words. *Republic. Prime Minister. John A. Costello.* I felt nothing. Just a kind of admiration, as if I'd watched a card trick that I couldn't figure out.

The hand grabbed the paper's edge but didn't pull it back.

I sat up.

—All yours, I said.—Fire away.

I was starting to understand again. It was years since I'd felt in charge, since I'd felt the slight swerve that was the act of deciding. I recognised it one morning, when I made up my mind which way I'd have my eggs.

—How d'you want them?

I looked at the waitress's jaw.

—Scrambled, I said.

And I'd felt it, just before I spoke. The swerve, the corner – the exhalation. I was going to eat scrambled eggs, because that was the way I wanted them.

I was in Los Angeles again, but not because I'd been brought

63

there. I'd chosen to be in Los Angeles. Because I needed to stay near Ford.

He'd fucked up.

—You look good, Henry, he said.

He was right. I did look good. I smelt and felt good. I woke up after I slept. I slept when I was tired. I ate when I was hungry, three or four times a day. I walked, turned the occasional corner, and knew exactly where I was. We sat on the step outside his studio office. It was the 19th of April, 1949. I'd been able to name the day of the week every day since the desert. I'd decided to shave and stop being the oul' lad. I'd seen the old rebels; I remembered them. They were still rebels, still dangerous. I'd seen old hard men, too shaky to shoot straight, but still hard. You had it, or you didn't. I reminded myself – I insisted: I had it.

He'd fucked up.

—What am I? I asked Ford now.

—What?

—What am I?

—My job, I said.—What am I?

—You're a goddamn writer, he said.

—Pay me.

—What? he said.—Nobody's paying you?

—No.

I'd found cash in my pockets, most of the times I'd searched in there for some. But no one had ever handed it to me.

—That's fucking outrageous, said Ford.—Meta?

—Just pay me, I said.

—Well, sure, he said.—We'll get you onto the payroll. Sure. But what'll you do with the money?

I bought a suit. I bought another hat. A fedora that wasn't heavy on my head. I bought boots.

—See them?

They were cowboy boots. They were hanging behind the head of the guy I was talking to.

He turned. He put one finger to one boot.

—These?

—Yeah.

—You want these?

—No.

It was dark in the store but the boots were shining.

—I want the leather, I told him.

—That's alligator skin, he said.

—Grand, I said.—Look.

He leaned over his counter, down at my boot. It was old, and timeless. A boot.

—I want a pair like this, I said.—But made out of the alligator.

I pointed back at the boots behind him. They were black and brown, and shining like they'd just been peeled off the beast.

—Can you do that? I asked.

—Nope, he said.—I just sell 'em.

—Who makes them?

—Guy behind this wall here.

—Well, I said.—Can he?

—Well, he said.—I've only seen him make the one kind. And that's cowboy.

He waved a hand.

—That's what we sell.

—Ask him, I said.

He looked at me.

—Alright, he said.—You wait.

I'd told the man to do something and he'd done it. No growl or bribe, just Henry Smart. The charm and danger. They were still in me.

He was back.

—Says No.

Too fast, too soon.

I hopped the counter – I nearly did it. My hand slid on the varnish as I hoisted myself, and I landed hard on my hip before I rolled off the counter, right against him. But I didn't regret it, and I didn't grunt.

—Excuse me.

He got out of my way; he pasted himself to the wall. The hanging boot heels were tapping his head.

—Good man.

I got past him, through the door to the left, and in. To the smell of a perfumed butcher's shop. Hides and skins hung like tobacco leaves, waves of them. They swung as I went under. I could hear the tap of a small hammer on little nails – *tap tap*. I could hear a man whistling his anger. I found him, the *cobbler* – the word came back. But he wasn't making a boot. He had a strip of dark brown leather, flat on the table, and he was chiselling words into it. The letters were coming out a lighter brown, and he'd nearly finished. KEEP OU —

—It's for my boy, he told me.

—Your son?

—That's right.

—For his bedroom door.

—Nope, he said.—For mine.

He tapped at the T.

—Keeps walking in on top of me and his stepmother, he said.— If this don't work she's leaving.

He'd finished the job.

—He's thirty-one years old, he told me.—And know what worries me?

—She'll go with him.

—You're ahead of me, he said.—What can I do for you?

I showed him my boot.

—One of those feet ain't bones.

—That's right, I said.—Can you do me a pair like this one, but alligator?

—Do?

—Make.

—Mister, he said.—I could make you a brand new foreskin with alligator, and it'd be a good'n.

—The boots will do.

—I'll do 'em, he said.—I like the notion.

—Two boots, I said.

—Two's good.

—How long will it take?

—Two days.

—Grand, I said.—I'll come back the day after tomorrow.

—It ain't going to be these next two days, he said.—I'm making two pairs for Alan Ladd. I'll get down to yours when I'm done with Al's.

They were mine in two weeks. The cobbler brought them out from under his bench. He took a cloth from a back pocket and flicked and rubbed the dust from the skin. He put the boots side by side on the bench.

I slid my wooden foot into the alligator. I thought I felt new softness. I stood up straight; I ordered my back to keep going. I looked down and watched my trouser legs slide over the new skin. I counted out the money. I folded the notes, once, and handed them over.

—Did a special job on where the wooden foot'll rest, he said.—
That boot'll outlast the wood.

—The wife still with you?

—Still with me, he said.

—That's good.

—Sure is.

I was gone.

The new man, the old man. The new man and the old man.
I was Henry Smart. I wasn't a ghost or a shadow, a leaking bag
of memories and bitterness. I was living. I was breathing in and
comfortably out.

I looked down at the boots. And so did everyone else. They
looked down, and up, and saw a man worth knowing. I could
keep it up for hours, before I'd have to hide.

—Good boots, said Ford.

—They're only the half of it, I said.

I saw it, seeping from under the lenses: worry. I was becoming
the man he'd been trying to get out of me. I was more than he
could handle.

He smiled.

He'd fucked up. *The Quiet Man* wasn't going to be his next
picture. There'd been a deal. I didn't know the details. I didn't
need them; the details would never make sense. But I did know
there'd been a deal with one of the film companies, RKO Radio
– something like that; the names changed, the faces changed. No
one wanted to make our picture, because no one had wanted to
pay for it. But it would happen, Ford would get the finance – I
liked the word, *finance*; I heard it, and always saw a woman swaying.
He'd get the finance to make *The Quiet Man*, but only if he made
another picture first, something that would roll quickly into profit.
Easy, simple – he'd been doing that since the start of the century.
One more film and we'd be on our way.

He made the picture, a thing called *The Fugitive*. I didn't see
it. (Although I'd been sneaking into the picture houses.) It had
Henry Fonda and some woman with a name that made me sit
up when I heard it, Dolores del Rio. I never saw her, but I knew
she'd be gorgeous. Ford, Fonda, del Rio – tits and horses. It
couldn't go wrong. But it did. The deal was off. There'd be no
money going to Ireland.

He still hadn't told me. No one had told me. But I knew.

—Come on, he said.

He stood up and walked into his office. There were cardboard boxes on the floor and the photographs that had filled the walls – the actors and horses – were gone. The empty squares made quick, sharp sense; he was getting kicked out of the studio.

Then I saw the chair – and the back of the chair.

H. Smart – Writer.

White letters, white words, across the back of the black canvas. I sat down. It was the same chair. It fell into shape exactly as it had before, whenever I'd sat into it. Only the letters were new.

And that was fine. I was H. Smart, the writer on the payroll. We were making a picture. He said nothing about the new letters. I could hear Meta Sterne, behind me. She said nothing either.

But I could feel them on my back.

—The I.R.A., said Ford.

—What about them?

—Forget about them, he said.

The interrogation had resumed. He was whacking me first; then he'd help me up and clean me. I kept my mouth shut.

—I've given those guys money, he said.—The I.R.A. I've donated. I know some guys.

He leaned forward.

—The fight's not over. Right?

The little hard eyes behind the lenses – I thought I saw them, jabbing at me.

—What do you want? I said.

—I want you to forget what you think, he said.—You've been through a lot. Given the chance, would you do it all again? My guess is you'd say No. Am I right?

—I don't know, I said.

He nodded, twice.

—Good, he said.—That's okay.

I wanted to talk now. But it was too early.

—Before, he said,—when you told us about the killings and the no-come-back jobs, you spoke like a man who'd learnt to change his mind. Like we already knew the ending, so there was nothing new to hear. Understand?

I nodded.

—You didn't even sound bitter, he said.

Meta Sterne still hadn't written anything.

—Bitter can be good, he said.—We can see the guy earning his bitterness. It's still a good story. And the girl can suck the

68

bitterness right back out of him. Bitterness in the first or second act is dandy.

He shrugged.

—Bitterness has life, he said.—Believe me.

He was forcing me to fill the hole he was digging. And I wanted to. It was on my back – I was the writer. The words were on my tongue – *but, then, bombs, guns, bullets* – I wanted to save the story. But still, I said nothing.

He sat up, quickly. He slapped his leg.

—There's one more picture in the old man. Right, Meta?

—Oh, yes.

—Yeah. And it won't be a Western, I'm sick of 'em. It'll be this one.

I tried not to sit up with him.

—But here's how it has to be, he said, as he let himself sink back.— We got the love story. We got the love and the bicycle. It's got to be Maureen. She can reach those pedals. You see Maureen yet?

I had.

—No, I said.

I'd seen Maureen O'Hara in Technicolor.

—You will, he said.—You've got to meet Maureen. Henry Smart and Mary Kate. We can write that script today. But it's not the whole story. Right?

I nodded.

I'd seen her in *The Black Swan*. I'd sat in the dark and watched Maureen O'Hara, in among the pirates and the fencing, all the bloodless swashbuckling. She was supposed to be English, but her accent crept through. She was a big, good-looking bird from Dublin. That was all.

—See, look, said Ford.—You're young when you talk about Miss O'Shea. And I want that when you talk about the I.R.A. Before you learnt the bitter truth. Let's get back there, to the beginning. Let's get Meta working here.

I was ready to talk.

—It's your story, Henry, he said.—But we need to see you learn the bitter truth. Before you knew there was a lesson to learn. Let's go. Ready, Meta?

—I'm here, Pappy.

—Alexander, I said.

—Who's that?

—I had a brother called Alexander.

69

—I thought we had all of them, and the sisters. Meta?

—There are some—

—He's another one, I said.—He came into my head.

—Fine. Got him, Meta?

—Got him.

—Alexander, he said.—Alexander the Great. You want time to get the name into your book?

—No, I said.—I'll remember.

I believed that.

—Okay, he said.—What was the first time?

—What time?

—First time you handled a gun.

—I don't remember.

—Then make it up, for Chrissakes.

He didn't tell me. No one did. But I read about it in *Variety*. He was making another picture. He'd told me he was tired of making Westerns. Fair enough, but he was about to make another one. His photographs were already up on another wall, in another studio. Republic Studios – for fuck sake.

Bill, Ford's driver, came looking for me. And I was ready. I knew what I wanted, words on paper, a script. I wanted to see and hear a typewriter.

—Ready, Mister Smart?

I picked up my hat.

—All set, I said.

We drove well out of what I knew of the city. I saw gulls above us. Bill parked the car. I didn't ask him where we were. There was a wooden jetty, built low, just over the water, and a smell of long-dead fish and oil. There were five or six boats – yachts – tied along the jetty, and action on the one that was the biggest and furthest away. There were busy men there, hoisting a sail or some fuckin' thing, five or six men. And one old man, dressed in white, staring at me. The old prick was wearing an admiral's uniform. Rebel, my arse.

I walked.

I didn't like the jetty. It wasn't solid enough for me. But I kept going.

It was some sort of a bay. The water was tame and old, but I could hear the real ocean in the air, lifting and breaking not far off.

70

I could feel it beneath me, the hum of huge waves, the power of the water.

Ford stepped onto the varnished plank that ran from the boat to the jetty.

—Welcome aboard.

He could fuck off; I wasn't going aboard. I stood at my end of the plank.

—We're ready to cast off, said Ford.

—Grand.

—We'll be taking her out for a day or two.

He stepped back, through the small gate on the boat's side, to give me more of the plank. The other men on deck stayed out of his way. I'd seen none of them before.

The boat's name, the *Araner*, was in black paint, on the side. He saw me looking at it.

—My old mother came from the Aran Islands, he said.

—Mine came from Bolton Street, I told him.

It surprised me, stunned me. I hadn't known I knew; the certainty. My mother lived on Bolton Street. My mother had been a child. I could see my mother.

But I was standing on the jetty. Staring at Admiral Nelson, staring back at me.

—I always get down to writing my scripts on the *Araner*, he said.— The sea air. Away from the producers and the goddamn mess.

I felt the sea beneath me, rising and letting me drop. I felt it pull at the leg.

He took another step back, to give me even more room. One of the other men jumped from the boat to the jetty – I felt his weight as he landed. And another jumped. I was ready to fight them. But they both grabbed the ropes that held the *Araner*, and untied them. They waited for the nod or the word, to throw the ropes aboard and jump back on after them. The boat was huge, a big long thing with two masts and a lot of white canvas, a Hooverville of the stuff. The varnished wood grabbed the sun and made the boat shine even bigger. It wasn't a boat; it was a fuckin' ship.

—Come on, he said.—We'll lose the tide.

—No.

—You scared, Henry? he said.—Something we should know about?

—No.

—Someone drown? You drown someone?

71

—No.

—So? he said.—What?

He came down off the boat. He stepped off the plank and stopped in front of me. I could see the eyes behind the lenses. They were weak but they could hold onto malice. I'd seen it before, but there was none of it in there now.

—I didn't tell you about my father's wooden leg, I said.—Did I?

—No, he said.—You didn't.

—He could find water with it, I told him.

—Felt it in the leg, right? A diviner.

—Yeah.

—What about you? You got that gift?

He looked down at mine.

—I don't need it here, I said.—It's fairly fuckin' obvious.

—That's right, he said.—But elsewhere?

I started to shrug.

—Great, he said.—We can use this. We'll start with this. And you can meet Maureen.

I ignored the name.

—No, I said.

—Why not, goddamn it? Tell me about your father's leg. How'd he get it?

He stepped back, nearer the plank. The two men still stood there, holding the ropes.

—He had it when he met my mother, I told him.—I never knew how.

—John Carradine will play him, said Ford.—John'd saw his own leg off for a part like that. Let's get this thing started, come on.

I was tempted now. I could pull the story in my direction.

—No.

—Goddamn it, he said.—This just might be the last time you get to say that fucking word to me.

—Fair enough, I said.

He was chewing the air right in front of my face.

—Jesus Christ! I want to make this fucking picture!

—So, why are you making a different one, called *Rio* fuckin' *Grande*?

—That's none of your fucking business.

The jetty sat on thick wooden stilts that had been hammered deep through the ooze to the solid stone beneath. But it still started to rock, under his canvas shoes.

—I have to make it, he said.—The fucking finance. I told you. I've hidden nothing.

—Grand, I said.—But we've been talking about it for – I don't know – months. Fuckin' years. And I haven't seen a page of a script —

Then I saw another uniform. There was a woman standing on the deck, looking straight into the sun. She was dressed in the gear of Cumann na mBan.

—That's Maureen, said Ford.

—What's she dressed like that for?

—Like what?

He looked over his shoulder.

—That's one of her costumes, he said.—She's trying it on, see if it fits.

He turned now, so he was looking straight at her.

—And I guess it does.

She turned slightly, and saw him. He waved; she waved back. Her smile was huge.

—No famine teeth in that girl's mouth, he said.

He was right. She outshone the varnish. The wind was there now, enough to lift her red hair and put it back in the right place.

—Where'd you get it? I asked him.

—What?

—The uniform.

—It's a costume, he said.—I don't know. Photographs, pictures. It's okay, right?

—Yeah, I said.—It's accurate.

The woman in the Cumann na mBan gear stepped carefully across the deck and began to sink; she went down some steps I couldn't see, into the gut of the *Araner*. She had to look down as she went.

—Does she fit the bill? Ford asked.

—She's lovely, I said.

—She's Miss O'Shea, right?

—No, I said.—She isn't. Be seeing you.

The sea air was doing me good, now that I was walking away from the sea. It was still hot but the breeze was on my back, patting me along. And the smell was good too; it was the soup I'd grown up with.

I was off the wood of the jetty now, happier on the solid ground.

But that wasn't why I hadn't climbed aboard Ford's ship and sailed away.

I'd made my mind up.

—I'm walking, I told Bill the driver.

—It's a stretch.

—I know.

The picture would be made, because I wanted it to be made. It was my story. And I was letting him know; he had to make his mind up too. I wasn't waiting. If he wanted the picture he'd have to come after me. Because I was more than the writer. I was the plot.

I knew it wasn't Bill before I opened the door.

I should have known. I *did* know.

—Where's your uniform? I asked her.

It was Maureen O'Hara standing there. And I wasn't surprised.

—Come in.

—Thank you.

She walked past me. Three good steps and she was in the centre of the room. She didn't look around and she didn't look uneasy.

—He's such a rude man, she said.

This was five days after I'd seen her on the boat.

—Ford? I said.

—Yes, she said.—Mister Ford.

She looked straight at me. She didn't smile.

—I have to warn you, she said.—Turn down Mister Ford and he's a demon.

—Grand.

—But he's right about one thing, she said.—You are the real thing, even at your age. A little Dublin gurrier.

—He sent you.

—He did not.

—Okay.

—I sent myself.

—Grand. Why?

—To meet you, she said.

—Why?

—I wanted to, she said.—And I thought I was going to, on *The Araner*. What part of Dublin are you from?

—All over, I said.—It's been a long time.

She was lovely, gorgeous – the words weren't there to put her together.

—Yourself?

—Ranelagh, she said.—Originally.

I nodded.

—You remember it?

—Yeah, I said.—Sort of.

I'd been in the water under Ranelagh with my father and, later, I'd cycled and crept through Ranelagh, in the crooked line of duty. There'd been safe houses there, tucked in under the leafy respectability. I'd robbed books from good houses in Ranelagh, for my granny; I'd more than likely lifted books from this woman's house, right from off her mother's bedside table.

—I hate that boat, she said.—I'm not a natural sailor at all.

—I saw you in *The Black Swan*, I said.—You looked alright.

—That was all done in the studio, she said.—Nowhere near the sea. The water in the tank is only two feet deep. Did you like *The Black Swan*?

—No.

—Why not?

She stared at me.

—You were good in it, I said.

—Thank you.

The stare became something softer.

—He actually does like to write his scripts on the *Araner*, she said.—Away from everything. And he really was hoping to get working on your script. And —

—What?

—Well, she said.—He drinks. Very heavily. It's disgusting, as a matter of fact. But he only does it between pictures.

—With you?

—No, she said.—How dare you.

Her anger was quick and impressive, and she had it back in her bag before it got properly out.

—He has his cronies, she said.—You'll meet them.

—I've met some.

—Grand.

—I'm not one of them.

—No, she said.—No. He keeps you well away. He has too much respect for you. He wouldn't want you involved.

She didn't look like an actress reciting the lines she'd been told to learn and deliver.

—So anyway, she said.—He sails off for a few days, clears the head after all the shenanigans, and comes back ready for work. He's home tomorrow. Then we're off. *Rio Grande* is the name of the new one. I'm in it.

—I know.

—Good for you.

She wasn't at the end of Ford's hook. There was something about her that made that obvious. It wasn't the beauty, although it was that too. It was the thing that made her so completely beautiful, and familiar – her independence, the strength in her eyes.

—Oh, she said.—There was me saying Mister Ford was rude and I didn't even tell you who I am yet.

—I know who you are.

—You don't, she said.—You know nothing about me. I'm Maureen FitzSimons.

—Grand.

—I'm Maureen FitzSimons of Churchtown Road and you're Henry Smart of all over.

—That's it.

—But we're both from Dublin and that's the main thing.

—Ah now, I said.—You're just being sentimental.

—And that's another thing I want to warn you about, she said.—I left before the war, twelve years ago now, and I'm desperately sentimental about the place. But no one —

She leaned forward, just a bit.

—No one is as sentimental as the Irishman who was never there in the first place.

—Ford.

—Mister Ford, she said.—Yes.

—Why is that a warning? I asked her.

—Well, she said.—He told me you won't read the story.

—*The Quiet Man.*

—Yes, she said.—You should.

—Why should I?

—I think you should know what's happening. I love the story. Mister Ford loves the story. Duke loves it.

No mention of Henry Fonda. I said nothing.

—We all love it, she said.—It's a love story, you know.

76

I nodded.

—And he wants to make it yours, she said.—And that's fine. It's easily done. He told me there was a lady in your life.

I nodded.

—Mary Kate, she said.

And I nodded.

—Was she lovely?

—Yeah, I said.—She was.

—And you know I'm going to play her?

—So he said.

—And how's that?

—Grand.

—I'm a tough Irishwoman.

—You're starting to sound like him, I told her.

She laughed. I could feel it flow past me.

—But, she said, and the laugh left her face,—he'll give in, you know.

—What?

—He'll give in to the sentimentality.

—What d'you mean?

—He wants to blend the two stories. *The Quiet Man* and yours. But *The Quiet Man* will win.

—How do you know this?

—I just do, she said.—I've been in this town long enough to know a thing or two. He's desperate to make it. He has been desperate, oh God – for ever. He asked me years ago. To play her. Long before he ever laid eyes on you.

Something heavy dropped through me. I waited a second before I spoke.

—What's going on?

—Nothing, she said.—Nothing sinister at all. It's just —

She looked away, for the first time.

—I wanted to warn you.

She looked at me again.

—I met a few of those quiet men, she said.—At home. Some of Daddy's friends. Never a word out of them about the things they did and saw.

I said nothing now myself.

—I've been away a long time, she said.—But I love Ireland all the more because of that. I admire the men who did what they had to do. And you were one of them. You and Mary Kate.

Her face was so big then, so enormous and bright – I thought she was going to fall back on the bed.

—That woman, she said.—I really want to play her. *Be* her. I want to fight for Ireland.

She stayed on her feet and looked at me – right into me.

—That's why I'm here, she said.—You have to fight for Mary Kate.

—Why?

—*Your* Mary Kate isn't in *The Quiet Man*, she said.—There's a good woman in it but she's no Mary Kate.

She moved to the window. She stood against the blind.

—Mister Ford is a genius, she said.—And he wants to do right by you. Don't doubt that, please. He'll bring the two stories together. But he'll come under the pressure to drop your side of it. Too violent, too real, too blessed tragic. But I want to be the woman in *your* story. A woman who fights. The love of your life. And that uniform – holy God.

She laughed.

—There's never been a woman like her, she said.—Never, ever. We'd be making bloody history.

—Grand.

—He's on our side, Mister Smart. But you'll have to fight.

She walked to the door.

—Is there any more fight in you, Mister Smart?

The answer came quickly.

—Fuckin' sure.

—That's the spirit.

—That story, I said to Meta Sterne.—In the magazine.

I was standing in Ford's new office, at Republic. I'd changed my mind about waiting for him to come after me, right after I'd watched Maureen FitzSimons's arse walk out my door. I'd walked to Republic, all the way. I was going to march straight in to Ford, flatten the cunt – I'd make him sit down and we'd write the script in one big go.

I'd thought of stopping a cab but I didn't know how it was done. I used to – I knew that; I remembered being in cabs. But I watched the taxis pass and both hands stayed deep in my pockets. I pursed my lips but I'd lost my whistling teeth; they weren't in my head any more. I knew how to get there, the boulevards and corners. But the journey took all day. Shadows were hard to read in this city but I could tell it was late afternoon. The sweat had crusted on my back; the pain was solid in both my legs. But I still meant business. I wiped the dirt from my crocodile boots before I marched up to Ford's door.

—*Saturday Evening Post*? she asked.

—I must have it put it down somewhere, I said.—I never got the chance to finish it.

She slid open a drawer and lifted out the clean-shaven coastguard and his iceberg. She held it out, across the desk.

I took it.

—Thanks.

I pointed at the closed door to Ford's inner office.

—Is he in?

—No, she said.—He isn't.

She smiled. Then she looked back down at her desk.

Other men had crossed him and been shunned for years; stars and stuntmen, any men or women who'd needed his work and love. Maureen FitzSimons had said it: turn down Mister Ford and he was a demon.

Fuck him.

I didn't wait.

I sat on the bed and I read it.

Shawn Kelvin, a blithe young lad of twenty, went to the States to seek his fortune.

It was right; I had been twenty. But what did fuckin' *blithe* mean?

And fifteen years thereafter he returned to his native Kerry, his blitheness sobered and his youth dried to the core, and whether he had made his fortune or whether he had not, no one could be knowing for certain. For he was a quiet man, not given to talking about himself and the things he had done. A quiet man, under middle size —

My arse.

with strong shoulders and deep-set blue eyes below brows slightly darker than his dark hair. That was Shawn Kelvin. One shoulder had a trick of hunching slightly higher than the other —

That was true. I did carry one shoulder higher than the other. But only after I'd been shot a few times and I'd fallen off a train. He'd got the eyes right too, although he could have made more

79

of them. The dates were way off, and the geography. I'd never returned, to Dublin or Kerry, or anywhere else.

But I couldn't be sure. There were holes in my life, holes that I still fell into. I'd been twenty when I left. I remembered leaving, standing on the deck of the night boat to Liverpool. I remembered myself exactly then. I stood in the wind and felt the rise and drop of the boat as it tried to cut across the waves. I'd left, but I'd never gone back.

But I had to keep reading. I couldn't be certain I wasn't in there. *The Quiet Man* was nearly twenty years old; it had been published in 1933. I'd had brothers, sisters I couldn't name. I'd done things I couldn't properly recall. I'd met people I didn't know. Was one of them this man, Maurice Walsh, the chap who'd written the story? Had I spilled my guts to him one night in Chicago or St Louis, or anywhere? I could say No, but only because I couldn't remember.

She was past her first youth into that second one that has no definite ending. She might be thirty – she was no less – but there was not a lad in the countryside would say she was past her prime.

That wasn't too far from Miss O'Shea. She'd been out of her young years when I'd accidentally caught up with her, at her mother's house in Roscommon. She'd been sick but she'd been beautiful, out there in the field, when – *Two and two?* – I'd turned and found her, much older than me but still a young one.

I kept reading, but the more I read the less I had to care.

On himself, and on himself only, lay the task of moulding her into a wife and lover.

I could laugh at the thought of moulding Miss O'Shea. She'd have boxed the fuckin' head off me. I could relax now. I read, because it was a story. And I finished it. I took the pages away from my face. It was dark.

I'd been worried. I'd been terrified that I'd be in there, with Miss O'Shea, my life already told. It was the fear that I wouldn't know it, that I'd read it and not know myself, no matter how often I read, or coaxed and battered my memory.

But it wasn't about me at all. I felt that certainty, and I stretched. I hadn't stretched like that since I was a young fella. The enjoyment of it, the pride – the sheer length of this fine man – I did it and heard no cracks. I could relax; I could rest. I was still intact.

Then there was the fury.

Your man in the story, Shawn Kelvin, a steel-worker and a boxer, came home to Ireland from Pittsburgh. He set up house and married Ellen O'Grady, a fine-looking bird with a tongue and a temper. Her brother, Big Liam – for fuck sake – wanted her out of the house, so he could bring another woman into it, a widow with a few quid. There was a dowry too – the fuckin' dowry that Ford had tried to shove into my life. Kelvin wasn't fussed about the dowry; he was happy enough with the woman. But Ellen was having none of it. She wanted what was hers. There'd have to be a scrap, because Big Liam wouldn't cough up. But Kelvin wouldn't fight Big Liam. Ellen was ashamed of him, and that was the start of the lockout; the legs stayed shut. So Kelvin demanded the money, in front of the wife and Big Liam's farmhands. He told him he could have the sister back; all deals were off. He more or less threw her into the muck in front of Big Liam. So Liam stormed off, and came back with the money. Kelvin took the cash without even looking at it, and made straight for the thresher – whatever the fuck that was, some farming machine with a coal-burning engine. Ellen went ahead of him. She opened the door of the firebox and stepped back to let Kelvin throw the readies into the fire. Big Liam came charging at Kelvin but, no surprises, Kelvin decked him with a few good thumps. Kelvin shook the sweat off his neck, turned to the missis, and they all lived happily ever after.

And John Ford thought he could force my life into that. That the life and even partially remembered times of Henry Smart could be reduced to a fight across a fuckin' farmyard, for a couple of quid and the right to ride a good-looking culchie.

I'd kill him. I'd give him his final scene. I'd batter him through the floorboards.

I went back out to Republic. I walked into a new, hot day.

But Ford wasn't there.

He was never there. And then there was no *there*. He'd moved again, to a different studio. There was a different director in Ford's Republic bungalow. A younger man, with a younger secretary. She'd never heard of Mister Ford, she said. She was a hard girl behind the gorgeousness, or because of it. The message was clear: I'd be found when I was wanted. I could fight when he was ready.

I walked to every studio; there was one at the end of every day-long avenue. Fox, Universal, MGM. I waited at the guarded gates. I climbed high fences after dark. I clubbed a German shepherd to death with the leg and its boot before I could get the thing off properly. I didn't have time, and neither did the dog. I fell on him as his last bark licked my face.

I gasped and laughed. I was living.

I crept under palm trees, behind the lines of studio bungalows. I peered through blinds, for photographs of cowboys and their leading ladies. I found plenty but none of them were Ford's. I jemmied locks and remembered how to get past window glass. I sat at desks and read scripts and script notes. I read in the dark. I looked for Ford in the lines. I resisted temptation; I added no notes of my own. I read all the hard men and war heroes, bad girls and heroines. But Ford wasn't directing any of them.

It stopped mattering, because every night I read. I learnt the codes and shortcuts. I knew what a script looked like now. I knew the layout and the language. I sat in the cave under Cecil B. DeMille's desk and read every script in his Paramount bungalow, using a torch I'd bought on the way.

I heard the key. The door opened.

I walked out, past the woman who'd opened it. I was carrying the waste bin.

—Grand morning, I said, the new janitor, in good suit and fedora.

—Yes, said the woman.

I dumped the rubbish behind a bush and brought the bin back in. I put it back beside her desk. She hadn't moved.

—See you tomorrow, I said.

I broke into Ford's house. I stood in the hall and knew he wasn't there. I looked in the hidden rooms. I looked for scripts – *Rio Grande*, *The Quiet Man* – but I found nothing.

I kept moving. It was the best time I'd lived in years. I was awake and younger. Over walls and fences, through wooden and cast-iron doors. *Singin' in the Rain*, *High Noon*. I read them all; I prowled the sets. I fed the horses and pissed in the water tank. Gene Kelly never knew what rained on him while he was singing. I roamed all night and slept through the days.

—Mister Smart.

I left Bill at the door. He followed me in.

—Ready? he said.

—For what?

—Mister Ford wants to talk with you, said Bill.

—Is that right?

—Yes, said Bill.

—Grand, I said.

—All set? he said.

And I told him.

—No.

He was shocked, then anxious and annoyed.

—You won't come?

—No.

—What do I tell Mister Ford? he said.

—It's up to you.

—You won't meet him?

—I didn't say that.

—Should I come back tomorrow?

—Fair enough.

—Tomorrow morning?

—Grand.

He walked to the door.

—Goodbye, Mister Smart, he said.

—Good luck, I said, and followed him to the door. He stopped and looked back. We could hear a fight going on, a few rooms away. A serious one – things breaking, angry people grunting quietly. Bill looked at me. He was hunting for reassurance, something solid to tell Ford. He shrugged and walked away. I watched him till he turned the corner to the elevator. I heard it start; the cables groaned as they pulled it to him.

I shut the door.

I was wide awake, alert. Trained killer – I never slept. Before, in the old days, I'd woken straight into every escape or confrontation. Nothing had been unexpected.

I was ready. I didn't move.

I couldn't hear anything beyond or beneath the usual. Early, pre-dawn morning – all the expected sounds. The corridor outside was empty. The hotel's clients were fast asleep or dead.

The crack on the head came before the grunt. Hands were on me, heavy on my head and shoulder. The hands had weight but the knocks to my head weren't meant to kill or even hurt me. One hand pressed my face hard into the pillow. Things seemed to squirm and shift inside it, right against my skin and

83

eye. I tried to push against the weight. I got my head up, but I knew it: I was being let move, an inch or two. There was enough power there to push me down, to smother me or even break my neck.

—The leg on, Mister Smart?

My face went back down into the pillow. Harder this time, longer – I was losing.

The leg was beside the bed. The sheet was off me; he'd have seen I wasn't wearing it.

That was what drained everything out of me. The sight of myself, what he must have been looking at. The old man, naked, the meatless arse; the old insect, one of the legs pulled off.

—Ready to get up?

I nodded – I tried to.

—Okay?

I nodded again. I could turn now.

—Sorry, Mister Smart, he said.

I covered myself with the sheet, for his sake and my own.

—Just following orders, Bill, yeah?

—No, he said.—Nobody told me to do this.

—Then what the fuck are you up to?

This time he really hurt me. He swung his open hand from right across the room; the crack filled the place. I hit the floor, between the bed and wall. I'd landed on the wooden leg.

—Put it on, he said.

He watched me carefully; he stayed close. I stopped holding the leg like a club, and I saw his feet shift slightly. But he wasn't giving me room. I wasn't going to get him now.

He watched me strap it on. He watched me get the clothes on. He moved, just enough. He stayed right with me.

—Why? I asked him.

I put my notebook into one of my jacket pockets. I remembered the fedora and I put it on.

—There's just so much a man should have to take, he said.

I was ready to go.

—I don't mind taking the orders, he said.—It suits me fine. Mister Ford is a good man.

I looked at him. Not for the first time, I'd underestimated a man. I'd never fuckin' learn.

—But you, he said.—Calling you Mister Smart don't come natural. Let's go.

84

He didn't touch me. He didn't have to. I moved; I did what he wanted me to. But he stood in my way.

—You're shit, he said.—Like me.

There was no aggression in what he said, and he wasn't trying to provoke me. That was what made it frightening. He believed what he'd said.

—I'm sorry, I said.

—Yeah.

—You have a passport? said Ford.

—No.

—You had one when you came here.

—It wasn't mine, I told him.—And I threw it in the Hudson.

—We'll get you a passport, said Ford.—You American now?

I didn't know.

—I don't want a passport.

It wasn't the same desert. It was the whole world, a vast land all around me, but still, it looked smaller than Monument Valley. The fort looked like the same one, a flimsy thing, picked up and dropped there. The walls were too low to stop anything. In fact, there was only one wall. There was a long line of army tents, brighter versions of the ones I'd seen in the migrant camps during the Depression years. There were trees here, a few of them, that made long vein-like shadows across the dust. We were in Utah, somewhere – the Moab. Somewhere I'd probably been through before.

—I'm just back, he said.

I said nothing.

—From Ireland, he said.—I was looking at some locations.

—The place is full of locations.

I hadn't been going to talk or get sucked in. But the mention of Ireland had been enough; the mouth had opened and the shite spilled out.

—Point is, he said.—I couldn't get there without my passport. Meta?

—Here.

She was under the same big hat.

—Let's get Henry photographed, he said.—And, Jesus. Is he Irish or American?

—I'll look into it, she said.

—He might even be Mexican, said Ford.

—He might have to be, she said.—If we need his passport any time soon.

—We do.

—Leave it with me, she said, but she stayed where she was, sitting just behind us.

(I found out later, I was American. There were no records in Dublin; I'd never existed.)

—So, said Ford.—We're on the home stretch. We have the finance, and Duke and Maureen.

—What about Fonda?

—Too poker-assed to be a convincing Irishman. We just need the script. You ready?

—For what?

—The work.

—I've been hanging around for three years, I told him.

I'd worked it out in the station wagon; it was still an angry shock.

—So you're ready, is my guess.

I stood up. I wasn't doing it again, listening to him force my life into *The Quiet Man*. The chair was the trap. I could feel it, on my back. *Henry Smart – Writer*. The words were glue, already drying. But I'd seen scripts now; I'd read a few. I hadn't written a word and I hadn't seen a line being written.

—Sit down, said Ford.

—No.

—Then listen.

—No, I said.—You listen.

And he did. He lifted his hat and looked at me as I spoke.

I told him I'd read *The Quiet Man* and that there hadn't been a sentence that I'd felt was mine. I told him I wouldn't give him bits of my life to make his picture a bit less of a travesty. I told him more and I think I spoke for hours.

I was ready to walk and I didn't care if I walked deeper in or out of the desert.

—You win, he said.

—What d'you mean?

—We'll make it your way.

I knew enough by now. In the world of Ford there was only one way, and it would never be mine or anyone else's.

He stood up now. There was no tension in his body.

—I'm sorry, he said.

Then he lifted his hand and slapped the words away.

—I understand, he said.—You've been hanging around. But that's not it. I know.

He shrugged.

—But, he said,—we got the finance.

I stepped back.

He was messing again, the salesman, the barker. But he saw me move and he slumped again, became a smaller man than me.

—Listen, he said.—I have the finance. I used *The Quiet Man* to get it. That's the package. And Duke, and Maureen. Now I have it. From that prick, Herb Yates. Took the fucker back to Ireland, showed him the cottage I almost starved in before I took the boat. Believed it myself. We were both crying. But I got it. And now I can do what I want. We'll be in Galway. He'll be in L.A. He'll scream down the phone when he sees the dailies but the dailies he's looking at will be three or four days late. We'll be finished before he knows what he's paid for.

He sat down again.

—So, tell me about the wedding.

I heard the typewriter; I watched it. I spoke, and saw the words being thumped across the page.

Meta Sterne had added a card table to the pile of things she carried everywhere. And the typewriter, a slick, low Underwood – she carried that too. I saw her walk across the parade ground and I remembered Winnie Carney, James Connolly's secretary, as she marched with the Citizen Army in 1916, down Abbey Street to the G.P.O., with her huge typewriter and a Webley revolver nearly as long as her leg.

We turned our backs on every set, and wrote.

I must have looked the part. I stood up as I talked. I paced the Utah desert.

—Where's Collins?

—His office.

—Boring.

—It's guarded.

—Okay.

—He's always ready to run.

—Great.

COLLINS
This might be a no-come-back job, Sean.

SEAN
I'm in.

COLLINS
Good man yourself.

—Where's the office?

—Bachelor's Walk. The quays. Overlooking the river.

—Those little Guinness boats, right? Army tenders skidding, braking. The boots, the Tans – we hear them land and run.

—We got out over the roof, once.

—That's a new scene. Who's on the roof? Heads down. On the hunkers. Collins, Seán.

—And Jack.

—Seán says something.

—I don't remember.

—It's a fucking story. Come on, come on. You're on the roof. In mortal danger. We'll make it night. Searchlights, crisscrossing there. Three good men on the roof, escaping from the might of the fucking Empire. Steep. Loose slates, all that. And you say —

SEAN
Grand night for a walk, lads.

COLLINS
It surely is.

I heard the deep tap of the Underwood keys bounce off the mesa walls and come right back over our hats. I saw the words dig their way down the page. I sat when a clean page was being pulled into the machine, or when Ford was up directing the film going on behind us. I turned the chair and sometimes watched.

Wayne and Maureen were good together; I could see that from where I sat. Wayne, like the last time I'd seen him, was made to look older than he actually was. And she, in the film, was a woman with a grown-up son, a gawky kid who'd enlisted and ended up in his father's regiment. Maureen and Wayne played two people

88

who'd met decades before but they looked at each other like the blood roaring through them was still a surprise.

The local Mormons were objecting, Ford told me. Half the extras were threatening to walk out of the fort.

—I guess that's the catch with that particular creed, he said.— You can have yourself a house full of wives, but you can't want to fuck any of them. Has to be a duty.

—Sounds like Ireland, I said.

—Not the part where that woman comes from.

He was talking about Maureen.

—Dublin's different, I said, although I didn't know if I meant it.

—Dublin, he said.—See, that's a problem.

I should have listened.

—Dublin doesn't really count, he said.—Folks just didn't get *The Informer* back then. Because it was set in the city. It wasn't Irish. Dubliners aren't really Irish. They're scum.

—And proud of it.

My head was full of the typewriter and the block of pages growing up beside it.

Wayne and Maureen FitzSimons stood and chatted as the camera and the lights and miles of cable were lifted and brought around them the long way. I'd seen it quickly this time, I'd understood, how the make-up and dirt could make men like Wayne older or younger. And Maureen looked, would always look, the one big, glorious age. I'd be Seán, and Wayne would be me. They'd make him young. Then they'd make him older; they'd give him the years and the beatings. Then he'd become the old, stiff man getting ready now to stand up out of his writer's chair, so he could punch out more of the lines of his life. Wayne could be all of the men in that life.

—Come on, said Ford.—Let's beat this son of a bitch. We're cycling into town. Seán and Mary Kate. Ready, Meta?

—All set here, Pappy.

—We got the camera on a hill there, we see them coming through the pass. Then they fly past one of the stone high crosses. And some other stuff, on into town. They're on the bike. They laughing?

—No.

—They're enjoying it. A day out.

—They're robbing the fuckin' post office.

—The devil may care. They cycle straight in there. What's he say?

SEAN

Good morning! No messing here and there'll be no one hurt.

MARY KATE

This post office is a relic of the British presence. And is now
closed.

SEAN

So, let's see the cash and God save Ireland!

It's there, in *Rio Grande*, if you look. You can see it in their
eyes. Wayne and Maureen knew there was something more important going on. They were delivering their lines but they were
listening out for the lines coming up off the Underwood. They
were already in *The Quiet Man*.

Maureen stayed away from me. She smiled her smile and played
the Paddyette for Ford, the headstrong Irish girl, when he called her
over to the opened-sided tent that was, that day, our desert office.

—You able to cycle a bicycle, Maureen?

—Of course, I am, Mister Ford, she said, like it was one of the
lines from the pages sitting upside-down beside the typewriter.

He looked at her not looking at the pages.

—Reckon you can handle a gun?

—Oh, yes.

—Just checking, said Ford, and he looked away.

She knew the routine; it was time to get out of the way. One
lifted eyebrow, very slight – that was all she sent me. I didn't
look, but I could hear her humming as she went.

He'd come back off the set, bawling new lines through the dust.
Not lines – he bawled to get the new lines out of me.

—They're in the bar – what's it called?

He was still a good distance away.

—Cohan's, said Meta Sterne.

—That's right, he said.

He was nearly at us.

—Having a drink, a break in the fight.

He stopped.

—And Red Will Danaher says – Meta?

—You know what? she read from the page still in the typewriter's roller.—This is a fight I'd come a long way to see.

—That's right, said Ford.

He looked at me.

—And what does Seán say?

SEAN
I hope you can stick around for the finish.

RED WILL
Don't worry about that.

It was give and take; I went along with it. I'd never been in the fight that Ford said was going to be the longest in screen history. I'd always fought quickly, to kill; rules were fuckin' stupid. But he was right and he kept reminding me: it was a story. I gave him the fight, and I enjoyed it. We dragged the fighting men and the watching population over fields and walls, through rivers. The fight eventually ended, victory to Seán. There was the cheering, the back-slapping. Then screeching brakes and pounding boots – the Black and Tans had arrived. Seán and Mary Kate escaped, hand in hand. They dashed across the field, over the dry-stone wall. Mary Kate got shot in the arm.

They run – they ran. Mary Kate took another bullet. Seán turned, to lift her onto his shoulder. The next bullet caught him —

—In the back, Meta, said Ford.

—Got it.

And Seán ended up on Mary Kate's fine shoulder, carried over another wall, into trees and a fade. It took three days for us to get that far, and another day to get Seán fixed again and on his feet, reunited with Mary Kate, also mended. We doubled back, and rewrote the recuperation. They recovered side by side, in single, sunlit, attic beds, nursed by the wise old widow of a Fenian.

Seán recovered first, and went back to the war. He got himself caught and tortured, and Mary Kate came over the wall of Kilmainham Gaol, to rescue him.

—We'll get some swashbuckling out of Maureen, said Ford.

—We'll give her a sword.

There was the Truce, the Treaty, the Civil War. The men in charge were now coming after Seán. He was on the run, with Mary Kate at first, and then without her. She's about to drop the baby.

—Stop, said Ford.

—What?

—She can't be pregnant.

—Why not? She was.

—Too physical, said Ford.—It means they fucked. The censor won't allow it. Maureen's fans won't want it.

—She had a kid in *Miracle on 34th Street*.

I knew my stuff.

—She *has* the kid. The kid's a ready-made kid, there from the get-go.

—Babies have been born in pictures.

—Tell that to the fucking censor, he said.—It's not the baby. It's the circumstances. They'll say she isn't a fit mother. She's a psychopath, for Chrissake.

—She's not —

—It's un-American.

—You'd know what that fuckin' means, I said.

He stared at me. He stared at me for a long time. He didn't chew the handkerchief. This was the real thing; real, white fury. The typewriter stayed silent and Meta Sterne stayed sitting at it, while the page in the platen baked and the words began to fade under the dirt.

Ford went away and filmed men riding past on horses.

I'd brought the outside world to the desert. He'd come here to avoid it. The Cold War, McCarthy, the House Un-American Activities Committee – where he stood and didn't stand, what was right and what was manly, what he'd said and wouldn't say, what stance would keep him in work. He was there to escape, into the nineteenth century, long before there was an un-America. He was inventing America while he tried to get away from it. He was defining the place, and I'd reminded him of that. There was America, and there was un-America. He was building America, with John Wayne and the desert. He was giving Americans the history they wanted.

He came back, much later in the day. His shadow arrived and cut across me for five, six deep breaths before the man himself sat down and spoke.

—All set there, Meta?

—All set.

—She can be pregnant later, he said.—When the Limeys are gone.

I didn't hesitate.

—Alright.

—So, he said.—Where are we?

—They're on the run.

—That's right, he said.—They're on the run. In a ditch.

92

—Okay.

—Together.

—Yeah.

—They're caught – he's caught.

—She's caught.

—No. Back. Neither of them is caught. He was caught already, right? She rescued him.

—That was the British, I told him.

—That's right, he said.—Now it's the Civil War. The Irish arrest him.

—Yeah.

—Tricky, he said.—Back, back. They're on the lam. They're running from the Irish, the other side, but still Irish. Jack, his old buddy. Why is he doing that?

—They want him dead.

—Why?

I wanted to tell him that he already knew the answer. Some of his old friends were un-American now, although they'd been grand and upright a couple of years before. It had happened in Ireland too; you could be too Irish or not Irish enough, depending on which side of the table you sat at.

—Why? he said again.—Why do they want to put a bullet in him? He's a good guy.

—They're the bad guys.

—No, he said.—They're Irish. They can't be bad. Outright bad, Limey bad. So, why does Jack want Seán dead?

—He loves Mary Kate.

—That could work, he said.—You're thinking now. He pushes the piece of paper across the desk.

Meta Sterne was typing again.

—Seán picks it up. And his name is on it.

JACK
Don't worry, Seaneen. She won't be a widow for long.

SEAN
That's the game, is it?

—No, said Ford.—Rip that out, Meta.

The sound of the paper being torn from the platen was a sudden relief.

—He gets out before the Civil War, said Ford.

—No.

—You're right, he said.—We can't avoid the story just because it's tricky. We need to see that piece of paper. I love that piece of paper.

—The Treaty, I said.

—Fuck the Treaty.

—My name on the paper had nothing to do with the Treaty.

—Go on.

—They had it in for me before the Treaty.

—Why?

—I was awkward. I'd be dangerous after they got what they wanted.

—Go on, said Ford.

Meta Sterne wasn't typing.

—I was fighting for more than they were ready to settle for. I was—

—A traitor.

—No, I fuckin' wasn't.

—That's the story. That's how Jack nails you. He frames you. You have to run. *We* know you're innocent. The people watching the picture know it. But Collins doesn't know it. They'll be shouting up at him. *He didn't do it!* Who's Collins, by the way? Chuck Heston. Or that kid, Bill Holden. We can put him up on a fucking box. That's for later, I'm distracting myself. Heston's too straight to be Irish.

He stood up and joined me.

—The folks who paid for their seats will know Jack has it in for Seán. They'll even be kind of sympathetic. Because it's Maureen he loves, not some broad. She's Ireland. He loves Ireland. They both love Ireland.

He stopped. He looked at me.

—Ready, Meta?

—All set, Pappy.

COLLINS
All those good men?

JACK
He gave their names to the British, Mick.

Mary Kate was arrested – Jack's doing. He arranged for her to be put into Kilmainham, to keep her safe, out of Seán's reach.

—He can't put her in Kilmainham, I said.—The British still have it.

—Fuck, he said.—Fuck, fuck. She isn't arrested.

—She is.

—She isn't.

—She is, I said.—The handover.

—What?

—We see the handover of power as she's being brought in the yard at Kilmainham – where Connolly was shot, earlier.

—Page 27, said Meta Sterne.

—The Union Jack comes down, the tricolour goes up, as they drag her past the flagpole.

—It works.

—It's an Irish jail by the time they get her to the door.

—Great, he said.—Let's get her there.

We wrote through a dust storm. I didn't see it coming, blackening the day. The walls of the tent were unfurled and tied by men I didn't know because they'd tied cloths across their faces, while myself and Ford shouted at each other. We had to shout; the wind was solid noise. We were alone, the three of us. The world outside was gone. The canvas walls stopped flapping; the weight of the dirt held them tight. We were lit now, yellow, by a storm lamp that swayed and rocked, then stopped. I couldn't hear the typewriter, but I could see it.

SEAN
Look for me!

MARY KATE
Yes!

SEAN
Look for me!

MARY KATE
I will!

He's spotted under the jail wall by a patrol. He runs. They fire. His feet on the cobbles – the bullets chip the walls. He escapes. He lifts a manhole cover, and drops. The lid is rattling, back on the hole, by the time they turn the corner. He's on the mail boat —

—New scene, Meta.

He's looking back at the lights of the city. He's aware that other men are watching —

—Stop right there, he said.

He didn't have to shout. The wind outside was dead.

—What?

—The boat, he said.

—What about it?

—That's our ending.

—What about the rest of it?

—Different story. Different country. We're done. The boat – it's perfect.

He was right. I saw that ending. I could feel it too now.

—Except, said Ford.—Let's go back to the jail.

—Why?

—He rescues her. They're on the boat together.

—No.

—Yes.

—There's already been a rescue. She rescued him.

—That's right, he said.—We ditch it?

There were two breakouts. She'd saved him, and now he goes over the wall and grabs her. They stand on the boat, together, and look back at the fading city.

They had to dig us out.

—Everybody okay in there?

Ford answered.

—We're okay.

I heard the shovels sliding into sand. I heard the labour, the grunts, the laughter. I saw the stain, sunlight, on one of the walls. It grew, and quickly spread.

—Stand back, said a voice, outside.

A knife burst through the canvas. I heard the rip, then saw the sudden, gaping hole, and white, blinding light.

I climbed out after Meta Sterne. She carried the typewriter, and the pages. The finished script, *The Quiet Man*.

6

Nothing had changed. The same roads and rocks. The leg was heavy. The ground was hard and uncertain. But I didn't care; I didn't tire. I knew where I was going.

There was copper in the air as I hauled myself out of Roscommon, into Mayo. I could taste it, like an old wet penny on my tongue. The farmers were spraying the spuds.

—The blight's back, an oul' lad told me.

He was fixing a wall, messing with the stones.

—The potato blight?

—That's the man, he said.

—Like the Famine?

—There was never anything but famine or the promise of it in this part of the world.

He held a flat stone in both big hands, as if he was thinking of taking a bite from it.

—Are the potatoes rotting?

—Maybe not, he said.—It's met its match in the spray.

He coughed till his face was wet. He stopped looking at the stone and stared around his yellow cataracts, at me.

—A Yank using his feet, he said.—That's a rare enough sight.

—I'm not a Yank, I told him.

—You've been across, though.

—Yeah.

He nodded.

—See now. And did you meet my brother there, did you?

—I don't think so.

—Willie O'Connor.

—No.

—He's a twin, he said.—I'm the other one. He'd look like me now, I'm betting.

—Never met him.

—In Pittsburgh, Pennsylvania.

—No.

He placed the stone on the wall. He stood back and tried to see it.

—I never liked him, he said.—Never. If he broke one of his legs this day, I'd feel fuck-all.

I'd had enough.

—I'll be seeing you, I said.—Good luck.

—A lamey leg like that would be hard going, he said.

—It's not too bad, I told him.

—You get used to it.

—That's it.

—Like nearly everything, he said.—Except walls made of bastard stone. I've been making the stone walls all my life, since I was smaller than the stones. Right back to the bad times before the English left us alone to make our own bad times. I'm still the best at it around here and further. But still and all I hate the bastard stone walls. They never stay built.

I was back, in among the walls and shite, loving and fuckin' hating it. I tried to fight it, the creeping, sugary thought: I was home. I wouldn't let myself feel or fall for it. I wasn't John Ford. I'd left a kip and I was back in a kip.

But it was my kip.

Bollix to that; nowhere was mine. That was the honesty. That had been the big lesson, the real words on the piece of paper that Jack Dalton had slid to me across his desk.

—Good luck, I said.

I headed west along the broken road, till I got to an untidy crossroads where I'd once ambushed a tender full of Black and Tans with Miss O'Shea. I didn't stop for old times' sake. I chose my next road and walked. The sun was at my left shoulder now, throwing my shadow over the wall and across the land. I could still hear the oul' lad.

—You're on your way to Cong.

I couldn't help it.

—That's right, I shouted over my shoulder.

—It's full of Yanks, he said.—You'll be at home there. With your boots.

—Go and fuck yourself.

—I did that once, I heard him.—When I was a younger man than I am now.

I didn't look back.

—It was like riding the bastard stone.

I kept my eyes on the ground.

—Full of big Yanks, it is. Making a fillum.

I was going the right way.

The first explosion was no surprise; it came with the geography.

I dived for the ditch. But I missed it by a yard and a half and had to crawl the rest of the way. I worked as I slithered. What direction had it come from? Who was it meant for? What war had I walked into and what fuckin' year was it?

I waited for gunfire, or the next explosion. But they didn't follow. Or the rubble and screams, or flying grit. The birds were still at it, like they hadn't heard what I'd just heard and felt. It wasn't a good ditch for hiding in. It was too shallow, and the wind from the Atlantic had shaved the top off anything green that wanted to grow. But I stayed where I was.

I was catching up; I hadn't walked into a war. The silence made no sense.

The film – the explosion had been for the camera.

But there were no bombs in the script. There should have been. There *had* been bombs, but they'd gone when I read the final draft.

Unless they were back in.

The second bomb was exactly like the first. It was muffled, careful, intending no harm or heart attacks. It was a Hollywood explosion.

I got out of the ditch and followed it.

I wasn't supposed to have seen the final draft.

The plane – my first time on one, and my last – charged down the Idlewild runway. I was pulled back into the seat. I felt the thing lift, and the end of the shuddering. There was nothing else I could do now; I was flying to Ireland.

It was at my feet. I'd felt it as the plane was climbing, and now I looked. A script. I parked my alligators on top of it.

—Anybody got my script back there?

It was Wingate Smith, Ford's brother-in-law and assistant director, a noisy, bullying fucker. I shut my eyes while, in front and behind me, hands and legs stretched under the seats.

—Nope.

—No.

—Nothing down here.

I kept my eyes shut. There was no one sitting beside me. No one ever sat beside me, except Ford. The empty seat was paid for, in case Ford wanted it. I was his I.R.A. consultant, and he might need me as the plane brought us closer to Ireland.

I waited until Smith was sitting down again. I hadn't looked, but I'd heard him as he'd pushed his way down the aisle, looking under the seats and ordering others to do it. I'd dropped a blanket over my legs and feet. I knew he'd leave me alone.

I let things settle.

I opened my eyes. There was a good-looking face very close to mine.

—How are you there, Mister Smart?

—I'm grand.

She was one of the hostesses. Her fingers were on my shoulder, gently digging.

I'd been asleep.

—Where am I?

—Nowhere yet, she said.

I remembered the script under my feet.

—I'll tell Mister Ford you're still with us, she said.

—Grand, I said.—You do that.

She was gone, back behind the curtain to the dearer seats. I waited a while, to see if the good news that I wasn't dead would bring Ford through the curtain for a chat. But nothing happened. He left me alone.

I picked it up. And I read it.

I knew I wasn't hiding from the Black and Tans but I crept along, behind the walls and the small bits of hedge.

It made no sense. I was moving away from where I knew Cong was, on the strip of land between Lough Corrib and Lough Mask. This was the place Ford had chosen to make the picture; it was going to be his Irish Monument Valley. I could see the town's two church steeples but they were smaller now than they'd been when the first explosion had sent me diving. The afternoon had travelled on; it was early evening and the sun was hanging over the sea. It was three or four hours to darkness but the light had changed.

I heard trucks on the road and I decided not to hide. I got over the wall and waited. A truck came over the bit of a hill. I heard its engine calm down, and it crawled nearer. It was open-backed and filthy, driven by a thick-looking lad sitting under a peaked cap. He nodded as he passed, without looking at me. I watched the muck trickle out both sides of the tailgate onto the muck already on the road. The next truck was the same, and the third one had an extra lad sitting on a heap of stones at the back. He nodded too, as the truck crept past. And he winked.

—Watching the work, he shouted.

—That's it, I shouted.

—Good man.

—What're yis up to?

—The electric, he shouted.

—What?

—We're bringing the electric to Cong.

I walked beside him. I was an old man with a wooden leg, but it was no big effort to keep up.

—What about the explosions? I asked.

—The fuckin' stones.

He nodded back, the way the truck had come.

—Blowing them all to fuck. They're making big holes for the pylons. Foreign lads with the gelignite. As if we didn't know a thing or two about that stuff ourselves. But that's the way. They bring in foreigners to handle the gelignite and we get to hold the fuckin' shovels.

I let him go.

There was no need to go looking at the new holes or the shiny pylons. So I pointed myself at Cong. Thirty years after I'd freed it, parts of Ireland still didn't have electricity. It didn't surprise me, and I didn't know if it should have. It was starting to feel like a very long day – it was my second day walking and hitching since I'd left Roscommon – but I pulled myself towards the town's two steeples. I climbed over the walls, and I remembered how I'd been able to get over them without having to trust or even touch them, and often with the bicycle on my back, how I could cross the broken ground without a complaint from my soles or the stone. Those days were gone. But I went carefully, like a man in a war. I knew I'd be doing some creeping when I got into Cong.

It was dark and so was I by the time I got to the outside of the place. I was sweating, clogged – but I'd made it. There was a granite high cross at the top of the road into the town. I stopped there, and looked down rural Ireland's idea of a street. I leaned against the cross. It fell over with me onto the road. The fuckin' thing was made of wood, as real as a *Fort Apache* cactus.

The plane brought me nearer to Ireland and I read the script I'd written with Ford. But I didn't. Because this wasn't the script I'd seen Meta Sterne thump onto white paper.

But it was. That was why the shame took me over so quickly and entirely. I wasn't entitled to anger. I thought I'd die – I wanted to.

But I kept reading.

I remembered a cold night in 1920. I was with a flying column, in a safe house outside Ballinrobe. There were seven of us, six local men and me, the outside man sent down from Dublin to teach them manners and soldiering. One of the men was only sixteen, and two of them were twenty, but they were veterans already. (I'd just turned nineteen myself, but no one knew it. They looked at me and saw the original Fenian.) These men had killed other men, and had been away from their homes for more than a year. They were farmers who couldn't farm, a teacher who would never teach again. They stared into the fire and talked about burning down Ashford Castle.

—There's no one living in the castles these days, sure. It's a long way to go, to put a match to a ruin, just because a Protestant used to live in it.

Ivan Reynolds was there that night, well on his way to being a frightening man.

—This one's different, said Ivan.

—How is it?

—Big people own it.

—Who?

—The Guinnesses.

—The people who make the porter?

102

—That's them.

—We've nothing against them, have we? They're fuckin' grand, sure.

They laughed quietly.

—We could shoot the lot of them, said Ivan.—And the porter would still get made.

—There's big money in drink.

—There is, said Ivan.

—So, will we throw the paraffin at it, so?

—We won't, said Ivan.

He stared across the fire, to where he knew I was sitting. I said nothing. The war needed Ivan and the other Ivans. I was doing my job, letting him grow.

The young lad broke the silence.

—Why not, Ivan?

—Too far, he said.—There's plenty we can be doing around these parts. There's more to rebellion than setting fire to big houses.

No one argued. Ivan was their man.

—And another thing, said Ivan.

—What's that, Ivan?

—We won't be at this forever, said Ivan.—We'll be the winners one of these days.

—Good man.

—And I'll tell you what, boys, said Ivan.—We'll tell the fuckin' Guinnesses to get out of that to fuck. And one of our own will move right in.

—That'll be the great day, alright.

Ivan sat there while his men slowly realised that he was talking about himself. They loved him for it, and it scared them. It wasn't a dream coming out of a cloud; it was Ivan's plan. They could see him walking up to the big wooden door. And they could see him giving it the boot.

So Ashford Castle had been spared, although Ivan never moved in. The castle was just outside Cong, and I was looking at it now. It was the real thing, turrets and all. But there was a tricolour at the top of the flagpole. The Guinnesses were gone and these days it was a hotel. I'd have no problem getting in. The door would be wide open. But I was waiting until it was properly dark, country-side dark, when I could see just enough and know I wouldn't be seen.

The Prods had always managed to convert their own patches of hell into some sort of England. Trees grew where none could; hedges flourished in places where finding muck to cover the spuds was the yearly struggle for the Catholics. I knew: it was the history of the place. The conqueror had taken the land that could support the trees and left the shite for the natives, and had even taken rent from them for it. I knew all that. But it was easy to fall for the alternative story: the conqueror was just better at it, more industrious, there because he deserved to be. Plants grew because he planted and tended them; he told them to fuckin' grow. I was leaning towards that version now, because I was well hidden behind some Protestant trees, fifty yards from the front steps of the castle.

The working day was ending, and a convoy had arrived. Cars, a truck, a green double-decker bus – I'd never seen one before. I was impressed. An Irish bus, a good shade of green. I watched men jump off the back of the bus, before it had finally stopped. They walked away in all directions, waving and shouting, over the lawn, and into the bushes. They were *The Quiet Man*'s extras, the Mayo Navajo, going home for their dinners. And some of them were heading towards me. I needed to keep looking at the castle, to see who was going up the steps. So, I stopped looking like a hidden man and leaned against the best of the trees, and let the extras come at me.

—You got back before us, said a young fella as he passed me and kept going.

—That's it.

—Good man, he said.—Taking the air before you go in.

I could hear him running at the wall behind me, and hitting it. It wasn't one of the dry-stone walls. It had been built high, not to keep sheep in, but to keep the natives out. I didn't look back, but he got over the top without much fighting. Two women strolled up, trailing bright shawls on the grass behind them. They hauled in the shawls as they stepped off the lawn into the rough. They carried them under their arms. They both saw me, and smiled.

—You brought the weather with you, said one of them.

She was young. They both were. They might have been thirty, but life hadn't knocked the bounce out of them. They were freckled and red-haired – I couldn't believe it – and lovely.

I kept an eye on the castle. I saw John Wayne going in, trotting up the steps. There was a wind now, coming off Lough Corrib. It took spray from the fountain; I could feel it on my face.

The girls were in no hurry to go.

John Ford was getting out of one of the cars. He stopped, and looked across the lawn, to where we stood. He was blind, but he stared.

—What are yis up to? I asked.

I nodded at the bus and the rest.

Ford had gone up a few of the steps. Meta Sterne was with him, lugging her table and a basket. He stopped on a step, and he was looking across at me. I didn't know why I wasn't hiding.

—What's up? I said.

—Are you not in it?

—In what?

—The film.

It was only one girl doing the talking.

—No, I said.—What film?

—Ah, it's great, she said.—*The Quiet Man*, it's called. We're in it, me and herself.

He was going up the rest of the steps.

—That's great, I said.—You're the stars, I'd say, are yis?

I was slipping into it.

—Go 'way out of that. We are not.

Maureen FitzSimons was going up the steps now, on her own. Something about the way she was lifting her feet – she was tired.

—So, what were yis up to today? I asked.

—We went to the beach.

There was no beach in my script. I'd once buried a spy up to his neck in the sand at Dollymount, while the tide tumbled towards us. He'd admitted he'd given big names to the G-men in Dublin Castle and we'd had to be quick digging him back up, so we could execute him in the dunes. But that beach hadn't made the script.

—Lovely, I said.—What beach was that?

—Lettergesh. D'you know it?

—No, I lied.—Is it nice?

—It's lovely.

—And what was happening on the beach?

—The horse race, said the talking girl.—At least, we think it was a horse race. There were horses. Weren't there?

Her friend nodded.

* * *

The race was still there in the script. The beach was new but the horses weren't. I'd let them trot right in. Somehow, somewhere in the tumbling of the story back and across from Ford to me, the early animosity between myself and my wife's cousin, Ivan Reynolds, had become a race between myself and her brother, on horses. I'd let it happen. I was born before cars became common, but I'd never been on top of a horse. I wasn't scared of much that I could look at, but horses scared me. They were too magnificent. I was always a tall man but I could never look down at a horse. The horse's eye was always there, always staring through me. I knew the horse would never let me stay in the saddle; it was the only fight I knew I'd always lose. But I'd seen what Ford had done with horses, the beauty of the trailing dust, the pounding of the hooves. I was a scriptwriter, and my life and times became a Western, for just five pages. The race went in, across the mountains and the bog, with guns. Ivan was after me; Red Liam was chasing Seán.

What was in the script now wasn't what we'd written. The race across country to save the rebel's life had become a race on a beach for a woman's bonnet, a hat.

I looked at the seat in front of me until its upholstery stayed still and the sweat in my hair felt cold. I looked back down at the script. I looked at the front page, at something I hadn't seen before. A name, under the title. Frank S. Nugent.

Who the fuck was he?

I went across the carpet, and lightly over the boards. I stayed close to the wall and I didn't stop to look at the art. I couldn't hear myself move. Till I got to the stairs. My feet were fine but the real knee cracked on every step. The stairs were narrow, not what I'd expected. Maybe I was taking the servants' route – I didn't know. I stopped at the top. I was on a balcony. I put my hands on the rail and looked back down at the oak-panelled room. I heard feet below, whispering over the carpet. I stepped back and sideways, into the dark. I could still see most of the room below, and the man who walked across it. He had the clothes and clip of a butler on a mission. I watched him as he moved away from me, through an arch, to another wing of the castle. I waited till the room settled back to emptiness.

But something strange was happening to the butler's feet.

His steps had faded; I'd heard him on a distant stairs, climbing further away. But now, still climbing, he'd turned. He was coming towards me. I had to move.

I got in behind a grandfather clock and hoped its shadow had me covered. My ear was up against it. Its pendulum joined the butler's feet, the countdown to his finding me. I wouldn't have to kill him – I told myself. I was in a hotel and this wasn't a war. His feet clipped over the floorboards, getting nearer. The pendulum got louder too. I felt the sweat on my chest and face.

He passed, an arm, a slap, away from me. I didn't breathe. A tallish, straight-backed man, ex-army, my age but moving younger. He was holding a bottle he hadn't had when I'd watched him crossing the room below.

I followed the bottle.

Ford never drank when he was working. But I still went after the butler. Up another stairs, down a narrow corridor. I heard the knock on a door. I couldn't see it, but I knew. I'd been good at this once; I still was. I knew it wasn't Ford's door, even from the length of the corridor. The door was hiding a small room. There was a big man in it, but the room itself was tiny. The butler's knuckles on the oak told me as much as I needed to know.

—Come in!

Victor McLaglen was in the room. I moved away, back, down the corridor. I listened at other doors as I retreated. A kid snored, a woman sighed. There was plenty of life along the corridor but the bigger rooms weren't up there. I went back down to the clock. The butler passed me, back down his hidden stairs. I stayed until I saw him cross the room below.

There was another corridor, off the balcony. Thicker doors, bigger rooms, the sounds of sleep more distant from the doors. I put the ear to one in time to hear a page being turned; someone inside was reading a book. But that was the only drama. I listened at each door, and chose my room.

The door wasn't locked. I held it tight to its hinges as I pushed it open.

It was a big room but it wasn't a bedroom. I stood back, against the door. Two windows – the curtains were drawn. Paintings of racehorses on the walls. Low tables, two good sofas, a fireplace – no fire. And steep steps to my left, to the bedroom.

I locked the door, slowly. I heard and felt the old lock tumble;

I made sure it went at my pace. I took out the key and put it into one of my pockets.

I looked at the floor. The rug was deep, put there specially for me. Five good strides to the steps, up to the bedroom. There was no door; I could see the bed. A four-poster job, and a grey old peasant lying on it.

I got up the steps, I was standing in the room. More good rug – I moved to the bed.

The curtains were drawn but it was Irish summer; the night outside was silver.

I'd expected him to be waiting for me. He'd seen me earlier; I was sure of that – he'd stared across the lawn and water. His eyes would be open – waiting, glaring. But he was asleep. His black specs were on the table beside the bed. I folded them – they squeaked – and slid them into the same pocket as the key.

He was lying on his back. His head was lodged between two pillows. The bedclothes were off, pushed away by his feet. He was wearing – I leaned across and felt them – silk pyjamas.

I stood straight, beside him. I thought about taking the leg off and pounding him with it, the boot still on it, till he sank through the mattress and the floor. I'd have to sit on the bed to get at the straps – and wake Ford – or sit on the floor and hope I could get back up. It was too much effort and I didn't want to ruin the alligator skin.

But I woke him.

I lifted my right arm and brought my fist down onto his chest. His face woke into a hard, open hand. I covered his mouth and pressed him back down to the bed. I felt his shock and pain push hard against my palm, and subside.

He knew it was me. He lay still.

I thumped him again. Felt his heart in my palm.

He knew I'd kill him.

I saw them – a string of black beads, hanging from the board behind his head.

He didn't fight. I felt him pull his body back to quiet; his heart slowed down and helped him. I felt his breath against my palm. I lifted my hand from his mouth. I was still looking at the beads.

—They were my mother's, he said.—You're going to kill me, right?

—Yeah.

He didn't sigh. He didn't move.

—Good, he said.—Great. Mind if I sit up?

—Don't fuckin' budge.

—I'm going to sit up.

I took a clump of his hair and pulled him up from the pillows. I grabbed the beads with my other hand. They weren't tied or looped; they were just resting on top of the backboard. I let go of his hair and got the beads around his neck. I felt the dry skin of his neck becoming wet against my knuckles. And I pulled. The crucifix was in my right hand; the beads locked in between my fingers. I felt bone beneath my knuckles now. He didn't fight. He didn't resist. Even as I killed him, he took control. I was doing what he'd ordered me to do. Even if I stopped, I'd be obeying him. He was still the fuckin' director.

I stopped. I loosened the grip on one end of the beads. He didn't fall back on the pillows. He stayed in midair for a while, a second, before dropping forward onto his legs. Three broken groans and he was breathing again. He pushed himself up. I could see the line of the beads, a pink river and its tiny lakes, on one side of his neck. But he didn't touch it. He was sitting up. I wouldn't have recognised him; I'd never seen him straighter.

—Why did you change your mind? he said.

The last few minutes were in his voice.

I didn't answer. I didn't know the answer. I hadn't killed him because he'd wanted me to. But I wanted to kill him – I could still feel that urge in my arms. I wanted him dead but he was sitting up, looking at me.

I tried to hate him, tried to reignite the rage. Finish the job and walk to Dublin. Become myself again.

He was looking at me.

It was a script meeting.

—Cat got your tongue?

I hit him. I drew back my arm and slapped him. I felt his head go with my swing. He fell back and stayed down, his head in one of the pillows – I could see one scared, uncovered eye. I was back in charge. The whack had done me good; it was still reverberating, and fading nicely along the walls.

—Why? I said.

Now he said nothing.

—Why? I said, again.

I saw his blind eye move. He was trying to look at me without lifting his head from the pillow. He couldn't do it.

—Jesus, Henry, he said.—That's a fucking question.

I agreed with him.

—I'm going to sit up here. You going to sock me?

—No.

—Okay.

He groaned now, made all the noises. Climbing back into his director's chair. Acting.

I hit him.

I punched him this time; I threw fifty years into it. I broke two of my own fingers. I felt them go; I heard them. He didn't fall back; his head stayed put.

My arm was breaking apart. I sat on the side of the bed. I herded the pain, pushed it back to my broken fingers. I let air go, and took it carefully in.

I opened my eyes.

The fucker was granite.

—So, he said.

Then I heard noise from his mouth, like he was gathering the words and putting them into the right order.

He was crying.

I held my hand up, brought it closer to my eyes. The fingers didn't look too bad. I'd stayed silent through worse torture.

He'd stopped bawling but he hadn't moved. He hadn't lifted his hands to wipe his eyes or his nose, or the raw line that cut across his neck.

I heard feet outside. They passed.

I asked him again.

—Why?

He sighed.

—Honest answer?

—Yeah, I said.

—I don't know what you mean.

It took a while. To know that he really was being honest.

—What don't you fuckin' understand? I asked.

—Why you'd even ask.

The words were bubbled. I'd done damage.

—I don't get it, he said.

But it wasn't just the floating teeth. His voice didn't have the bark. He was talking, not performing.

—We wrote a script, he said.—So we could make a fucking picture. After that, I don't know *why*. Ask yourself.

I started to answer, several times. I got ready to let him have it. But —

—Yeah, I said.

It was all I could manage, at first.

—It wasn't just a picture, I said.

It sounded right, and it was right.

—It was never just a picture, I said.—You told me that. It was my fuckin' story.

He sighed.

—Yeah, yeah. Great. Listen.

He moved, but not much. He turned his head. He hadn't looked for his glasses; they were still in my pocket. But he looked at me as if he saw exactly what was in front of him.

—It was a picture, he said.—It was a picture. Your story, my picture. I hid nothing.

—You said —

—I hid nothing, Henry.

I heard a slurp, like he was knocking back soup.

—I hid nothing, he said.—You were with me all the way.

He didn't move again. He didn't even touch his mouth or face. He couldn't see me; I knew that. But he still knew how to use his eyes.

—I'm not apologising, Henry.

—I don't want your fuckin' apology.

—Yes, you do.

He wasn't challenging or provoking me.

—You want me to take on some kind of blame, he said.— Fucking guilt or something. But I won't.

He let that settle.

—It was work, he said.—But we knocked it into shape. Accept that.

A spring beneath him groaned and the noise had me up off the bed, standing ready to deal with the attack.

—Jesus, Henry, he said.—Do rebels never retire? I'm going to lie back here, no funny stuff.

More springs joined the first one.

—You really shouldn't be socking old guys like me. You broke a couple of fingers is my guess.

He didn't lean his head or shoulders against the backrest. He was lying down, ready for the coffin.

—Where were we? he said.

111

I didn't hit him.

—It was honest work, he said.

He wasn't looking at me now. He couldn't, because his head was back between the two pillows.

—Or what passes for honest in this business. You cut it to fit. And that is what we did. We wrote a script and here we are, making the picture. You should be fucking proud of yourself.

I hit him again.

But I was stopping myself, or trying to. And it wasn't the pain already humming there that pulled me back. I was smacking him to stop him, not to punish him. I knew that, quickly, and I didn't want to do it. But I hit him anyway, slapped him like a cissy, gave him a fright and sent the pain snarling back up my arm and neck.

—Fuck!

—Jesus, Henry. We wrote the picture but we are not in the fucking picture. Calm down.

—Sorry.

—Fine, great. Sit down. Here.

I heard the springs again, then saw him lift, and drop again, making space for me.

—Lie back there, he said.—I bet you walked all the way here, right?

—Yeah.

—Henry-style. From Dublin.

—No.

—Roscommon.

—Yeah.

—I could do that myself, he said.—Sit down.

I sat on the bed. I lay back; I let myself go. I left the pain in the air for a while. I stretched out on the bed. We were lying side by side.

He had me beaten. I couldn't blame the man for what I'd let happen; I couldn't beat my own guilt into him. I closed my eyes.

—It'll be great, he said.

The name was suddenly there, lit and throbbing.

—Who's Frank S. Nugent?

—Writer, he said.—A damn good one.

—His name's on the script.

—A formality.

—Fuck that, I said.—What's that mean?

—It's about credit, said Ford.—The Writers' Guild. Frank was the last guy to work on the script, so his name goes on the front page. That's how it works. But it's just the working draft. We'll sort it out. Your name will be there with his, up on the silver screen.

Each word was the blade of a shovel. He was digging himself out of a hole. He was acting again. He'd forgotten about the new name on the front page.

—Frank tidied it up, he said.—He did a good job. You read it, right?

—Some of it.

—Most of it.

—Yeah.

—On the plane.

—Yeah.

—Yeah, that's Frank. He tidies up.

All references to the war and to the I.R.A. had gone. The Seán in the picture wasn't a kid of the Dublin streets, and all the killings had became one big punch in a boxing ring. The tommy gun had come off the bike, and the bike had become a Protestant vicar's tandem. He'd tidied up alright.

—Is he here? I asked.

—Frank?

—Yeah.

—No, he said.—I don't allow the writers near the set. They get upset.

—What about me?

—You're different, Henry, he said.—I need you. You're my I.R.A. consultant.

—You took the I.R.A. out.

—I'm putting them back in. We don't want to waste all of those trenchcoats.

I was pulled between fury and sleep. I counted to three.

—No more messing, I said.

—Great.

The old trickster was back beside me on the bed. I wanted to kill him again. And he wanted that – I could feel it and smell it in the cockiness beside me. He even put his hands behind his head.

I didn't touch him.

I wasn't going to find out. I could torture him and kill him very slowly, but he was never going to tell me. Because he didn't

113

know why he did what he did, made pictures, once or twice a year. There was the finance, the pressures but, really, he wouldn't have been able to tell me. He was just making a picture.

I could feel it in the bedsprings; he'd calmed down. He'd be up again, play-acting, if I asked him another question. So I didn't.

We lay there. We didn't sleep and we didn't talk. We didn't budge. He sighed occasionally, like a man looking back at something good. And that was all. The light from outside crawled across the curtains. I heard feet, more feet, movement from below and above. The birds outside were breaking up the night.

A hand outside turned the doorknob.

—Mister Ford?

The hand turned the knob again, tried to twist it further. The other hand knocked, softly.

—Mister Ford?

The next knock was firmer.

—Mister Ford?

—What?

He spoke to the ceiling.

—Your door's locked, sir.

—That's right.

—Your coffee, sir.

—Don't want it.

—Mister Ford?

The voice belonged to a posh culchie, probably the butler I'd hidden from earlier, wrapping up his shift by delivering the great man's coffee.

—What? said Ford.

He still hadn't moved.

—Are you alright, sir?

—Yeah, said Ford.

—Should I call someone?

—No, said Ford.—I'm fine. I just don't need the coffee.

He didn't have to shout.

—I'll go, so, said the butler.

—Right, said Ford.

I listened to the feet; I hadn't heard them coming. It was the same guy, the same clip. Some doctor's son, the black sheep, who'd done his stint in the R.A.F. or the British Army. He was gone.

—The coffee's shit in this country, said Ford.

It was full day out there now. There'd soon be Yanks knocking hard on his door.

—I'm sorry, Henry, he said.

I moved my head now; I looked at him.

—You said you weren't going to apologise.

—And you said you didn't want my fucking apology. I'm not apologising.

—What then?

—I'm sorry you're like this, you feel like this.

—Fuck off.

I put my hands behind my head and my fingers reminded me that they were broken.

—Shite!

—You need them looked at?

—No, I said.—I'm grand.

—The last of the rebels.

He wasn't slagging; I could hear it there, respect, and even envy.

—What about your neck? I said.

—I'm fine.

—The hard man.

I felt his smile in the springs beneath me.

—I can see it, you know, he said.—How I fucked up. I can see why you'd see it that way.

He nudged my side.

—But, you know, he said.—There's something else.

There were important feet coming our way.

—Wingate, said Ford.

His brother-in-law.

The feet stopped; the fist started.

—Pappy?

—Here we go, said Ford.—What?

—All set?

—Yeah.

He started to get up; he groaned and so did the mattress.

—I'll need my glasses, Henry. I can direct blind but I have to deal with Technicolor here.

—Who's in there with you?

—No one.

—You're talking to someone, said Wingate Smith.

Ford lay back down.

115

—I've changed my mind, he told me – he whispered.

Smith could still hear him.

—What?

He tried the lock; he shook the door.

—Win, listen, said Ford.—Leave the door alone. Are you listening?

—Yeah.

—Great, okay. So, listen. I feel like shit. Fever or something. Flu. I can't make it today.

—I'll get a doctor —

—No, said Ford.—No doctor. Listen, Win.

There was silence outside.

—Still there?

—Of course, I'm fucking here, said Smith.—I'm getting you a fucking doctor.

—Win.

—What?

—Listen.

—Pappy? You been at the fucking sauce?

I got the glasses out of my pocket and handed them to Ford, but he didn't seem to see them. He was gazing up at the ceiling. His glasses were in my good hand, four inches from his face.

—Okay, Win. Now listen. You know the rule about me and the booze and work. Ever known me to break it?

—No.

—I feel like shit. I'll just stay here for today and I'll feel significantly less like shit by tonight. And tomorrow morning you'll be outside that door again and I'll feel just great. What we got scheduled for today?

—Why is the door locked?

—I guess that's because I don't want you to come in. So, I'll say it again. What we got scheduled for today?

—Same as yesterday, Smith shouted.—The horse race on that beach.

—Let Duke do it.

—Duke?

—He wants to direct his own pictures. Here's his chance. Let him see how easy it is.

—I'll get a doctor.

—Get yourself an air ticket while you're at it, said Ford.—You hear that?

116

There were more feet outside now – three more men and a little woman – and a lot of urgent whispering.

—I heard, said Smith.

—Great. Get Duke.

—Duke's gone. Will I bring him back?

—No. Just tell him. Tell him he's ready. Tell him I say so. You still standing there?

—Yes.

—I'm fine, Win. I just need a rest. Tell the hotel to stay away.

—You want some water?

—What the fuck would I do with water? Go on. And I don't want to see you on a ladder at the window. You'll see me tonight. Go on.

Smith moved, and stopped. The other feet moved, kept moving, including Meta Sterne's. But Smith hesitated.

—Still there, Win? said Ford.

—No.

—Go, goddammit.

I heard him hurry down the corridor and onto the stairs.

—I got the day off, Henry, said Ford.

He took the glasses from me and put them on but he still looked at the ceiling.

I stopped looking at him. I put my broken hand on my chest.

He was awake when I woke. The light had shifted. I'd been asleep for an hour and a half. And he was exactly where I'd left him.

—I'm going to move now, Henry, he said.

—Alright.

—I knew you'd tear my throat open if I moved while you were out for the count. So, I'm standing up and I'm going to the john over there. I'll be shutting the door but I won't lock it.

—Fair enough.

—Great, he said.—I'm going to wash some of this mess off my face. I haven't seen it but my guess is I'm a mess.

—You don't look too bad.

—Fuck you.

He groaned as he rose. He rubbed his neck, the first time he'd acknowledged any pain. His feet were on the floor and he sat for a while with his back to me. He coughed, as if testing his pipes. He stood.

I watched him shut the jacks door. I saw the mirror, and the

117

window. I'd never seen that before, a jacks tucked inside the room, another little room, a cell. With a good-sized window.

I stayed where I was. He'd said he wouldn't lock the door, and he didn't. I listened. He didn't touch the window. If he started whistling I'd be over there quick, although I wasn't sure why. If he climbed out and fell, if he stretched a leg to some ledge – none of it mattered. I'd come to Cong to murder the man but that seemed like a long time ago.

I heard the chain and the flush. I heard water running. I heard nothing extra. But the water kept running. And now I saw the steam, leaking up from the edges of the jacks door.

My broken fingers hopped as I got off the bed. I fell – I made it to the door and pushed it open. He was sitting on the jacks and he was crying. I was drenched already; the steam was dragging me to the floor. There was barely room – I had to shove his legs out of my way. I turned off the hot tap and managed to unlock the window one-handed. It was already a hot day outside, so the steam made no dash to the open window. I looked again at Ford. His glasses were two white clouds and the tears ran, straight and quickly, from under them. His pyjama bottoms were up and his hands were clasped and caught between his legs. He was leaning forward, but not slumped like he often was. He looked like he was trying to hear properly, trying to catch the words. But there weren't any. There was nothing, no noise at all, now that the tap was off. There wasn't the sound of an engine or animal. The hotel was absolutely empty, and the country outside was empty.

—Alright?

He didn't answer. He didn't hear.

I stepped back, into the bigger room. It was like walking through drizzle, and the condensation on all the wood and glass. I got back up onto the bed and scooted across to my side.

He was crying. But fuck him. I'd remembered why I was there in the first place and why I'd strangled him with the beads that I now pushed off the bed onto the floor.

I didn't give a shite.

He came out. Walked out of the edge of a cloud. Like an ancient angel, in his silk pyjamas. He leaned against the door frame, like I'd seen Wayne do in one of his films.

—I love this country, he said.

—For fuck sake.

—Fuck you.

He climbed onto the bed like a kid, knees first, then turned over and lay back.

—That's the problem, he said.—And that's your answer.

—What?

—I love this country, he said.—You never did.

—How can you love a fuckin' country?

I was angry again, but I was curious. I'd done the fighting, but he was the one doing the crying.

I pointed at one of the curtained windows.

—What's out there that you can love?

—Nothing.

—Exactly.

—You don't get it.

—Trees and water and trout.

—You don't get it.

—Explain it to me.

He pointed to the side of his head, inches above the raw line I'd put on his neck.

—I love what's in here, he said.

—What's that mean?

—What I grew up with. I was Irish from the start. It was the stories my parents told. And the dancing and music and the drink. We were never really American. We were Irish but Ireland was thousands of miles away. And fifty years away. I grew up loving a place that didn't fucking exist. I just knew it was a hell of a lot better than where I actually was.

—What about America? I asked.

—I love America.

—You're a cranky old cunt, for a man who loves so much.

—I love America. You do too, Henry. You fucking know it. It's impossible not to. When I went across it that first time, on my way out to California. To meet my fucking destiny. I loved it. The plains and the deserts and the old-time religion. Everything. But it never really let me in. I was always Irish. Even my wife wouldn't let me be American, even after I married her. And her fucking brother out there, Wingate – Jesus. I fought in two fucking wars. I made some of the best pictures ever made. I conquered the Wild West single-fucking-handedly. I gave them John Wayne and a brand new history. I changed my fucking politics. But, you know, I'm not really American.

119

—You are.

—No, he said.—I'm Irish. But I guess you'd dispute that.

I shrugged, and the pain shot up my arm.

—That's the problem with America, he said.—And I'm guessing it's going to get worse.

—What?

—It's full of folks who'll never be American. They'll try their damnedest but they'll never make the grade. They'll die in all the corners of the world. They'll dye their hair and bleach their skin but it won't work. They'll grab at new religions or they'll try to buy their way in. But it'll be never be enough. That's the secret. And I'll tell you, Henry. I'm content enough keeping it.

—The secret?

—Yep. I keep the secret. I help hide the fact that there's a secret. I give 'em Duke and Jimmy Stewart and all that hokum about the American way, and I get honorary membership.

It made sense. But America was big enough for any kind of sense. I'd done it myself, invented America, after I'd landed on Ellis Island; I'd done it every day.

—But I have my Ireland, he said.

He tapped the side of his head.

—In here, he said.—Take it out of me and I'm dead.

I heard his head move on the pillow. He was looking at me.

—I tried, he said.

I looked at him, but not for long.

I didn't know what he meant yet; I didn't know if I wanted to. I was ready for sleep again. It was good there, on the bed; I'd never been relaxed like this. I thought about closing my eyes, and thought about trying not to.

He nudged me – a soft prod to the shoulder.

—What?

—Wake up.

—I'm not asleep.

—You came all this way to hear me, he said.—I took the day off. First time in my life.

—Right; go on.

—I intended making the picture. I fully intended doing it. When we met, in the Valley, back then. I loved that story. I knew the story before we even met. It was in the can, already made, as far as I was concerned. You remember that, don't you?

—Yeah, I said.

—That's right.

—I remember.

—Great, he said.—But I couldn't do it. The killing.

—Fuck you anyway, I said.—You've killed hundreds of men in your films. Fuckin' thousands.

—That was different.

—How?

—Soldiers and Indians. Mostly Indians. They don't matter. The Indians love me, but they don't matter. It's sad but fucking true. No one cares about the Indians. Not even the Indians. It's propaganda, I guess. All the how the West was won. Indians, Japs, commies. I played my fucking part. And, like I said, they gave me my honorary membership. I knew exactly what I was doing. I invented a place that would take me. Understand me?

—I suppose so, I said.

—But I couldn't do that here, he said.—I won't have this place covered in dead Apaches and Navajo.

—What are you on about?

—I could tell it to a point, he said.—The fight, your part in it. The Limeys would be the Apaches, but worse. Bad palefaces. I'm getting a bit mixed up here. I suppose, we – the Irish – would be the Apaches.

He was years ahead of the Provos.

—The rebels, he said.—You'd be Geronimo. And we'd win. But I'd have to make it happily ever after.

—Why?

—I'm a cartoon Irishman. Like all the other Irishmen and women in America. Look, he said.—Listen to this.

I looked through the black lenses, to the eyes behind them. For a second or two the lenses weren't there. Ford wasn't hiding.

—Without our nostalgia we would die, he said.—We'd be nothing. Landless. The place mightn't exist, Henry, but we need it. And the Italians, and the Swedes, the Russians and all of those people. They need the home in their heads. You too.

—No.

—Yes.

I didn't repeat the denial. The first No already sounded hollow.

—You too, he said.—You colluded. I told you why I'm doing it. But what's your excuse?

He was right. I'd colluded with him, long before Frank Nugent rounded up the diehards and drove them off the pages of the script.

—I couldn't have an Irishman shoot an Irishman, he said.—That doesn't happen in Ireland. No one gets shot in the back. No one gets shot at all.

—What about *The Informer*?

—No one paid their ten cents to see it, said Ford.—They stayed away and they were right to. We all know the fucking truth but who wants to pay for it? And, listen. There's something else.

—What?

—I'm doing the right thing, he said.—Making this leprechaun Ireland. I'm doing the right thing here, Henry.

—What d'you mean?

—You'll see. Can't say now. But it's part of the plan. You retired from the fight, right?

—Right.

—I never did.

—You're talking shite.

—That might be, he said.

We lay there.

I didn't feel bad; I didn't feel good. I was in Ireland, the real place, not Ford's. I was lying on a fat bed in a well-kept castle, but I was still in Ireland. And I was more than likely staying. I hadn't thought about that. I didn't think about it now.

—I could use some food. You hungry?

It took a while – where and who I was; who was talking.

He was standing beside the bed, beside me. A sudden thought, a fact: he'd kissed me. It was on my forehead, left from the dream that had burst, collapsed when his words came through.

I knew where I was.

He hadn't touched me. It was all that was left of the dream, all I could keep hold of. A child – a daughter – had kissed my forehead. But Saoirse, my daughter, had never done that. But maybe she had in my own Ireland. It was still there on my forehead.

Sentimental shite.

—Yeah, I said.—I'm starving.

—Anywhere else, there'd be a phone and I could ring for some breakfast. Here, I have to put on my pants and walk.

—Off you go.

—I'm locked in.

—Oh, yeah.

I pushed myself up, one-handed.

—Someone will have to fix those fingers, he said.

—They're grand, I told him.—No one fixed them the last time they were broken.

—Younger bones back then.

—The same fuckin' owner. Leave them alone.

—Okay, he said.—But I need the key.

It was in one of the pockets of my American trousers, the same side as my broken fingers.

—Need help?

—Fuck off.

I had it; I pulled, and heard the lining rip. I shook the loose threads from the key and held it out for him.

—Anything you don't like to eat?

—No.

—Just cooked.

—I'm easy.

—The fucking rebel.

He wore his cap but he hadn't put on shoes. He leaned on the wall as he went down the small stairs to the big room. He looked down at each step. He left the key in the lock; he wasn't going to lock me in.

—And coffee, he said.

—Yep.

—No tea.

—Never touch it.

—Limey piss.

He shut the door.

I'd eat and go.

I'd tried to tell the truth but I'd ended up inventing another Ireland. Just like Ford had done to America. He'd sold them the story – the good fight their people had taken to the frontier; the Yankees and southern rebels, and the Irish and Swedes, all united —

—AND IF YOU ASKED HER —

WHY THE HECK SHE WORE IT —

They watched, and saw themselves ride out of the fort, to push savagery back, across the heartland, all the way to the Pacific.

The covered wagons stocked high with provisions and civilisation, they made the land theirs – because it was theirs. The men and women in the picture houses were out there with John Wayne and Maureen FitzSimons and the others that Ford had chosen to be the faces of America. They sat in the dark and accepted their American destiny. And the fight went on – Bataan, Normandy, the 38th Parallel. Ford's stories were all the same story: America was right.

He was taking his time with the fuckin' food. I was starving.

And that was what was happening here as well, in Cong. Dublin and the slums didn't exist; Ireland was a village called Innisfree. The tommy gun was off the handlebars, and the bike now had two saddles, a foot and a half between them. *The Quiet Man* would be the emigrant's dream, soft and green. And Ireland was going to play up to it. The rest of the world would see the film, and Ireland would give the world what it had seen. The village, Cong, was outside the castle window. I'd walked through it and I'd seen the hungry faces; they hadn't changed since 1922. But they wouldn't be making it into the picture. The extras would all be red-cheeked and smiling. That would be Ford's Ireland.

But he was right. I'd been with him all the way. Ford wasn't to blame, and Frank Nugent wasn't to blame. I'd let in the blarney long before Frank Nugent.

I could hear feet outside, more than one pair.

I was the one to blame.

Silver trays came into the room, and the two men in white jackets carrying them. They saw me propped up in Ford's bed but they refused to look surprised.

There was no blame. My daughter had kissed my forehead. I'd invented a place where that could happen. Ford had invented a place where the Irish could be at rest. Where fists didn't hurt, where drink did no damage, where there was no real pain to hide. A monstrous fuckin' lie, but a nice one.

There were the usual bits of business now. It was a film set and Ford was directing. The bell lids were lifted off the trays. He showed them how to pour the coffee. The butlers watched and learnt.

I got out of the bed – they didn't look. I came down the steps; I'd slept with my boots and leg on. I grabbed a full cup.

—Thanks, lads.

I heard myself; I was in the fuckin' film. And I was happy to be in the film. I went back up the steps.

The lads closed the big door very quietly and Ford carried my tray up to the bed. I watched him take the steps carefully; I could hear his determination. I took off the boots but I left the leg on. He put the tray across my lap.

—Good man.

—That enough?

—Looks alright.

He went back down and got his own tray.

The plate was huge and white. Sausages, rashers, black and white pudding, a couple of eggs, fried bread – even the food came out of *The Quiet Man*. I was loving my country.

Ford had just climbed onto the bed, pushing his tray ahead like he was holding onto a lifebuoy.

—That fit the bill? he asked.

—It's alright.

I was eating one-handed. Our forks, his knife, tapped the plates and the old men swallowed as quietly as they could. The edge off the hunger, I asked him a question.

—Why me?

—What?

—Why did you bother dragging the story out of me?

—It's part of the process.

He was fussing with the fat on the rashers, cutting it away from the proper meat. I leaned across and took his fat up with my fork. I shook it at his face.

—You're not fuckin' Irish.

He looked caught for a second. He was thinking of taking it back, grabbing it off my fork.

—I knew that, he said.

—My arse you did.

—I was saving it.

—You said it was part of the process.

—Fine, he said.—I won't repeat myself. But here. We started out with your story. And we got that down. We blend it in there with the Walsh story. And we're ready to roll. But then the question arises, and the question gets bigger and more insistent. Wait.

He picked up his coffee. He pulled most of it into his mouth. He rolled it, and swallowed.

—Jesus, he said.—The question. Is this. What exactly is Henry fighting for? Or Seán. We have to see it. This place that's worth dying for. See, that's what's great about Monument Valley.

125

The most desolate place on earth and yet it's worth the fight. The sheer fucking size of it, and the sense that this is the worst land in the world, so the land behind the Apaches and beyond that horizon must therefore be the best. It's all America. Right?

I nodded.

—So, he said.—Is it Dublin? Is there one fucking brick worth fighting for in that town? It ain't a city. Well?

It had never been about bricks – I'd wanted to demolish the place.

—No, I said.

—So we get you out of Dublin.

He nodded at the window.

—And you're right outside there. Now it's worth it. It's God's own country and it's been taken from you. The lake out there and all that Technicolor green. The castle with the wrong people in it. It's worth fighting for. We're all with you.

He held his tray, leaned out, and lowered it to the floor. Then he straightened up and sat back.

—You let it happen, Henry.

—I know. I'm thinking of going back to sleep. I might give it a bash.

—Good idea, he said.—A bit of shut-eye. We've a busy week ahead of us.

I pushed the tray to the end of the long bed. I could lie down without shoving it over the side.

—You understand? he said.

—What?

I stretched out. I thought about taking the leg off.

—The war, he said.

They weren't the words I'd expected.

—What war?

—Well, both wars, he said.—The War of Independence, then the Civil business.

—You didn't want to put them in, I said.—I heard you the first time.

I was going to sleep.

—But that's what *The Quiet Man* is actually about, he said.—It's what happened after we won the war. Paradise.

—Who d'you think you're codding? I said.—I'm only back a few days but it isn't fuckin' Paradise.

I was just talking, counting the sheep.

126

—But it could be, he said.—The real thing. The emigrant's dream.

—Rural, Gaelic, the simple life.

—That's right.

—Remember the piece of paper? I said.

—With your name on it. *Smart, Henry.* Sliding over the polished desk.

—That's right, I said.—My execution order.

—That would have been a hell of a scene.

—That's the shite they said they wanted, I told him.—Jack Dalton and the boys. A rural Ireland, the simple life, spouting fuckin' Irish. That's what they hid behind. I'll tell you what you're up to and then I'm going asleep.

—Give it to me.

—You're taking the war to Ireland, I told him.—Your fuckin' Cold War. You're making Ireland part of America and you've sent in John Wayne. Ireland will be the land worth dying for.

I was talking through my hole, but I believed every word. I was back there, in my heyday, selling freedom and hooch in brown paper bags.

—So fuck you and the Ireland in your head, I said.

—Maybe you're right, he said.—But it'll bring in the tourists.

—I'll be waiting for them.

—The rebel.

—I'm going asleep.

—Me too.

I drifted for a while, aware that I wasn't asleep. I wanted to talk some more, make it up and convince myself. There were things ahead of me now. Years, life, people I could find. There was no fight; there was no one I wanted to kill. I was a happy man, freed by the cranky old cunt beside me.

He spoke.

—Asleep?

I didn't answer.

—Henry? You're awake. There's more to it.

I woke.

He was asleep, and loud with it. His neck was at a bad angle; I could see the strangling I'd given him earlier. I got out of the bed. The tray tipped over the side. The noise woke the world.

But he stayed asleep. I put on the boots, laced them up. I rubbed the dust off them with a corner of the sheet. It was early evening outside; the cast and all the crew would be coming back soon. Wingate Smith would be marching down the corridor, the posse right behind him.

I came out of the castle, past the two lads who'd carried the trays earlier for Ford. They studied me slowly and kept their fags in their mouths. But they stood back.

—Taking the air, sir?

—Something like that, I said.

I stood at the top of the steps and saw the convoy heading towards me, turning in at the hotel gates, the black cars, the vans, the trucks, more of them squeezing slowly through, filling the narrow road. The black cars and the big people in them – I didn't want to take them on, or to see them recognise me. I didn't want to look at Maureen FitzSimons. I'd let her down; she wasn't going to fight for Ireland.

I turned to the lake and walked. Lough Corrib. Fifty years later it poisoned Galway. But that day, as I strode in and sank, it welcomed me and took me under. I climbed back out twenty years later.

But those days were gone. There was no more magic. I swam; that was magic enough for a one-legged man with a broken hand – out of the castle's gaze. I climbed back out on the far bank, into the rest of the sun. I walked into the trees and found the castle wall. I climbed it easily enough. I dried quickly as I walked. I heard the leg creak and shrink.

I walked.

PART TWO

7

I felt the bomb before I heard it. I didn't know what it was. I was in the air, smashed into the wall, when the noise came. This was something new. The dust, the screams, the shredded metal – I'd seen them before. But it was the size of the thing, the depth of it. This was a bomb that didn't care about numbers. I couldn't move. I was still on the street. But the street was gone. The air was dirt and screams. I knew who I was. I was Henry Smart. I knew where I was. I was on Talbot Street. Where Talbot Street had been.

I lay there and waited.

I had cash that dried quickly in my pocket as I walked away from Ashford Castle. I was going right across the country, to Dublin, but I wasn't going to walk. There were green buses now. There were trains. I wouldn't be hiding.

I got off the train at Kingsbridge and wandered. I listened for voices, looked out for faces. But that stopped; I copped on. It had been more than thirty years. I walked until I knew again where I was going. Some of the streets had new names – Pearse Street, Cathal Brugha Street – men I'd known and sneered at. Other streets had been demolished. Not just the street, the line, the streets off it – the whole area was gone, replaced by a shape I'd never known. And that was grand. I wasn't coming back; I was arriving. I cried out for nothing.

The slums were still there, like broken teeth in a rotten mouth, but far worse now because I'd been away and seen different. I walked past some of the steps my mother had sat on every night. I walked past gaping doors that had brought me safety and women. Piano Annie's house was roofless, the front door and the windows bricked up. I walked past men and women I might have known once, but I didn't examine the crumbling faces. *Gracie*, *Lil*, *Alexander*. I didn't look too carefully.

I stood at the railings and looked in at the school that had given me my two whole days of formal education. This was on the fourth day back. I saw young teachers, grim-looking girls, but no old ones. I stayed an hour, and left it at that. *Two and two?* She was dead.

I stood on Gardiner Street and looked through the gaping hole of a door – the skylight glass was gone – at the peeling wall and the black pram parked against it, and the big stairs leading up to darkness. I heard the noises, laughter, the bawling, the final coughs, exactly as I'd left them, still floating around in there, and constantly kept fresh. Consumption was killing some man on the second floor. A young one was crying behind the door to the backyard. A gang of kids came tumbling out, down the steps, and all around me. Some wore canvas shoes – runners – but there were others who had nothing. Bare feet slapped the pavement. This was 1951.

I made my mind up: I'd stay away from the old places. I'd stop feeding the anger.

I walked down Marlborough Street – some street names had stayed the same – and I found a line of the green double-decker buses, on Abbey Street. I got on one. It took me north for twenty minutes, and I got off it in the village of Ratheen. I didn't know it; I'd shot no one there. I'd stay.

I got work that became steady, and a cottage that became my home. I cut grass in the gardens of the big houses that stood on both sides of the long Main Road. I bought an old bike and went from door to door. I didn't cycle – I couldn't, unless the hill was steep and I could freewheel down it – but I tied a stolen rake to the crossbar, and a spade I'd found leaning alone against a gate. I put an old sack across the handlebars, and I pushed my new office along the Main Road, to where it came out at the coast. I cut grass and came back and cut it again, and waited to be asked to do more. Two months after I'd cut the first grass, I took the spade down from the crossbar and began to dig. I became Henry, and Old Henry, and How's Henry, and, at the back doors of the Protestant houses, I became Dear Henry.

And that was it for years. A living. The outdoor life. I'd kneel on the sack and pull away at the plants that looked like the weeds, and I was never wrong.

—You're a jewel, Henry.

—Thank you, missis.

132

Did I see the beauty that others saw, in the years that I tended the Northside's bigger gardens? I did like fuck.

—What would I do without you, Henry? *Your own fuckin' gardening, missis.*

I pulled the weeds – none ever got away from me. But, really, I could never tell – I couldn't *feel* – the difference between the weeds and the flowers.

But the life was good. The work was steady, and more than steady in the summer and autumn. I took it easy in the winter. I had my own name, and no one looked at me twice when they heard it. I was Henry Smart, dear Henry, the gardener. And then I was Henry Smart, the caretaker. I was Henry Smart and I never had to think about it.

There were shoes in Ratheen; there were no gaping Georgian doors. The black prams were pushed by well-fed mothers, and they were pushing babies, not coal. No one begged, no one hugged the walls. There were huge green trees that stayed there, swaying but solid, as the building took off and continued, and filled the fields behind the Main Road and gave me more grass to cut and weeds to murder. I had two suits now, and boots I wore only for work, that killed me by the end of every day because they'd be muck-heavy and twice the weight of the wooden leg I was already carrying. I went through six or seven pairs in the twenty years, but the alligator boots stayed fresh, under the bed six days a week, because I only wore them on Sundays, to mass.

I went to mass.

The city followed me out to Ratheen. The City Corporation took over a large tract of land near the sea, surrounded by everything good, and built houses for the people. The sons and daughters of the corner boys I'd had to fight and batter came out with their mattresses and prams. A good house for each family; a house full of kids, and a brand new school just up the road.

I began to wonder if my fight had really been a total waste. The city centre – I'd begun to think of Dublin as *town* – was still the kip I'd climbed out of. But here, twenty minutes away, the children had parents and coats. There were bedrooms and electricity, the certainty of dinner. Women stopped and chatted to each other, and none of them stood at wet corners, waiting desperately for business. Men came home from work at the same time every day. It was boring, but maybe freedom was supposed to be boring. I was home, myself, by six o'clock every evening.

There was one day, too early in spring, too damp, too cold, I got up off one knee, the one that carried the wood, but I couldn't manage the other. The knee had locked; I was stuck. I watched the knee sink deeper into the muck, and it started to fuckin' rain. This was March the 21st, 1963. I was only sixty-one, but my gardening days were over. I knelt in the front garden of one of the flat-roofed German houses – called German by the locals because the houses didn't look Irish. The rain made the ground even softer; I could feel the water seeping in between the wood and the meat of my leg. I knew I was in for hard pain. But I couldn't get up. The rain got heavier and the hole got quickly deeper. I was being swallowed – I fell forward.

And that was how the oul' one saw me. She was looking out the window, checking to see that she was getting value for her money and she saw the gardener trying to turn over onto his back, so he wouldn't drown in her flowerbed. Both of my knees were bent, my feet were in the air – an ancient baby trying to stand up in its cot. *What about me!* She came straight out. I heard her squelch across the lawn. She had ten years on me, but she still managed to pull me out of the muck and carry me to her kitchen, around to the back of the house – she didn't mind a bit of rain but she wasn't going to let me dirty her hall. She carried me, my arms around her neck and one of hers under my knees, all the way, right over the fuckin' threshold. I could tell immediately I wasn't the first dead man she'd carried.

She sat me down in the kitchen, on a white-painted chair. She put old newspaper under my feet. She lifted each foot, no bother, and didn't flinch or even pause when she held up one hard leg and realised what she was holding. She put it back down on the paper, and stood up without grunting. I looked around me while she went off somewhere for a towel – I knew; she'd gone looking for an old one – and I saw the photograph. I could just about see it in the hall, past the open kitchen door. A young woman, in the Cumann na mBan uniform.

She came back in with a thin, grey towel. I dried my head; the towel nearly fell apart on my face.

—What happened you?

She wasn't a Roscommon woman, or she hadn't been in a long time.

—My knee, I told her.

I looked at the water still running off me, onto the *Irish Press* at my feet. The print was going to stain her lino.

Her name was O'Kelly and she'd been married to the man I'd seen her walking with, past my door, every Sunday afternoon, until just before Christmas the year before. The Widow O'Kelly, still dressed, I noticed now, in black.

I looked at her.

She'd never been Miss O'Shea.

—Did it lock on you? she asked.

—It did.

It did, I'd said, and not just *Yeah*. I was in *The Quiet Man*. (There were cinemas near enough to me, in Sutton and Killester, but I'd never gone to see it.)

—It happens to us all, she said.—All you can do is wait. You'll have a cup of tea.

I didn't tell her I never drank it. The cold was in me; I could still feel the muck on my lips.

She came back with some of her husband's clothes. A pair of corduroy trousers, a jumper and a flannel shirt.

—What do you think?

—Thank you, missis.

—He'd be glad you have them. He thought the world of you.

—He was a good man.

—Ah, sure.

She stepped out of the kitchen. She brought the door with her.

—The kettle will be ready by the time you've changed.

Bending down was a killer. The laces put up a fight; they were soaked fat and ignorant. But I got the boots off and managed to keep them on the paper. The trousers were tricky – the kettle was boiling, starting to rattle; she was right behind the door. My knee was still locked, so I had to change them sitting down. The kettle steam was getting into the corduroy. The fuckin' things were wet before I got them on.

—How are you getting on in there?

—Grand.

I was buttoning up the shirt.

—Are you decent?

—I am.

She came in through the steam, and I was sure it was my woman. *Ah, sure.* The thin hair up in a bun. I stopped being old Henry and asked her.

—Were you ever a Miss O'Shea?

—No, she said.—I wasn't.

She didn't hesitate or raise a grey, wet eyebrow. She went straight for the kettle.

—How's the knee?

I told my leg to straighten, and it did. One slight click and I was back in action. She wasn't looking. She was messing with the teapot. I could have cheated; I could have stayed. But —

—Grand, I said.

I didn't want to be helpless.

—You'll have the tea before you go, she said.

—I will.

I will. I hoped she'd look, and admit it: she was Miss O'Shea. But she wasn't. And she didn't.

She gave me a couple of fig rolls. She watched me eat them. They were stale but I said nothing.

—Redmond, she said.

—That was your name before you got married?

—Yes, she said.—I was twenty.

—Young enough.

—Young enough, she agreed.

I stood up.

—Thanks very much, I said.—I'll bring the clothes back to you.

—They're yours, she said.

I was wearing a dead man's clothes again.

—Thanks.

—They fit you.

It was true.

I went out the back door, after she'd slipped me a ten-shilling note.

—I'll see you next week so, Henry.

—Yeah, I said.

But she wouldn't. She'd see me, but not knee-deep in her garden.

I went to mass.

I went, and stood and kneeled – and sometimes groaned – and sat, and listened to the hum of the Latin around me. I looked at the mothers in their Sunday best. I stood up and left with everyone else. I even stood around outside and chewed the rag with the other oul' lads and louts leaning against the church wall, waiting

136

for the Manhattan, the pub across the road, to open. I went to
the church every Sunday, so the priest would see me there, clean-
shaven, clean-shirted, a widower, well able to look after himself.

There was a job going, and the priest had it. He stood in front
of the bike one day, late afternoon, getting dark, when I was going
downhill, towards the high cross – the real thing, stone, not a
film prop – at the junction, the last steep stretch before home. I
saw his new black shoes and I stopped.

I'd nodded before, two or three times, but I'd never spoken
to him.

—Not a bad day now, he said.

—No, I agreed, although I was sick of the day and the weather
that came with it.

He stared at my hands on the handlebars, and looked back up
at me.

—You're a hard working man, he said.

I said nothing back. I didn't understand priests; I hadn't a clue
what he was doing there.

—Henry, isn't it?

—Yeah, I said.—That's me.

—Henry Smart.

He was used to being listened to; he was used to stopping
traffic.

—That's right, I said.

—I've been asking around about you, he said.

He was a lucky man; thirty years earlier, he'd have been dead
for doing that.

—Why? I asked.

Then I made a quick decision.

—Why, Father?

—I have a job you might be interested in.

—Is that right, Father?

—That's right, he said.—Caretaker of the boys' school. Are you
interested?

—I don't know, I said.—Why me, Father?

—People speak highly of you, he said.—And good men are
scarce. You'll be kept busy. But I don't think you'd mind that too
much.

I nodded.

—The last incumbent wasn't too fond of hard work, said the
priest.—Or children.

I looked at him.

—I don't mind hard work, Father, I told him.

—You've had children yourself, Henry?

I thought quickly about it.

—Two, I said.

—Are they nearabouts?

—They're in America. Father.

—And the grandchildren?

I shrugged.

—You've lost count, he said.

I didn't kill him. I stood up straight beside my bike. I pushed it an inch; I was ready to move.

—Will you think about it? said the priest.

—I'll think about it.

—You're interested.

—Yes, Father, I said.—I'm interested.

—Good man, he said.—Good. When I see you at mass a couple of Sundays in a row, I might even offer it to you. There are one or two other candidates I want to talk to first.

He stood aside.

—I'll let you go.

He walked off, up the hill. I thought about going after him with the spade off my bike; his neck was an easy, red target. But it had started pissing down, black fuckin' rain. A job with a roof – it was already keeping me dry. I went home and polished the alligator boots and I wore them to mass the next Sunday. I liked the company and the Latin. And five weeks after I kneeled at my first mass, the priest knocked on my door.

—The job's yours, he said.

I took a breath. I kept my hands at my sides.

—When, Father?

—Tomorrow, he said.

—Thanks, Father.

He held out a fat set of keys.

—I won't bother you with the which-one-is-which palaver, he said.—You can learn by trial and error. Eight o'clock tomorrow morning. You're expected.

—Grand.

I liked the neat click of the lock in the front gate. It was new; it wanted to give. The railings were new too, and silver. The path along the perimeter was sharp and new, where the handsome

mammies parked their prams while they wrapped up their eldest
boys and sent them in to learn. The tarmac from the gate into
the yard was new; it held onto my soles for just a welcoming
second before letting go of me again. Everything was new. The
teachers were young. The headmaster was a gentleman. The walls
inside still gave off the good smell of new paint, even on the wet
days when the corridors shrank between lines of damp, hanging
coats.

I'd finally found a school that wanted me. I was maintaining
a building that wasn't falling apart. And I caught myself thinking,
just the once: James Connolly would have liked this. I copped
myself on; it was only a fuckin' school. But I was content enough
as I did my daily rounds, swept the yard, fixed the leaking tap,
threw disinfectant at the cement urinal and listened to it hiss and
eat the tiles.

The quiet life was mending me.

—You've abandoned us, Henry.

I looked and saw her, Missis O'Kelly. Outside the butcher's on
the Main Road. I'd just bought a load of calf's liver. It was heavy
and wet in my hand, beginning to seep through the brown paper.
But I wasn't going to take out my net shopping bag. It stayed
safe in my coat pocket. This oul' one had been in Cumann na
mBan; men carried rifles, not shopping bags.

—Hello, Missis O'Kelly, I said.—Grand day again.

It wasn't raining. The only thing dripping was the blood from
the bag in my fist.

—Have you retired? she said.

—No, I haven't, I said.

My back was as straight as I could get it.

Her eyes were brown, and younger than the rest of her.

—I've just moved on, I said.—A new job.

She looked down at my knee – at both my knees.

—It's grand, I told her.—No bother since. I'm looking after
the boys' school.

—Looking after? she said.—Caretaking?

—That's it, I said.

—But who'll take care of my garden? she said.—It's already
growing wild.

She was well able to go into her own garden and beat back
nature. She'd carried me into her house without sweating. But
that wasn't the point. A good garden looked better with a handy

little man standing or kneeling in it. And I'd seen the way she'd looked at my knees.

The suburban life was doing things to me. I was grabbing back the years.

—I could drop by on Saturday, I said.

—Good, she said, like I'd finally seen reason.—That's arranged then.

I heard the explosion from out on the roof. Some poor little fucker had dropped the bottle of ink.

By the time I got down the headmaster was showing the young lad how to use a mop. The kid was still snivelling, still half expecting to be hammered. But he wasn't going to be hit, and his body was beginning to know that. The headmaster – I'll give the man his name: Mister Strickland – he'd swept the broken glass to the side of the floor, and he was running the mop across the block tiles like a man who'd done it before and liked being useful.

—Good man, Henry, he said.—I beat you to it.

—I was up on the roof, I told him.

He said nothing to that and dropped the mop-head into the bucket and sloshed it around. He squeezed it out.

—Come over here now, Peter, he said.

Peter was small and probably ten. He pulled himself away from the wall and slowly made his way to Strickland. He kept his feet out of the blue-stained suds.

Strickland held out the mop handle.

—Your turn, he said.

Peter hesitated – I waited for the quick jab, the mop handle to his gut. I knew it wouldn't happen but I still expected it. Peter took the handle. He was tiny beside it.

—Off you go now, said Strickland.—Let's see what you're made of.

He stood back and gave the kid his elbow room. Peter held the mop like it was a leper's prick; he wasn't happy at all.

—Go on, said Strickland.

We both watched Peter as he sent the mop out over the floor, and dropped it. He picked it up. He gathered up the suds. The ink was cheap – dyed water – so it didn't stain the wood.

—Good man, said Strickland.

He took the mop from Peter.

—Now, Peter, he said.—Listen to me now. If you work hard in school, that might be the last time you'll ever have to use a mop.

—Yes, sir.

—Off you go.

—Thanks, sir.

—And mind the wet floor there.

Peter didn't move.

—The ink, sir, he said.

—What about it?

—Mister McManus sent me on the message, sir. To get the ink.

—Go back to Mister McManus —

I saw the fear hop into Peter's face. So did Strickland.

—Tell him the bottle was empty, he said,—and I'll bring the ink up to him myself in a few minutes. But I'll have to mix some more first, tell him.

He watched Peter.

—Got that?

—Yes, sir.

—That'll be fine, he said.—Off you go.

Peter slid over the wet tiles. He tried not to run because he knew he wasn't supposed to.

—Poor Peter, said Strickland.—He's a bit of a worrier.

He picked up the broken neck of the bottle. The spout, for pouring the ink, was still jammed in it.

—Can you get that out, Henry? he said.—And I'll find a new bottle.

The bell was rung every morning. Strickland lifted it over his head, held it there for a long second, then let it fall, his arm held straight – it shaved his knee. It went up again, and down, four times, and the boys, cold and giddy, got into their lines and waited for the go-ahead, permission to walk in, out of the cold, in to the hissing radiators and coloured chalk. They turned up every morning, and they were let in. No boy was stopped at the front door. The nuns were safely next door, in the girls' school, and they never climbed over the railings.

These boys ran out of the new houses every morning. Most of them had been born in rooms like the one I'd been born into – *What about me?* But their parents had brought them out to clean air, fresh paint and free primary education. The houses were good, and built by the state. The school was good, built by the state.

It was a national school – although this was Ireland, so the manager was the priest – and this was my reward. I'd been run out of the country before the state was founded. But now the state was looking after me. And I looked after its little lads. They'd be waiting, some of them, when I took the block of keys from my jacket pocket and found the one I wanted, and opened the front gate.

—Hiya, Hoppy Henry.

—Jesus, lads, you're early.

Hoppy Henry – I fuckin' loved my name, the cheek and life that went into it. And I thought the boys were like me, and that they loved the place. It took me a while to calm down, to notice the shivers and malnourishment, the ringworm, the bruises. It took me a while to accept that poverty could also be suburban. And it was a while before I noticed the disappearing boys. That last lesson came with a cough.

I heard it as I crossed the yard, on my way to the outside jacks with a bucket of disinfectant. The yard was closed on three and a half sides, by the school itself, the hall and bike shed. The wind was trapped in there and made to do laps. It went clockwise, always, and so did the kids. All games, the chasing and the football, went from left to right. That morning was a windy one, the middle of April but still winter, even if there were pink blossoms being whirled among the running boys. I was the only one walking into the wind, from my windowless office in under the hall, to the jacks.

—Howyeh, Hoppy!

The top layer of the disinfectant was being shaved off by the wind and thrown back into my trousers. There was a slate, fresh-smashed, on the ground, near the front door – dangerously near it. I'd get rid of the disinfectant first, clear the jacks of kids and throw the contents of the bucket so hard it would smack the back wall and roll back, chewing the old smell with its new one. Then I'd go in to Mister Strickland and warn him about the flying slates. I looked up now to see if there were more slates missing or on their way down. There was the bucket of disinfectant pulling the arm off me; I was going to have to climb out onto the roof and into the strong, mean hands of the wind; I'd found rat droppings on top of my desk, when I was mixing the disinfectant. It was a fuck of a day already. But I was happy.

Then I heard the cough.

It came straight out of my memory, like one of the slates. Came out, and down, and sliced me. My mouth, my eyes – I was split in half.

Victor. My brother, and his last cough – I'd woken to its dying echo but he was already dead. And I'd just heard it again. I'd heard a cough that had opened flesh. There was a dying child in the school yard.

The yard was full. Every boy under twelve from the Ratheen estate was in there. But I saw him immediately. There were invisible hands holding him up at the shoulders. His face was white and disbelieving – he was climbing out of his own mouth. He knew it but he didn't understand why his own life was leaving him. He was trying to close his mouth, but couldn't.

The wind whipped around me; I could feel the disinfectant splashing on my hands, over a lifetime's cuts and damage. I didn't put the bucket down. I wanted to move, but I couldn't. The kid's mouth was closing, slowly. His eyes were back; his shoulders were coming down. He was alright, for now. He'd cough again. I'd be given another chance.

Strickland came out with his bell. He saw the broken slate and stepped back into the school, the corridor behind the glass. I saw him shout, and immediately his staff, the country boys, came running out past him, ready to herd their lads out of the yard.

I finally moved. I went over to the jacks and threw the disinfectant. The bucket went with it; I couldn't hold on. It clattered against the far wall, above the urinal. The hand stung, and I let it sting. I took my punishment, but it wasn't enough.

I got up onto the roof. I hoped the wind would grab my arm and throw me down into the yard. But it wasn't as strong up there; it wasn't trapped and angry. I looked down at Strickland walking back across the empty yard. He had the kid with him, trotting along beside him, happy now with the big bell in his hand.

It was called consumption when it got Victor. Now it was T.B. And it was under control, well on the run. There were sanatoriums, and a man called Noel Browne. No one coughed to death in the new Ireland.

But I knew what I'd heard.

There was just the one slate missing. The others were well tacked down. I got off the roof; it was easily done, even with a wooden leg. I went down the wide stairs to Strickland's office to tell him the good news, to lick up to him and hear him say *Good man*. To make sure he hadn't seen me standing by while the poor kid was breathing his second last. I nearly ran along the corridor. I knew it; I was pathetic.

I'd been lots of things in my time, but never pathetic. Never in my own eyes. I'd been stupid and magnificent, and all the little countries in between. But I'd never seen myself as pathetic; I'd never been on that island.

When I got to his office he was coming out, with the kid. He had his coat on.

—I'm bringing Seán home, he told me.

Seán looked quite excited. He was going home early, in a car. His lungs were sleeping; he was grand.

Strickland locked the office door.

I kept an eye out for Seán after that. But he didn't come back. I asked Strickland.

—Young Seán, I said.

—Poor Seán, he said.—He'll be fine.

—Where is he?

—Wicklow, said Strickland.—In the sanatorium up there. In a room all by himself. His mother, God love her, can look in at him every Sunday, through the glass. And his father's there too. In another room.

He clapped his hands, once.

—But, he said.—Seán will be back.

I believed him. But I woke up. I began to see and hear. I still saw the progress, and smelt it. It came from the walls, and from inside the classrooms. But I knew I wasn't in a republican heaven. Bad lungs weren't left at the gate, and bad bastards occasionally crawled off the farm and became teachers. I kept hearing Seán's cough, every time I crossed the yard, even fighting the loudest wind. Every time I walked along one of the corridors.

I declared war, a guerrilla war. I declared, but no one heard me. I always carried my excuse – the mop or a spanner – and I patrolled. Quietly, lightly – I went easy on the limp. I roamed the corridors, upstairs and ground floor, and the three extra rooms hidden away at the back. I stood among the hanging coats. And I waited. All the training came back; I'd never lost it. Boys and staff went past but they didn't see or hear me. I could stand still for hours. I could withstand the pain that ate its way all through my leg; I could even ignore it.

I listened, and heard the slaps. I counted them. Four, five, then the sixth. Six was as many as I'd tolerate. Six of the famous best. Three whacks on each open hand with the leather strap. The limit: I'd allow no more. But then I heard the seventh, and the eighth. The ninth, the tenth. I heard the objections, killed in the throats of fifty-four witnesses, the silent outrage. And the terror. I was outside. The boys were inside, watching a brute lose control of himself. Living it, and being destroyed by it.

The three o'clock bell – *go home, go home*. I stepped out from the coats as the door opened and the boys came out, in a long, slow line. Still pale and scared but ready to laugh and pretend it had been nothing. It was hard to tell which of them had been the victim. But I saw him. And I'd remember him.

I made my move.

I filled the door before the teacher could get out. This was Mister Mulhare. I didn't know his first name. The job was easier without it.

He spoke first – I wasn't going to.

—Henry, he said.—I'll leave you to it.

He had his bag, the *mála scoile*, under his arm. He tried to walk around me.

I didn't move.

He was young, still in his twenties.

—The latch on the window beyond needs looking at, he said.— Good man.

I still didn't move. Then I stepped straight into him and shut the door with my heel, just rightly weighted, no big bang or ricochet. He stepped back, nearly fell, to get out from under me. His bag slipped from under the arm; he held it now in both hands.

—Fuck the latch on the window, I said.

He was short and broad. He came from a line of mountain men. But he was scared. He tried to look outraged but nothing came out of him.

—If, I said.

I stepped on his foot and brought the rest of me forward to meet it. I was a tall man again.

—If I ever hear you slapping any of the boys again, I said.

I stayed still now, hung right over him.

—I'll kill you, I told him.—Slowly. D'you hear me, Mister Mulhare?

—What do you mean?

I hit him.

I back-handed the cunt, sent the slap bouncing around the walls and maps.

—You know what I mean, I said.—If a kid misbehaves, you can slap him.

He was still clutching the schoolbag. He hadn't touched his face, where I'd whacked him. It was turning red, and his eyes were catching up.

I stepped a bit closer. He was backed up to his desk now.

—To a maximum of six, I said.—Three on each hand. But only for the mortal sins. Once in a blue fuckin' moon. D'you understand me, Mister Mulhare?

I laid off the sarcasm. I threw no extra weight into his name or the *Mister*.

He nodded.

—Good, I said.—I'll be outside. Always. Counting. If I hear more than six, you're dead.

A sharp dig to his gut; my fingers reminded me that they'd been broken before.

He dropped the bag.

—Or you'll wish you were dead.

I stepped back.

—If anyone else hears about this, I said.—Do I have to say more?

He shook his head.

—I know, I said.—It's a bit of a shock. I'm the caretaker. Yeah?

He nodded. He wasn't ready to talk.

—Your daddy told you all about the War of Independence. Yeah?

He nodded.

—And I bet he told you he was in the thick of it, I said.

He nodded.

—Yes, he said, as he picked up his bag.

—And I bet you never really believed him.

—He has a medal.

—They all have fuckin' medals.

I didn't hit him.

—I was there, Mister Mulhare, I told him.—And I never got a medal. And I didn't have a fuckin' farm to go home to.

I hadn't planned this, but it was coming from somewhere sore right behind my ribs. I moved in close again – I parked right up

146

against him. The schoolbag was back on the floor. I shoved it aside with the wooden foot, no twinge or protest from the knee.

—If your da was ever in the thick of it, it was because I ordered him to be in the thick of it. Where are you from, Mister Mulhare?

—Kilkenny.

—I know every inch of it, I told him.—Every ditch and hiding place. Is your da still alive?

—Yes.

—That's because of me.

—Thanks.

—No problem. You understand me.

—Yes.

—Your da and his brothers and cousins took their orders from me. And so do you.

—Yes.

—Remember that, I told him.—All those stories your da told you, I'm in every one of them. I was there. And now I'm back.

I stepped away.

I was tired now. I'd gone too far. I was a gobshite. But the teacher didn't think so. He was shaking. Trying to gather himself and stay whole.

I opened the door.

—I'll be listening, I told him.

I left him there and went up to the roof, to do some shaking of my own. I watched Mulhare walk across the yard, to the gate and the bus stop up on the Main Road. I shook till I stopped, and got down off the roof. I locked up and went home.

I passed him the next morning. I made sure I did.

—Morning, Mister Mulhare.

—Good morning, Henry.

—I fixed that latch for you, I said.

—Oh. Thank you.

—No problem at all, I said.—It's why I'm here.

I watched him stand at the door of his room. He smiled at the boys who walked past him. He smiled big at every one of them. He looked at me and closed the door. I did the bits of business that made my job, and listened. Mulhare didn't use the leather strap at all.

I didn't overdo it. I left him alone, and the others too. I knew they had a few pints on Friday, the younger ones, after they'd emptied the school and cleaned their blackboards. I saw them

147

gathering around the cars, giddy for drink, boys again, laughing much louder than they had to. They all pushed in – there were three cars, and seventeen of them. They didn't drink local. They wisely kept going, on into town. I wished them well and I knew: Mulhare would eventually yap. He'd move on to the small ones one Friday night, and it would all come out. In one of the culchie pubs, on the shoulder of a fat nurse from home. He'd tell them what had happened. Or he'd tell her – he'd whisper it wet, into her ear. And she'd pass it on, when he'd gone into the jacks to vomit; she'd whisper into the ear of her off-duty pal, who was sitting beside, or on the knee of, another of the teachers, or his cousin, the Guard. It would be all around the pub and out the back door by the time he'd finished puking and cleaned himself. The band in the corner would be putting it to music.

I slowed down and let the job go at my new pace. I made more of my limp; I did less work. No one complained. The place didn't collapse. The emergencies were rare and easily conquered – a leaking pipe, blocked jacks, the odd broken window.

I was standing in the yard, under my fedora, and shoving a brush handle down into a drain that was blocked with the pebbles that were the props in a game the boys had been playing for months. It was raining, and warm. The yard sloped very slightly on all sides, to the shore and the drain at the centre. The rain was heavy, the first of the new summer – this was early June – and the yard was starting to flood. I'd been down on my knees, and I'd scooped handfuls of the pebbles out of the hole, along with sweet papers and cigarette butts and old bits of bread crust, and woodlice and long worms. But there were still enough of the pebbles down there, a dry-stone wall of the fuckin' things, enough to keep damming the rainwater. I was pounding them into wet dust with the butt of the brush. I wasn't enjoying it; each bash was a boy's soft head.

I saw bubbles, and more bubbles – I'd dislodged enough stones, and the rainwater rushed for the hole. My working day was more or less over. I started to walk across the yard to my office. The fedora was low on my head. So I didn't see the man. But I saw the feet, the sudden change of direction – the skid – to avoid me. I looked up and saw O'Naughton, the teacher in charge of the High Babies. He smiled back, terrified.

It was out. Mulhare had cried into his pint and told them. The caretaker was one of the men who'd mattered. Young Mulhare

148

would have recovered as he told them the story; he'd have enjoyed the attention. The girls from home, the nurses and clerical officers, would have been there too, with their fizzy minerals. He'd have wiped his nose on the shoulder of one of the nurses. He'd probably got his hole later, in her digs, a quick, mad ride, still in his shoes and socks, before she had to get him out and let in the rest of the girls who were waiting outside in the rain.

So, the lads in the staffroom were scared and impressed. They were careful. They'd learnt Mulhare's lesson. But there was also the luck I'd brought; they'd seen that as well. Mulhare had got the ride from a fine girl because of me, because of my presence in the story he'd been blubbering that Friday night, in one of the new lounge bars where country girls with jobs could sit and stay. He'd have told the lads about that too – proudly, secretly, over the biscuits on Monday morning in the staffroom. It had worked for him; it could work for them. The word from old Henry, the benediction. They just needed something to bring with them the next Friday, a story of their own. Not even a story; a greeting or nod, or the rub of shoulders as we passed in the corridor. That would get them sorted. I saw it, after the early shock of Mulhare's story had faded. His big eyes had told them that, as he leaned closer to them and whispered the muck through the steam that rose from their tea.

I became their leprechaun and pimp. I set them up with birds I never met. I was a very busy man on Friday afternoons. I patrolled the corridors after the break; I kept that fear in the air. I'd got a cobbler in Killester to add nails to one of my boots. They'd hear me coming at them over the wood tiles – *tap, tap*. The old I.R.A. man who'd lost his leg for his country – their country. It didn't matter that the hobnails were on the good foot. The noise was what mattered; the nails kept the peace.

Some of them got brave and they'd start to shout when they heard the extra nails approaching. They'd fill their rooms with sudden, badly acted rage and sometimes the real stuff too, kept in all week till now.

—Do you call that a straight line!

A duster hit the blackboard.

—No, no, no! You *amadán*!

Sometimes I'd take their bait – just to let them know that the school's flying column was still active. I stood at the doors of their emptied rooms and I waited till they knew I was there. More

149

often than not they'd be waiting for me, trying hard not to look too delighted.

—I heard you shouting there, I told him.

I was talking to McCauley, the man in charge of the top sixth class, all forty-two of the scholarship boys.

—Did you? he said back.

—Yeah.

—And? he said.

He was a bit older than the others, and under pressure. It was in his eyes, even in the way he walked. He was given the same class, the scholarship lads, every year, because he was good enough and frightening enough to drag results from boys whose parents couldn't read. He was on his own, under a unique pressure – even his room was away from the others, up its own short stairs – pushing these kids out to secondary school, creating a middle class on the Northside of Dublin, for his own good name and the school's. It was relentless. And he'd been under even more pressure since I'd whacked Mulhare, because I wouldn't let him be as frightening as he'd always needed to be. He hadn't biffed a kid in weeks.

—I don't mind the odd shout, I said.—But *amadán*. That means eejit, doesn't it?

—Broadly speaking, yes.

I hit him. I punched the side of his face, enough for a bruise, but not hard enough to break or squash anything. His glasses went up over his hair, but they stayed on his head.

I stepped right up to him. He was wiping the blackboard with the back of his jumper.

—You've your job to do, I told him.—But no kid is an eejit, in any language.

He nodded.

—You agree with me.

—Yes, he said.

—Good man.

I watched his face – the terror, delight. He couldn't wait for the bell and his turn to drop a story onto the lounge bar table. He was an ugly cunt but it wasn't going to matter.

—Look, I said.—I understand what you're doing here. But this isn't a war and those kids aren't the British. You understand me.

—Yes.

—I'm on your side.

He was salivating – he was.

—Both of us are in this thing together, I told him.

Mulhare and the boys would be outside, waiting for him. One of the cars was his.

—Enjoy your weekend, I told him.

He didn't have weekends. He brought the boys in on Saturdays – he had his own keys – and he did all his corrections on Sundays. But he had his Friday nights.

I walked out.

For fifteen years the boys' national school in Ratheen was the most civilised place in the country. No child was slapped, except on the days when I stayed at home. I'd made my own republic, inside the railings of the school.

It was a good life.

—Howyeh, Hoppy.

I was tempted to ban subtraction. Addition and multiplication were grand – *Two and two?* – but there'd be no place for taking away in my republic. But I didn't do it. I couldn't ban reality, the hard knocks and grief that were waiting beyond the railings. Two and two was four, two from two was fuck-all – it was the complete package. I didn't want to mould them; they'd be well able to do that by themselves. They eventually left, for secondary school, or the tech, or the building sites – and the poor little fuckers didn't know what happened, as the Christian Brothers and other outside forces got their maulers on them. But the years in my school were enough. There was another way and they went through their lives knowing that.

I lived in my country and liked it. I woke up beside a woman, once a week. An old woman, older than me, but she was the first woman I'd touched in more than twenty years. I cleaned up her garden on Saturday afternoons, for two quid and my dinner.

Nothing was said, and there was no kissing or awkwardness. I just didn't go home the second Saturday. She went out and hid the bike. She came back in, turned off all the lights and I followed her up the stairs. I wasn't excited; I didn't give a shite. She filled a bath and left me at it. I took off the leg and climbed in.

She said nothing. When I followed her into the bedroom, when I sat on the bed and put the leg beside me on the rug. When I put on the pyjamas she'd left there. When I lay back beside her and grunted, and covered myself with the sheet and blankets and eiderdown. When I looked to the side and tried to see her. I could see her sharp nose, aimed at the ceiling. I could hear her breath.

She spoke.

—You'll have to be out early.

—Grand.

—Very early.

—Grand.

—And the bicycle with you.

—No problem; grand.

—Quietly. Carry the bike till you're down the road.

—I'm ahead of you, don't worry.

—I'm too old for romance or any silliness.

—I'm still ahead of you.

—Do you need the alarm clock?

—No.

—Sure?

—Yeah. I'll be grand.

That was it. We listened to each other breathing, and we slept. I woke in the dark. I got out of the house, got the bike from the shed, carried the thing on my back to the front of the house – there were no lights in the neighbouring houses, or across the road. I walked a bit further. Then I put the bike down and pushed it the rest of the way home.

The following Saturday I brought the bike straight to the shed. I left it there and took out the lawnmower.

—You don't cycle the bike, she said.

She always came out for a chat when she saw that I was there. She chatted outside, never really in the house. She chatted to Henry the gardener.

—I can't, I said.

—Your leg.

—That's right, I said.—Too tricky.

She never asked where the leg had gone. I never asked her about the woman in the Cumann na mBan uniform, in the photograph on the wall. It wasn't a good picture, and the photographer had parked the camera too far from the subject. She caught me staring at it, when she was coming down the stairs. She said nothing. I walked back into the kitchen. I dried the dishes she'd already washed. She turned off the lights. She lay on her side, and put her arm across my chest. We slept.

Some months in, I asked a question.

—Do you have any children?

—Yes, she said.—I've one. A girl. And you?

152

—A girl too, I said.—And a boy.

We were in the bed, in the dark. We said no more.

Mister Strickland stepped out of his office just as I was limping past. He grabbed my arm and held it.

—Listen to that, he said.

I knew what he meant but I pretended he'd have to give me more.

—Listen to what? I said.

—Just listen, he said.—What do you hear?

—Nothing.

—Exactly, he said.

He still held my arm. I hadn't tried to free it.

—I haven't heard the *leather* being used in months, he said.

—That's good, I said.—Is it?

—Oh, yes, he said.—I hate the things.

He carried a leather in his jacket pocket. It gave weight on his right side, like a gun. And he'd once sent me into town to buy a box of the things, in a shop on a street off Marlborough Street that sold clerical outfits and straps. I'd brought them back on the bus, on my lap.

—Don't get me wrong, he said.—I've used one, and I'll use it again, I'm sure. I hand each new man a leather of his own when he comes in to see me in September. But I always tell them to keep it on the desks. Visible, you know?

I nodded.

—A warning to the boys, he said.—But only to use it when it's absolutely necessary. And there's the problem. Because, Henry?

—What?

—What's necessary?

I didn't answer.

—Good man, he said.—There was a time there when I wondered if maybe I'd failed to make my point. Because there was a hell of a lot of slapping going on. It was like applause some afternoons, all the way down to the bottom of the corridor there.

He let go of my arm.

—I spoke to them, he said.

He was tall. I made sure I was too. We were tall together, looking back along the silent corridor. There was a bulb down there needed changing.

—I spoke to them, he said again.—They're nice lads, I like them all. And top-class teachers. There isn't a real dud in my staffroom. They agreed with every word I said.

He smiled.

—And it worked, he said.—For a little while. I've been in worse places. And so have you.

I said nothing.

—But gradually it came back, he said.—Usually in the afternoons. The last hour before the bell. One started, and they all had to join in.

He stopped. He looked at me.

—And then it all stopped.

—That's great, I said.

—But why?

I looked down the corridor, half hoping some teacher would take a swipe at a child and save me.

—Because it's unusual, he said.—It's nearly the end of the school year. It gets wild around this time.

It was graveyard quiet down there.

—And Tom McCauley's scholarship lads, he said.—They don't really appreciate how important that Primary Cert is to them. How their whole futures depend on it. It has to be beaten into them. Usually.

He held my arm again, gently.

—What's going on, Henry? he said.—Any theories?

—No.

—None at all?

—You said one of the teachers started and they'd all join in. With the leathers.

—Yes.

—Well, maybe that's what after happening this time, in reverse.

—One of them stopped using the strap.

—And the others joined in.

He let go of my arm.

—But *why*?

—Don't know.

—You have eyes and ears, Henry.

—So do you, Mister Strickland.

—Yes, he said.—I do.

*   *   *

154

—Your daughter, I said.

We were eating the dinner. It was stew, but with better meat than I'd found in any stew before.

She looked – she stared.

—Yes? she said.

—Is she here? I asked.—In Dublin.

—No, she said.

—Grand.

The spuds were great too. I could forget the awkwardness I'd just dragged into the kitchen.

—I don't know where she is, she said.

—Oh, I said.—Right.

—What about *your* daughter?

—America.

—And your son?

—The same.

—It's far away.

—It is.

I ate, and she did too.

—This is great, by the way, I told her.

—Thank you.

—Lovely, I said.

I looked at her. I waited.

—Did you ever eat griddle cakes?

—No.

—Really? I said.—Never?

—No, she said.—Not where I grew up. They wouldn't have been the thing.

—Grand.

—We'd gone past griddle cakes, she said.—That would have been the thinking.

—Fine.

—Why do you ask?

—I was just wondering.

—I could find a recipe.

—It's up to yourself.

We ate.

The priest was sweating. It was another hot day out there.

—Father, I said.

155

—Henry.

I didn't know why he was there. He was my employer but it was his housekeeper who handed over my pay at his back door every Friday night.

—I was passing, he said.

—Grand.

—How are you?

—Fine.

He was trying to see past me, into the gloom behind. My home was like a cave. It had been built when men were smaller and the builders even meaner. Each cottage got a window at the front and a much smaller one at the back. There were three small rooms behind me. The jacks was out the back. The water pump was on the street, right behind the priest.

But I liked it. The word *home* had begun to mean something. I didn't own the place – the Corporation did. But it was mine.

—I hear great things, he said.—I had a chat yesterday with Mister Strickland.

—I'm glad he's happy, I said.

—He's happy, alright. He's more than happy.

He clapped his hands.

—And that, now, makes me happy.

I'd been seen. Sneaking out of Missis O'Kelly's, with the bike on my back. Someone had told him, some insomniac gawking out at the dark, or the dawn – it had been bright enough when I'd left the previous Sunday. The priest was letting me know. He was threatening me.

—Will you have a cup of tea, Father?

I didn't move to let him past. I was letting him know there was no one hiding behind me.

—Ah no, he said.

I didn't have any tea. I never drank it.

—I was just passing, he said.

—Grand.

—And you're happy?

—I am.

—With the job, he said.

—That's right.

—Because, he said,—there are people who'll be very happy to hear that. Cheerio now.

I wondered who these people were but I was happy enough to

156

see him go, back up the hill. I wasn't so sure now that he'd been threatening me. But what he'd just said had sounded like a much bigger threat.

He didn't look back. He slowed down; he was struggling on the slope. But he kept going. He looked in the open door of the cop shop. (It had been the R.I.C. barracks in the fighting days, but not one that I'd ever set fire to.) He kept going, past the barber's, up on to the Main Road.

I told her nothing. There was a risk now but I didn't want to give it up, the bath and the grub and the breath beside me in the bed. But I took different routes home, dog-early on the Sunday mornings. I climbed over her back wall, dragged the bike over with me, and dropped into the soft field – it would soon be a building site – behind her house. Or I climbed into the garden next door, and the next one, the handlebars biting into me, and I came out on the road by a different front gate every time. It looked like I was riding every oul' one along the road. I didn't really know why I did it, all the creeping and climbing. The bit of excitement. It did me good and I did it for years.

I spoke to the priest just three times in the next ten years.

—How are you?

—Not too bad, Father.

—I hear great things.

—That's good.

She never made the griddle cakes.

8

Louis Armstrong came to Dublin, but I stayed away. I saw the photos in the *Herald*, Pops at the National Stadium. He looked well. He looked like the man he'd been. But I didn't. He wouldn't have known me. The bouncers wouldn't have let me near him.

Kennedy came, and stayed a few days. *We need men who can dream of things that never were.* His day in Dublin was a day off work, a day to be loud and Irish. I stayed in the house.

Then there was 1966, and the fiftieth anniversary of Easter Week. Another right time to be loud and Irish – the Golden Jubilee. I was tempted. I looked at the parades of oul' lads in their cleaned suits and bits of uniforms. I looked carefully at them all. I didn't know half of them, or a quarter or an eighth of them. With their medals and their slouch hats. I made sure I was in the Manhattan when the news was on, and I sat up close to the brand new television, right on top of the thing. I looked for the faces I'd known. I saw one or two – I could see the young men looking out of the old heads. I recognised two or three, maybe four, out of the hundreds, the thousands who'd claimed their medals and their I.R.A. pensions, and who marched, or tried to, up every street in the country. I watched them march in parts of the country that had never given a flying fuck about the freedom of Ireland and probably still didn't notice that the postboxes had been painted a different colour. Those medals were mine.

They even met in Ratheen village before mass on Easter Sunday, to march into the church together. I walked through them and heard voices remembering the time Dan Breen had nearly been caught in the safe house on the Main Road, how he'd taken a rake of bullets as he was going over the back wall and still managed to leave three Tans in the back garden, bleeding into the pond. All of them nodding away: they'd all been there, climbing over the wall with Dan. I knew those gardens; I'd been up and over most of the back walls. There wouldn't have been room for all these chancers. None of them had been in the G.P.O., or anywhere else that had mattered that week, those five days, or the six big years that followed them.

I went into the church and I noticed: my limp was worse than usual. It was worse than it had ever been, even in the days when the absence was new and I'd had to learn to walk. I was dragging my excuse in with me. *I was there*, I wanted to shout. *I was in the G.P.O. I was up on the fuckin' roof. I got my hole in a room full of stamps!*

Missis O'Kelly marched in with them, in her Cumann na mBan uniform and a neat line of her own medals. The only woman in the gang. And her now, I believed: she'd been there – somewhere. It was in her back and eyes. I'd known her fifty years before. I was sure of it, but only now, even after sleeping with her every Saturday night for years. I'd known her voice, years before, when she was young and I was younger, in the G.P.O., and years before that too. I'd known her before she was Missis O'Kelly. I was sure of it now, nearly positive. I knew her people; I knew the mud she'd come from. But I looked at her skirt as she passed. There was no sign of the tear she'd inflicted on the material when she'd climbed onto the bed of stamps. Her hair was grey and too thin now for a decent bun.

It was a hard week to get through. I had a Bush transistor at home, and I heard Éamon de Valera. *We cannot adequately honour the men of 1916 if we do not strive to bring about the Ireland of their desire.* That was the end of the first day; there were another six to go. But I didn't turn off the radio. I'd even bought a spare battery, just in case.

I recognised voices, and faces. Seán Lemass, the Taoiseach – 'The Boss'. He'd been a kid in the G.P.O., a few years older than me. But, unlike me, he'd looked like a kid. I saw him now, all week, looking out from behind his pipe-smoke. De Valera was there too, everywhere, blind and ancient but with no sign of the madness I'd stood beside in Richmond Barracks in 1916 while the photographer, Hanratty, took the snap that became the famous one, the father of the state-to-be, undaunted and straight, a foot taller than his English guards. I was right beside him, smiling for Hanratty, but the useless bollocks only got my elbow. I saw them all week, and a few others, the ones who'd survived. They'd lost the Civil War but they'd ended up winning. The country was theirs and they stood to attention as the flags went up and the old men marched past.

I even saw Ivan Reynolds. I sat up and laughed.

I was in the pub, hugging a slow pint.

He was on a panel, some sort of discussion, looking huge and breathless, being swallowed by his own flesh. But I couldn't hear him; the sound on the telly was down. He was a minister. Post and Telegraphs, or something like that; Fisheries, Local Government – a step or two from the big jobs. He looked like he'd made the most of his days in power. The television was black and white, but Ivan still managed to look red and shiny. I'd had him down for an early death, back when I'd last seen him, sucking Rémy Martin from the bottle. That was in 1921. But Ivan was far from dead. I looked at him and I wondered if I wanted to meet him again, shake his hand, slag his shine.

I didn't.

And I didn't want a medal. I didn't want to march or hop.

But I was tempted.

I lay beside her. And I wanted to tell her. *I know who you were.* But I didn't.

Easter Week went away. The Proclamations stayed up, on the school wall and behind the bar of the Manhattan. But most of the flags came down, or frayed and rotted in the wet and the wind.

I looked at Missis O'Kelly, and I wasn't as sure as I had been. She was just an old woman who missed her husband, once a week. A fine, straight-backed oul' one. But no more. She'd never been anyone else.

I wasn't sure.

Once a week, I became her husband. Once a week, she could be my wife. It was grand. And I always liked the time when I was sneaking home. I was getting older, but it got no harder. I kept on climbing walls, and more walls. I'd drop into brand new, grassless gardens. I was nearly sixty-five but I kept on loving the challenge, slouching home, past more and more suburban windows, with the black bike on my back.

Life stayed good in the Republic of Henry. There'd been a sharp increase in the use of corporal punishment in the weeks leading up to Easter Week. Rebel songs and laments had to be learnt, and time was running out. But I let most of it go. I knew it would poison the boys, that they'd always associate *A Nation Once Again* and *Kevin Barry* with being skinned alive by some mad culchie teacher with spots across his forehead, bouncing up and down with a tuning fork in a cloud of chalk dust and dandruff. It would make real rebels of them later, as they grew up. So I stayed outside in the weather and gave the football pitch its first cut of the year.

Then it was all over and I advised one or two of the teachers that the time was right for a ceasefire. They looked at me and heeded the advice, and life at the school slipped back to its normality. They didn't know – though Strickland did, I think – that they were producing a brand new middle class, quick-witted and hungry, who'd grow up soon and make the country theirs. Dublin kids, the sons of parents from the slums. I'd sit back and watch them take over. It would be the pleasure of my real old age.

There were lost days. I'd wake up on the floor. I'd know: I'd been gone, wandering. I'd search my pockets, look out the window at the light. I'd touch my chin and read the stubble. One day gone, or two. On my own floor. Never at the school, or on the street. Or I'd wake on my bed, my clothes still on, jacket off and collar loosened. There'd be food on the table, in the kitchen. Fresh bread, a pint of milk.

Someone – people were looking after me.

I'd look at faces I'd come to know and sometimes like, the ones I saw every day. I saw nothing that said they knew.

I woke up in Missis O'Kelly's bed. I knew where I was, but it was bright day outside. I hadn't seen the room in light like this before. I could hear movement from downstairs, and the radio – afternoon music, one of the sponsored programmes. I was dressed, but not for gardening. She'd left the leg alone, and the boot still on it. It was digging into me; it hadn't been off for days.

—What happened? I asked.

She was in the kitchen, baking. But she wasn't happy.

—I found you, she said.—Outside. On the road.

—Sorry, I said.—Passed out?

—No, she said.—Just lost.

—I thought it had stopped, I said.

—What is it?

She hadn't looked at me properly. She was bent down, staring into the oven. She closed it and stood up straight, no grunt or crack. She still didn't look at me. She was too busy, and furious.

—I don't know, I told her.—Amnesia, I suppose.

—Why were you outside my house?

—When was it?

—This morning, she said.—In the garden – the front garden.

—You said the road.

—The garden, she said.—You were in my garden.

—I'm your gardener.

—Not on Tuesdays, she said.—And not dressed for Sunday.

She was right. I was wearing the good suit and the alligators. I rubbed my chin. I'd shaved that morning.

—Sorry, I said.

—You were standing in the garden, looking in my window.

—I don't remember that.

—You're too old to be Romeo, she said.—And I'm much too old to be anyone's Juliet.

She was looking at me now.

—I won't have it.

She was angry, furious that the neighbours might think that she was rubbing against the hired help, and furious too with herself.

—I'll stay away, I said.

I meant it; I didn't give a shite. Fuck her and her snobbery. What the fuck had she fought for, when she'd worn the uniform? I wasn't going to ask.

—You can get someone else to look after the garden, I said.

Ratheen was full of old men.

—I can, she said.

—What're you baking? I asked.

But she didn't answer.

—I'll see you on Saturday afternoon, she said.

—Grand.

I went out the back door.

I couldn't move. The air was dirt and screams. I was still on the street. But the street was gone. I knew who I was. Where I was.

Another bang, another bomb, from further off. People near me screamed and ran. I couldn't see them. I could smell fire in the air. I was under bricks, and looser stone. Big dust still landed on me.

—There's one over here.

I heard the voice, but I couldn't see the man.

—Over here! Jesus, his leg!

I tried to tell him. He was forty years too late if he wanted to save it. But I couldn't talk – there was no real air.

I could feel hands now. Lifting weight from off me. I could hear feet, and gasping. The screaming around me didn't stop. The crying, gulping. The smell, the noise, of burning. I could see a face; a handkerchief covered the mouth.

—You're still with us.

I tried to nod. I tried to move.

—You're grand, stay still for a bit.

He wasn't a professional – a doctor or an ambulance driver. I could see that through the dust that caked him and his uniform. He was a postman.

—Bomb, I said.

—Bombs. All over the place.

I could hear sirens.

—I can't see much, I told him.

—Mister, he said.—Believe me. You're lucky.

He was crying.

There were more men now, and a stretcher.

—I think this wall is going to go.

—Let's get him out of here. Jesus, this is terrible.

He wasn't talking about me. I could see that. He was looking around, trying to find a door out of the nightmare.

I tried to get up.

—No, no, stay still. We'll do the work.

They'd thrown rubble out of the way; the stretcher was right beside me. They grabbed my feet and shoulders and started to lift me – the leg slid out of my trousers.

—Oh, fuckin' Christ —

—It's grand, I said.

I could talk; I sounded fine.

—It's a wooden one. I've had it for years.

—Are you serious? said the poor fucker holding the leg.

—Yeah, I said.—A train went over me.

—Fuckin' hell, he said.—And now this.

They'd dropped me sideways onto the stretcher; the man with the leg couldn't get a proper grip. But they moved fast, through hard dust, through the walking and the dead. I watched as they carried me. It was worse than anything I'd seen. It made no sense. This was Dublin, in 1974. A warm day, late afternoon. I'd been thinking about taking off my jacket. And the whole thing, the place and everyone around me, had disintegrated.

I was gone from there before the smoke had cleared. Thick walls of grey and yellow smoke. I didn't see much – I couldn't, although some of what I had seen hit me days, years, later. I'd wake up in it again; the smoke and grit would be at my mouth and nostrils, in my own bed. Sleep scared me, for a long time.

I heard the crunch of shoe leather going over broken glass. It was ankle-deep where the shop fronts had once been. I heard the groans and screams, of pain and disbelief; bodiless noise, last words and gasps, still hanging there after death. The fierce breath of men who didn't want to breathe. The sirens that couldn't get nearer.

I told the lads carrying me to go back for my leg. But they wouldn't stop. They were brave, as long as they could keep moving. That was the fear; there'd be more bombs. I'd heard two more explosions, one of them quite close, while I'd waited for the stretcher. (Weeks later, I saw the pram. When I was thrown, a black pram had passed my face. I waited to see the baby, or the mother. Every time I closed my eyes, I expected the baby. But he or she never flew or landed. Babies died that day, but I only saw the pram.) They didn't stop, and I couldn't blame them. I wanted to get away; this was my past. I wanted to go home.

They kept going. It wasn't far, but they were moving through mangled cars and people. I was one of the first to be brought out of the smoke. A harmless old man, with his leg blown off.

—It was gone already, I told the photographer, who was on his knees beside me.—There's no blood; look it.

He didn't hear me. He didn't even look at me. I was sure I was talking; I could hear myself. I thought we were on Amiens Street. But it was hard to tell – I never knew. It was years before I'd go back there.

—What's his name? I heard the photographer.

Now he was looking at me.

—What's your name? he asked.

—Henry Smart, I said.

He heard me.

I lay there for hours. There were no more explosions; the ground stayed solid. I lay beside other stretchers. I spoke to no one. I stopped listening.

It had been a beautiful day. I still remembered that, and the street and women with their jackets off – before it all disappeared. It was night now. There were lights, torches, camera flashes.

I was lifted.

—You're grand, said a voice right behind my head.—You'll be grand. We're just bringing you to the hospital.

—My leg, I said.

—It's not too bad, said the man right behind my head, carrying the stretcher.—Someone cleaned it up nicely.

—I left it back on Talbot Street.

—You should see what's left back there, he said.—It's unbeliev-able. There's more than thirty dead. Three bombs here. And another one in Monaghan.

—Who did it? I asked.

His face was even nearer now, because himself and the young lad at the front were lifting the stretcher into the back of an ambulance.

—The U.V.F., he said.—That's what they're saying.

—Who are they? I asked.

I'd hadn't paid attention to the Troubles; I'd been living in my own contented republic.

—The U.V.F.?

—Yeah.

—The Ulster something or other, he said.

—Ulster Volunteer Force, said the other lad.

He was strapping me to a plastic mattress.

—Unionists, I said.

—God, yeah. Our own lads wouldn't do something like this.

—Not down here, an'anyway, said the other man.

—My leg, I said.

—Be brave.

—My fuckin' leg.

I always wore the good boots when I was getting the bus into town. (I remembered, years later: the buses were on strike. That was why I'd been on Talbot Street, on my way down to get the train home.)

—I need the boot, I told them.—It's alligator skin.

I lifted the other leg – I tried to. But I was strapped down. They were shutting the back doors.

—Like this one, I said.

I was alone.

But I wasn't. There was another mattress beside me, on the other side of the ambulance. I could touch it; the upper strap was across my chest but they'd left my hands and arms free. I could move my head, turn enough to see that I was sharing the ambulance with a dead body. Man or woman, I couldn't tell. Adult, I could. The body under the blanket used to be a grown-up. I stopped looking.

I was taken out of the ambulance, and carried into the noise made by people trying to climb out of their wounds. Trying to forget, to shut down, get back to the weather and the afternoon and the promise of the night ahead, a bag of chips, a woman or a boyfriend. A priest stood beside me. A young lad who'd shaved just before he'd got the call. I could smell the aftershave. He prayed – I think – said things in Latin, put an oily finger on my eyes. I let him do it; I said nothing. He was getting me ready for death. I didn't object.

I didn't know the hospital. I don't remember if I ever found out. It could have been the Mater or the Richmond, or Jervis Street. The Rotunda, the maternity hospital, was even taking in the wounded. The Northside's newborns dropped into hell that night. I don't remember leaving the hospital. I never knew how long I was there.

People came looking. Mothers, husbands, daughters. I wanted to be the one they were searching for. I wanted to take the terror from their faces. I watched them pass, and leave. And others came too. They saw the shape the absent leg gave to the bedclothes, and they sat beside me.

—What was it like?

—Dreadful, I said.

The word seemed feeble – all the words were. But it was the best I could do. It sounded right.

I should have kept my mouth shut.

—You're Henry, aren't you?

—That's right.

—It must have been a shock.

She was a young one – very young. Too young to be sent off to interview the dead.

—Dreadful, I said, again.

—Henry Smart, she said.

—That's it.

I'd been Henry Smart since I'd come home, more than twenty years before. I hadn't hidden.

—I've heard all about you, she said.

—Is that right?

I couldn't sit up. I knew who I was but I couldn't feel the pain that everyone saw when they glanced at me.

—Did it remind you of 1916? she said.

—You know about that, I said.

Was I pleased? I was fuckin' delighted.

—Yes, she said.

I tried to sit up.

She put down her jotter and she leaned over; for a second I thought she was going to climb up onto me. I fell back on the bed, to give her the room. I actually did think that I was in for my first big ride since the late 1930s, with a young one who hadn't even been born back then. In a ward full of broken men who were trying hard not to die.

It was a bit of a shock when it didn't happen. When one of her hands held one of mine, and the other one cupped my elbow, and I looked and saw her sympathy and some of her disgust, and I let her help me sit up. She thumped the pillows behind me, and I could smell whatever perfume or deodorant she'd sprayed on before she'd run out of her flat to meet me. I could see the flat too. She was showing me around – I was some fuckin' eejit.

She'd picked up her jotter and pen again.

—You were in the G.P.O., she said.

—That's a long time ago.

—What was it like?

—You'll need more than that jotter if you want to know.

She smiled.

—Go on.

I crammed a big week into five minutes. I got to watch as she filled the pages with her shorthand. And I got to feel guilty too, quickly. She was a kid, doing her homework. This was her break. So, I talked. I filled her jotter for her. She looked up and smiled, and nodded.

—Go on.

And I did. I went through it day by day. I told her how the place had started to burn from the inside, how the melting glass of the dome had dropped onto the men and women beneath it.

—That's amazing, she said.

—It didn't seem that way at the time, I said.—It was just one of the things that happened.

—Still, though.

—You're right, I said.—It was amazing. But I think we were all a bit mad by then.

—With the bombing?

—And the rest of it; yeah.

—Like now.

—Am I mad now?

She didn't answer that one.

—You still had your leg then, didn't you? she said.—After the G.P.O. and that.

—Yeah, I said.—But that's a different story. A long time ago too.

167

—I knew it, she said.—They said you'd lost it in the bombing. You know, a week ago.

A week? There were men all around me who were moaning like it had been an hour ago. I couldn't go back the seven days; I could only account for one. But that was nothing new; I'd been dead before for weeks, and much longer.

—Who said that? I asked her.

—Everybody, she said.—But I could tell. By your face. You didn't have your leg amputated six days ago.

—No, I said.—It's been gone a while.

The triumph was gone from her face. She looked a small bit angry.

—It's a bit awkward, she said.

—What is?

—I'm supposed to talk to the old I.R.A. man who lost his leg last week. After all he'd – *you'd* – been through.

—No, I said.—I lost the leg in America. Sorry about that.

—Still though, she said.—It is a bit much, isn't it? To be blown up again. At your age.

I slept – I must have.

She was gone. It was dark. Injured men moaned less in the dark. I'd been in the bed for six days, she'd said. I wondered now how long I'd been sleeping. She'd have looked up and seen my head falling back. I hated that, even when I was on my own, at home. Falling asleep before I was ready to – like dying. I wondered how long she'd waited, and I lifted my hand to my chin, to check if I'd been drooling.

Something was immediately different.

I felt it when I lifted my arm. The slight shift, the rearrangement – there was something on the bed, something had just rolled against me.

I sent my hand under the sheet. I went slowly – I didn't like this – but it didn't take long to hit the thing. Wood – my fingers knew it. Metal – smooth, cold. And leather.

There was a leg tucked in against me. I knew before I saw it: it was new.

I woke.

The priest was beside me. He'd been given a chair with arms. There was a cup on his lap, and half a biscuit sitting on the saucer.

—There's no doubt about it, he said.

—Howyeh, Father.

—The men of your generation are made of stronger stuff, he said.

I closed my eyes. He was gone when I opened them. The chair was gone too.

He came again, another day. I was sitting up, on the mend. Sore where I'd never felt pain. This time I saw the young nun deliver the chair, and I watched him let her drag it till it was right behind him, so he could sit back safely without breaking his arse. He didn't thank or even look at her.

—You're a brave man, he said.

—I was only walking down the fuckin' street, Father, I told him.

He looked at me, hard. He didn't move, but he was shoving me back into my box. And I went; he was my boss.

—You're a stoic, Henry, he said.

—Thank you, Father.

—You know what a stoic is.

—I do, yeah.

I wanted to go home.

—And it's nice of you to call me one, I told him.

—You've read the papers.

—No.

—No?

—I've been sleeping a lot.

—Recuperating.

—That's right, Father.

—Good man, he said.—You spoke to a little girl between your naps.

—She wasn't that little, Father.

—She gave you a great write-up, he said.—All your deeds of derring-do.

I had to listen carefully. I'd been drugged to fuck – I suddenly knew it. I still was. I'd been knocking back every pill they'd given me.

—There are people outside who can't wait to meet you, he said.

I wanted to drift – I didn't want to face this. What was he telling me?

—Friends, he said.

—Old friends? I asked.

—New friends.

169

I didn't want to meet the old friends, even though the times had changed and nobody wanted me dead – except the fuckers who'd planted the bomb. That was something I suddenly realised: I hadn't thought about them at all. Not since I'd been lifted into the ambulance.

New friends.

What had I told her? Everything – I thought I had. My entire life and times.

I had to be careful.

—Did I say anything I shouldn't have, Father?

—Nothing substantial, he said.—There was mention of a married woman who helped you hide from the foe.

—Annie.

—That's right. And a piano.

—Sorry.

—She was off the page for the late edition.

—Who managed that?

—Your new friends.

—Why?

—You're a hero, Henry. But you're tired. I'll leave you to it.

He stood.

—One thing, Father.

—Go on.

—It's a blunt question.

—The right ones often are, he said.

He fuckin' loved himself.

I looked straight at him.

—Do you think I'll be shot when I leave here?

He looked at me.

—No, he said.—Why would you be?

The bus strike was over by the time I left. I know this, because I was on the bus.

I'd braced myself for something different. A small crowd, a quick burst of clapping as I came down the hospital steps. Some of the new friends the priest had mentioned, or the priest himself, his car door open for me. The odd photographer, and women with jotters. But there was no one.

I don't know any of this.

I've no memory of leaving the hospital, or the moment when I knew I was being discharged. I still don't know which hospital I was in, or if there were steps at the front door. But I was going home on the bus. I was wearing a suit that fitted me but wasn't mine. I'd seen the old suit, already in bits and smoking, being cut away from me with big silver scissors. I'd watched as the scissors went straight up the full leg, cut through the waistband without any extra effort, and moved on up the jacket, to the shoulders. I'd stared at the hand holding the scissors. I was on my back, on a trolley, right under heavy light. But my head was propped up, pillows under my shoulders, to dam the bleeding I couldn't see or feel.

I must have walked to the bus stop. I must have known the way. I wasn't worried – this wasn't new. And neither was the leg. I'd known that when I'd picked it up, to strap it on a week before, when I'd been ready to stand and go for my first piss since the bomb. It was the same leg I'd brought with me from America, polished up and cleaned, a lovely job. Someone must have gone looking for it, must have crawled across smoking rubble to find it for me – the same way I'd searched for my father's leg after I'd escaped from Richmond Barracks in 1916. Who had done that? I didn't really care. It was my leg and I wouldn't have to learn how to walk all over again. I'd have missed the creaking feel of the straps, and the weight of the leg itself – every bit of me knew it off by heart. I was able to stroll to the jacks.

And I saw myself in the mirror. I looked at the ghost of the damage that must have nearly killed me. There were three thin gashes that ran into my hair. There was bruising, calm now, down the length of one side of my face. And a general swelling, still just there – I turned my head; the profile of a slightly different man. But, fuck it, the damage suited me. I was going out a better-looking man.

I thumped my chest, and knew that there was more. Beneath the striped pyjamas. I unbuttoned them slowly, and saw what I'd missed. Raw red and yellow blots, across my chest and stomach. The heat had threatened, but it hadn't burnt too badly. I was getting away with the warning, and a shaved chest. I was slower going back to the bed. I was in pain for the first real time since the bomb.

My alligator boot was under the bed – the boot I'd left in the wreckage, with the leg. It had been polished too, and looked fresher than it had when the alligator had owned it. It made the other one look dull and ordinary, the skin of a local animal. I looked at them now, downstairs on the bus. I was wearing odd boots. I'd work on the dull one when I got home. I'd exhaust myself doing it.

I had no key, and no idea where it was. In the gutter on Talbot Street, in a box back at the hospital – which hospital? – I hadn't a clue. I went through my pockets again. I'd the remains of a fiver, and nothing else.

But I knew: I was being looked after. And for some reason – no reason – it didn't scare me.

I went to the back door of the priest's house. The housekeeper gave me a house key, newly cut, and the pay I was due for the week I'd worked before the bomb. There was no money for the time in hospital; I didn't ask about it. The priest wasn't my landlord but he had the key to my house. I didn't ask about that either. She handed me the fistful of school keys too.

—You're glad to be back, I'd say, she said.—Are you?

—I am, yeah.

—Out of that place.

—Yeah.

It was the first real time she'd spoken to me.

—I hate those hospitals, I do, she said.

—Ah, sure.

—And I seen you in the paper.

—Did you?

She was a Dublin woman, and that seemed unusual. The priest's housekeeper should have been a culchie, a peasant, bred to be a slave. I wondered was he riding her. I guessed he was – there was something too meaty about him – but I didn't care. She was a skinny thing, standing there, trying hard – too late – to be nice.

—Yeah, she said.—I read all about you.

—Was there a picture?

—There was, yeah. You in the bed.

She was looking down at my legs, trying to guess which was the wooden one. I gave her no help.

—And there was an old one, she said.

—Old one?

—You, out in 1916, she said.—In your uniform and all. A handsome young lad.

—Which paper? I asked.

There was no photograph of me in 1916. I'd been cut out of the only photograph.

—Father's *Independent*, she said.

—You don't still have it, do you?

—It might be in Father's office, she said.

172

—Any chance —?

—I can't go in there. It's locked.

—Grand, I said.

I wasn't going to charm her; I wasn't going to try. I wanted to get home.

—It's Father's golf day, she said.

From another woman, that might have been an invitation. I'd have been up that step in an oul' lad's flash. But this was the priest's housekeeper. I wasn't going to mess with the boss's secret missis. Even if she was looking better than she had been a minute or two before.

—He got a good day for it, I said.

—He plays off ten.

She didn't know what that meant, and neither did I. She was trying to lure me into the kitchen, to take her into the stuffy dark of Father's office. She'd find the key – I'd wear his slippers. I was seventy-two; she was a girl in her forties. She was looking at the man who'd been in the G.P.O.

—Good for him, I said.—I'll be seeing you.

I went down the deep step, put there to prove I was a cripple. But I was fine; I kept my hands in my pockets. I went around to the front of the house. There were no eyes holding me up now, so I was dog tired, exhausted. But I made it down the hill. The new key worked, and there was fresh bread and milk on the table, and a packet of Wholegrain.

I was being looked after.

There was a copy of the *Irish Independent*. It was open, folded, on page 9 – an old, grainy photograph of a skinny kid in a Volunteer uniform, standing out in his parents' back garden. It wasn't me, and it was the wrong uniform. I was still right. I'd been sliced out of the only photograph.

I slept all night; I didn't dream.

I went to work. It was the last week before the summer holidays.

—Good man, Henry, said Strickland.—You're back from the wars.

I shrugged, and smiled.

—That was a dreadful thing, he said.

—It was, yeah. Terrible.

—I should have been in to see you.

—You're grand, I said.

—Father Devine said you didn't need visitors, he said.—But you're alright?

—I am, yeah, I said.—I'm grand.

And I was. I was a bit stiff, but I was grand. And I knew why. The secret was out. I was Henry Smart again. I was side by side with the boy I'd been in the G.P.O. People knew what I'd been and what I'd done. They looked at me and saw their country.

The kids in the yard played near to me.

—I'm Henry.

—No, I am!

—Fuck off, you. It's my turn.

They played 1916, a yard full of Henrys knocking fuck out of the British. They fell dead. They got up and died again. They wanted me to see it, their readiness to die for Ireland. To shoot a gun, to die and live, forever.

The teachers knew they'd been right all along. They grew as they came up to me. They nearly fuckin' saluted. One of them definitely genuflected. He kept going and pulled his socks up while he was down there.

I saw Strickland looking, trying to figure me out. Why wasn't I in the Dáil, a shadow minister, the father of the opposition? (There was a coalition of Labour and the Blueshirts in power in 1974.) Or an old diehard, a last link to the country's birth and death, living up a country lane where the electricity hadn't gone, or in a flat in Ballymun, refusing the respectability that could have been my due? He knew his history – why hadn't he known about me? Why was one of the country's heroes the caretaker of his school? No one liked questions they couldn't answer, and there was a line of the things waiting in the corridor every time he opened his door. He kept a new distance. He didn't stop to chat.

Women kept their distance too, but it was different. They looked at me in a way that hadn't been familiar for a long time. They stared at the man I'd been, and they could see some of him in my current features. They were curious, but it was more. I made sense now – the scars, and the leg. I was Celtic mythology walking towards them. I was fuckin' biblical. I was the quiet man, and suddenly a fine man. The women smiled.

I was being looked after.

9

The smile was big, but controlled. Everything about him was under tight control. The beard, the eyes. The teeth were perfect, too big and even.

Whoever grabbed hold of me just kept going, pushed me ahead.

I'd been locking up the school, hauling myself upright after bending at the keyhole. There was the pain, tangled and old, across my shoulders. I took my time, breaking through the ache. I was nearly there, when the blow came and I was being brought across the yard. By a strong man. I wasn't given the time to turn and face him. But he wasn't being brutal.

And he wasn't trying to hide himself.

—There's a man wants to meet you, Henry, he said.—Sorry about the drama.

I knew who was shoving me towards the van that had now appeared at the mouth of the yard. It was McCauley, the man who'd taught the scholarship boys before they'd brought in the free secondary education. It was mad McCauley, but he was suddenly someone else.

The back door of the van swung open. I didn't fight or try to. There was more strength in the fist holding my jacket than I'd have been able to manage. The door kept swinging my way, but McCauley didn't slow me down or help me dodge it. I walked right into its swinging path. It caught me, and hurt.

—Sorry, Henry.

I shut my eyes against the pain – more fuckin' pain – and felt the hood go over my head. Warm cotton, a pillow or something; it wasn't clean. I vomited. A hard hand pushed my head down, as McCauley kept shoving me into the van. I fell in, onto my stomach – I didn't have time to use my hands – and I was pulled and pushed the rest of the way, across a metal floor that stank of rust and oil.

—Sorry about this.

It wasn't McCauley who spoke this time. Someone put a knee on my back. His feet were huge, right at my face. He was climbing over me, to pull the door closed – I thought. The van was moving – it had started while I was being dragged into it. I felt it turn left when it got to the front gate. The knees and weight were off my back. A hand took one of mine, and guided it to some sort of handle or grip. I held on as the van took quick corners – I lost count; I never started – and then got going on a straight stretch of road.

My hands weren't tied. I wasn't a real prisoner.

—I've been sick in here, I said.

No one answered.

I'd no real idea where we were; I'd been driven off my map. We weren't heading east; that was the sea. And we weren't going south, into town, because the van picked up some speed and didn't slow down for quite a while. I was being brought away from the city, west – or north. The rest of the country.

There was only one other man in the back of the van. McCauley hadn't come with us. I knew, and was pleased I knew: I hadn't heard the van's front doors being opened, at the school. McCauley hadn't got in. There was me and the man who'd put the hood over my head, and the driver – and maybe a passenger beside him.

I guessed we'd been going for ten minutes. But I'd been stepping out of time all summer, since the bomb. Wandering in the dark. Waking up, not having gone asleep. I could have been in the van for hours. But the smell in the pillow was consistently desperate; it got no worse or better.

—I'm after vomiting in here, I said.

—Won't be too long now.

It was a Dublin accent, and it wasn't delivering a death sentence. I'd been kidnapped, but I was still being looked after.

—How long?

—Not too long. You'll be able to clean up in a wee while.

It was a Dublin accent but it belonged to a man who'd spent time in the company of men who said *wee*. We were heading north, up to the wee six counties. We wouldn't be stopping soon. Or, if we did, it would only be to change vehicles. The small bits of

176

news I'd listened to in the last four years had been full of abandoned cars.

The van turned, and we were off whatever main road we'd been on. There was no real slowing down; I had to hold on as the van took the swerves and potholes of the smaller roads. My guess was North Dublin – Man o' War, the Naul – wild places I'd known a bit more than fifty years before.

The puke was crusting, cementing my head to the pillow, sealing the pores of the cotton.

—I can't breathe in here, son.

—We'll be changing in a minute.

—Changing?

—Swapping cars – vans.

I was right: we were driving out of the Republic. I let go of the handle – whatever it was I'd been gripping.

—I'm taking this thing off, I said.

—That wouldn't be wise, said the voice.

The words were plain, but there was no threat in the tone. I started to pull at the hood.

The van was still moving when I woke. My head was on the floor, bouncing as the van bounced. Beating the pain in deeper. I'd been whacked.

My hands were still free.

I thought I'd been whacked.

I managed to sit up. I wasn't sure – my whole body was agony. Was it even the same van?

—That shouldn't have been necessary.

I'd been whacked. It was official. Most of the pain was new, and real.

But the experience was old. I'd dragged men into the mountains. I'd hit them across the head with the gun-butt and told them not to struggle; it wasn't necessary. Then I'd put the gun to the backs of their heads and shot them.

The same hand took mine and guided it back to the handle.

—Thanks.

—You're welcome.

—Where are we going?

Get them talking.

No answer.

—Who am I meeting?

No answer. I went back to the easier question.

—Where are we going?

—Can't tell you.

—How long?

—Not long. Nearly there.

—Where?

No answer. Then the voice.

—Don't worry.

The van was slowing; the left-side wheels were off the road, on a ditch or something. It stopped.

The man in the back with me pushed against me – getting past me, I guessed. I still wasn't tied. I heard the driver's door open. One door. Only the driver. The passenger was staying put, or wasn't there. The driver and the man in the back. I'd been whacked, and it hadn't been a fist. I'd been hit with the back end of a gun.

Two men and one gun.

The back door opened. I felt the breeze. Sea air.

—Out you get.

He grabbed the wrong leg.

—Fuck, sorry.

—No problem, I said through the cotton and puke.

I was able to fumble my own way. I was given the space to do it. I felt soft ground under my foot. Had I been brought to a field? Or the edge of a wood? I could hear and smell the sea. But we weren't in sand dunes. I was pretty sure we weren't near mountains. It was a long drive to any mountains north of Dublin, and we hadn't been going uphill. It was still a hot day. I could feel the sun burning through the hood. Heating the vomit.

—This fuckin' thing, I said.

—Right.

The voice was new, and hard.

—You'll have to keep your eyes shut, said the old voice, the one I'd travelled with.—It's important.

—Okay.

I felt his hands – both hands: he wasn't holding the gun – as he grabbed the cotton at my neck, about to pull.

—Here goes.

I screamed – I didn't. The pillow did. It ripped as he pulled and took half my face with it.

—For fuck sake!

It was years since I'd heard myself laugh. I'd be laughing as they shot me.

I'd kept my eyes shut.

There was something against my hand, being pushed against it.

—Clean yourself.

The hard voice. The accent belonged to a man who'd spent long periods of his time in different places, or pretended he had. Belfast, England, the east coast of the States. They were in the layers of each syllable, and no layers were fat enough to hide the fact that this was a man who had killed and believed he'd done the right thing. It was a voice from way back, although the man who used it was young.

I put the cloth to my face, and kept my eyelids locked. It was velvety and thick, too heavy to be an old shirt or pillow. It felt like well worked leather. I smelt the polish before I buried my face in the cloth. It was a shammy, a chamois leather, for polishing a car or van. My quick guess was that it hadn't come out of the van. The polish was fresh, still there in the leather. The hard man had been going at the paintwork while he'd been waiting for me.

I polished my neck and face. I stank of old Goldgrain and beeswax.

—We have to change cars, said the hard man.

—We didn't have to do that in my day, I said back.

The silence was brief, respectful.

—Right.

The hard man.

—We'd better get going.

I held out the shammy. It was taken.

—Am I supposed to keep my eyes shut? I asked.—Or d'yis have a clean bag or a pillow?

—It's for your own good, said the man who'd travelled with me.—The less you know and that. You know yourself.

The bag went over my head. A plastic bag.

—You're fuckin' joking.

—It's all we have.

—It'll smother me!

—I cut wee holes in it.

Wee again.

A hand gripped my elbow, a gentle shove.

—It's just over here. Flat ground, don't worry.

The plastic bag was dreadful. It was a hot, wet lick every time I inhaled.

—No, I said.

179

I stopped walking. The hand pulled at my elbow, then stopped.

—Get into the car, said the hard man.

—No.

—Get —

—This fuckin' bag.

—Get in first, and I'll put something else over you. I've a jumper in the boot.

The car door opened. The hand protected my head, gently pushed me down, and in. I was their guest. The I.R.A. – I knew it was them.

I was out of touch, and I regretted it.

Someone climbed in beside me.

There were two I.R.A.s. The Provisionals and the Officials. There'd been a split – another one – a few years back. I knew that much, but that I was all I knew.

—Shut the eyes again, Henry.

He ripped through the bag; it fell away from my head. And he hung the jumper over my head. It belonged to a man who smoked forty a day.

—Can you see anything?

—No, I said.

I felt the engine fight, and the car moved; it was climbing off a soft slope. Then we were going. I didn't know which I.R.A. had taken me. I didn't ask.

—D'you like Planxty, Henry?

The hard man – driving.

The man beside me laughed. I didn't answer.

—I have the album here, said the hard man – he was talking to the man beside me, talking to someone he knew.

—Good man, said the head beside me.

—I'll stick it on, said the hard man.—See what Henry thinks.

I heard a click – all clicks sounded like triggers being cocked. Then the car was full of diddley music.

—What d'you think of that, Henry? the hard man shouted.

I knew the right answer.

—Good.

The two lads laughed. By the time the hard man stopped the car I'd heard the thing, the whole long player, three times through. I'd given up trying to position the car on the map. I might have slept; it didn't matter. They'd brought me north. Either that, or the north had come to me. I knew that much:

the I.R.A. had migrated north since my day. And this was I.R.A. business.

The car had stopped. I heard the head beside me yawning. An elbow to his neck, and I could have been out of the car and zigzagging, running from the bullets.

But I didn't want to escape. I couldn't – and I didn't want to. I was curious. More than curious. I liked these men; I'd missed them.

It was true. I felt good in the car. At home.

—Where are we? I asked.

I didn't expect the answer, but I wanted to hear the voices.

—See if you can guess, said the hard man.

He opened his door.

The air that came into the car was cold. More sea. We'd hugged the coast, north. I was alert, wide awake.

I got out under my own steam; I pushed away the offered hand. I tried to stand straight, quickly. I managed it too. I knew I was being watched. There were new eyes there, new men watching the old man.

And I knew something else: I wanted in. I could feel it still down in me, still there. I'd been angry since the bomb; I knew that now.

But why did they want me?

I was still waiting. The men – I didn't know how many now – had gone downwind. They whispered, spoke softly. Northern accents – I wasn't sure of it.

The jumper still covered my face. The wind flicked at the sleeves but it wasn't strong enough to lift the whole thing off me. I stood there for silent minutes. I'd been bombed, but I only really knew it now, and knew it as a rage I could master and depend on. A useful, easy rage. They'd nearly killed me. They'd killed thirty-three people. The loyalists, the U.V. – whatever the fuck they were. And the British – someone had whispered that, as I lay on the bed in the hospital. The British had been behind it. But I only heard it now, the voice of a girl. Meaning had arrived, months after the bomb.

I stood there and I didn't doubt.

Shoes through grass. Fag smoke arriving. I was surrounded.

—Henry.

Another new voice. A Belfast voice.

—*A chara.*

181

—You can see me, I said.

The jumper was off, and I was looking at a tall man with a beard. I made sure I didn't need to squint.

—My God Almighty, he said.—It's great to finally meet you.

The smile was big, but controlled. Everything about him was under tight control. The beard, the eyes. The teeth were perfect, too big and even. I'd never seen teeth that white in a Catholic mouth before.

He'd smiled, and the other men smiled. Six men. I immediately spotted the ones who'd brought me. I'd been good at this before, telling a man's worth by the shape of his head. The two Dublin lads were standing off to the side. They'd done their job; they weren't the big men in this company. They smiled at me – old pals. I nodded back. They'd looked after me well, no hard feelings. I didn't smile.

I looked back at the man with the beard. The strength was in his chest, inside the Aran sweater: here was a man who'd built himself while he'd done his time. Here was a man who'd been interrogated and had given them nothing. A man who'd had his teeth kicked out and hadn't even bled. He'd got himself a bigger, whiter set and he'd smiled back at the fuckers the next time they'd pulled him in. He was young, in his twenties, but there was nothing young in him.

He held out his hand. I took it. The manly grip, all that shite. Big spades softened by gun oil.

(You think it was Adams. But it wasn't. It was a different man. Adams was in Long Kesh, in Cage 11, becoming Gerry Adams. He'd be in there for another three years.)

—*A chara*, he said again.

They were probably the only Irish words he knew. *My friend. My bollix* – I pushed back the sarcasm; I didn't want it. I looked back at him.

The other men drew a bit closer. I shook hands with them all, the Dublin lads at the back of the queue. In my day, Dublin had been the centre of the new place we were making. This wasn't my day.

—Do you know who you are, Henry? said the man with the beard.

He didn't want an answer. He had his own.

—You are our republican dead, he said.

No one laughed. No one smiled.

—Back from the dead, I said.

—Exactly, aye. The real thing.

—I'm not the only one still alive, I said.—There are hundreds of them. Us.

—Ach, but. Those lads have always been around. We grew up with them. Good men, many of them. But comical. Shrunken wee lads. It's hard to separate the real thing from the chancers.

He smiled.

—But you're Henry Smart.

—What do you want?

—See now? he said.—You're not on for flattery. I can see that. You're still active.

I tried not to look flattered.

—Nothing, he said.—We don't want anything.

—So you've brought me for a picnic, I said.

He laughed. They laughed.

—Good man, he said.

He laughed again. We were all friends, beside the sea. He stopped laughing.

—You want something, I said.

—Aye. We do. But we know.

He stared at me. He let me match the stare; he let me join.

—We don't have to ask, he said.

He was right.

But he did ask.

And I nodded.

They drove me back to Ratheen. I sat in the front passenger seat this time.

—Where are we?

—Balbriggan.

—The Tans burnt it.

—That's right.

—It hasn't recovered.

—It isn't the worst, said the driver.—I've a brother lives out here. He says it's alright.

—I've a cousin of mine out here too, said the man behind me, in the back.

—What's he think?

—She. I don't really know her that well. I chatted to her a bit at a wedding there last year. My sister, like. Got married. But the cousin. She said she lived out here.

These were the Dublin men I was with. I was already ashamed of them. I was on my way home, but half an hour before I'd been sitting on a rug with three big men from the Provisional I.R.A.'s Army Council while we ate republican sandwiches and I listened to the one big man explain my part in the long war.

—We're in it for the long haul and we want men who know what that means. We might be old men or even old dead men before the British realise that the time has come to go. Old empires are stupid. You know that.

The other men stayed back and leaned against the cars, and looked north and south. There were guns near if the Guards or the Special Branch came at us through the dunes or along the flat stretch of road. I could feel the stiff grass under the rug as the man with the beard told me who I was and who we all were.

—We're the legitimate government of Ireland, Henry, he said.— And you're the living proof of that.

He breathed deep, and his chest pushed against the Aran sweater.

—This is a great day.

The other men nodded.

—Aye.

—It's a strange one, though, he said.—Have you thought about this, boys?

I knew he was saying something he'd said before, and the boys had heard before; he'd rehearsed it with them.

—If it hadn't been for that bomb. If the U.V.F. hadn't parked the car *there*.

He looked at me now.

—We'd never have found you.

I knew: I'd have to be wary again, and scared. Because he was lying.

What about the priest? I wanted to say, to catch him out and prove I was more than their link to our glorious past. *He's been looking after me for years. And what about the teachers?* I knew now, they'd been keeping an eye on me, waiting.

—Enough, he said.—We can't be sentimental. It's a long way home, especially the long way we've to go the night. Crossing that scar across our land.

He was talking about the border.

I didn't groan when I sat up off the rug. I let them watch the leg, and how I owned and manoeuvred it.

—It's not the same leg, is it, hey?

—No.

—Still. It's powerful.

We shook hands. We even hugged. He held my shoulders and looked at me again, like a proud father sending his eldest off to his first day's work.

He spoke and, again, it sounded like something he'd rehearsed.

—*Tiochaigh ár lá.* *

It was dark when the car slid out of the country onto the streets. I was tired but I'd never sleep again. I was a hero and a fraud, elated and a bit terrified.

They dropped me at the house. I didn't have to show them where it was. I half expected – I fully expected to see the priest sitting there when I turned on the light. But the house was empty.

I sat there till daylight. *You got me wrong.* It wasn't too late. I could tell McCauley or the priest; I could go up to his house. I could put them right and tell them: I hadn't been elected to the First Dáil. I hadn't been there in January 1919, in the Round Room of the Mansion House, when the Dáil had ratified the 1916 Proclamation and adopted the Declaration of Independence. What they thought I was, I wasn't: the sure, tight link, the man who'd actually voted. There was no Henry Smart M.P. The day of the vote, I was cycling through Roscommon and a wall of sleet; I was going through Strokestown, to Rusg, and the house that would give me my wife. Further east and south, in Soloheadbeg, Dan Breen shot two rozzers, the first official killings of the War of Independence. And back in Dublin, hands were raised – most of the elected men and women were either on the run or in jail – and Ireland became the Republic. I was always on the run and I'd done more than my share – but it didn't matter. They thought one of the raised hands in the Mansion House had been mine. They were wrong. But these men were never wrong.

I stood up and looked out the window. There was nothing out there. I put on the kettle.

I'd thought they were after a mascot. When the man with the beard told me I was their republican dead, I thought they'd parade me, bring me to the odd meeting. Bodenstown, and the

* Our day will come.

185

other holy places. I was ready to argue – I could still fight, I was still a soldier. An old man was like a pregnant woman; he could slip through any checkpoint. I'd be useful, vital. But I'd listened, and the realisation came, the reminder – the man with the beard had actually said it: this was religion. They thought I was Moses, someone who'd actually spoken to God. I wasn't a symbol: I was an old, rediscovered fact. The eleventh commandment.

But I was a lie. And a bigger, more frightening lie because I was keeping it to myself. *Hang on, lads.* I could have put the hand up and confessed. *I wasn't in the Dáil, I never stood for election. I was only seventeen.* They wouldn't have shot and buried me in the dunes. (I found out soon enough, those dunes and other dunes and ditches and bog holes were filling up with renegades and informers, men and – worse, and new – women who got in the way, joining all the informers we'd thrown into the same holes nearly sixty years before.) I'd still have been useful. A veteran, recently wronged, an old man still hungry for freedom. Whatever they wanted me to be.

But I'd said nothing.

Because I'd wanted it. Despite the mistake, and the lie that it quickly became. And the danger. The fresh death sentence it would become if it stayed unsaid. I wanted to be who they thought I was.

And I was. I was the Henry Smart they'd been told about by their fathers and grandmothers. The man with the beard had looked at my leg: he knew who I'd been. I *was* Henry Smart.

But I knew. I'd learnt it years ago. It was religion and, so, it was madness. It was the sanctity of the words. *Republic* or *free state*. Choose the wrong one and you were damned. Choose the right one and you were dead. It couldn't be both and it couldn't be neither; I knew that too, even when I'd got out of the country. But at least back then, at the dawn of fuckin' time, it had been a real decision. It had been a vote.

It had been a vote, but never my vote. Hands were raised and counted. But not my hand. I wasn't in the Mansion House. And that was all that mattered. I was their walking legitimacy, but – for now – I was the only one who knew it was a lie.

I drank the Nescafé. I even tasted it. I ate the cornflakes. I did most of the things that were normal. I made sure I had my keys and I went to work. I knew I was being watched.

I had no idea how they'd made the mistake. I'd be able to point that out, if I lived long enough. The mistake was theirs, not actively mine. They'd jumped to their own quick conclusions. The old I.R.A. man in hospital. A familiar name. Henry Smart? *The* Henry Smart. Not a name from the history books, but spoken of in the right, tight circles; old men passing it on down to the little lads, the gun runners of the future, around the tables of the republican clubs, singing and crying, eyes closed. *The Bold Henry Smart.* They looked at the photo on the front page, the old bandaged man sitting up in the bed, defiant. Was that the same man who'd smacked the Big Fella? The same. The man who never gave in or gave up – that's him. The man who was elected to the First Dáil. I could hear the conversation, up in Belfast. Some shell-shocked oul' lad got his rebels mixed and I ended up one of the anointed, the last man standing. Fuckin' Moses. The link to God. And what about the time before the bomb? The mistake was older than the bomb. But that didn't matter.

I opened the school gate, and realised it was Saturday. The day off. The hall was being used, but not till later, a cake sale, for a parish trip to Lourdes. The woman in charge – I couldn't remember her name; I hadn't paid attention – would be collecting the key from my house. Going to Lourdes felt like a good idea. I could hide among the mad and the lame. I'd done it before; there was nothing to it. I could limp to France, and disappear.

I locked the gate and walked back through the village.

I was being watched.

I thought about Lourdes and the Spanish border, and the woman who was organising the trip. I worked on the limp as I went; I gave it a swing. I'd need a new passport. My old one was American and long out of date. I had money in under a floorboard. I'd make sure it looked like I'd be coming back. The school was full of Provisionals. The parish priest was a Provisional – and my plan was in tatters already. The priest would be going with them, half a planeload of his sick parishioners. He'd be flaying them with the rosary. We'd end up sharing a room, or even a fuckin' bed.

I'd ask the woman, whatever her name was, which of the priests would be carrying the holy water on the trip. I'd go if he wasn't the one; the parish was young and had three priests. The old church had been abandoned to bingo; the new church across the new Main Road was a huge thing that was packed five, six times every Sunday. If I couldn't escape to Lourdes, I could take the boat to Holyhead or Liverpool. I wouldn't need a passport. I could go back the way I'd gone in 1922.

I was near the house. I was struggling. I wasn't acting. I was an old fool, caught again.

I'd go back down to the hall while the sale was in full swing and I'd buy a cake. I'd help them clean up after. I'd talk to the woman, charm her; I'd even ride her to get onto the plane for Lourdes.

I brushed my teeth. I polished the boots and the leg. I thought about leaving the front door open. *Come in, come in, it's always open. The bit of heat helps the lumbago.* But the door was never open. There was no garden or gate; it was straight onto the street. It would have been like living in a stationary boxcar, sitting at the door while the rest of the world rolled by. The door had always been shut. I couldn't change that now.

There were two boats a day to Liverpool. I could get on the bus, going into town. I hadn't been in town since the bomb, but no one else knew that.

I had money. I could reach it without climbing out of my chair. I owned nothing that was worth bringing with me, nothing that wouldn't fit into some of my pockets.

I sat there. I made myself sit there. They'd find out the truth, and they'd come after me. I wasn't going to Liverpool and I wasn't going to Lourdes. I'd take what was coming. There was no reason to run, other than to save my life. But I'd lived it. I'd lived most of it running – no more of that. I was angry again, ready to shout back.

The knock came, and it was grand. I knew the soft tap of a woman's knuckles. It wasn't a man with a gun, or a man pretending he didn't have a gun. It might have been a woman with a gun but it was definitely a woman. She knocked again. I got up and went to the door, to meet her.

But I met a different woman.

—Two and two? I said.

She didn't answer. But she didn't look surprised.

—I'm here for the key, said Missis O'Kelly.

—I was expecting the other one.

—The other one?

—I don't know her name.

—We're a committee, she said.

—Grand, I said.—Come in.

She didn't.

I stood well back. The door was as wide as I could make it.

—Come in.

She leaned in a bit closer – she hung over the step. Her forehead might have been under the roof, but that was all.

—The kettle's on, I said.

—There's a bit of a rush.

—I miss you.

I thought I was falling; there was nothing beneath me. I was naked, sad.

—I miss you too, she said.—We're ridiculous.

—I suppose we are, I said.—But fuck it.

She smiled, although she didn't want to.

—Come in, I said.

—No, she said.—I really can't. I came for the key, you see.

—That's right.

It seemed like years ago, my plans to seduce her pal on the committee and run away to Lourdes. I was in a different life.

—They'll be waiting for me, she said.—The other ladies.

—Yeah.

—At the school.

—We can't have that.

I picked the keys off the table and took the big one she wanted off the ring.

—There you go.

—Thank you.

—No problem, I said.—She said something about yis finishing up at half-five.

—If there's anything left, she said.—It might be earlier. The raffle's at four, I believe.

I looked at her. She'd stepped in properly. Both of her feet were in my house.

—Why do you do it? I asked.

She put the key in her jacket pocket.

—You were a rebel once, I said.—And now you're baking cakes, for the church.

She stared at me.

—You were a rebel yourself, she said.—And now you go around to the back of a priest's house, to collect your wages.

I smiled.

—Fair enough.

She didn't smile back.

—I'm not who you think I am, she said.

—Okay.

—I'm not.

—Yeah.

—You can come to the house to collect the key.

—Tonight?

—If it suits you.

—It does, I said.—It suits me.

—Good, she said.—Fine.

—I'm your boyfriend again, am I?

—You're the scut.

She *was* who I'd thought she was. And she was letting me know it.

She left the door open. I went out onto the street, to gawk after her. She walked away like a young one. There was an arse under the skirt; the hill did nothing to slow her down. I stayed there for ages, long after she'd gone. The sun moved. The grass grew.

I'd changed the world. *I miss you.* I'd said it, and all the mistakes were nothing and I was back where I'd been when I was happy and hanging onto the side of a slow train. *You're the scut.* She was Miss O'Shea.

—What was he like?

—My husband?

—Yeah.

This was in her kitchen, later. She was feeding me. She looked at me wolfing what was on the plate.

—What's this called, by the way?

—Lasagne, she said.

—It's good.

—Thank you.

—No problem, I said.—So, what was he like?

—He had manners.

I looked up. It wasn't Miss O'Shea who was staring at the floor. It was the other woman, and she was missing her husband.

—He was a good man, she said.

—Was he?

—Yes, she said.—He was. He had great integrity.

She looked at me now.

—But no sense of humour.

—None?

—Whatsoever.

—You bought no cakes.

—What?

I nodded at the table.

—You were at the cake sale all afternoon, I said.—But you bought nothing.

—What makes you think that?

—There's nothing on the table.

—There's more to the house than the table, she said.

She *was* Miss O'Shea.

—Maybe I'm keeping the cakes for those that might be worthy of them.

—Griddle cakes, I said.

—What are they?

—They're the only cakes I ever gave a fuck about.

—Is that right now?

—It was a long time ago, I said.—The first time I ate them, I thought they were worth dying for.

—Ah, now.

—I meant the right to make them and eat them, I said.—The freedom. They came from one part of the world, and I thought that was important.

—And is it still important?

—This is some fuckin' conversation.

—Is it?

I gave her the answer she wanted.

—Yes, I said.—It's still important.

—Life goes on as normal, the big man with the beard had told me.

—Stay healthy, say nothing. You'll know, when the time comes.

As we sat that day on the blanket beside the sea.

—We'll get good mileage out of you, don't worry.

—I'm not going to be a fuckin' mascot, I said.

He looked genuinely upset.

—No, he said.—Henry. *A chara*. Don't misunderstand.

He grabbed my arms.

—I'm a fool, he said.—An *amadán*.

He rubbed my sleeves, consoling me.

191

—This is a big day for us, he said.—Hey, boys?

The boys nodded – a big, big day.

—To be meeting Henry Smart, he said.—Ach, you're the reason we're here. Why we are what we are.

More nods and grunts.

—I want to fight, I said.

—Yes.

—I can.

—We see that, he said.—But we have to be a wee bit strategic. It's not an even fight.

—It never has been, I said.

—Aye, he said.—And it was even worse in your day. They still had the Empire. They ruled the waves.

I nodded.

And he nodded.

—After what those fuckin' bastards did, I said.—In Talbot Street and the other places.

—Aye, he said.—We're forgetting none of that, don't worry.

He let go of my arms.

—I'll tell you what it is now, he said.—Why we're here. Why *you're* here.

He took a gulp of the sea air.

—Religion, he said.

—Fuck religion.

His mouth tightened. He was wondering if I was worth it.

He took a breath.

—Our religion, he said.—Our own religion.

—Martyrs.

—Aye.

—And victims, I said.

—You know the score. And prophets.

—Prophets?

—You're the prophet, he said.—Don't be modest.

—How am I a prophet? I haven't opened my mouth in sixty years.

—That doesn't matter, he said.—All the better.

—How come?

—It'll be fresh news and sixty years old, he said.—You were there.

I said nothing.

—In the Mansion House. You voted for the Republic. And the Declaration of Independence.

The mouth stayed shut.

—You're more than a prophet, Henry, he said.—You're our direct line. To God.

He smiled. He laughed.

I went to the jacks, came back, sat down beside her. I hoped she'd lean my way, that my arm would go around her and I'd get to call her *Miss*.

—What's this? I said.

The telly was on. Black and white.

—A film, she said.

—What film? I said.

—*The Quiet Man*.

—It's supposed to be in colour.

—Is it now?

—Technicolor.

—Well, she said.—There's not much we can do about that.

It was shite in any colour. We sat and watched the whole thing and nothing in it made her move nearer to me. And nothing in it moved us to share a knowing look. Wayne and Maureen on the bike, a saddle each and no machine-gun on the handlebars. No sign of an ambush or a shoot-out. It was like nothing or nowhere we'd lived through, together or alone. It was exactly as I'd read it in the script, before the plane touched down in Shannon in 1951. *The Quiet Man* and the Provisional I.R.A. – the two faces of Ireland, and they were both invented by me.

I stretched when the film was over. I sent my arms out far, and they came back empty.

—What did you make of that? I asked.

—It was lovely, she said.

—Lovely?

—Yes.

—What was lovely about it?

—Everything.

She wasn't Miss O'Shea.

I opened the school gate. I looked after the leaks and breakages. I watched the school grow older. The damp stains crept down the walls outside, and moss crawled up to meet them. The shine went off the floors. Paint cracked and flaked. Small cracks that were no one's fault appeared in window corners. I watched, and I couldn't stop it. I couldn't keep up. The new damage had brought new life to old damage. The Talbot Street wounds had joined the bullet holes and the scars and hollows left by torture, and years of lying in ditches and falling under trains. I was an old man with an older life to drag around. All movement was difficult. My days were numbered.

But I couldn't show that. I was the sleeper, the walking relic. The teachers, the ones on the inside, genuflected when I passed. But they aged too. Hair changed colour and fell out. Some left, to take control of the big schools being built in a hurry in the new suburbs to the west. Strickland avoided me, but when he couldn't, when there was no quick way past me, he talked about retirement – his – and looked over my shoulder to the place where it was waiting for him. His shoulders collapsed inside the suit he'd worn the first day he'd walked into his brand new school. The boys in the yard got bigger. They were the first generation of the well-fed. Even the runts were huge.

The nightmares got worse. There'd been none in the early months, immediately after the bomb. The pain had been welcome. I could take it all; I was alive. For a year, more, the dreams stayed away. But then they came and hauled me out of sleep, and didn't let go till I had to sleep again. Sleep – the terror was tucked in behind its thin, breathing wall. My eyes would close, and the hands were there, at my mouth, pulling it open, tearing it from my face. Pulling out the cry before I could let it into the air.

—Is that you?

It was dark. Pitch dark.

—Was that you?

It was the woman, Missis O'Kelly. I knew where I was and where I'd fallen asleep.

—Did you make that noise? she asked.

—I must have.

—It sounded like you were being strangled.

A car went past. I could make out curtains, a wardrobe.

—I was, I said.

I wasn't convinced I was awake. The dreams had become more real than the waking hours. They never gave up. I felt my face for the blood. I was still gasping, appalled; my chest wasn't there. I was up on an elbow. I didn't want to lie back down.

194

—Do me a favour, I said.—Turn on the light.

I felt her shift in the bed, and she groaned as she leaned to get to the light switch beside her. The room was there now, and I lay back.

—Sorry about this.

I closed my eyes. Shame pushed at the lids.

I felt her hand on my forehead. It wasn't a shock; it wasn't unwanted. Still, I moved from under it. It was too like the hands in the dream – the dreams – shrapnel that became iron fingers at my face and mouth, pinned me down and held and pulled till I dried and crumbled, but never enough to fall away from under the fingers.

—A nightmare? she said.

—Yeah.

—You're alright now.

I said nothing, but I nodded.

—The bomb, she said.

It was the first time she'd mentioned the bomb.

—Yeah, I said.—The bomb.

—You poor thing.

Still, I kept my eyes closed. I wanted the light on but I didn't want to see her looking at me.

—Would you like some water?

—No.

—I knew it was you.

I kept my eyes shut.

—When I saw it all in the paper.

Something had happened. She wasn't interested in hiding any more. But I was: I couldn't look at her.

—I knew all along, she said.

A finger poked my shoulder.

—I knew.

The time had come.

—Of course you fuckin' knew, I said.—You knew it was me when I was cutting your fuckin' grass. How many other Henry Smarts were you going to confuse me with, for fuck sake?

—Stop that.

—You knew —

I counted back the years, to the time I'd arrived.

—More than twenty fuckin' years ago. And now you tell me you *knew*.

195

—Stop.

—For fuck sake.

It was strange, letting go of the temper with my eyes clamped shut. Shouting at someone I wouldn't look at.

—All these fuckin' years!

I was shouting straight at the wall and the bedroom window.

—More than forty, I said.—Jesus Christ, I'm seventy-four!

—You're a teenager, she said.—Compared to me.

She'd always been older than me. She'd been my teacher, the lady up at the blackboard. I did the sums now. I was in bed with a woman of almost ninety.

I laughed. I still hadn't opened my eyes. I burst my shite laughing. I heard her laughing too.

And I looked at her.

—You're well preserved.

—I always was, she said.—Not like you.

—True, I said.—Why did you pretend?

—I wasn't pretending, she said.—I was never pretending.

—You knew it was me.

—But it wasn't me.

I said nothing. I was wearing her husband's pyjamas.

We got up. I put the leg on. We went downstairs. I counted the steps. I looked at the streetlight, the way it coloured the ceiling in the hall. She bullied the kettle. We sat at the table.

—Well, she said.

—Well.

—Will I start?

—Go on.

—You remember, she said.—When you went under the train.

—Funny enough, I do.

—That train never stopped. It went on and on, you remember yourself the way they could be. And I couldn't jump. Poor Séamus Louis had nearly gone under it with you. We couldn't jump. A day and a night and another day. I never knew the name of the town where we finally got down off that blessed train. It wasn't really a town. I don't think it was ever a town. I can still see it. And feel it. The dirt all around us. And poor Séamus.

—What about Saoirse?

—Ah, she was grand. It was Séamus I was worried about.

She looked at me.

—Do you know about them?

—No.

—Oh God. This is terrible.

—They're dead.

—No, she said.—Yes. Poor Séamus is dead. He died. Not then. It wasn't news; I'd known it, carried it.

—A year later, or so, she said.

—How?

—Everything, Henry. And nothing. A cold he couldn't shake, God love him. Because he'd nothing left in him to shake. He just died.

—And Saoirse?

—She's in America, Henry. I think.

—You said you had a daughter.

—That's her.

—She's mine too.

—I know. I should have told you. Sooner.

—But I was your fuckin' gardener.

—And not a very good one, faith. I had to spend the rest of the week getting rid of the weeds you'd missed.

—That's a fuckin' lie.

—It is not, she said.—I haven't heard a thing from Saoirse in years. I don't know where she is.

—She'd be fifty-something.

—She would.

—But she's alive.

—I think so. She never took to my husband. She couldn't like him. It was hard. And she said all along you were alive.

—Well, she was right.

—Yes. I have an address but I don't think she's there now.

—Where?

—Chicago. She phoned me once, in 1964. But not since.

—I was here in 1964.

—I know.

—I was out there, cutting your grass.

—I know that, she said.—And I'm sorry. As sorry as I can be. But listen to me, Henry. We'll have to stop this upstairs-downstairs business if we're going to get anywhere.

—What the fuck is upstairs-downstairs business?

—It's a programme on the television, she said.—The masters and the servants. It's very good.

—She's alive.

197

—I'd say so.

—You'd say so?

—She's like me, she said.—I saw that the minute she left.

She stood up without creaking and went back to the kettle, and kept talking while she worked.

—She's a survivor.

—We all are.

—Except Séamus.

I cried.

She held my head against her old stomach. I cried into her dressing gown.

—I loved him.

—I know.

—I loved him.

—I know, I know. And you saved him.

—He died.

—Yes, she said.—But he saw you saving his life. Not many fathers get to do that.

—That's just sentimental shite, I said.—That's all that is.

—I know, she said.

She let go of my head.

—It was a long time ago.

—D'you have a photograph? I asked.

—No, she said.—I've nothing.

She went back across to the kettle and the breadboard.

—There was nothing, she said.—No keepsake. Just himself and the clothes he was in. And they were too worn to take off.

—Where?

—Kansas, she said.—Looking for you.

—I was in Kansas.

—It's big.

—It fuckin' is.

—He died on the side of the road, she said.—I'm ashamed to say that.

She sighed.

—But there you have it.

She put a teapot on the table, beside me.

—I don't drink tea, I said.

—Who said it's for you?

She walked back to the counter.

—I've only the instant coffee.

—What about the percolator over there?

I'd noticed it before, a big old silver American one.

—Too much effort, she said.—The instant will have to do you.

—Grand, I said.—You were looking for me.

—I was, of course. For years.

—I heard stories, I said.—And Wanted posters. Dark Rosaleen. Lady O'Shea.

—I knew you'd see them.

—I saw them alright. Too late.

—I heard about you too, Henry. I knew it was you. One-Leg O'Glick.

—We must have been close to each other.

—We must have been.

She was sitting now, beside me. Holding my arm.

—But then it stopped, she said.

—I knew he was dead. I felt it.

—I came home, she said.—I thought you would too.

—I did.

—Eventually.

—I thought you were dead.

—Our lives could have been very different.

—Yeah.

—But I have to tell you, Henry.

She patted my arm.

—I've no regrets.

I let that settle.

—I married a good man, she said.

—You were already married to a good fuckin' man.

—D'you know what, Henry Smart? she said.—In all the years I was married to him, he never said *Fuck*. Not once.

—That must have been nice, was it?

—Not even once.

—Listen, I said.—You knew what you were getting when you married me.

—That's true.

—What was it like?

—What?

—Being married twice.

—It was very different, she said.—He was a different kind of man. And, I have to say, I became a different kind of woman.

—And no regrets.

199

—No.

She sighed.

—None.

—Go on, I said.—You're lying.

—I'm not.

It was a new day outside. I could see the sun against the back wall, creeping down towards the flowerbeds. The grass looked cut and there were no weeds climbing out of the muck. She had a new gardener, the bitch.

—I was destroyed when I came home, she said.—I didn't grieve till I got *here*. Not *here*. Home.

—It's gone, I said.—The old house.

—I know that, she said.

—I went looking for it.

—And me in it?

—Yeah, I said.—In 1951.

—I was married in 1943.

—You're a bigamist.

She laughed.

—I am, she said.—I'm a bigamist. Or I was. Did I stop being a bigamist when one of my husbands died?

—You're not a widow now either.

—You might be right.

—I am fuckin' right, I told her.—You're married to me and I'm not dead.

—I can't cope.

—You'll be grand, I said.

—I stayed down home for a while, she said.—Then I came up to Dublin. This was at the start of the Emergency.

—The what?

—The war, she said.—The Second World War.

—I missed it, I told her.

She didn't ask me what I meant. She was doing the talking.

She'd moved up to Dublin with Saoirse, because Saoirse was going to the College of Art, all fees paid by her Uncle Ivan. They had a flat in Rathfarnham. She met her husband at a bus stop, in town.

—Was he younger than you? I asked.

The old eyes stared at me.

—It's only a question, I said.

He was younger than her, but not that much younger. He was

200

a bachelor and settled in his ways. Until he met her. He sat beside her on the bus and he was at the bus stop the next day, and the day after. And the next week, he was waiting at both bus stops, in the morning and the evening.

—I don't know if I want to hear any of this, I told her.

She took him home and she gave him a fry and the ride of his life.

—The first one? I asked.—His first ride?

She nodded.

—He was very grateful.

—Did he pay you?

She slapped me. It didn't hurt, but had some clout for a woman of her age.

He'd bought a new house in Ratheen, way off on the other side of the city. He'd bought the place but he hadn't moved. It was too big and empty.

—So you married him.

—I loved him.

She looked at me staring at her.

—I did, she said.

We were sitting side by side. There was only a couple of inches between my eyes and hers.

He was handsome, shy, and a civil servant, in the Department of Agriculture. A big man in a big department. Her cousin Ivan was his boss for a while. The war was on and his work was vital; we were feeding England and we had to feed ourselves. He was sending cattle out onto the Irish Sea, to outrun the U-boats, to Holyhead and Liverpool. He'd come home late and he'd ride her for hours.

—Why are you telling me this?

—I want you to know, Henry, she said.—I don't want you to cod yourself. I haven't been waiting. I had a very good life. It wasn't about sitting by the fire.

—Did you have any more kids?

—Will you do your sums, for God's sake? It was more than thirty years ago. I was nearly sixty.

—Still riding.

—Yes.

—Good girl, I said.—Was there anyone else?

—What do you mean?

—Men, I said.—Or man.

—Between you and himself?

—Yeah.

—Of course there were.

—How many?

—Oh, stop that, she said.—Fine men, they all were.

—When?

—Stop it.

—I'd ride you now.

—What's stopping you?

—My wooden leg, my bad back, the shrapnel in my chest.

—They're just excuses.

—I know. You're still the same woman.

—I am.

—What're you looking at? I asked.

—Your forehead, she said.

—Are they still there?

She was looking for the pockmarks her nipples had dug, on the bed of stamps in 1916.

—No, she said.—There's so many holes, sure. It'd be too hard to tell.

—They're there alright.

—I left my glasses upstairs.

—I hear great things.

I'd seen him the odd time since I'd sat on the rug beside the sea, but he'd never stopped. He'd wave and keep pushing on, up the hill to the church and his house beside it. He was a walker. He knocked on the doors. He knew all the names, the holy communions and approaching deaths. He knew his parish. He didn't drive unless he was leaving it.

I knew he was watching me. But I knew something else: he wasn't the boss.

—Yes, he said.—Great things.

He sat there, looking at me over his glasses, pretending there was something more important than me in front of him.

I'd been summoned. Mister Strickland had given me the message.

—He'd like to see you now, he said.

—Grand.

—He stressed *now*.

Strickland knew his school was an I.R.A. cell, and he didn't like it. It was the priest – the manager – who'd brought in the new teachers: whenever there'd been a vacancy, some young lad would arrive with top marks and a brand new briefcase. Most of them had been good and eager teachers. But Strickland began to realise it at the same time I did: they were Provos. He looked back – like I did – and realised what an eejit he'd been. He remembered tension in the staffroom some years back and, only now, he got it; the split, when the I.R.A. had divided into the Officials and the Provisionals. He remembered wondering where he was going to get a substitute at nine o'clock on a Monday morning, just before a call from the priest would save the day; there'd be a young lad on his way, to fill the gap.

I was in on it. That was what Strickland thought. And he was right – although I only found that out at the same time he did. But I couldn't tell him. He wouldn't have wanted to hear. He ran a very good school, not a hidey-hole for the I.R.A. And that could stay the story, if nothing was said. The Provisionals had never used the classrooms for recruiting. They didn't need to. Once I started paying real attention to Ireland beyond the parish, I realised that it was 1920 again. Every stupid decision, every shooting, every rubber bullet – internment, Bloody Sunday, every strong rumour – British collusion in the planting of my bomb on Talbot Street and the other bombs that afternoon – all of these sent young men and women queuing up to join. Approval was in the air, everywhere. The British were back, on the telly every night, taking over the streets eighty miles up the road. There were dead bodies, there were refugees. Reprisal and counter-reprisal, terror and retaliation – it had gone on for three years, in my day. It went on for decades this time – and it was still my day. The priest behind the desk confirmed it.

—Great things, he said.

—Mister Strickland said you wanted me.

He looked at me over the specs.

—That's right.

There'd been a shift in the balance. He could look over his glasses as much as he liked, but he still had to look up. He'd been patronising me for years. Not now, though. Not while the I.R.A. thought that I was their last man standing. And not while I was pumped full of the fact that I had a wife who loved me. A secret wife – an even better secret. I'd look at her smiling at the kitchen window as she watched me slide over the back wall into her garden, with the bike on my back, the handlebars digging into the old spine. (I wasn't the gardener any more, so I had to sneak in as well as sneak out.) The fields behind the wall had filled up with new, still soft houses, their windows full of mammies and daddies walking angry babies back to sleep. I wasn't getting any younger. But that, too, was a big part of the crack. I was much too old for any of this, and so was she. I'd burst into the kitchen, she'd put on the kettle and we'd go in to the couch and watch *The Late Late Show*, and fall asleep watching. But not always. Sometimes there was some life left by the time I fell into the kitchen. I'd fall into her arms or she'd let herself drop into mine and she'd kiss and our mouths would open and we'd laugh as our old breaths met and we'd look into each other's eyes and try to see. And then we'd go in to the couch and the telly. On Saturday nights, and sometimes Wednesdays too.

I wasn't taking shite from the priest.

—I haven't seen much of you lately, Henry, he said.

—You've seen me, I said.

He dipped the head a bit more, so the glasses were well out of his way.

—It's my busy time of the year.

—Grand.

It was Holy Communion and Confirmation time, the spring, and two years since the bomb.

—How have you been?

—Grand.

—Everything's as it should be?

I remembered my manners.

—Yes, Father.

He looked at me.

—Be patient, he said.

He said it again.

—Be patient. You understand me?

—Yeah, I said.—I do.

—That's the message, he said.—You know what it means.

—Yes, Father, I said.—Do you?

A finger shoved the glasses back up along his nose. He looked uncertain – the fucker looked beaten.

—Yes, he said.

—Grand, I said.—I'll go out the back way.

He was sitting at the desk but I was the officer in the room.

I got to the door, through the empty kitchen. His housekeeper was staying well out of the way. She'd lost her pulling power a few years before. I was paid by cheque these days, by Strickland, the tax and P.R.S.I. deducted, even though I was much too old to be working. I didn't have to stand on her poxy step in the pissing rain and wait till she opened the door a chink and slid my money out to me.

I got to the door, and it hit me – I understood. The priest had been in on it from the beginning, and the beginning wasn't the bomb. I'd known that for more than a year, but I hadn't looked at it properly. It went back years, to the time he'd come looking for me. He hadn't just stopped me in the village and offered me the job. He'd been told to. Before the Troubles had started again, before 1966, long before the bomb that was supposed to have brought me back, the priest – a young man then – had been told to get me the job, to keep a close eye on me. For later.

It hit me, but not enough to stop or slow me down. They'd been waiting for me when I got off the bus in Ratheen the first time; they'd been keeping an eye on me all those years, when I was gardening. And before that – back to when I came down off the plane at Shannon with John Ford.

I was still walking as steadily as an old man with a wooden leg could walk as I got to the end of the priest's drive and kept going, onto the Main Road. The thought was mad – Irish history was all about *me*. I let go of the thought, and it scurried away happily enough. I wasn't going after it. Irish history could fuck off; I was in love.

I fell over the wall one night. I got out from under the bike and sat on the grass till some of my breath came back. I could feel the damp climb into my trousers. But I couldn't get up – I couldn't manage the thing. The light was off in her kitchen. But the blinds weren't drawn. She was standing there, watching, waiting. I rubbed my eyes, and stood. I swam a bit – my face felt gluey – and the lights and houses swerved and melted. But I stayed up. My mouth grabbed air and held it. The lawn was just a patch of grass, twelve good steps to the back door with only the empty clothesline in the way. I got there – the cold air was good on my face again – and I opened the door, into deeper gloom. There was no light at all, none from the hall or the landing above it. The house was completely dark.

My head caught up.

—Oh fuck.

There was something wrong.

She was upstairs, dying or dead. Maybe since Wednesday, the last time I'd gone back over the wall.

I made it to the light switch, beside the door to the hall. I turned on the light.

She was sitting at the table. In her Cumann na mBan uniform. She was smiling, nervous.

—Did you think I was dead, Henry?

—Not at all.

—Were you worried?

—No, I said.—Not much. Is it the same one?

—It is, she said.—Though the skirt is newer. It still fits.

—Why wouldn't it? I said.—You were a lanky oul' one back then too.

I sat down too – I had to.

—Hat and all, I said.

—Hat and all.

She stood up. She looked at the clock on the wall.

—It's late enough, she said.—Come on.

She went out to the bike. She picked it up out of the flowerbed.

—I can't manage the thing, I said.

—I'll do the pedalling, she said.—And it won't be the first time. You can get up on the crossbar.

—I can in my arse.

—Exactly.

We cycled through the village when the pub and the chipper were safely shut. We met no one, and nothing big got in our way. We stayed off the hill, so we wouldn't have to hear the rattle in her chest. I held the bars and she held me. I pushed my old arse back at her and I knew it was me who gave her the power to push down on the pedals. She hadn't cycled in years —

—Not since I became respectable.

Talking nearly killed her.

But she talked.

—What if they come along now?

—Who? I said.—The Garda?

—Oh God. What if —

—Sorry, love, I said.—I can't hold onto the bars and talk. It's one or the other.

She laughed. I felt the shaking in her arms.

—It's a pity the post office is shut this time of night, she said.—
We could have gone in, for old times' sake.

—We'd never be able to ride back out, I said.

—That's probably true.

—And we couldn't manage the kerb, I told her.

She got us onto the new Main Road. It had been built on an
easier slope; it didn't go into the old village. She could just about
manage it. I turned us onto the old road again, and we free-
wheeled down the hill and felt the wind grab at our clothes and
cheeks. Her hat stayed on and so did I.

—Better than *The Quiet Man*, I said.

—God, yes, she said.—Those ol' tandems are good for nothing.

—Except cycling.

She stopped at the bottom of the hill.

—I'm finished, she said.

So we swapped. She got up on the crossbar. I put the weight
I remembered down on the pedal, and went. I couldn't cycle
because of the leg – but I did it.

—Still alive?

—Fuckin' sure.

But I couldn't take us far.

—The leg's fucked.

—You've had enough.

—What about you?

—I'm grand.

—Good girl.

She got off the crossbar. I watched the pain cross her face. I
looked away as she slowly assembled herself. But I stopped – I
made myself look. And I loved her.

—I'm exhausted, she finally said.

—I did all the fuckin' work.

—Always the smart answer.

We were three steps from my door.

—Will we go in?

—No, she said.

She looked at me.

—I'm not who you think I am, she said.

I looked at her.

—Fair enough.

We walked back to her house. We both leaned on the bike. I

had to. This was the pain of a fresh-lost leg, and worse, every time I moved it – a new cut every step. But it didn't matter. We struggled together, back up the Main Road.

We got onto the bed. I gave her a hand. She let me take off her second boot. She lay back on the bed in the uniform. She let the hat drop to the floor. I lay beside her. I didn't take the leg off yet. I didn't want to face the mess.

We lay there.

—What if they come in now?

—They'll find two old people afraid of closing their eyes.

—They will not, she said.

I felt her head move. I felt her breath, then her lips touch the skin at my eye.

—There now, she said.

She lay back again.

—I won't climb up on you tonight, she said.

—Thanks.

—You scut.

—Tomorrow, I said.—Get up on me tomorrow.

—I might, she said.—Are you happy, Henry?

I thought about it.

—Yes.

—Good, she said.—So am I.

We slept.

No dreams – no fingers.

We both woke up.

PART THREE

10

I waited for four years.

I was too old and wrecked for the job but no one was going to sack me. The school started to fall apart, and so did republicanism. The pub bombings had started before I was bombed, and the kidnappings. One after another, after another – Guildford, Birmingham, half the pubs in Belfast. Reprisal and counter-reprisal became tit for tat – murder was trivialised. Bank heists became the daily thing, and every housing estate knew a Provo with a red car and a stiff leather jacket. The rebel songs stopped, except in some of the pubs. Little boys stopped singing about Saxon gore and the men behind the wire. The portraits of the republican dead were taken down off the classroom walls. The Provisionals were losing but only a few of them knew it.

—They didn't have that in our day, I said.

—What? she said.

I pointed at the telly.

—That, I said.

It was 1980. We were watching the news.

—Kneecapping, I said.

—No, she agreed.—We didn't have that.

While the Provisionals were emptying the country's banks, they were kneecapping kids for robbing shops.

—Did we do that kneecapping? I asked her.

It was a real question. I wanted to know. I'd shot men so their outraged pals would shoot other men. I'd fired off rounds so that people would be terrified and grateful. I'd left a dead body on a street, so that fury would drop solid and blinding onto the surrounding streets. I'd murdered men because I'd been told to.

—We didn't, she said.

—Are you sure?

—Maiming our own? she said.—We never did that. Why would we have?

—Okay.

—We didn't.

—Good.

—Only them that were looking for it.

I looked at her. I sat up – it took a while.

—You still believe in it, I said.—Don't you?

—When I remember, she said.—Yes. Sometimes.

She tried to sit up, to match me.

—It's there in me still, she said.—And what about you, Henry?

—Not really.

I'd never let her in on the secret. It had nearly killed me, but I hadn't whispered the fact that I was one of the men that mattered. I'd been told to tell no one. I'd been reminded of that, the day before.

—*A chara*, he said, when I finally got the door open.

It needed to be taken off its hinges and given a planing – the weather had fattened the wood – but I wouldn't be doing the job.

He was by himself. It had been more than five years, and the beard was gone. But the teeth and the accent; I knew who he was. He followed me back into the house.

—How's the health? he asked.

—Grand, I said.

—You're looking well, he said.

—I'm not, I said.—But I don't look.

—That's the spirit.

It took a while – everything took a while; nothing came quick any more – but then I knew how I felt when I saw him: delighted. I was being rewarded for my patience. I was the sleeper, being called into action at last. Miss O'Shea was going to be proud of me.

I remembered: republicans loved their tea.

—Will I stick on the kettle?

—Don't bother yourself.

—Grand, I said.—I've biscuits.

—No, he said.—No.

I had Goldgrains, but so did the mice. Their droppings were all over the plate on the table. I could hear the bastards but I hadn't seen them in years.

—I'm on my way up to Parnell Square, he said.

He looked less sturdy without the beard. He was still the man, though – even the mice were listening.

—And I thought I'd drop in, say hello.

—What's in Parnell Square? I asked.

I remembered singing on Parnell Square, with Jack Dalton.

—Headquarters, he said.—The political wing. Has to be done.

—I bet it works, I said.

—What works?

—The shaving, I said.—I bet you can go anywhere without being stopped.

He smiled.

—I can, aye.

—The same here, I told him.—I put on a suit and they didn't know how to find me.

—A suit would be too much for me, he said.—I'd nearly prefer to be sent back to the Kesh.

—Long Kesh?

—That's right.

—Looks like a kip.

—It's a kip, right enough.

It was man to man stuff and I loved every word. He pushed the door shut. It closed with a whinge.

—So, Henry, he said.—I don't want to attract attention. So I'll just say my piece.

—Go ahead.

I didn't sit down. I was ready to follow him straight back out the door, to Parnell Square, to the walls of Long Kesh. I wouldn't need a bag.

—There's something big on the way, he said.—Something very big. It could change everything.

—I don't like this kneecapping, I told him.

—I don't like it myself, he said.—But listen now. I can't give you details. And it's no insult to you. No one knows the details. No one.

Your secret's safe, I wanted to tell him. *I'll have forgotten it before you're back in your car. Just tell me.*

—The timing's vital, he said.—And it might be a while yet. Are you fit?

I nodded.

—I am.

I could climb over walls, although I went over Miss O'Shea's front wall these days; the high back wall was beyond me – I couldn't look up at it.

—Good man, he said.—Ignore what you hear. On the news or from any other source. It's a smokescreen. The armed struggle. You understand?

I nodded.

—Behind the armed struggle, Henry, there's another struggle going on.

He was making sure his eyes were locked to mine.

—That's where you'll come in, Henry, he said.—At the right time. The exact right time. The word from you, Henry. You have no idea.

—What word?

—You'll know when the time comes.

He was at the door.

—We'll meet again soon, he said.—Keep fit. Be patient.

—I'm not going with you?

—No, he said.—Not this time.

The teeth lit the room.

—But you will.

The door was open.

—*Slán*.

I stayed where I was. I heard feet joining his feet, car doors, an engine, two engines.

—Is there anything good on after this? I asked her now.

But she was asleep. Fair play to her, she still slept with her mouth closed. Not bad for ninety-three. I wanted to kiss her but her head was right at my shoulder, tucked in like the butt of a rifle.

—I was lying, I said.—I'm involved.

She stayed asleep.

—I love you.

I retired. No one told me to. No one announced it. A young lad of about fifty passed me by in the corridor. He was the new care-taker. And I didn't mind. I cared – but I didn't mind. Good luck to him; he had a job.

That was another thing. The country stopped growing. The dizzy spell was over. There were fathers and grandfathers collecting the little lads at the school gate. They'd no work and no chance of work, and their wives were off cleaning houses or working up in Cadbury's. And the kids in the school began to change as well – they were looking ahead to nothing. Even that young, they knew they were fucked.

But I was gone and I didn't have to look at them. I handed over the school keys to the priest. He was starting to show his age as well. He was prosperous around the jowls. His head was slick, and he'd stopped wearing the dog collar, except on Sundays. He looked filthy.

—We'll have to give you a good send-off, Henry, he said.

There were more keys on the ring than there had been when he'd first handed them to me. More locks, more security, extra prefabs out the back – more kids but no money coming to pay for proper classrooms.

—No, thanks, I said.

—Ah now, we'll have to have a do, he said.

—No.

He shrugged. It was a strange gesture, coming from this man. He'd never shrugged before; he'd never had to. He'd known everything; he'd always got exactly what he wanted. It was as if the action, the little shrug, hurt him, a muscle pain that scrabbled across his eyes.

I turned, and left him to it. The housekeeper was in the kitchen, sitting there, growing a beard. I'd come in that way but I went out by the front door.

Shrugging was what dying slowly was all about. I could have told the priest that. And I could have told the men at the school gate and the kids on the other side of the gate. Not understanding, or pretending not to give a fuck, the whole country was shrugging, killing the time that was left.

But I'd retired, a few months shy of my seventy-ninth birthday. (Strickland had gone two years ahead of me.) I could do my shrugging on my own. I'd actually gone past shrugging – the shoulders were fucked, seized up around the ears. I'd become a shorter man.

Except when I was meeting my wife. Then I had the zip to stand up properly.

I rang the bell. There was no more wall-climbing left in me. My last go had been a disaster. I'd tried to get over the front wall, but I'd ended up stuck under the bike, lodged between the top of the wall and the fuck of a hedge behind it, while I listened to an ambulance siren getting nearer, and I had to listen to the cop and the woman from next door who'd done all the phoning as they tried to figure out how a man of my age could have cycled into that position, or how a car could have swiped me without breaking a single bone or the light on the bike. I'd spent that Saturday night in the Mater A&E, and kept having to explain that the missing leg was an old, old story and I just wanted to go home. But I wasn't able to get off the trolley. I think I delivered my final shrug that night. And I saw what happened to a dying city when the shrugging stopped: I saw my first Dublin junkies.

I gave the bell another go.

I lay on the trolley and I watched a junkie die. Her friends, the ones who'd come into the A&E with her, didn't notice. The drunk and the mad I was used to. But this was new.

I'd no more climbing in me. I'd even had to get a taxi from the village to her house, five hundred yards – for one pound ninety.

—D'you want the change? the driver asked.

He'd let the car roll a bit as I opened the passenger door. He was a young guy, twenty-five or so, with a tattoo, *Eire Nua* and the tricolour, on the arm that was holding my change.

—Yeah, I said.—I do.

I'd put one foot out on the road. The wooden leg was still in the car.

—It's only ten fuckin' p, he said.

—It's my ten fuckin' p.

This was right outside her front gate. She'd be waiting, looking out the window. It was Saturday night again. I'd shaved – I thought I had. I was ready to drag him from the taxi. But he surrendered the money.

—Good man, I said.

He'd stopped the rolling. I was able to get out smoothly enough. I slammed the door. It didn't work. I gave it another go, just as he leaned over to do the job himself. The boom of the door and his trapped *fuck you* were music to my oul' lad's ears. There was nothing wrong with my hearing. I was tempted to give the wall one last go. But I resisted. I knew the woman who'd phoned for the cops a few months before would be looking out her window. Two women were gawking as I went up the driveway, Miss O'Shea and Neighbourhood Watch. I didn't know what she looked like, but I remembered a voice, and tits in black wool – *Are you alright*

216

there? Hello? It wasn't too far to the front door, although the driveway was on a slope I hadn't noticed when I'd been the gardener. But the lungs were grand, and I felt my shoulders start to shift and grow. I had a neck, I had a chest.

I rang the bell.

A beautiful evening. I turned and looked out at it while I waited for Miss O'Shea. Blue sky, unbroken, over the Old Shillelagh, the hotel across the way, a bit further along the road. It was an I.R.A. spot, someone had told me once, back when I didn't care. Escaped internees and other lads on the run hid openly in that place, free of charge, and they were left alone by the Guards. But that was years ago now. The place looked innocent enough from where I stood. There was always a wedding on, in a big room around the back. I'd often seen men in suits vomiting against parked cars, and young ones with young lads up against the same cars. There were three young ones now, three fat girls, uneasy on their heels, going through the car park towards the steps to the bar. A young lad came out as they were going in. Even from across the wide road, I could see he was terrified. There was nothing wrong with my eyes either; they weren't blue any more but they worked. And I could see the red in the young lad's eyes. Three girls together made one big scary bird.

But I was waiting for my own bird. I turned, and expected her shadow on the glass, her heels on the floor inside.

There was nothing. I rang the bell again – tried to count back the number of times I'd rung it already.

I stopped looking at the door.

The girls were gone inside. The lad was standing at the bus stop.

I was supposed to be patient. I couldn't die. I'd get the call, and I was going to give the word. And I'd know the word; I wouldn't have to ask for it.

It was quiet now, across at the hotel. The lad at the bus stop was gone. I hadn't noticed the bus. I looked the other way, but he wasn't walking – I couldn't see him.

She wasn't answering. I put my face to the glass. But I gave that up and smashed it with my elbow. It went first time but I smothered any satisfaction. The smell of old food rushed through the cracks in the glass – old porridge, I thought, and not cooked that morning. I hadn't seen her since the Wednesday before. Three days. I battered at the loose glass with the elbow. There was a shirt and a good tweed jacket sleeve between me and a bloody death. The jacket was one of her husband's old ones. I was able to reach in and get the door unlocked.

I didn't bother with the kitchen. I knew she'd be in the bed. I was racing against something – I could feel it turning – time, breath. I was off the stairs and into the bedroom.

She wasn't there.

No one had been there, for days. The air moved sluggishly, woken by me when I shoved the door.

She was in the kitchen. On the floor. There was blood around her head. It was dried, baked, sticking her face to the lino. But she wasn't dead. There was an eye looking at me – at my foot. Looking, staring. Watching as I got down to touch her face and kiss her. She wasn't cold – she wasn't dead. The house was warm, she was fully dressed. Cardigan, tights. But the blood wasn't flowing or trickling; it was dry and cracked on the floor.

She looked at me – the one brown-black eye. The frightened, living eye.

—Can you hear me?

The eye stared. No blink. No movement at all.

She was breathing. My cheek was at her mouth. I could feel her breath – the room was warm, the breath was faintly wet.

—You'll be grand, I told her.—You'll be fine. Hang on a minute.

She must have watched as I got myself upright again. It took most of the minute I'd asked for. She'd have heard me on the phone in the hall, calling for an ambulance. She'd have heard me on the stairs again, and again when I struggled back down with the blankets from off her bed, and a pillow. And she could see me again as I lifted her head – I looked to see pain in the eye as her skin and hair fought with the glue that the blood had become – and I forced the pillow under her head. But I saw no pain. I covered her with the blankets, and myself as well, beside her, to warm her. I closed my eyes. Then opened them – I was stupid, I had to stay awake.

I got out from under the blankets. They were heavy; they made me wheeze. I put my hand on her forehead. I hoped to feel her shake. She was still, absolutely still – but her eye still looked at me. Open – alive. Frightened. Angry.

She'd fallen – I'd worked it out. Earlier in the day, or the night before. Or the afternoon, the morning, or the night before that. She was dressed for the day – but the end or the start of the day, or what day, I couldn't tell. She wasn't cold.

It annoyed me now – it upset me – that we hadn't lived properly, that I hadn't pressed her to let me move in. But we'd never lived like that. Even in Chicago, in the short time we'd shared a roof, it hadn't been our roof and I'd rarely been under it. Our happiest years had been just after we'd got married, when we were both on the run and the rampage, and the years after we'd escaped from Chicago, still on the run, with a growing family brought up in ditches and boxcars. But we should have settled down. I was already wearing her other husband's threads. I should have gone the whole fuckin' hog. I should have smashed the door glass years before.

I stood up properly – I tried to.

Age came at me in sudden, angry waves. I'd be grand, and then I'd suddenly be crippled, folded, bitten by pain in every part of me that had to move. My wrists, my back – everything hurt. But it didn't matter.

She'd fallen. There was no kettle on the floor, or a pan or a plate, no burning porridge. She'd just fallen, and knocked her head against the edge of the table. The blood had gushed from the side now buried in the pillow. I wasn't going to move her again, to get a good look at the damage. I wasn't going to bend again. The eye was still there, wide open; I didn't want her looking up at me gawking back down at her. She had pain of her own; she wasn't going to stare up, trapped, at mine.

I looked around. There was no rug that could have tripped her, or slid from under her. She'd fallen and hit her head on the way down. She hadn't been mugged. The back door was shut. I went across – and it was locked.

My voice stopped other noise.

—I'll go and see if I can hear them coming.

I went back to the hall. I should have stayed with her – she needed to see me. But I kept going. I spoke as I went. I walked over the broken glass.

—Hear that?

I loved the crunch and bite. I'd broken the door. I'd saved my wife.

I stood in the porch. I heard nothing – just the usual. Passing traffic, the odd shout from the hotel car park. I couldn't hear a siren.

Then I could. I definitely could. I left the door open. I went back to the kitchen.

The eye was open. I got down on the floor. I sat beside her.

—Good girl.

I was lifted – easily. Put sitting on a chair beside the table. Eyes stared into mine. A man's mouth, remembering to smile.

She was already on a stretcher, being carried out to the hall. I tried to see past him, to see if her face was covered.

—Is she alright?

—Was it yourself called us?

—Yeah.

He nodded at the hall, and the broken glass.

—You're a neighbour.

—I'm her husband.

—She locked you out.

—Is she alive?

—She is, yeah, he said.—Just about. Where were you?

—We don't live together, I said.

I tried to get past him – I tried to stand up.

—You don't live together? he said.

He'd never heard of anything like that. He was only a young lad.

I got up from the chair. He let me. He'd no right to stop me; he wasn't a cop.

—Did yis have a fight, or what?

—Just get out of my fuckin' way.

He did – quickly, although some of the smile was still hanging there.

—I have to ask, he said.

—Ask away.

I followed the stretcher. I went over the glass, out to the drive. The ambulance was out on the road. I went down the drive. The mouthy fucker from inside passed me.

—I'm coming with you, I told him – I thought I told him.

By the time I got out on the road, the ambulance was finishing a U-turn and heading back towards – I didn't know which hospital.

—Where —?

I tried to shout.

She was gone.

I had to tell them all. Her neighbours, the hospitals, the Health Board – I was the widow's husband.

220

The priest didn't look surprised. He'd had bigger shocks.

—You married out of the parish, he said.

—It was a long time ago, I told him.

—Her surname isn't Smart, he said.

—She thought I was dead, I told him.—She thought I'd been dead for years, before she met the other man.

—But she'd no proof of your death.

—Well, look it, I wasn't dead. So no, she didn't. But she could never have found it. There were dead people everywhere. It's a long story.

—Keep it to yourself, so, he said.—It can be another of our secrets. Am I right?

I nodded for him. I thought he'd give me something back.

—Do you know where she is, Father? I asked.

—No, he said.—I don't. Why would I?

—It's your parish.

—I'll bury her when she's delivered to me.

—But she's definitely alive?

—As far as I know.

—Where?

—I told you. Her cousin dealt with her, I'm told.

—Her cousin?

—Her cousin, he said.—Another powerful man. But, like us all, Henry Smart, not as powerful as he used to be.

—Ivan Reynolds.

—Ivan the Terrible, he said.

He made sure I knew he was sneering.

—He'll tell you where she is, he said.

—Ah, fuck off, I said.

He said nothing to my back as I walked out.

—I'm not sure where she is, the woman next door to her told me.

This was the woman who'd phoned for the ambulance when she'd seen me under the bike, lodged between the wall and the hedge. She was a good-looking woman. I'd seen her waiting at the school gate for kids who were more than likely living and working abroad now, in England or America. She wasn't unfriendly, but she was wondering what the retired caretaker was doing, looking for straight-backed Missis O'Kelly. (I'd stopped being the gardener before she'd moved in.) There was something small but cruel on her face: she knew what I wanted to know.

—I'm her husband, I told her.

She grabbed hold of the shock, and managed one word back.

—Husband? she said.

—Yeah.

—But you don't live there.

—Where is she?

—And your name isn't O'Kelly, she said.—Sure it's not? What is your name?

—My name's Smart, I said.

—Henry.

—That's right, I said.—Please. Where is she?

—You worked in the school, she said.

—That's right, I said.

—When did, she said.—When did you get married?

—In 1919, I told her.

I couldn't help it; I smiled. But she didn't.

—What about the other man? she said.—The man who died. Her husband. Mister O'Kelly.

—A misunderstanding, I said.—I'll tell you another time. Do you know where she is?

—No, she said.

—No?

—Not really, she said.—I mean, a lady in the butcher's told me she was in a nursing home.

I'd tried all the hospitals; I'd gone to them all. But it had taken me days. There'd been no Missis O'Kelly, no Missis Smart, no Miss O'Shea, and no records of any or all of those old women. Ivan Reynolds had got there long before me.

—Where's the nursing home?

—She didn't know where, exactly, said the woman.—And I've never really known Missis O'Kelly that well. Are you really her husband?

—Yes, I am. Where's the nursing home?

—Howth, she said.—I think she said Howth – the lady.

—Thanks.

She wanted more but I turned away. I had a taxi waiting at the gate.

I found her. Just twenty minutes in the taxi. To a nursing home in Howth. With a view of the Bay that she was never going to see.

She was lying on a bed, under the window, with her one eye open. Still alive – the only thing left living in her. Looking up at the ceiling.

—I'm her husband, I told the nurse.

—She's a widow.

—She isn't, I said.—She used to be.

—Oh lovely, said the nurse, a gorgeous fat young one from the country.—Did ye get married recently?

—No.

—Was it years ago?

—Years before she met her other husband.

—God.

She loved it. She watched me holding the dead woman's hand.

—Will you have a cup of tea?

—No, thanks.

—Sure?

—Yeah, I said.—I'm grand.

She didn't leave. She sat on the end of the bed, her toes just tipping the shining floor.

—There's never a peep out of her, she said.—Was she always a quiet one?

—You're jesting, I said, the proud husband.—She was mad.

—Was she?

—She was out in the War of Independence.

—Fighting?

—Yeah.

—Shooting?

—Absolutely.

—God.

Bad noise from another room sent her jumping off the bed and running. I watched her arse as she hit the hall.

—Back in a minute, she called.

But she left me alone for a while. I sat and watched the eye, and hoped. And hoped for weeks.

The pride became anger. I wasn't angry at her, not just her. I was angry at both of us. We should have done the sane thing. We should have grabbed the last few years and lived them in the normal way. She'd done that with the other man, for years. I should have made it my turn.

I went there every day. I didn't have the money for taxis. I got the bus to Howth and hitched my way up the hill. In O'Kelly's tweed and cotton I looked like I lived in that posh world above Howth village. I was never long waiting for a lift.

I sat there and held her hand. The fat nurse and the other nurses and kitchen staff all took their turns and looked in at us. I knew they were there without having to turn and hear my bones crack. I'd hear the squeak of their work shoes, or the romance and sadness of it all escaping in their breath. I'd know they were there and I liked it. The curiosity, the attention, and the soapy smell of the nurses.

Then, one day, the squeaks were sharper. I knew Ivan Reynolds was behind me. The man I'd trained to kill, who'd then tried to kill me. And the man who was paying for my wife's bed.

This time I turned.

—Who are you? said the woman at the open door.—Why are you here?

She was an old woman now, but I was looking at my daughter. The hair was grey but that was my sixty-year-old daughter standing at the door, straight-backed as her mother used to be. It was her face, puzzled but sure, and angry. And something too, behind it – in her eyes. It was the face behind the face I recognised. But she hadn't a clue who I was.

—Who are you? she said.

—Well, fuck it, I said.—I think I'm your father.

—My God.

—Now you're talking.

She stood there. For ever. She didn't look at me – not properly.

—You took your time, I said.

—Excuse me?

—I said, you took your time.

—I didn't know, she said eventually.

—You phoned, I said.—1964, was it? Nothing since.

She stepped into the room.

—And what about you? she said.—My father?

Her mother lay dead on the bed – maybe listening. The eye was open, but I wasn't sure about the ears. I believed she could hear, because I wanted her to, just as I believed she could see me when I hung my face over hers. But she hadn't squeezed my hand when I'd held hers, not even slightly. And she'd never blinked when I'd asked her to – one for yes, two for no.

—So, said the daughter.—Here we all are.

She was standing beside me. She looked too, to see if her

224

mother was listening, if the eye was up to anything. It was open, but nothing else.

I'd no idea who this woman was, only who she'd been. She stared down at me like she'd found me on her shoe.

—It must be a bit strange, I said.

—What?

There were years of American living in the accent that carried her question. But the question itself was Irish.

—Finding out you've got a father, I said.

She didn't answer. She looked at her mother but made no attempt to get closer, to muscle me out of her way. She had a man's watch on her wrist and she kept looking at it.

—Where's Ivan? I asked.

—Uncle Ivan?

—He isn't your uncle, I said, and I felt stupid as I said it.

—He was more of an uncle than you were ever a father, she said.

If this was a war, she'd won it already. I looked at her mother. But the eye wasn't backing me up.

—That's how you remember it, I said.

—That's how it was.

—You saw me fall under the train, for fuck sake.

—But I never saw you crawl out from under it, she said.—But you must have.

—You know what happened.

—Clearly, I don't, she said.—You were dead until a minute ago. And forgotten.

—I didn't know —

—The world's a small place, Mister Smart, she said.—Nobody is very hard to find.

She was making sure I wouldn't like her. And she was good at it. I could have killed her. *Mister Smart*. Had she really forgotten the good years? I was too old to re-examine them. I needed them as they were, solid and mine.

—Where is he? I asked again.—Why isn't he here?

—He is, she said.

—Is he outside?

She didn't tell me to follow, but I knew I was supposed to. She was still in the hall by the time I'd made it to the door. She was going into the next room.

He was on the bed – *in* the bed – both eyes open. Wide awake and dying. I'd forgotten: I was the man who trained Ivan for leadership but he'd always been older than me.

He was smiling – before he saw me, before he knew there was someone else in the room. The smile, for my daughter, took all the energy he had and it was gladly given. I envied, but I couldn't hate him. The fucker loved her – it was clear and shocking. He loved the child she'd been and he didn't mind the fact that she wasn't a child now. He'd seen her grow.

I'd been waiting for this, wanting it, for years. Eyes locked to Ivan's, the confrontation. Now, though, I wanted to step back out of the room.

He saw me, and he knew me. The terror that ran across Ivan the Terrible's grey face did me no good at all. But the way he flicked it off did; he was still thinking, still on the make. It took less than a second. He could look straight at me.

—Captain, he said.

He was using his death rattle, hiding behind it. She stood beside him.

—Ivan, I said.

—A long time.

The rattle again, and a cough. I was too late if I wanted to kill him.

—A lifetime, I said.

—That's right, he said.—More than the one lifetime, faith. You're looking well, Captain. Still the handsome man.

—Fuck off, Ivan.

—You've come to see me off, he said.

—No, I said.

—No?

—I came in to say hello.

—You'd be doing me a favour, he said.—If you helped me on my way.

—That's grand, I said.—But I'd hate to think I'd ever done you a favour.

I didn't look at her.

—No grudges, so?

—None, I said.

—Hard feelings?

—No.

—You got the looks, Captain, but I got the land.

I shrugged – I tried to.

—You still have the land, I said.

—And the looks fucked off on you many moons ago, said Ivan.—I told the lads to go for your face. Make him ugly, I told them.

He was still Ivan.

—And no hard feelings?

I saw her hand pat his shoulder.

—No, I said.—None. It's good to see you.

I looked at him, but I spoke to her.

—I wish this had happened years ago, Ivan.

—Do you now?

—Yeah, I said.—But better late than never. I still have time to thank you.

—For what?

—Looking after my family.

—Sure, aren't you family yourself, Captain?

—And you tried to kill me.

—For Ireland, he said.—It was all for Ireland.

—Was it worth it?

—God, it was. Sure, look at us.

I watched while two of the people who'd made this country died. And, outside, the country was already dead. I was in the nursing home most of the time, or coming to and from the place, but I couldn't ignore what my eyes still made me see.

Ratheen had always been a village of walkers but they'd been old men and young mothers, pushing themselves or their prams, killing the slow time before death or the time before the school bell freed their kids. I'd avoided the oul' lads but the mothers were a great idea: women with time on their hands, still young after three and four children. They, as much as their kids, were the measure of my success. I'd created the land that fed them – me and Ivan and Miss O'Shea. These good-looking girls who wore trousers and threw back their heads when they laughed. They blessed themselves when they passed the big church but they weren't going to cringe or hide. Early summer took the fuckin' years off me, as they gathered at the school gate, chatting and laughing. The smell of idle Irishwomen – it was my victory.

And the oul' lads too. When I was born, at the start of it all, forty was the ripe old age. My parents never got near it. Working

227

men and women who crawled across the forty mark often wished they hadn't. Crippled, toothless, broken-lunged, they sucked the Dublin air and hoped for the end, even as they fought it. But when I came back it was different. Women of forty were vital and solid – fine things with decades of sex and madness still ahead of them. And old was properly old now. Men could walk up to sixty, and seventy, and still chew raw carrots at eighty. I stayed clear of the oul' lads but I liked them. They had their pensions and enough of their health. They were walking success stories, written by me, secretly happy with the work that strolled and hobbled past me every day. The young arses and the old ones – I signed them all. *Best wishes from Henry Smart.*

But then it changed. It didn't happen suddenly but, for a while – for years – I didn't want to see it. The walkers were joined by men I hadn't seen before, because they'd been at work. The builders, the plasterers, the young lads who'd gone into the offices – there was no more building and no new offices. The working men were killing the day.

They didn't walk. They stood. Outside the bookies, outside the pub, outside the new library. Their backs to everything; nothing belonged to them. Staying out till they could go home. And now that the streets had been taken by their husbands, the women stayed at home – and aged. They couldn't go out while their husbands did nothing. They couldn't laugh while they worried about food and where the money would come from. They worried about their husbands. They worried about their children. The country became the old place again, killing everything young. The children were leaving, or staying. They were going to the old places – London, Liverpool, Boston; and to the new ones – Luton, Sydney, Düsseldorf. The ones who stayed were finding their own new country, where the dead walked – until they died too.

I knew this but it didn't get in my way. Not in 1980, while I watched my wife die. I'd found needles in the school yard, in the last years before I retired. Thrown over the wall the night before, or used by ghosts who'd climbed the wall. I knew it was happening. I knew what a hophead looked like. I'd seen my share; I'd known them when I'd lived the life with Louis Armstrong. But they'd been jazzmen, irritating, sad, but never a mass, never a fuckin' generation. They'd have filled a club but not the world. These kids, in Dublin, were grey. And yellow. Kids I'd seen running around in the school yard, whose mothers I'd wanted to pick up and bite. They were ancient teenagers, derelicts still in their early twenties. Taking over the corners that their fathers hadn't already taken. While their mothers went to work and only laughed now when they needed to hear themselves, to prove that they still lived.

I noticed the boys – noticed, and ignored – and then the girls. Young ones being punctured and pumped up, fat and skeletal in the space of a week. Traces of their mothers in their faces, lovely women turned desperate. Junkies pushing buggies, making early grannies of the women I'd adored from the safe side of the school gate. I saw it while I waited for the bus and decided that the place was worse than it had been when I was the young, hungry king of Dublin's corners. Poverty then had seemed natural, but this was just atrocious.

But I didn't care. I couldn't.

—Do you know what I regret, Captain?

I looked in on Ivan every day.

—What?

—The time I said *Fuck you* to God, said Ivan.—D'you remember that time?

—I do, yeah. I made them all say it.

—That might be true now, he said.—But it's myself I remember saying it. Fuckin' shouting it, boy. To the high fuckin' heavens. And here's me now.

—There's no God, Ivan.

—Not for you, maybe. But there'd have to be God for me and the likes of me. There's no point to it all if He isn't up there, waiting. With the account book out, like.

—Maybe you're right.

—I'll be telling Him it was you put me up to it, Captain.

—That's grand, I said.—I don't mind.

—It's true, though.

—I know.

—How's herself? he said.

—The same.

—It's hard to think of her up to nothing.

—It is.

—And the young one?

—The young one's sixty, Ivan.

229

—Well now, I wish I was fuckin' sixty. And yourself?

—I'm happy enough where I am.

—Go on, yeh liar, he said.—You'd love to be the lad again. Is she around? The young one.

—No, I said.—She's not.

—Gone back?

—Yeah, I said.—She's gone home.

But I didn't know.

There were two men blocking the door.

—Back in, said one of them.

It was a Dublin accent but he wasn't one of the Dublin boys I'd met before. I didn't know him, although there was something about him that seemed familiar – the way his body took over the place, a shoulder in each high corner of the kitchen.

They were both in the room now and the door had been quietly closed.

—Do you want to sit down? said the other man.

He was a culchie and the fat was new on him. He'd come up to Dublin from west of the Shannon, and south. I'd cycled through his granny's townland.

Nothing about these men frightened me. I was ready for them. My heart was grand. My lungs were too.

—I'm fine, I said.

—We might be here a while, said the culchie.

He was from north Clare, I decided, with five or six Dublin years under the belt. He had a rat's head, on top of a bear's body. I looked again at the other man. They both looked bright. There was nothing thick or lazy about them.

—Right, I said.—I'll sit.

—Good man.

I sat on one of the hard chairs at the table. There were only two chairs. The other man, the big Dub, took the other one. The Clare man stayed standing. His toes were up against mine.

They were badly dressed, for professional revolutionaries. Bad jackets, cheap trousers. I could see the weight of their guns. The police would have them easily spotted. But maybe the rules were different these days. The trick was to blend in, wear the uniform of the respectable unemployed. The Provisionals I'd met at the sea had been dressed like these men here. No one stood out.

Elegance had got off the island long ago. I hadn't bought or stolen a shirt in years and I was wearing a dead man's trousers.

One big face was close to the side of mine. The other was hanging over me. They'd come with the instructions, and I was ready for them.

—We decided to have a chat with you here, said the Clare man.

—Grand.

—Instead of bringing you down to the station.

I made sure the shock didn't show. But I was the thick in the room. They were cops. Of course they were. The long arm of the state, in plain clothes, but not hiding behind any disguise. They were Special Branch – the G Division all over again. The new, quick shock was that it had taken them so long to come for me.

—So, Henry, said the Clare man.—What are you up to?

I gave him the honest answer.

—I don't know what you mean.

—Serious? said the other voice, right against my face.

—Yeah.

I expected it now. The fist to my head, the chair kicked from under me.

Nothing happened.

—You're off up to Howth every day, said the Clare man.

—Yeah.

—Why?

—Visiting my wife.

—The O'Shea woman.

—O'Kelly, I said.

—Fuck off now, Henry, and stop messing. We know all about her.

—She's my wife.

—But you live here, said the Dub at my ear.

—Yeah.

—And her house is down there.

—Yeah.

—She's the ex-wife then.

—No, I said.—The lost wife.

—She's been living there for forty years, said the Clare man.—And you're here thirty. We've done our homework, Henry. So think before you say anything.

—She's my wife, I told them.—We were married long ago. But we drifted apart. It's a bit of a story.

—Okay, said the Dub.

—Grand, said the Clare man.—I'll tell you a different bit of the story.

He was the boss. But I might have been wrong. I had to accept it: I was out of touch.

—So, he said,—Henry Smart is walking down Talbot Street on a sunny afternoon some years ago when a car bomb goes off close by and throws him right into the hospital. He ends up in all the papers, sitting up in bed. His picture and his name are seen and you get visits from interesting people. He even goes on a trip to the seaside. Bettystown, no less. Am I right so far?

He was bang on, although I hadn't known it was Bettystown. I didn't nod.

—So there's great excitement, said the Clare man.—Great bowing and scraping. The boys of the old brigade are wetting themselves. It's Henry Smart, one of the last survivors of the First Dáil and the Second Dáil. Their route back to Connolly and Pearse. Their link to the Lord God Almighty in heaven.

—Fair play to you, by the way, said the Dub beside me.—We think you're great too.

—That's right, said the Clare man.

He tapped my boot.

—We're no revisionists.

I didn't know what he meant.

—We know how it was, he said.—It was wild in my part of the country.

—My grandad was in the G.P.O., said the Dub.—As well as yourself.

—What was his name?

—You wouldn't have known him.

—Grand.

—Enough now, said the Clare man.—We're only distracting ourselves. I'll go on with the story, will I?

—Grand.

—This happened – the meeting in Bettystown – a while back, a good few years ago now. When myself and Detective Sergeant Campion —

—Howyeh, said the big man beside me.

I didn't look at him.

—We were only young lads, said the Clare man.—We weren't actually there. But there were eyes and ears there, if you follow.

And keen to help. Only, the eyes saw plenty but the ears were a bit too far away.

I tried to remember the faces of the men who'd been there, especially the ones who'd had to stand back while the real talk was going on. There must have been an informer in the van and the car that had carried me to Bettystown and back. It might even have been an informer who'd hit me with the butt of his gun.

—So, said the Clare man,—we don't know exactly what was said or planned. But we do know that there was ham in the sandwiches and that the soup wouldn't have been the best. And we know it was a happy enough meeting and that contact was to be maintained, between yourself and our friends in the north. Sporadic contact. Very sporadic. So we waited.

—Six years, said Campion.

—Six years, the Clare man agreed.

There wouldn't be any heavy stuff. I didn't think they were building to a beating, although these lads would have been knee-deep in the Heavy Gang. They'd have been bouncy recruits six years before, eager to show their bosses that they could kick and stomp with the best of them, defending the state against terror.

I was enjoying the attention.

—So, said the Clare man.—We're nearly up to date.

—And then you start hanging around with gun runners, said Campion.

I felt his lips at my ear.

—Gun runners? I said.—My wife?

—She'll do for a start.

—She's in a coma, for fuck sake.

—She is when you're looking.

Now I looked at him.

—Fuck off, I said.

He slowly withdrew his face. His knees were still against the side of my chair.

—Sorry, he said.—I shouldn't have been disrespectful.

He meant it; I was looking at him.

—It's alright, I said.

—And I'm sorry for your troubles, he said.—The coma and that.

—Thanks.

—Nevertheless, said the Clare man,—it has to be said. Your wife has a history, stretching back to when the guns were needed.

—That was long ago, I said.

—You don't think they're still needed?

—You're trying to catch me out, I said.

I was breaking rules, talking back to the men who were interrogating me.

—No hope of that, said the Dub.

He kept his face the respectful distance. He seemed to have given up.

—There've been mutterings, said the Clare man.—Down through the years. Leopards and spots, you know. That she was still up to it. And then there's her cousin.

—Ivan Reynolds.

—The same.

—He's a politician, I said.—Fianna Fáil. He was a minister and all.

The Clare man stared at me.

—You seem to be lacking some basic information, Henry, he said.—Because I can't believe you're messing with us.

—What information?

He was making me talk; I couldn't help it. I wanted to talk.

—The arms trial? said the Clare man.—Does it ring a bell?

—No, I said.—Not really.

—1970. No bell? Ding-a-ling.

—No.

—You were living here. In this bloody house, sure. There's a radio beyond. But you missed it?

—Must have.

I saw the anger climb onto his face, then saw it pulled back.

—Ivan Reynolds T.D., said the Clare man,—the Minister for Foreign Affairs, was charged with importing weapons illegally and handing them over to the newly formed Provisional I.R.A. You missed that, did you?

—Was he guilty?

—Oh, he was, said the Clare man.—But he was found innocent. But, more to the point, you're telling us that you didn't know about it.

I didn't answer. There wasn't an answer.

—You're letting yourself be set up on a pedestal, said the Clare man.—You're on standby, all set to help them win their five demands. But, hang on, you know nothing about that either, do you? The five demands.

I said nothing. There was nothing in me. I'd thought I'd be getting something out of them, something to pass on to the man with the beard.

—The hunger strikes, said the Clare man.

I shook my head.

—Is he senile?

—I don't think so.

—Just ignorant. God almighty.

He tapped my foot. He wanted my attention. I wanted to apologise. I wanted them to go away and come back in a few days. I'd do my eccer, and we could start again.

—You'd need to brush up on your current affairs, Henry, he said.—Forget the history. Are you listening to me? You might be living in the past. I can't blame you there, I suppose. We're a terrible fuckin' country for the history. But it's not good enough. Sure, man, you walked right into a bomb, only a few years ago. Did you ever find out why?

—Not really.

—Jesus.

He wasn't just angry; I worried him. I was like his old uncle or something, fading away in front of him.

—Well, listen, he said.—This is important. Your pals, the Provisionals, take this stuff very seriously. The chain of events that led them to where they are today. From history to here. There's 1916, and you were there. You remember that?

—Yeah.

—Good. And the First Dáil and the Second Dáil and the men who walked out and brought the legitimacy of the Declaration with them. And handed it over, eventually, to your pals, so they can claim to be the only legitimate government of this country. It's religious. You know that. You're holding the chalice.

I nodded.

—So, they want to use you. Your go-ahead means everything to them. Literally everything. They go on about Marx and science but they love the religion. They love the certainty. Giving the orders. But, better than that, taking the orders. Obeying. That's what they're into. So, you tell them armed struggle is the one true path and they'll be more than happy to kill anyone who tries to stop them.

I spoke now.

—You want me to say that the armed struggle isn't the true path.

—No.

—What?

—We don't care.

—I'm lost.

—Oh, we know.

He sighed.

—Look, he said.—It's simple. We want you to tell us what happens. Keep in touch. Wherever they bring you.

—You want me to spy.

—That's right.

—Turn informer.

—That's it, he said.—But if spying fits you better than informing, that's grand. You can be a spy.

—Why would I do that? I asked.

—Well, he said.—Because we're in the right and the Provisionals are wrong. We're all for elections and letting people make their own minds up.

—We already live in a republic, said the Dub; his voice beside me was a shock.—Most people down here would lean that way. Even if it is a bit of a kip.

—But we know, said the Clare man.—It's a complicated world. And we could spend the rest of the day debating the pros and the cons of liberal democracy. So I'll give you a more compelling reason for keeping your ears open and reporting back to us.

He stood back, a few steps.

—Henry, he said.—Look it. If you don't do what we want you to do, we'll let them know you're a fraud. You were never in the First Dáil. You weren't anywhere near the Mansion House when the Declaration was ratified, and you were even further away when the right lads walked out.

—You knew, I said.

—I've a degree in history, sure.

—So do I, said Campion.—Trinity, no less.

—So, there you go, said the Clare man.—We'll tell them. They'll kill you. And your wife will die alone.

He stepped back.

—Hang on, though, he said.—There's the daughter. She visits the mammy too, doesn't she? When she's here.

I didn't answer.

—She's what? Sixty?

—Yeah.

—She's your daughter too, so.

He looked happy again.

—Yes, I said.

—They'll kill her too, he said.—Nothing surer. If they find out you're an informer as well.

—I'm not.

—You already are, Henry, said the Clare man.—So, what have you got for us?

I caught my breath and the shelves stopped swaying. I made it to the desk in a line that was nearly straight.

—The papers.

The young one behind the desk pushed back in her seat. She thought I was going to vomit on her. I heard the wheels squeak, and stop.

—Sorry? she said.

—The papers.

—Newspapers?

I nodded.

—On the rack over there.

I grabbed the *Independent* and the *Mirror*, and I kept moving till I got to the first empty chair. The library was full of men, waiting till nearer teatime when they could go home. I waited myself, until the sweat dried and the shakes backed away from my hands and arms.

The five demands were easy enough to find; the hunger strike was on the front page. There were men starving themselves to death for the right to wear their own clothes, and the right not to do prison work – fair enough, I thought; the right to associate freely with other prisoners – grand as well; the right to full remission on their sentences. I'd never been sentenced to jail-time in Ireland; I'd been locked up till I escaped. And ninety days' hard labour in America had been hard and had lasted ninety days. The final demand was the right to visits, parcels, and educational and recreational facilities. There were names too, the starving men. They were well on their way; the country was counting down. Bobby Sands. Francis Hughes. Raymond McCreesh. Patsy O'Hara. There were words from Francis Hughes, written on tissue paper and smuggled out under someone's tongue. *I don't mind dying, as long as it is not in vain, or stupid.* The names were vaguely familiar – I'd heard of Sands – and the fact of the strike too. They'd been on the radio, floating around in the kitchen.

I hadn't been paying attention.

I sat beside her bed. The eye was open. I held her hand every day, in case she knew I was there. I held it just for a few minutes, and tried to feel the fingers move, press themselves into the warmth of mine, respond to the cuts and calluses – something a bit more than the pulse I could feel and see, barely, at her wrist and, when I leaned in nearer, in her neck.

We were alone. I'd looked in at Ivan. He still had life enough in him to snore. She didn't snore; she didn't sleep. But, still, the heart was beating. I wondered which of them would give up first, or if this was a fight, each cousin determined not to be the first to go. I looked at Miss O'Shea but saw nothing like determination.

The nurse, the fat beauty, told me that Ivan hadn't woken up since the day before, that he hadn't eaten in three days.

—What does that mean? I asked.

—Only what I'm telling you, she said.

—I mean, is he on the way out?

—God sure, Mister Smart, aren't we all?

Then it was darker in the room. There was a man at the door. His gaze went straight past the nurse. He didn't see her.

I knew I was right to be frightened.

This was two days after the G-men had told me that I was their informer. My new career was about to start.

The nurse didn't know he was connected, but he was virtually the first man who hadn't gawked at her since she was fourteen. She knew he was dangerous but she wasn't sure why. She might not have recognised the ideology, but I did. I'd slept in ditches with men who'd cried in their sleep for an Ireland free. She wanted to go. Her common sense was screaming but her vocation wouldn't let her budge.

He stepped into the room. He seemed to be alone but I knew he wasn't.

—Out, he said.

—Are you talking to me? she said.

His jacket creaked. He took another step.

—It's alright, I told her.—He's here for me. We'll only be a minute.

—Do you know this man? she asked.

—I do, yeah, I lied.—It's grand.

—Are you sure?

I was already out on the corridor, and so was he. He held my elbow, lifted me along. He carried me down the stairs, giving me speed I hadn't had in years. He was hurting me. But it didn't matter. A part of me – a big part – was delighted. We were falling into each other's traps, but I was the one who knew it.

We were in the hall, near the front door. Past oul' ones on Zimmers, through the smell of soup and piss.

The back of another car. No pillowcase over my head this time. My escort pushed me in and slammed the door. Then he got in behind the wheel.

There was another man sitting beside me. I knew him.

—*A chara*, he said.—How are you?

—Grand, I said.—*Go maith*.

—Good.

I'd read enough in two days to know I wasn't going to be shot. Not on this trip. The man beside me was the voice, one of the important faces. There'd be no one killed while he was near.

—Would you be up for a drive? he said.

—Where to?

—Bodenstown, he said.

—Grand, I said.

Bodenstown was a graveyard near Sallins, in Kildare. The big grave in the yard belonged to Wolfe Tone, the leader of the United Irishmen, who'd given the Brits a scare in 1798. The march to Bodenstown had always been a big date on the republican calendar. I'd stayed away in 1918 because I was a wanted man and by 1919 I'd had enough of marching.

—It's not June, I told the man beside me.—Is it?

I wasn't sure.

—No, he said.—It isn't.

—It's not Sunday.

—Aye, he said.—It is.

—Oh, I said.—Grand.

—One day must be like the rest of them beyond in the home, he said.

The small talk wasn't natural. He looked out his window as the car flew down the hill, through Sutton Cross and along the Strand Road, through Baldoyle.

It was up to me.

—Terrible business, I said.

239

—What's that?

—The hunger strikes.

—Aye, he said.—Difficult.

—Difficult?

—Aye.

I began to feel a sneaking admiration for some of the men I'd shot in the head. There was obviously more to informing than just listening. My arm was hopping, sore, where the bollix driving the car had gripped it as he'd hauled me out of the nursing home.

—Is your belt on, Henry? the man beside me asked.

The beard was back. It was dark but well managed, like a Protestant hedge.

—No, I said.

—Best put it on, he said.

We'd gone past the airport. I didn't know where we were. We drove on country roads that suddenly widened, the hedges fell away, showing off new, unfinished housing estates, before the car dived back into the country and the gloom of the high hedges.

—How is she? he asked.

—The same, I said.

—Tough business. And Mister Reynolds?

—Deteriorating, I said, a bit surprised as the word came out.

—Sad.

—Yeah.

—A good man.

—Sometimes.

—Ach, that's all of us.

—Why are we going to Bodenstown?

—Same reason we always go to Bodenstown, Henry, he said.— To renew our vows.

—It's not June, I said.

—Aye, right enough.

—What make of car are we in?

He looked a bit lost, annoyed. Then amused.

—D'you know what? he said.—I don't know, myself.

—Toyota Corolla, said the driver.

—There you go. Toyota. Why d'you ask?

—Just wondering, I said.—I was thinking of investing.

—Tired of the bus, hey?

I looked at him.

—You've been watching me.

—Aye, he said.—You're a popular man.

I was in trouble.

I tried to read my own face, tried to see what he'd be looking at. Made sure no shock or fear got through. Felt no heat beneath the skin. Skin so hard and weather-beaten, a knife couldn't have got through it, let alone embarrassment or terror.

I looked out my window. I gave it twenty seconds.

I'd seen no one following me, nobody standing near the house or sitting behind a paper in a car – like a Toyota – as I passed. Except the unemployed and the junkies. Men and boys I knew to see and nod to; men, I knew, I'd written off. Maybe the spy was one of them, shooting heroin for Ireland. Pretending to be worthless. Fitting right in and doing a good job.

—What colour is it?

—The car?

—Yeah.

—Can you not see for yourself?

—The name for it.

—Silver, said the driver.—It's a bit on the dirty side.

—A wee bit, aye.

—Less conspicuous, I said.

—Aye, said the man beside me.—Unless there's too much of the dirt. Then it becomes noticeable.

—Like a suit, I told him.—In my day. No suit at all and you were stopped by the rozzers. Too flamboyant and you were stopped as well. It's the balance.

—Right enough.

I felt my chest loosen as I spoke. I knew what I was talking about. I was safe in the words.

There were no more housing estates. The driver was taking us by the scenic route, hugging the hedge on narrow roads that hopped and twisted beneath us. There was something else I began to notice. He'd slow down, almost stop, on some of the straighter stretches, and wait before putting the foot down again. I sat up, to see better. There was another car, about two hundred yards ahead. It was approaching a bend. It slowed down, or seemed to. Our driver slowed. Then I saw lights, once, the hazard lights. The car disappeared around the bend and our car started going at a decent clip again.

—The car ahead up there, I said.—Is he scouting for us?

—Spot on, aye, said the man beside me.—Looking out for the peelers.

—I thought so.

—Did you put the belt on, like I told you, Henry?

—No.

—Do that, like a good man. We need you alive for a wee while yet.

He gave me a smile full of teeth. Then he dropped the lip over them.

—I'll tell you why we're on our way, he said.

The car and the sudden heat – it was a quick, hot day; I was fighting my eyelids, dropping into sleep. He rolled down his window. Then he leaned across me and rolled down mine.

—There we go.

He sat up again.

—That's a bit better.

The air was good. I was awake again and on the case. We passed pig shite and a crowd of cows, then hedges too wild to see over. I could hear soft branches scrape my side of the car.

—So, he said.—The hunger strikes.

One of the blanket men, Bobby Sands, had stopped eating on the 1st of March, at midnight – I knew that now – and other men had joined him, one by one. No man had died yet but the country was waiting. *They won't break me because the desire for freedom, and the freedom of the Irish people is in my heart.* An M.P. in the north, Frank Maguire, had died, and there was talk of running Sands in the by-election. I'd read the morning's paper. Two days on the trot. I was bang up to date.

—A bad business, he said.

—Yeah.

—Like in your day, Henry, eh?

—I never went without food, I said.—If I could help it.

I'd go for his head and knock out any doubts he had about me.

—I knew hunger all my life, I said.—And it was never a fuckin' strike. Only the middle class could come up with starvation as a form of protest.

I stared back at him.

It worked. I could hear the big teeth grind. But it wasn't anger. He was reversing, back-pedalling furiously, reassessing the oul' eejit beside him in the silver Toyota. He'd have to be interesting now.

—I disagree with your analysis, he said.—I disagree fundamentally. But —

He didn't hesitate, exactly. But he dropped the voice.

—There's no persuading them, he said.—Bobby and the other boys.

He sighed, but the noise wasn't theatrical.

—We have to make the most of it.

The smile was small now, shy.

—It isn't the route I'd have wanted, he said.—Your class analysis is way off the mark, Henry. But I understand, you came out of different times. But the doing without food – there I agree with you.

I had my information. I'd made my day.

—What's on in Bodenstown? I asked.

—The usual, he said.—And the unusual. We honour our republican dead. And we plant something too. For tomorrow.

—What do we plant?

—You, he said.—We plant you.

I was sitting in front of a window. It was mid-afternoon out there. I could feel the heat but I could see absolutely nothing. It was paint. The window had been painted black, recently. There wasn't a scratch or a hint of the day outside.

I'd been told to sit there, facing the blackened window. There were men behind me. At least two of them. Probably more. There'd been quiet coming and going. The door behind me, to the left, had been opened and closed. Another door further away had just been closed.

Politely, firmly, I'd been brought to the chair. It was ready, alone, facing the black window. I looked for rope in the gloom, or straps. Strong hands told me to sit. I did, but I wasn't tied down. Nobody said, *Don't turn*. Nobody had to.

I waited for it to start.

Then a voice. I didn't know it. Northern. How far north, or west or straight ahead, I couldn't tell. In my day I'd have been able to pin an accent to a town and a street. I wished now that I hadn't been so bigoted. The north had never featured. I never gave a fuck about the north, or the strangers up there. They were foreign then, and they were still foreign.

The voice. A smoker, in his forties, carrying his share of lost life. He was speaking for the benefit of other men. There was more than one other man behind me in the room, and the talker didn't know them very well.

—So, Henry, he said.—Welcome. This is standard procedure, nothing to be concerned about. You understand? You have no need to fear.

—This isn't Bodenstown, I said.

That got no reaction, at all – not a foot moved or a sock pulled. I was in a room with experienced interrogators.

—Give us your name.

—Henry Smart.

—Age?

—Seventy-nine.

—Where do you live?

—Dublin, I said.

—Exactly?

—Ratheen.

—What's your line of work?

—I'm retired.

—What did you do before you retired?

—I was the caretaker, in the national school. The boys.

—You're a fair age, Henry.

—I know.

—Why do you want to join the I.R.A.?

—I don't want to join the I.R.A.

—That's not what —

—I never left.

—What?

—I've been in the I.R.A. since 1917, I said.—I never left or resigned, or anything. And I was in the Citizen Army before that. Before there was an I.R.A.

The men behind me knew their history. They knew about the Citizen Army, and James Connolly. They'd read him and revered him. He was up on their walls, with Che Guevara. They'd be looking now at the back of my head and thinking, *He knew Connolly.*

I was in control.

The shout appalled me. Right into my ear.

—Why!

I'd heard nothing. No one had crept up on me. But he was there. I could feel his breath while the shout still burrowed into

244

my head. He didn't touch me but I couldn't get away; I couldn't lean away from his weight.

I couldn't budge.

—Why?

I couldn't talk. I wasn't there.

—Why were you talking to the peelers?

I couldn't talk – I'd have spilled everything. I was choking.

—Answer now.

My head was coming back to me.

—What did you talk about?

This wasn't interrogation. It was a test. Say nothing – keep the mouth shut. That was the rule, and it wouldn't have changed – since my day.

—Answer!

Say nothing, don't listen. The shout was solid but it wasn't a shock now. The real shock was the fact that I was still sitting, that I wasn't being dragged across the floor. I hadn't been touched. And that was the torture.

I decided to breathe – I had to decide.

They knew that the G-men had been at my door. I could talk my way out of that. Or they knew that I'd never been Henry Smart M.P., and they were working themselves up, to get past my age and history, so they could kill me. But there wasn't enough sense in that. They'd have shot me already, or left me alone. This was a test. They had business in mind and they were checking to see if I was up to it. One of their big men had travelled here with me – wherever we were – in a silver Toyota. They weren't here to execute me. He wouldn't have gone near a condemned man.

—Stand up!

I didn't know if I had the life in me; I expected the hands to pull me up.

—Stand up.

Refusing to speak was resistance. Refusing to stand was a sign of nothing but the probable fact that I couldn't. I gave it a go. I left the chair, tried to make sure my legs didn't knock it back. I could feel the man's breath on the sweat that soaked my neck. It was the hardest thing I'd ever done. But I made it. I stood.

—Turn.

It was the difference. The stance. The difference between my time and theirs. The modern gunman, legs apart, the arms pointed straight ahead, at me, at my mouth. In the half-light, it took a while to see that there was actually a gun his hands. I hadn't a clue what make it was.

I stared back at him, over his hands and the gun. At the man who had shouted into my head. The man who'd been driving the car. He was wearing a black balaclava but I'd seen his eyes in the rear-view mirror, when he told me the car's colour.

He should have looked a bit thick or at least sheepish, because he wasn't going to shoot me. But he didn't. He stared at my mouth. Whether he shot me or not didn't matter. I wasn't there; he didn't give a shite. I didn't know why he bothered with the mask.

The first voice spoke again. I looked at him, and I let them know: the pointed gun wasn't bothering me that much. It was still a test and I thought I was passing.

—Sit down again, Henry.

—Face to the window?

—Yes.

There was one other man. He was wearing a balaclava too. I could just about see him in the corner near the door; the light coming from under it gave his shoes a good shine. I didn't stare at him. He wasn't to be seen. My guess was he'd been sitting beside me in the car. He was two men, two roles. Two paths to Irish freedom.

I sat again.

More questions followed, because they had to be asked. They went through the catechism, even though I'd already passed, or failed.

Had I ever sung rebel songs publicly?

—Yeah.

Had I ever attended marches or republican funerals?

—Yeah.

Did I have a criminal record?

—Yeah.

Had I ever been arrested?

—Yeah.

—What for?

—Being Irish.

They loved that one; I heard them behind me. If I'd been in charge, I'd have slapped the head off the man who gave that answer. The sentimentality nearly made me puke.

—When was this?

—Well, I said.—That particular time would have been in 1916.

—Of course.

The shout was a bigger surprise.

—Why?

I was gone again, dead.

—Why did you talk to the fuckin' peelers?

I found the words from somewhere deep; I could feel the slime on my fingers as I pulled them out.

—What peelers?

The wrong words – I knew it.

—Why? You cunt!

—Steady, said a different voice.

—Don't fucking waste our time!

Hard hands were clapped beside my ear. Or it might have been the gun. There was no cordite. Did spent bullets still come with cordite? I didn't know.

The glass in front was still black and intact. The day was still outside.

—Talk.

—I didn't talk to anyone.

—They were at your house.

—I didn't talk to them. I told them nothing.

I had my grip. I could choose the words; I was climbing, grabbing each one.

—I didn't have anything to tell them, I said.—Nothing recent. They already knew about 1916.

I was sitting on the chair. I could feel it again, under me. I could feel it against my back. I shouldn't have been talking. But this wasn't the police. This was my side.

—They said they'd be back, I said.—I'll tell them nothing then either.

I could hear a baby crying downstairs. Definitely in the same house, under me. It was a farmhouse. I hadn't been blindfolded before we'd arrived. They'd let me see the lane, the new gravel – I'd have heard it hopping under the car if I'd been blindfolded – the wide yard, the whitewash on the walls. The walls reminded me of a photograph I'd carried for years. But I didn't let it. I concentrated. There were two greyhounds tied to an iron ring in one of the walls. They had plenty of rope, but they looked bored and too skinny. There were slates missing off the farmhouse roof, and another dog, a mutt lying on the step at the back door. No one came out to greet us or see who we were. There was nothing going on in any of the outhouses. I'd got out of the car on my own steam. The man beside me had stayed put. The driver didn't lay a hand on me, but he'd been right against me, straight in and up the stairs, into the room where I sat now, facing the black glass.

I could hear nothing behind me. Absolutely nothing. And I wanted to. Badly. I wanted to hear – I needed to hear a chair or a foot scrape, even another blast into my ear. Anything except the fact that they'd gone and I'd been talking to myself. Or they hadn't been there in the first place.

I waited.

I didn't look.

I heard nothing on the stairs. And nothing from downstairs. The baby was gone, or asleep. The radio was off. There was nothing being cooked, no livestock out there protesting, cows crying to be milked.

Nothing.

I hummed. No one told me to stop. I gave them *Kevin Barry*. I even sang the odd word. *In Mountjoy Gaol one Monday morning*. No one joined in, took the bait. *High upon the gallows tree*. I hated that song. I hated all songs.

I sat there until I could do nothing else. Until I heard steps on the stairs and the door behind me opened, and the voice told me that I could come and join them downstairs. I couldn't turn and look.

The hand on my shoulder released me.

—Are you awake at all?

The hand, and the excuse. I could confirm his gentle suspicion.

—I must have dozed off, I said.

I sounded the part, cracked and slow. But the hand on my shoulder had broken the spell. I felt the loosening and the pain. I knew the aches, and I loved them. I could stand up. I could groan as I did it.

—Good man. Hungry?

—Starving, I lied.

The same man who'd brought me here, who'd sat beside me. I groaned again as I followed him to the door. I looked at his feet, at the shoes. They shone in the sudden daylight. He went slowly down the stairs, in front of me. His hair was thick, hard.

He was fit, and considerate. Keeping pace with the old man. I wanted to grab his hair and pull it out of his head, pull him back and stamp on his face.

I wanted to hold his hand and go everywhere that he went.

He was off the steps now, in the little hall between the back door and the kitchen.

—Come in and meet the boys, he said.

—Grand.

I followed him in and sat down at the table and pretended I'd been out – checking on the cows, feeding the greyhounds – and had just come back in. There were no nods, or nothing – I was one of them.

—That's a fair good piece of ham.

—Aye.

—Strong tea.

—Aye.

—This soup didn't come out of a tin.

—No. Right enough.

There was no sign of a baby or anyone who'd obviously made the soup. I hadn't touched my own bowl yet. I didn't want the men to see the soup dance off the spoon. I picked up a sandwich and took a bite. The bread was soft – just as well – and the ham broke up without a struggle.

Eyes were waiting.

I nodded.

—Grand.

I took another bite. I even managed to get the spoon to my mouth. I was an old man; a bit of a shake was alright. As long as they wouldn't have to trust me with a gun.

—You can't beat vegetable, I said.

—Right enough, said the man who'd asked most of the questions upstairs.

The fuckin' quizmaster. He was older than his voice, and somehow smaller. He ate between drags from his smoke; there was a packet of Major at his elbow.

—When it's fresh, I said.

—Aye.

I'd had enough soup. I'd had enough of everything. I was tired and still terrified.

The man with the beard had been talking. He was looking at me now. They all were.

—We're heading into a summer of it, he said.

—Aye.

They'd kill my daughter if they found out. If the men here knew I wasn't Henry Smart M.P., she'd go into the ditch after me.

—Once or twice a week, said the man with the beard, to me.— We don't want to tire you out.

I didn't even know her surname.

They were going to show me off. The ancient activist, the man from the song. I'd make sense of the young men starving themselves, racing to become as old and as noble as me. I'd be their living saint.

And I'd tell it all to the G-men. To keep my sour daughter alive.

—And you'll say the few words?

—No problem, I said.

I'd been a veteran before, even when I was still a kid. In the first years after 1916, before the war became the War, I was the man who'd been in the G.P.O. As the story grew and the Easter days became glorious, I walked into crowded rooms with Jack Dalton. Gaelic League dances, fundraisers for the men still jailed in England. The hush and buzz. And the eyes.

I wondered what was going to happen this time, when I walked into a packed room or climbed onto the back of a lorry. Who would they see this time? What would they see? Would the young man be there behind the rheumy eyes, or in the oul' lad's shoulders? (The eyes were rheumy but I could still see plenty with them.)

—A fedora, I said.

—What?

—I'll wear a fedora. And I'll carry a wooden leg.

They'd see the oul' lad being helped up onto the platform. They'd see the leg – they'd know the secret story – and they'd see the young man stepping fast through the century, right in front of them. Like Oisin falling from his horse into Irish muck and ageing hundreds of years in a couple of seconds. They'd see me bettering Oisin, doing the trick in reverse, young Henry shimmering behind the oul' lad, walking back into quick republican life.

They looked pleased, settled.

—The wooden leg, aye, said the man with the beard.—But why the fedora?

—I look good in a fedora, I told him.

I was still the sandwich-board man.

The voters of Fermanagh/South Tyrone elected a dying man. Bobby Sands became Bobby Sands M.P. *I am a political prisoner because I am a casualty of a perennial war that is being fought between the oppressed Irish people and an alien, oppressive, unwanted regime that refuses to withdraw from our land.* Bobby's election would bring about a settlement. Thatcher would never let a British Member of Parliament die on hunger strike.

Thousands of people marched slowly behind his coffin to the republican plot in Milltown cemetery. Thousands more stood at the roadside as we passed. In Belfast this time, not Dublin. 1981 this time, not 1917. Bobby Sands, not Thomas Ashe. There was the tricolour on the coffin, the black beret and leather gloves. The cameras were everywhere, and I stood in front of them. And the surveillance helicopters – I was in among thousands of people but I could hear them clearly, the blades battering away at the silence.

The coffin was taken from the hearse somewhere near the graveyard – I didn't know Belfast – and out of the crowd three I.R.A. volunteers emerged, just as I'd done at Ashe's funeral, and fired three volleys. They removed the berets and bowed their heads for a silent minute. Then we moved again. A hand took my elbow; I went where I was brought.

It was a slow march that nearly killed me, the final half-mile. A strong hand held me up, into the graveyard. I was kept at the front, in among hard men in new suits. A man I was told was Gerry Adams – the name was whispered into my ear like a secret – folded the tricolour and handed it to a woman who must have been the mother. There was a little lad there too, the son. Then another man stepped forward. Owen Carron, I heard the whispers – Bobby's election agent. He was a young man trying not to look young. He spoke and I thought I'd stood there before; I'd already been at this funeral.

—Irishmen and women, he said.—It is hard to describe the sadness and sorrow in our hearts today as we stand at the grave of Volunteer Bobby Sands, cruelly murdered by the British government in the H-Blocks of Long Kesh. Bobby has gone to join the ranks of Ireland's patriotic dead.

Later, I recited the lament I'd written with Jack Dalton in the Gravediggers pub in Glasnevin after we'd buried Ashe. *Let me carry your cross for Ireland, Lord. For Ireland is weak with tears.* Men and women listened, as if the words were brand new. I saw tears, and held back my own. I looked out through the smoke, at my audience, at the crying, big-eyed women, and I wondered if any of them would want to know me like they used to in the old days.

—We took the crusts off for you, said a woman, another voice into my ear that day, as she put the plate of sandwiches in front of me.

The bus was waiting for me at the gate of the nursing home, two hundred yards from the bus stop. It had no conductor, and the driver was wearing sunglasses and – I was guessing – a bulletproof jacket. The lower deck was empty, until I sat down. Then the G-men came loudly down the stairs, and smiled. The Clare man took the seat in front of me, and Campion pushed in beside me.

—Shove over there, he said.

—Henry Smart, said the Clare man.—The star of stage and screen. How are you?

—Grand.

—And how's the missis?

I stared at him.

—The same.

Exactly the same. She hadn't moved or blinked in months. She was alive because I was told she was alive. I couldn't feel a pulse now, and I hadn't been able to see her chest take in a breath. But I knew she was alive. It was on – *in* – her face, the old look, up on the bike, on her way to kill for Ireland. Her colour was a shade deeper, a happy anger. And the eye, still open. She was looking at me – I knew it. She knew what I was up to.

They kept her nails and hair cut – the gorgeous nurse had told me. She'd given me a lock of hair, in a small plastic pill bottle. I stared into the bottle. I pulled out the grey hair – horse hair.

—Is this yours? I'd asked her.

—Go way out of that, she'd said.—It's Missis Smart's.

—Miss O'Shea's.

—Missis O'Kelly's.

She loved the names, the stories they were telling her. She'd even made romance out of the way I'd been pulled from the home by the I.R.A. driver months before; she'd forgotten the violence, the threat.

—It must have been urgent, she'd said, weeks later.—Was it?

She'd seen me on the television – fedora, black armband, leg held high, for as long as I could hold it. (They'd let me hold an Armalite, at the back of one of the republican clubs. The weight of the thing; I couldn't get it near my shoulder. A hand took it gently from my hands. No one said anything.) We sat side by side and watched my wife.

—The same, I said now, to the Clare man.

—Ah well, he said.—We've been watching you on the telly, Henry.

—Yeah.

—What have you got for us?

—The bossmen don't like it.

It wasn't the first time they'd met me since they'd come to my house – I'd sat on a bench beside the pond, in the park near my house; I slept, and woke, they were sitting beside me. But it was the first time I'd be giving them something big. I'd been holding onto it for months.

—Don't like what?

—The hunger strike.

—Why not?

—They're afraid of it, I said.

—Are you reporting here, or theorising?

—It's what they told me.

—We're talking Army Council here, are we?

—That's right.

—What are they afraid of?

—That it'll get out of control.

—How so?

—The impetus didn't come from them, I told him.—Adams and the Army Council.

I was pleased with myself. But I wasn't sure why.

—There was a groundswell, I said.

—That's the cliché, alright, said the Clare man.—You're telling us nothing new.

—They've had to jump in and take over, I said.—But they didn't want Sands running in that by-election. Or the other men.

—What other men?

And I told them.

There was a general election on the way in the Republic and there'd be hunger strike candidates, men dying on polling day. It would be well known soon; I was giving nothing real away.

—Who told you this?

I gave them the name.

—You spoke to him?

—Yeah.

—He told you this?

—You've been watching the telly, I said.—You've seen me with him.

—He talks to no one. He's famous for it.

—He talks to me.

—He talks to you, said Campion.

—Yeah.

—And tell us this, said the Clare man.—Why would he do that?

—I was in the G.P.O., I told him.—I freed this fuckin' country.

I'd reminded them: they were on the bus with history.

—And he thinks I'm harmless, I said.

We were on the coast road now. It was raining on the other side of Bull Island. It was early May.

The Clare man stood up.

—I'll get him to slow down, he told Campion.

—Right.

I watched him hold the bars as he went to the front and the driver.

—What are they afraid of? asked Campion.

—Who?

—The lads, he said.—The Army Council.

—There's fighting going on, I said.—Inside the organisation. It's the old fight and they're being stupid about it.

I spoke quietly to Campion as if this was for him only, although I knew the Clare man had left us alone, all pre-arranged, in the hope that I'd spill some better beans.

—Some of them are afraid that if they go too deep into electoral politics there'll be a change of direction, if they keep winning like they did in Fermanagh. And that the armed struggle will be parked.

It was the first time I'd heard the words out of my own mouth – *armed struggle*.

—Parked, he said – it was a question trying not to sound too like one.

—That's right, I said.—Parked. So he said.

—He.

—*He*.

—Adams or the other fella?

—I'm not sure, I said.

—You're —

—I'm not sure whether he's talking for himself or others higher up.

—Oh, he said.—Good man.

There were men who wanted nothing to do with elections, even if the candidates were their comrades, friends, relations on the blanket. And there were others, as far as I could make out, who wanted these elections to be the start of something new. I sometimes knew that I was in the centre of a fight; I was refereeing a boxing match I couldn't see or properly hear, a bare-knuckle fight with no bell or rules.

The man with the beard had asked me the question, in the bar of the Imperial Hotel in Dundalk. He'd waited till we were alone. He'd given the nod to two skinheads in zip-up jackets, and waited till they were outside in the foyer.

—How did you manage it? he said.

I tried to tell him. And, basically, I told the G-men on the bus the same thing. I shifted the geography from Dublin to the north, but I told them what I'd seen and known – or thought I'd known – in 1920. I changed the tense from past to present and informed on men who were long dead.

—He's no time for elections, I told Campion, of the man with the beard, in 1981, and of Ernie O'Malley in 1920.—Or parliaments, or giving the people artificial choices.

—We know that, said the Clare man, who'd come back.

He spoke as he sat.

I stared at him again.

—Sorry, he said.—Go on.

The bus stayed on the coast road, instead of going right, for Ratheen and town.

—The hunger strikes scare him, I said.—Because they're working. They're queuing up to join. But they're joining Sinn Féin and the H-Block Committees, not the I.R.A.

—Same thing.

255

—No.

—Go on.

—It's a fight, I said.

The bus turned left, onto the Causeway Road, to the island. It had to slow down as it went across the dips, where the new road was already sinking back into the lagoon. The weather was over us now, dark and suddenly wet.

—Will you look at that, said the Clare man.—What a fuckin' country.

He looked at me.

—Why you?

—I'm their link, I said.

—There are other links, he said.—There's Denis Archer. He *was* in the First Dáil. And he's endorsed all the splits for the last fifty years. They've always used him before. What's the story there?

—Don't know.

—Have you met him yet?

—No, I said.—Not in years.

The last time I'd seen Denis Archer M.P. – Dynamite Dinny – he'd been standing outside Jack Dalton's office, on the other side of Mary Street, just after Jack had slipped my death sentence across his desk to me. Archer was outside, waiting to execute me. I'd nodded to him; he'd nodded back. And I'd run.

—You know him? said the Clare man.

—I do, yeah.

—He's their reliable man, he said.—He's sanctioned everything, given his blessing to everything, as long as it's violent and pointless. Why do they need you?

—Are you sure he's alive? I said.—He'd be older than me.

—He's alive alright, said the Clare man.

—You're sure?

—We saw him this morning, said Campion.

—We did, said the Clare man.—Coming out of mass. He's a great man for the mass.

—He's eighty-seven, said Campion.—And still has all his teeth.

—Did you fuckin' count them?

—We know his dentist, said the Clare man.—So why you, Henry? Why did they come looking for you?

—Maybe Archer won't sanction the hunger strike.

—He loves hunger strikes. He's gone on hunger strike himself a couple of times. Brought himself right to the brink. Twice, I think. Mister Archer has been their walking monument through every split and campaign. Since the days of black and white. So. Henry. Why you?

I was tired. I was cold.

—I don't know.

I was holding the steel bar that ran across the back of his seat. He put his hands down on mine.

—Find out.

Francis Hughes died on the 12th of May, after fifty-nine days. *The light he kindled will never burn out.* Raymond McCreesh and Patsy O'Hara died on the 21st of May, after sixty-one. I sat alone beside my wife's bed and wondered – I suddenly wondered – if that was what she was doing. She was on strike and she wouldn't wake till the others had died and Ireland was free. The eye was open to let me know: she was waiting.

It made sense. But I knew it wasn't true. I'd found her on her kitchen floor. She'd been put there by a stroke, not a decision. But it still made sense. I held her hand for the first time in weeks. I thought I felt slight heat; I thought something moved – a muscle – in behind a finger. I didn't like the hunger strike as a tactic but it was honest – it was absolutely clear. The striker chose silence, emptiness, the step forward into nothing. Nothing was better than what was on offer. It was full freedom, or death.

I'd often wanted to die. I'd crawled to my own grave in Monument Valley, but only because I hadn't wanted to live. But these were young men. They weren't tired of life, or beaten by it. They were giving it up, refusing to continue. Refusing to exist. And their silence impressed me more than anything I'd met since Citizen Army men ran out the side door of the G.P.O. and took the bullets for the men who were right behind them. Now, again, I felt it; men I admired were dying for me.

Men and a woman.

I was thinking through my hole. She was an oul' one in her nineties, doing what all old women did if they made it that far – dying.

I felt her slap across the back of my head. *You're the go-boy, Henry Smart.* I squeezed her hand.

She was dying – she was already dead. Her hand didn't sweat.

I heard no feet, but I turned.

My daughter was at the open door. She didn't fill it – she was another woman on hunger strike. She was gaunt, striking – skinny. Bone angry. Looking in at me and her mother.

My daughter. I couldn't see Saoirse. It wasn't fair – I knew that. Saoirse was a child I'd loved fifty years before. This grey-haired woman wasn't her. There was nothing there, not a trace of the child or the girl.

—D'you remember going to see *The Gaucho*? I asked the woman who'd stepped into the room.

—Yes, she said.

She dragged a chair across the floor and put it beside mine. She sat beside me. We looked at her mother.

I'd never hated the English. I'd never killed a man because he was English, or British. It would never have made sense.

Then Thatcher came among us. Thatcher. Spelt c.r.o.m.w.e.l.l. Spelt that way in 1981 by people who didn't like Sinn Féin or the I.R.A., by people who were disgusted by the hunger strikes and dirty protests, who changed direction whenever they heard a northern accent. Thatcher was our greatest success of the campaign, our most potent weapon. The Iron fuckin' Lady. We invented her.

She'd been Prime Minister across the water since 1979, but I'd missed her arrival. If Miss O'Shea had ever mentioned her, I couldn't remember it. If she'd ever appeared on the screen while we watched the news on a Saturday night I didn't know. Then I was back in the fold and up on the backs of lorries and the name was hissed, all over the country. *Thatcher*. It was a name to stop a man in the middle of his ride, the name that made faces crumble into fast and ugly rage. It was weeks before I knew she had a first name.

We finally met in 1981, in June.

—Crime is crime is crime, said Margaret Hilda Thatcher.

—A cunt is a cunt is a cunt, I said.

—It is not political, said Margaret Thatcher.

—Oh yes, it is, said Henry Smart.

I shouted it from the back of a lorry. It got a cheer and – a rare thing in those months – it got a laugh. I waved to the faithful and lifted the new wooden leg as high into the wet air as I could manage. It was chipboard, darkly varnished. It would have broken under the weight of a small child, but it was made for an old man with a small child's muscles. (The humiliation of it, when the I.R.A. engineer explained it to me, like your man in the James Bond films, before he handed it over. I was tempted to skull him with it but I knew it would have broken on his head. This, by the way, was the same man who had invented the fertiliser bomb.) I finished. I'd earned my soup – two protest rallies, two dashes across the country. I'd done well. But I felt a strong, mean hand on my arm and I was quickly dragged aside; I was pulled off the back of the lorry.

There was a ban in the Republic on broadcasting anything said by members of Sinn Féin – the ban was called Section 31. But I was their face and voice – one of the few voices – because I wasn't a member of Sinn Féin and, with the big old head on me, with the rheumy eyes and see-through ears, I was no one's idea of an active Volunteer. I'd become a bit of a star. I was recognised on the bus and when I went to collect my pension.

—Are you the man on the telly?

—That's the oul' fella with the hat and the leg.

Even the junkies stopped to chat.

But now, the man with the beard gripped my arm. The lorry hid us from the crowd. There was shite on its wheels. I knew, because I was pushed up against one.

—They won't be broadcasting that wee speech, he said.

The anger was in his fingers, not his voice. I knew I'd been stupid.

—You won't get away with calling the Prime Minister of Great Britain and Northern Ireland a cunt. Three times.

He let go of my arm. But he was capable of killing me. He pointed a finger, like he was joking, scolding a child he loved but wouldn't hesitate to murder.

—And don't dare, he said.—Don't dare say she is one.

I saw him put the pillowcase over my head. That second – he'd do it.

I'd been getting cocky, stupid. But Thatcher gave me energy. I was a few months off eighty, and Thatcher had woken seven hundred years of racial hatred. She kept me wide awake at night. I shovelled spuds into me, thinking of Margaret Thatcher.

—The more men die, said the man with the beard,—the less shocking it will be. The country will stop being outraged and the softies down here will look at the kids fighting on the streets of

Belfast and go back to thinking that they're just wee savages. The strike will fail. These weeks are crucial and you've just blown one of them, Henry.

—I thought that's what you wanted, I said.—You said it yourself. Political ambition and armed struggle are mutually exclusive.

I was pleased as I spoke – as I heard myself. I remembered clearly what he'd told me months before. I remembered thinking that he was saying nothing new, that Ernie O'Malley had argued the same thing, whenever I'd been too slow to see him coming. And another thing: I knew that by arguing now I'd get something out of him, something with juice to bring back to the lads from G Division.

—If the strike fails, I told him,—you'll be able to put the struggle back on track.

I didn't believe a word I said.

—It's too late!

It was a whisper but he shouted. I was back up against the lorry wheel.

He took a breath.

—It cannot end in defeat, he said.—We're too far in.

He took another. I wondered if he had asthma or something else that grabbed his breath.

—The armed struggle can go on for years, he said.—It already has. We cannot be beaten. But this is different. The weapons in this one are the men themselves, not bullets. We're not going to get replacements from Libya or the States. They're men. If they keep dying, people will get bored.

—No.

—Yes. And they'll turn on us. Why are we letting it happen? Why are we letting them die? Now, it's Thatcher – she's to blame. But give it a couple of months, give it the summer, and see what happens. You don't actually know any of these men, right?

I didn't answer. He didn't want me to.

—I do, he said.—I knew them before they went in, and I was in there myself, with some of them. Four men have died. That's four good friends of mine. And there are more friends of mine in the queue. I don't want this but I'm stuck with it, and it is horrible. The thought that we are killing our own. It's horrible. So, don't you dare joke when you're up on that platform representing republicanism, d'you hear me?

260

He looked at me again; he held me up with his eyes. He patted my shoulder.

—You mind that wee tongue of yours, he said.

The general election was on the way. The man with the beard didn't want to run any candidates. He didn't want the infection that would come with success. And he wasn't alone. There were four men sitting at the table.

—A trap, said the man who usually drove, and all heads nodded.

—But it's a trap we'll have to walk right into, said the man with the beard.—The pressure's on. Bobby won.

—And he died.

—Aye, said the man with the beard.—But he won and Thatcher let him die. She killed him, that's the way of it. He was dying anyway, with or without the by-election. So it worked. That's the thinking.

—And now there's another chance.

—Aye.

—Does it have to be blanket men who run?

—What about Henry here?

No one laughed. They looked at me. And no one said No. But No it emphatically was; the three seconds' silence nearly took the roof off the place – we were in another farmhouse. I was off the ticket before I could turn down the honour. And that was grand. There was no hurt there, nothing in me screaming.

The man with the beard washed the cups and dishes. He wouldn't let the others help.

I gave the G-men the candidates' names two days before Sinn Féin gave them to the press.

We were sitting on the bench, at the pond. I was the man in the middle.

—You're sure about these?

—Yep. Unless they die in the meantime.

—Is that a stab at humour, Henry?

—Men who don't eat die, I said.—That's the tactic.

He looked at me. The men in my life had started to look at me.

—You're enjoying yourself, Henry, said the Clare man.

I thought about this.

—Yeah, I said.—I am.

* * *

261

—You were dead for fifty years, she said.

—I looked for you.

I nodded at the woman on the bed.

—I told her that too. I looked for years.

—We waited, she said.—It was our lives. Even after she married that O'Kelly man.

She sat up.

—Séamus would still be alive if we hadn't waited for you, she said.

I looked at her and, Jesus, it was much easier to love my son, the boy who'd always be a boy. She was right. But I had to deny it.

—How do you make that out? I asked.

—We'd have come home sooner, she said.—He would have had a bed, and food. Instead of dirt. And the wind.

She was right. I didn't try to change that. I didn't want to. She was my daughter.

She looked at her mother.

—How long has she known about you?

—Years, I said, and regretted it.

I'd have to become a father again. I was being crueller than I'd ever been, even with a gun. But I didn't know what to say.

—I'm sorry, I said.

She sighed. Her hands were up around her head, grabbing and prodding.

—About ten, I said, shaving two decades off the figure.—We met accidentally.

She looked at me.

—I moved to Ratheen, I told her.

How did I hug a long-lost daughter, lost so long she'd caught up with me? A thin, angry woman whose life I'd destroyed by coming back to life. It was ridiculous. I didn't love her, and I couldn't see the girl I'd loved. The room was full of the dead.

We looked at each other. We tried to see something we knew. Neither of us smiled.

—I saw you on T.V., she said.—There was a report, on N.B.C., I think. On that hunger strike.

—In America?

—Yes, she said.—It's a big deal. Especially with the Irish.

I wondered who else in the States had seen me. Louis would have been a telly watcher. He'd loved gadgets and new things. He'd have had colour and the works, a remote control. Sitting there, flicking through the channels. (I didn't know that he'd been dead for ten years.) Or Ford. I saw him in front of a colossal telly, talking to it, giving out and loving it, searching for old John Ford films. (But he was long dead too.) And the women I'd known – did they sit up, those who still could, when they heard the name and saw the fedora?

—You were holding a wooden leg, she said.

—That's right.

She was looking at my feet.

—Not that one, I told her.—Another one.

She knew the story; her mother would have told her.

—Do you have to do it? she said.

—Yes, I said.—I do.

There were nine candidates, nine big constituencies. The candidates were prisoners, four of them on hunger strike. I was their ancestor, their breathing link to the pure days. I was the rightness of their actions. And they ran me ragged. They dragged me through the wild border counties where, north of the line, the British ruled the air but none of the land, where, south of the line, the locals rode their livestock and smuggled out of principle. I had to stop shaking hands because my own hands and arms were loose in their sockets. I couldn't hold a soup spoon. I couldn't put on my own coat. There was rioting every night in Belfast and Derry, and tension you could lean on in the south. Ireland was dead, a failure, a third world country in Western Europe – I heard this every night. And we knew why, and who to blame. People voted for starving men because they hated Thatcher. She'd done this to us, in Cavan/Monaghan, in Sligo/Leitrim, in Dublin North-Central, in Kerry North.

Two of the men were elected, Kieran Doherty and Paddy Agnew.

They carried me on their shoulders, because there were no elected candidates to carry. The heroes were dead or in Long Kesh, so they carried me and Dinny Archer.

I finally met him.

Under a streetlamp. Two old men on the shoulders of the young. Right under the lamp. Someone just arriving would have thought they were going to hang us. We faced each other, under the yellow light. I knew him first.

—Dinny, I said.

He was older than me, and blind.

—Who are you? he said.

—Yeh cunt, I said.—You know who I am.

He was sharp, and fleshless. He must have been well past ninety. There was no blood working under the skin; the mouth was a rip across a yellow skull. He was a better-looking hermit than I was. And he was terrified.

He knew me, alright. And suddenly I knew – now, under the yellow light, it clicked: he was as big a chancer as I was. I knew why he hadn't exposed me as the fake M.P. and insisted on his own status as the only surviving real one. Because if he got me, then I'd get him. The republican legends would bring each other down.

We stared across at each other, two trigger men who wouldn't be drawing their guns.

When I'd come down the stairs from Jack Dalton's office, onto Mary Street, Dinny Archer had been there on the other side of the street, waiting to execute me.

And that was it.

Now, in June 1981, on a damp night in El Paso, County Louth, I laughed into his face. And he, the blind old fucker, knew exactly why.

He'd been on the wrong side.

Jack Dalton had been clearing the way for the new respectability. That was why I'd been destined for the ditch with a bullet in the back of my head. He knew there was a treaty coming, and he knew there'd be the compromises that men like me would never accept. If he'd listened, if he'd wanted to know, I'd have told him that I didn't give a shite. My war was over, and I only had one man left that I needed to kill: Alfie Gandon. (But Gandon was going to be part of the new respectability too. Gandon was actually their first respectable man.) But Jack hadn't wanted to know. There'd be the Treaty, and the split. I'd be on the wrong side, so he'd get rid of me a few months early, before it got really busy. Jack would be on the pro-Treaty side; I'd be against it. So my name came at me on a piece of paper and his executioner, Dinny Archer M.P., was downstairs, waiting for me.

Myself and Dinny had been together before. His credentials were impeccable. We'd been together when I shot Detective Sergeant Smith, of G Division. We'd gone into the same hotel room in the Gresham, on the morning of Bloody Sunday, and we'd shot the man we'd gone there to shoot while, in other hotels and bedrooms, other men did the same. The young lads holding us up knew all about that day and our part in it together.

I laughed again.

—Good man, Dinny.

Somehow, after I'd lost touch, after I'd sailed away to a new name, Dinny had changed sides. No one alive knew that he'd once been a hit man for Jack Dalton and the other men who betrayed the Republic. No one except me.

—Been down Mary Street recently, Dinny? I asked him; I shouted across the noise and polished heads.

He didn't answer.

Commandant Denis Archer. Some time after Mary Street, he'd changed his mind. Dinny had converted to diehardism and, as the other diehards died off, he'd become the last of the breed and the one surviving member of the only legitimate Dáil and, in the eyes of the faithful, the true Republic's only elected representative. He even claimed to be the man who'd put the last bullet into Jack Dalton. (Although he wasn't the only man who claimed that one.) In 1938, Dinny and the few other diehard T.D.s had handed over their authority to the I.R.A. Army Council. The I.R.A. became the legal and lawful government. All other parliaments were *illegal assemblies, the willing tools of an occupying force.* In 1969, when the others were all dead, Dinny endorsed the Provisionals' break from the Official I.R.A. The Provos became the true government – because Dinny said so.

—The cat got your tongue, Dinny?

For the last six months they'd been using myself and Dinny, the holy relics, parading us up and down the country, at candle-lit vigils and election rallies. And, now, finally, we were face to face. Maybe by accident. But maybe deliberately – we were always watched; no one in the republican movement was trusted.

They separated us now, the fat and skinny lads who were holding us up, and they brought us back, and did it again, and brought us back. *Ooh-Ah – Up the 'R.A.!* Then we were side by side, like the chariots in *Ben Hur.* Two old men on the shoulders of the Republic's sweating future, doing a lap of the square. We were neck and neck most of the way, our legs bashed and rasped. *Ooh-Ah – Up the 'R.A.!* Wood collided with bone. Did sparks fly when the dead met? I saw them that night.

And I won. I was waiting for him when the lads got tired and dropped us to the ground. I watched the face, the uncertainty that his blindness couldn't hide, as he was held in midair, and lowered.

We were being watched. Eyes, and eyes. And other eyes. And ears.

I put out my hand.

—Good to see you, Dinny, I said.

He was genuinely blind. He wasn't Ford, who hadn't needed his eyes to see. Archer couldn't see a thing. He couldn't see my hand. A younger hand, much younger – a grandson's? – took Dinny's and brought it to mine. The younger hand let go, and Archer now felt mine. He felt me grab it slowly.

I leaned closer to the face, and the big ear – the streetlight shone right through it.

—Will I tell them now, Dinny? I said.—Will I tell them all about Mary Street?

I got away from the ear, to watch the face. Nothing changed there, but the grip did. He was suddenly the man doing the holding. My grip became his, and he was leaning across to me as the pain climbed up my arm and ate into my shoulder. I felt his breath. I smelt it – he'd had an egg for his tea, and some chips.

—You won't, he said.

His other hand found my head and pulled it even closer to his mouth.

—You were never anything but a renegade, he said.—We'll say nothing.

I might have broken his fingers but they were still all set to break mine.

—We'll call a halt when I count to three, he said.

His face hadn't budged. Mine hadn't either – old nerves were slow in registering the pain.

—One, two. Three.

We both let go, and the night was full of clapping hands and whoops. The young hand that had guided Dinny's hand to mine now took his arm and stirred him away. It belonged to a girl, not a boy, and she looked back at me and smiled. I wanted to be Dinny.

The man with the beard was beside me.

—That was extraordinary, he said.

I nodded.

—Great to see Denis again, hey.

—Ah, yeah, I said.

I'd survived. I was still the last of the rebels. But so was Dinny.

—Denis Archer once changed his mind?

—Yeah.

—For the one and only time in his life, said the Clare man.—Jesus.

He looked at Campion.

—You know what we have here, don't you? he said.

—A brand new historical fact, said Campion.

—If it's true.

—It's true, I told them.—He was on the pro-Treaty side. He'd have shot me if I hadn't been quicker than him.

—Pro-Treaty, said the Clare man.—But before there was a Treaty. But, fair enough now, let's not quibble.

—We could bring them down with this, said Campion.

—The whole shooting gallery, the Clare man agreed.—We could go home to our beds.

They looked delighted, giddy, kids with a frog in a jar.

We were on the bus again, the only passengers. The Clare man looked at me.

—We could end it now with what you've told us, Henry. You're a fraud. And now Archer's a fraud as well. The republican religion is built on two whoppers.

Campion patted my back.

—But Dinny *was* an M.P., I reminded them.

—But he changed his mind, said the Clare man.—He's tainted. Think of all those gobshites who adore him. Literally fuckin' adore him. O'Brádaigh. O'Connaill, with his fuckin' trenchcoat. The priesty fellas. They'd be devastated if they ever found out. Archer changed his mind. Imagine. Changing your mind. It's the mortal sin. It's worse than compromising, sure.

He laughed.

—A few words with our colleagues in the Garda press office. Or, better yet, a chat with an eminent historian who'd write something erudite for the *Irish Times*. 'Archer Changed His Mind.' Or, 'Archer Shot Opponents of the Treaty.' We'd have Adams and wee Danny running for the dictionary, looking for a new definition of 'legitimacy'. And where would that leave you, Henry?

I shrugged.

—The last man standing, he said.

Campion patted my back again.

—But a quiet word from one of our inside men, 'Smart wasn't in the First Dáil, check it out.' And that leaves them with no one. No rock left on which to build their church. They'd whack you, Henry.

—No, they wouldn't.

—Why would you think that? Of all people?

—Bad press, I said.

I was wide awake, enjoying myself. I'd just spent two hours with my daughter.

—Killing an old man, I said.—They wouldn't do it.

—You're naïve, Henry. After all these years.

I shrugged – I tried to.

—No, I said.

—Sure, they wouldn't give it a second thought, man. They shoot housewives, they kneecap children. They don't care about bad press. They'd shoot the journalist.

—I couldn't give a shite, I said.

—If they whacked you?

—No, I said.

And then, there, I meant it. They could shoot me, or do me in with a mallet. I'd lived a life. I was full and happy enough.

—They'd hurt you, said the Clare man.

He meant *he'd* hurt me. The old man in the jar.

I shrugged.

—They'd be able to get at you, Henry, said my pal Campion.

I shrugged again. And I knew I'd overdone it.

The Clare man looked at me like he was delivering a promise.

—A pillow over your wife's face while they made you watch, he said.—That would hurt, I'd say.

—Take it easy, said Campion.

—Or your daughter, said the Clare man.

His face was right in front of mine, so close I couldn't see him.

—They'd blow her brains out right in front of your eyes, he said.

He took a smoke from his pack. I had to wait till he lit it.

—Just as *we* get to know each other again, he said.

He was quoting my daughter, saying exactly what she'd said to me an hour before, as we sat beside Miss O'Shea. The room in the home was bugged and I was a clown.

—And they'd rape her first.

—They wouldn't, I said – I managed to say.

—Wouldn't they now?

—They wouldn't do that.

—You're right, he said.—Faith and family, isn't that it? They'd strap her to a fertiliser bomb but they'd never touch her where they shouldn't touch her. Because that would be a sin. But killing her clean, because she's the blood of your bad blood. They'd talk their way around that one.

He smiled.

—So, Henry, he said.—You can't die on us just yet. We're depending on you. And so is someone else.

He patted my cheek – he slapped.

—Okay?

—Easy, said Campion.

I nodded.

—Good man, said the Clare man.—But d'you know what? We still don't know the answer to the question we really need the answer to. Why you? Why have they canonised you? When they already had Archer. They go and bloody manufacture you. They had to make you up. Why?

I had an answer.

—The hunger strikes and the elections, I said.—It's too much for one man.

—That's possible, he said.—But it's not enough. It's not the answer.

He patted my shoulder.

—I want the answer. Or we'll just have to give up on it and move on. Are you with me?

—Yeah.

—I want the answer, Henry. I'll even tell you what I think.

He waited until I looked straight at him.

—There's more than one man changed his mind in this, he said.—That's my theory.

She'd talked for hours.

No one came in to check on her mother. There'd have been no point. She was as stubborn as she'd always been, and solid now as well. She looked like she'd been carved from lovely wood. She was dead but she'd outlive us.

I sat and listened, and I began to like my daughter.

She lived in Chicago, she told me.

—Where?

—Oak Park.

—You went back.

—Well, yes, she said.

She'd lived there, with her mother, when I'd found them – when her mother had found me.

—In the same house? I asked.—Missis What-was-her-name's?

—Missis Lowe, she said.—No. Not there.

—She'd be dead now.

—Long dead.

—Go on.

She was married to a man who was fifteen years younger than her. Your mother's daughter, I nearly said – but didn't. She told me this in the American way, a sigh, a complaint that was actually a boast. At the age of sixty, or somewhere near, she was trying to provoke her father. She liked to think of herself as an artist – she *was* an artist – but she also sold real estate. Fabrics were her thing. Her life was very ordered, she told me. Her life was her loom and her dogs.

I looked to see if her mother was listening. She wasn't.

The dogs had names. And she gave them to me. Taft, Max, Holly. Not Connolly, Pearse and Collins. Taft, Max, Holly and Satchmo.

—Satchmo?

—Yes.

—Is he black? I asked.

—Please, she said. *Pull-ease.*

She stared at me, the mouth dramatically agape. It was hard to watch. The wizened girl, the ghost of my child, was in there.

—That just does not happen, she said.

Why then? I wanted to ask her. Why had she done it? To bring her back to the first time she'd lived in Oak Park – when her father had packed a carpet bag and left, to follow Louis Armstrong?

I didn't ask.

She didn't look at me while she spoke. She addressed the window, and her mother's feet. But she glanced at me now and again, and saw the oul' lad sitting straight, trying to hide the fact that his back was at him. Trying to hide the fact that he was bored, but happy to be bored.

I went out to the corridor while she'd gone to the jacks, and I saw the G-men's bus outside, parked across the entrance, blocking it, the engine humming, grey exhaust sliding out the back.

She came back and carried on. She was a woman whose life began in her twenty-fifth year. She didn't just deny or bypass her childhood and wandering, or the weight that had come with her name. She'd erased them. They just weren't there. She'd managed what I'd failed to do when I'd gone to America; she'd invented herself, new-born and ready, with no history or anything dragging her back. It must have taken her years, and she must have been mad.

Her fabrics and her doggies.

I heard the bus being revved outside. I heard the rain beginning to pat the window.

She was American. She spoke about her dogs and she knew she was fascinating. Her world was *the* world.

—What's your husband called?

—Benjamin, she said.

—Is he with you?

—No.

—Looking after the dogs?

—Yes, he is. He adores those dogs.

—Grand.

She rarely left Oak Park, she said. She very rarely had to. Her day was the block and a half from office to home. The dogs went with her, and to the houses and apartments she sold, all of which were in or near Oak Park. The clients loved to see the dogs in the empty homes; they heard their future happiness in the clatter of those paws on the polished floorboards. The doggies sold the houses.

I grinned – I felt the pull of old, forgotten muscles. She sounded like me, the young man back then, with the shoulders and the sandwich-boards. Selling the new world, with my back to the old one.

She worked, she came home.

—Do you have any children? I asked.

—No, she said.—I do not.

She said nothing for a while. And I said nothing. I wasn't a grandfather. The rain was thumping now.

—When I saw you on TV, she said,—it was the stance, I guess.

271

You stood that way at the boxcar doors. Watching the world. As if you owned it.

I said nothing – I kept the mouth shut tight.

—It's funny, she said.—I had to see it on the TV before I'd accept it. But there you were. And the word popped open in my head. *Father*.

—I didn't die.

—Yes, you did, she said.

She shook her head, like she was trying to disperse those words, break them up before they formed.

—No, she said.—I know.

She spoke so softly, I saw the words more than heard them.

—At least, I *knew*. You were alive.

She still didn't look at me.

—But you didn't come back.

I wanted to explain, justify. But I knew it would be wrong. Fifty years too late, I was thinking like a father.

—I looked out the window every morning, she said.—To see you there, waiting for me to open the door. I kept looking behind me – for years. You have no idea how often I was asked if I was looking for someone. How many people – men! – gave up on me because they couldn't live with the man who was over my shoulder. And my mother —

She didn't look at her now, either. She was staring at the window, past it, through the rain.

—I don't blame her now, she said.—She had to move on. But I would not budge. You were alive and it was simply a matter of time before you came home.

There was nothing for a while. I patted her mother's arm. I looked at Saoirse – that was her name – and she was looking at me.

—*She* found you, she said.

—I suppose she did.

—That's good.

—Yeah, I said.

It was feeble – she deserved a lot more.

—We —, I started.

I looked at Miss O'Shea, and held her hand. It did nothing in mine.

—We wasted a terrible lot of time, I said.—We both *knew*. But we were stupid. I was, anyway. She had more to lose, I suppose. Her name and her – I don't know – her reputation. She should have fuckin' killed me, to be honest. But, anyway, she was the one who knocked on my door.

—But you did look for her, I said.

—No, I said.—No. I didn't. Not by then. I went to Roscommon when I came back first, half hoping you'd be there. The three of yis.

She nodded.

—There wasn't a trace, I said.—The old house was gone. But that's no excuse. Finding her here, I mean in Ratheen – that was a fluke.

—Did it ever occur to you to go further down the road that time in Roscommon and knock on Uncle Ivan's door?

—Yes.

—But you didn't.

—No.

She sighed.

—Well, she said,—I *am* glad you found her.

—But I wasted it.

—Well, that's why I'm here, she said.—Too much time has been wasted.

—Yeah, I said.—You're right. This isn't your home, though. Don't wreck your life for me.

—Don't worry about that, she said.

It struck me: she was a nice woman. It made me laugh. She didn't join in, but she smiled.

—You're trying to send me back, she said.—Just as we get to know each other again.

—Grand, I said.—Fair enough. That's good.

She stood first, and I got up and followed her into Ivan's room. He was on his way out too, and he was going faster than the woman next door. He looked ripe, the colour of a hoor's curtains. He was rotting already, before he'd finally stopped. The smell was something no old man should have had to endure. But I said nothing. Saoirse loved him. He'd found her alone, a baby, with her dead grandmother, after I'd run from Ireland and her mother was in jail. He'd given her a home while I was in the desert pretending I had a story that needed telling, letting myself be conned, and happy to be conned.

I stayed standing beside her as long as she wanted to stay and hoped to fuck she wouldn't sit down and expect me to join her. I wanted home and the bed, a night's sleep.

She stayed a minute – maybe she prayed. Then she walked out. I followed her. She stopped at the front door as she rooted in the big shoulder bag she always had with her. It was some sort of hairy, unorganised wool that looked as if it stopped being a bag when you weren't looking.

—Did you make it yourself? I asked.

—My bag?

—On the loom.

—Yes, she said.—I did.

—It's nice.

—Thank you, she said.

She took out some keys.

—Can I offer you a ride anywhere?

She must have hired a car, or she was driving Ivan's – I didn't know.

—No, I said.—No, thanks; you're grand.

She looked disappointed. But she smiled. I could tell now: she was used to smiling.

—Tomorrow? she said.

—Sound, I said.—I'll be here.

Why didn't I take the lift? I was walking away again. The bus was waiting for me.

11

The strike was lost but they kept me working. Not as relentlessly as during that period in the spring and summer of '81, when the hunger strikers had become the candidates, before the deaths became harder to count. Much more of that would have killed me – the pinball charge around the country, the soggy bags of chicken and chips at two and three in the morning – no one outside of Dublin knew how to cook a fuckin' chip. The race against death, trying not to acknowledge the pointlessness, the obscenity of it, especially when the election was over and the victories were followed by nothing. But the men kept dying – Joe McDonnell, Martin Hurson, Kevin Lynch, Kieran Doherty, Thomas McElwee, Michael Devine – and I stood on platforms and looked out at smaller crowds. There were the riots every night in Belfast and the other northern towns – more dead boys – and a big riot in Dublin on a hot Saturday afternoon in August. A disaster. The plan was to burn the British Embassy for the second time in ten years. (The last time had been in 1972, a few days after Derry's Bloody Sunday.) But it ended in a rout, when the rozzers took off their badges and got stuck in with the boots and batons. I was escorted – I was carried – out of Ballsbridge by three big men in bomber jackets who managed to stay standing as their heads and arms were smashed. I tried to tell them that we could go under the street, that the river below could get us away, like it had when my father had rescued myself and Victor from the batons of different rozzers, the fat grandas of the fuckers in the riot gear – that we just had to get over a wall down the lane there across the street, and behind a bush and down a hole; we'd be under Beggar's Bush in no time. But they didn't hear or they didn't understand. Maybe I was only talking to myself. Because they took us the hard way, through the sweating fury of the state. I was covered in the lads' blood and none of my own when they put me down and into the back of a black van, in Sandymount. I could hear the riot behind us, but we were out of it.

It sickened me. Not the riot – the riot was always coming. The riot was the start of nothing; it was the strike's last shout. What sickened me was myself, my uselessness. The fact that I could do nothing. Get stuck in, observe, bear witness – I couldn't even walk away on my own.

—Photograph me, for fuck sake. Look! I'm drenched in blood. An old man! It's fuckin' scandalous.

The van kept going.

—There's plenty of blood today, said a new voice.

It seemed new; I didn't recognise it. I couldn't keep up with my minders. There was a core of five or six men and, except for the man with the beard, I couldn't remember them long enough to describe, either to myself or the G-men. I heard the names – they weren't kept from me – but never managed to keep them.

—You're above all that, Henry, said the voice.

I couldn't see the man at the front of the van. I was in the back, lying across a damp mattress.

—We don't want you to be seen bleeding, he said.—You're not flesh and blood.

—I fuckin' am.

—No. You're not.

It was over. The families started to intervene; they wouldn't let their sons and husbands die. Unconscious men were drip-fed back to life. Other men saw it was over and took food before they slipped out of the world.

The lady, the miserable cunt, wasn't for budging. The Famine Queen herself. Thatcher would have let every man and woman on the island die. But there was that, at least. The hatred. Defeat was always victory, another telling of the old story, to lure the latest young lads into the movement. Defeat was impossible. It was just a horrible kind of victory, the victim's wheezy triumph.

I gave up, again. I couldn't face another day. They were hammering on my door the morning after the Ballsbridge riot but I wasn't getting up to answer. I couldn't. I slipped below – I was gone. Far away from fact and hunger strikes. Back into the burning heart of Monument Valley.

I knew who I was again one afternoon in November. I didn't

sit up in the bed; I was already doing that. I saw the woman standing at the kitchen table. I saw her through the open bedroom door and I knew who she was, because the knowledge, the name, beat back the thought that it might be Miss O'Shea.

It was Saoirse. She was peeling cooking apples. I knew her, as if I'd been watching her at work for hours. There was a strong beam of sun cutting across the room, lighting two of the table legs. Her head was out of the light but I still knew her. Miss O'Shea was in the nursing home – I knew that. (I didn't know yet that it was months since I'd seen her.) Saoirse was there in the kitchen, peeling apples. She'd never been in the house before and I didn't have an apple peeler. But grand. I'd been sick and my daughter was looking after me. I was a lucky man. I was a happy man.

Ivan was dead and buried. The hunger strike was dead and buried. The coalition government that was formed after the June election was about to be buried. I fell asleep, and woke up the same man. I woke and saw a man beside me, sitting on one of the kitchen chairs.

—Benjamin.

—That's right.

—When did you get here?

—This morning.

—Good man.

I closed my eyes and slept. *We're in the money – we're in the money.* I loved Saoirse, first thing, every time I woke. Whether she was there or not. I loved her mother. I couldn't wait to see her, to look at her solid, dark red face.

—Is it Ben or Benjamin?

—Benjamin.

—Grand.

Then he was gone.

—Where?

—Home.

—To the dogs.

—That's right.

—Will he be back?

—Perhaps.

—Grand.

I'd wake up alone, or she'd be there, somewhere in the house – it didn't matter. The radio was quietly on.

I leaned out of the bed to hear.

—Turn it up a bit.

—I could bring it in to you.

—No, I said.—Just give the volume a bit of a twist.

I could hear the news from a safe distance. The Red Brigades were kidnapping half of Italy and Jaruzelski declared martial law in Poland. I listened for news from Ireland. The Society for the Protection of the Unborn Child was calling for a referendum to protect the rights of foetuses. And corporal punishment was about to be banned from Irish schools, twenty-five years after I'd banned it. I heard nothing about the H-Blocks and little of anything from north of Swords. The north was far away again. It was safe to get out of the bed.

I felt fine but I fell over. I hadn't walked in months, and I'd forgotten that I'd only the one leg. I'd been young again, a father – *We're in the money, we're in the money* – before I'd gone under the train. There was no self-pity, just a bit of catching up. I was ancient and my daughter was an oul' one. She had to grunt as she helped me off the floor.

We talked. But there was no making up for lost time. She was happy enough in the small talk. And so was I. I sat beside the Superser. I listened to the news and I didn't shout back at the radio.

I knew it wasn't over. The hunger strike had been lost but I was still the talisman. I'd seen the struggle before, the split between the gun and the vote, and I had a good idea of what was going on out there in the land of the Provisionals. They'd be re-enacting our glorious past. I knew I was in the middle of it. Sinn Féin had sudden political clout, on both sides of the border – the border they insisted didn't exist. The strike was over but seats had been won. I knew they'd come knocking – they'd all come knocking. I didn't mind. I was rested.

She drove me to her mother.

She turned left, onto the coast road. I couldn't see the Hill of Howth, because the weather was in the way. The wipers worked but they weren't much help.

—It's lovely here, she said.

—I suppose so.

She took us through the nursing home gates. There was no Special Branch bus there, waiting. But they'd be knocking soon. They'd be following us now, I thought. But the thought did nothing to make me sit up or worry. I was ready for them too. Until I forgot about them.

—A big funeral, was it?

I'd stopped at Ivan's door. There was someone else in there, a little oul' one shaking inside her nylon dressing gown, standing at the window and staring at her hands.

—Very big, she said.

—A good send-off.

—Yes.

—He wasn't the worst, I said.

—He was great.

—Did he leave you anything?

—You are such a horrible man, she said.

She meant it; I'd upset her.

—I'm sorry, I said.

She walked away, back the way we'd come.

—Sorry, I said again.

She stopped and turned.

—You were there, she said.

—What?

—You were at the funeral.

—Was I?

—Yes.

She knew I wasn't messing. She followed me into her mother's room. I sat beside the bed.

—Did I behave myself?

—Of course you did.

—Because we had our differences, me and Ivan.

—I know, she said.—He hated you.

I wanted to cry – I fuckin' did.

—He was scared of you.

—That's better, I said.—I don't remember it at all. Did he die here?

—No, she said.—At home.

—Grand.

There was no change in the bed. Miss O'Shea was maybe deeper, darker, but I couldn't really judge. I leaned over her, slowly, managed to hold the creaks, and I rested the side of my head on her stomach. Nothing gave or settled back. I lifted my head, very slightly. The blanket touched my ear, and dropped. Touched, and dropped.

—She's breathing, I said.

—Yes, said Saoirse.

She must have dressed me for Ivan's funeral. I was trying to see what had happened, making it up. I'd been sick and she'd helped me get the togs on. Some sort of a fever, the works; it was only natural that I couldn't remember. I'd insisted on getting out of the bed and off to Roscommon to make sure that they did a proper job burying the fucker.

—You're quite the celebrity, she said.

She was driving us into town, another day. We were going to the pictures.

—Yeah, I said.—It's gas.

—There were people who wanted to shake your hand, she said.—My God, a queue.

It was she who'd taken me to the burial, not the man with the beard or one of the other northern men. Ivan would have been on their long list of renegades. All he'd done in the War of Independence had been cancelled out when he'd decided to stand for election. He'd stood, and won, and he'd recognised the state. He'd been clever, Ivan; he'd always been very clever. He knew there'd be more than one split, that the more interesting splits always followed the first one. He went with the wrong side, de Valera and the diehards, at the start of the Civil War, because he knew they'd end up winning. He knew his history and he knew his own people. He lost the war and sat back. He was a young fella, and he could still get fat while he waited. Then the second split came, and his timing was perfect. He went with de Valera again, into the arms of democracy, and it wasn't long – 1932 – before the former rebels took power from the other former rebels and started to run the place. But Ivan had already been running the place. He was a gas man. He soon had his feet in under the Cabinet table and he helped stir the country through the Economic War and the Emergency and everything else, even up to the steps of the Common Market. But then there was the Arms Trial – maybe he'd felt guilty; maybe he'd felt old – and he'd lost his place at the table. He'd run guns for the Provisionals, but they still wouldn't go to his funeral.

—That man, Haughey? said Saoirse.

—Charlie Haughey?

—He shook your hand, she said.—But some of the other political guys stayed well away from you.

—That suits me fine.

—You're a hot customer.

I saw her smiling.

We went to *Chariots of Fire*, the first time I'd been inside a picture house in this country. It was hard to get worked up about posh Brits trying to outrun one another. Ford, I knew, would have hated it. There was too much talk, and no place in the script for Maureen O'Hara. After the film we went to Bewley's on Westmoreland Street. She held the tray. My wrists wouldn't take the weight of two full plates and a pot of tea. And I didn't mind at all. My daughter was looking after me. We both had the shepherd's pie and I ate my own and most of hers. Then we walked back slowly – there was no choice there; I was fucked and full – up to Parnell Square, where she'd parked her car. On the way home, as we crawled with the traffic over the canal bridge at the North Strand, I realised something that shocked me: I'd just lived the perfect day.

There were more good days and empty days. She was gone for a long time and I was back on the bus, up the hill to sit with Miss O'Shea and the wallpaper, and more sitting alone at home waiting for the bang on the door, the boys, or the lads who were chasing the boys. They hadn't gone away. I often knew that.

I kept the radio on low, but I listened. Lenny Murphy put on some weight when two lads with a sub-machine-gun put twenty-six bullets into his head and body. A Prod with a Catholic surname, a young man with a lot to prove, Murphy had been slaughtering Catholics, cutting them to pieces in the back rooms and front rooms, the romper rooms, of Shankill drinking clubs – *Romper, bomper, stomper boo. Tell me, tell me, tell me, do.* His pals in the U.V.F. told the Provisionals where Lenny would be on the night he swallowed the bullets – it was a complicated war.

That was in 1982, coming up to the Christmas. I remembered it, and other deaths and goings-on. I made it to 1983, most of the days accounted for, in the proper order. I woke up every morning and remembered the day before. I knew where I was and who I was. I had a calendar on the wall in the kitchen. I didn't know who'd put it there, but there it was, to the left of the cooker. I marked off each day, put a thick line through it, and made sure I was waking up in the day after the last one. I bought myself a new calendar, for 1983, with a woman on it, some skinny one called Olivia Newton-John.

Saoirse looked at me when she saw the calendar. It was a deliberate while before she spoke.

—Does that ever stop?

—It was half-price, I told her.

I'd bought it in early February.

—Were there none with cute dogs or horses? she asked.

—I just grabbed the first one, I lied.

I'd climb out of the bed and stroll, or try to stroll, across the kitchen to Olivia Newton-John. She wasn't my kind of woman at all but I still tried to make sure that my pyjamas were clean, when I remembered. And twice, before I'd made it to the woman, I'd know that there were days missing, whole clumps of the things. I'd know by the slant of the light, or the lack of it, or the fact that I was starving, too weak to make it across to the calendar. I hated that – I fuckin' hated that.

I met Saoirse at the airport. I knew the date. The 23rd of February, 1984. I knew she was arriving. I had the time of her flight on the calendar – it was Kathleen Turner up on the wall that year, and she left poor Olivia in the halfpenny place. I was dragged by my wet heart out of the bed by the alarm clock I'd bought specially. And I was waiting when she pushed her trolley into the arrivals area, my sixty-three-year-old daughter. She was flaked, I could see, but she grinned.

She came and she went. She never stayed with me. She had a place, she said. She had a car. She brought Benjamin with her, or she came alone. He was a nice, dull lad – like one of the dogs, she said. She wasn't joking. She loved him because he was like none of the men she'd known before him. He'd given her peace and I liked him for it, and I liked him anyway. He was quiet but he wasn't hiding anything. I saw him once or twice a year. I could measure his visits in those terms because the years were passing and I spent most of them in bed or sitting beside my wife's bed.

—Is this unusual? I asked one day.

—What?

—This, I said, and I nodded at my wife.

The gorgeous nurse had gone, off to California. More money and sun, she'd said as she'd kissed me on the cheek and let me gawk at her arse one last time as she carried it out the door and down the corridor and the stairs. I heard her rubber soles, and I missed her. She'd gone and been replaced by other girls I couldn't remember till I saw them again. It was one of those I was talking to now.

—Being unconscious, I said.—Dead and alive.

She looked uncomfortable, and red around the nose.

—Missis O'Kelly is not dead, she said.

—I know, I said.

—There's no life-support machine, she said.—You can see that.

—Yeah.

—This isn't a hospital, she said.—We feed her and clean her. Everything else, she manages herself. Do you understand me?

—Yeah.

—She's perfectly alright.

—I wasn't asking you to turn off any fuckin' machine.

—Language.

—She's used to it, I said.—And look it, I'll sit here forever, I don't mind. But it's been a long time. It's like a fairy tale or something.

She was looking at me now, properly.

—I've even kissed her, I said.—To see if that would work. But it didn't. You don't know any handsome princes, do you?

—They're all working on the building sites in London, she said.

—*Is* it unusual?

—I'd say so.

—Is she listening?

She stepped away from the bed, as if the consequences of her answer had just whacked her.

—Is she? I asked.

—I don't know. She's the way she should be. She'll go in her own time.

—Okay. Fair enough.

Maybe she was right. She'd go when she was ready. But when would that be? After I died? When the Brits got out of Ireland? I wouldn't fall for those ones, the romance and religion. The hunger strikes were over. She was nearly a hundred years old. She was dying slowly, and the only thing I wondered now was when I'd know she'd died. She didn't know I was sitting beside her. She didn't know anything at all.

But sometimes I didn't believe that.

They were out there. I knew that. But there was no bang on the door.

He was sitting beside my bed. The man with the beard.

—Are you well rested, Henry?

283

—Yeah.

The beard was gone.

—You're looking well.

—Thanks.

It was good to see him.

He brought his face closer to mine. I knew there was no one else in the house. He was alone.

—This is where it starts, he said.

The hunger strike had been lost. But it hadn't. Defeat was always more valuable – the better songs came out of it. Thatcher had done what she'd always been supposed to do. She'd let Irishmen die. They nailed themselves to the cross and she sat in the shade and watched. Cromwell came, slaughtered the innocents, and left. The surviving Irish, in the absence of a grave, pissed on his memory. But Thatcher came, and she stayed. The strikers died in 1981, but she was still Prime Minister years later. She killed Argentinians, she broke the heads of her own coal miners. She was the Provisionals' greatest asset. She was living, breathing evil and she was on the telly every night.

I knew the story. I *was* the story. I knew how the stupidity of 1916 had been turned to glorious success. The British had helped there too, when they'd executed the leading men instead of kicking them in their holes and sending them home. This new story had the same plot – but it was different. I didn't know why yet. But I knew.

There was desperation with a smell off it, as if the outlaws sensed that their days in the wild were numbered. They went from robbing banks to kidnapping. They grabbed supermarket magnates and the wives and kids of businessmen, anyone they thought might be swapped for a few spare quid. They kidnapped racehorses. They snatched poor oul' Shergar, the Derby winner.

I sat in a farmhouse in Leitrim one wet night after a republican funeral just across the border, in Fermanagh. I listened to the men in the kitchen talking bombs and diesel prices with the local priest, when I heard a sharp neigh from the other side of the kitchen wall.

The talking stopped.

—Was that a horse? I asked, before I'd mustered the cop-on not to.

—No, said a man with a Dublin accent who hid himself behind huge sunglasses.

—The mice are hoarse, said someone else.

—Shut the fuck up, said the hard man with the sunglasses.—All of yis.

I pretended I was falling asleep. I wondered later if my question had killed the horse.

—I'm going to tell you some things, the man with the beard now said.

This was a month after he'd called me out of retirement. We were off the main roads. He was staring ahead. His left hand was murdering the gear-stick. It was the first time I'd seen him drive.

—Alright? he said.

He didn't look at me.

—Yeah, I said.

—You're an informer.

I said nothing.

—Aren't you?

—Kind of.

—Don't kind-of me. You're a tout.

—Yeah.

I wasn't scared. I was weightless. I was dead.

—Listen to this, he said.

He was flying now, taking the corners like a mad thing.

—Are you listening?

—Yeah, I am.

—It doesn't matter.

He took us through an open gate, into a field. He didn't slow down. My head hit the roof. He was bringing us through the spring barley. I was in a getaway car but I didn't think there was anything behind us. I didn't think at all – the jolts and bangs wouldn't let me.

He did something with his feet, and the car died. I wasn't thrown forward. He'd stopped on some kind of ridge. He was on the raised side and his weight shoved me against the door.

It was quiet. And hot.

—You know the score, he said.—You shot touts yourself. Plenty of them.

He was calm; this was nothing unusual. He was tenderising me – I knew that.

—Yeah, I said.—I did. That was the excuse.

—Lay off the revisionism now, Henry. You shot informers.

—Yeah. I did.

—It was war, he said.—You did right.

—Okay.

—Good. Now you've joined the ranks of the turncoats and I'm telling you now, it doesn't matter. Is that in your head?

—Yeah.

—There's nothing much you've told them. I'm right?

—I'd nothing much to tell them, I said.—They threatened me with —

—Fuck off.

He wasn't a curser.

—Don't give me your excuses, he said.—From here on in, I'll be feeding you the information. I'll tell you what you can tell them. You'll tell them nothing else, from any other source. D'you understand?

—Yeah.

—No one else.

I tried to look at him; I didn't have room.

—You're informing, yourself, I said.—Through me.

—Aye.

—For fuck sake.

—There's a lot more to this, he said.—Just get what I told you clear in your head. You tell them exactly what I tell you and nothing more. Got that?

—I haven't seen them in years.

—You will, he said.—And you'll do what I tell you.

—Yeah.

—Why?

—You have me by the bollix.

—Aye, he said.—There's two games being played, Henry. This one – me and you. And the other one. This conversation never happened.

—I'm ahead of you there.

—Good.

—Why don't you talk to her?

—What?

—You never talk to Missis O'Kelly, said the new nurse.

—She wouldn't hear me, I said.

286

But I felt the rightness of the idea, and the guilt: I'd never spoken to her in the years I'd been sitting beside her, waiting for her to die properly.

—You'd never know, she said.—And there's no harm in trying.

I waited till she went. She'd been changing the glucose bag, or whatever it was.

The room was empty.

—How's it going? I said.

I didn't sound right; I was talking to no one. I took her hand. It stayed dead in mine.

—How's it going?

I couldn't ask questions; it wasn't fair.

I stood up. I leaned over and put my hands on each side of her head. I didn't look at the open eye. I tried to turn her, so she'd face me when I sat again. But she wasn't having it. She wouldn't budge. It was the first time I'd touched her face in years. There was warmth under the wood. I could see and feel the woman there.

I brought the chair right up against the bed, and my mouth right up to her ear.

—I'm an informer, I told her.—Can you fuckin' believe it?

The room was bugged – or, it had been. The G-men had quoted Saoirse back to me. That was two or three years before, and I hadn't seen either of them since. Did they collect the bugs when they were finished with them? Or did they just turn them off? I hadn't a clue.

I coughed and listened for a buzz or echo. There was nothing.

—An informer, I said.—If that bit of news doesn't wake you, missis, nothing will.

I was a bollix, pretending to talk to her.

I sat back, to see her a bit better.

—It hasn't rained in a few days, I said.—The sun was even out there, when I was at the bus stop. They're putting up a shopping centre, you wouldn't recognise the place. It'll have everything. So the woman at the bus stop said. Off-licence and all. She was about twenty years younger than you. Not in bad nick either. Her coat matched her trolley. Making the effort, you know.

I watched her face, the side of her mouth. For a twitch or a blush. Her skin was too livid for blushing, and nothing twitched.

But she was listening. I decided that. I wanted her to sit up and grab me. I wanted her to go for my eyes. I looked at her nails. They'd been cut. Her hair was clean and silver.

—I'm a fuckin' tout, I said.—The worst kind of cunt there is. D'you remember the bike?

I leaned in and kissed her ear.

—Why are you doing this?

She could hear every word.

—Get up, I said.

But she stayed put.

—I've a wee message for you, said the man with the beard.

—They haven't made contact with me.

—I told you, they will.

—Alright.

—Come outside, he said.

The day was beginning to seep into the room. He made his way to the back door and unlocked it. Fresh air rushed in, followed quickly by the stench from the bin I hadn't put out the week before. It was too heavy. I couldn't manage it, through the kitchen to the front door.

—Jesus Christ, he said.

The smell was my shame: I couldn't look after myself.

—It's grand, I said.

—We'll have to sort this out for you.

—It's none of your fuckin' business.

—Come here to me.

I followed him out.

—I'll be brief, he said.

He was breathing through his mouth.

I shook the age off my back and tried to see him clearly.

—Why are we out here? I asked.

—The walls, Henry, he said.—I'd say they might have ears.

The house was bugged too. But it was only now that I knew.

—Right, I said.—Go on.

—Tell them there's dissent.

—Grand.

—Dissent inside the leadership, he said.—Tell them you've heard that.

—Dissent inside the leadership.

—Exactly that.

288

—They'll want a bit more.

—Tell them that's all you've heard so far.

We went back in. There was a plastic bag, from the H. Williams up the hill, parked beside the fridge. He'd brought it with him. The supermarket didn't open till nine. So he'd bought whatever was in the bag the day before. He had the look of a man who'd slept in his car.

—So how are you, Henry?

—Grand.

—You're looking after yourself, are you?

—Yeah.

The bug was beside me, under the table. Or above, taped to the inside of the light shade. Or in the socket beside the toaster. I had three-prong sockets now, all around the house. Saoirse had arranged the work. For three days the electrician, a young lad from Finglas, had pulled back the skirting boards and rewired the house – and rigged the whole place for the Special Branch.

I didn't believe that.

Did it matter if they heard? Why didn't he just say it now? *There's dissent inside the leadership.* Why was I the messenger boy? The questions were climbing over each other while I tried to look like more than the harmless poor eejit who couldn't look after himself.

He stood up.

—I've left you a few wee items.

He pointed at the bag.

—Grand, thanks.

—Ach, I couldn't come empty-handed.

He put his finger to his lips. It was a childlike gesture but he might as well have slid the finger across his neck. Every gesture was a message; he wasted nothing.

He closed the door behind him.

And I waited.

He couldn't talk directly to them. Not even accidentally. He had to be able to deny. *There's dissent inside the leadership.* He'd come across the border with a message he couldn't give, and he'd be slipping back across. By himself. I was the one who had to hear the words and pass them on. I was the bug.

—Saoirse's coming next week, I told Miss O'Shea while the nurse worried the glucose in the bag.—She phoned last night.

The phone was new too, beside my bed.

—In case you ever need it, Saoirse had told me.

I didn't tell her that I didn't sleep any more, that the new sheets on the bed were there just to fool her.

—She'll be staying till Sunday, just, I said as the nurse slowly left us alone.—She's coming on her own this time.

I looked over my shoulder, and back to Miss O'Shea.

—They've been calling again, I told her.—I'm too old for it. I'm hearing things that could get me killed.

I put my head on the bed. I smelt the dust and the medicine. I pretended to sleep. I could feel nothing in the mattress springs, no breathing life from the woman in the bed.

The G-men didn't come, but Saoirse did. We sat with her mother.

I knew they were listening. I planted little bombs.

I yawned; I stretched till I cracked.

—You look tired, she said.

—Ah, I'm grand.

—I hate that word, she said.—Every time you people have to face something honestly and directly, you look away and say it will be grand.

I was using her, making her play a part.

—I've had a lot on my mind, I told her.

—What?

—Ah, nothing, I said.

—There we go, she said.—If it isn't grand, it's nothing.

—Just something I heard, I said.

I hated myself, the little whinge in my voice. I did in my hole – I thought I was doing alright.

—Something I was told at a meeting, I said.

—Well, what meeting are we talking about? You never alluded to any meetings when we spoke on the phone.

She was a pain in the arse when she had the hump. *Alluded to* – she was hiding behind her own *grands*.

—You're not still attending those republican – I don't know – happenings. Are you?

—The odd one.

—For God's sake, she said.—You're too old to be so vain.

—It's not vanity.

—What is it then? If it isn't vanity, or stupidity?

Sit up and defend me. I roared it silently at the woman in the bed.

—Your mother would understand, I said.

—You know what? she said back.—You are absolutely right.
She stood up but she didn't go anywhere.
—Why won't they just leave you be?
I loved her.
—You gave them everything, she said.
Her voice was softer this time.
—Is it something the police should be told?
—No, I said.—No way. I'll be grand.
I lifted my hands.
—I will.
She went home to Chicago. I waited. Another day and another week. I groaned, so they'd hear me.
—It's killing me, I told my wife.—They keep at me. The opposing wings.
The wings were an invention of my own. But I'd lived my history and I knew: there were opposing wings.
The nurse came in.
—How's Mister Smart?
—He's grand.
I heard her drag the chair. She sat beside me.
—You're chatting away to her?
—I am, yeah.
—Great, she said.—Tell me about the opposing wings.
I wasn't surprised. And that shocked me, later.
—Did you get rid of the last nurse? I asked.
—I didn't know her, she said.
—Was she one of youse?
—These wings, Henry? We're talking about the Army Council here, are we?
—You're the technology, I said.—The eyes and ears of the state?
—I suppose I am, she said.
—Are you even a nurse?
—Sure, the gang in here are easily looked after. Like herself. She's lovely.
—She hasn't budged in years.
—What have you for us?
—Is that really glucose?
—Of course it is. She'd be dead if it wasn't.
—Is she even alive?
I stood up.
—She is, of course. Calm down.

—Fuck off.

—None of that.

She pulled me back down beside her. It was desperate, so easy. She could have cracked my neck or broken my back. She could have put me across her lap and slapped my bony arse.

—Talk to me, she said.

—What happened Campion and the other fella?

—Before my time, she said.

—What happened them?

—One of them emigrated to Australia. And the other one is – he's important.

—So you're who I talk to.

—That's right.

—And what if I don't?

She shrugged, but she didn't smile.

—Life goes on, she said.

I could stand up and walk out.

—There's dissent in the leadership, I said.

—Thank you, she said.—What else?

—That's it.

—Dissent about what?

—Don't know.

—Who told you?

—No name.

—Army Council? Insider?

—Yeah.

—Dissent, she said.—It's old hat.

—It's serious.

—I hope so.

She stood up, patted my shoulder.

—The great fella, she said.—Look at you.

She stopped at the door.

—I'll be wanting more. Are you with me?

—Yeah.

—Good, she said.—I'll be seeing you here every day.

The whole place was a front, built to fool me. Even the seagulls outside were G-men. My wife was dead but it still killed me to know that she'd seen all that had just happened.

—Sorry, I said.—Sorry.

★   ★   ★

Wars were won or lost, or they just stopped, but a struggle could go on forever. Wars were dreadful but a struggle was always noble – especially when the enemy was one of the world's big armies and you were just a couple of hundred men and women. When you could point back to when it had started, past Vietnam and the Second World War and the War of Independence, to 1916, and further still if necessary, to the Fenians and the Famine and the United Irishmen, to pikes and wigs and the French Revolution and Cromwell and Drogheda, to Elizabeth and the first of the plantations and the Norman landing in 1169, and up again through Cromwell back to Thatcher. By 1985, it was eight hundred and sixteen years of struggle.

Where was the dissent? Thatcher had united the country more than anyone else had ever managed. People who didn't give a shite about the north felt the sweat climb out of their necks whenever they heard the voice. *A unified Ireland was one solution – that is out. A second solution was a confederation of the two states – that is out. A third solution was joint authority – that is out.*

It wasn't just the message; it wasn't really the message – very few actually cared. It was the voice, the reminder of who and what we were. Nothing. No blacks, no dogs, no Irish. We were nothing and Thatcher told us that every time she spoke. She was in her hotel bed in Brighton when the hotel blew up all around her. She lived and climbed out, a bigger, sharper version of herself. There would be no solution. The murder was there, like the rain, sad but Irish. It was part of what we were, a big, sore lump on the tragedy. With the Guinness and the crack – we sold it.

It was August before I saw the man with the beard again, on a hot, glaring day. His face was yellow-white, and shining wet. The beard itself was dirty and the man looked very sick.

—Henry.

He'd knocked on the door, although I knew he had a key.

—What happened you? I asked.

—Can I come in?

The way he moved, I quickly knew: he'd been shot. I looked out as I shut the door, but there was no trail of blood running along behind him, or the echo of a gunshot.

—You've been shot, I said.

—Aye.

—Are you alright?

He didn't answer but I heard him choke a groan. He was wearing a tweed jacket, on the hottest day of the year. He'd forced his right arm into it. The pain should have killed him but something more urgent was keeping him upright.

I had to get rid of him but there was nothing I could do. It was the first time he'd been shot; I could tell that.

—You're doing well, I said.

—Aye. Thanks.

—I gave them your message, I told him.

I was hoping he'd give me the next one and go.

—Good man, he said.

Saoirse was home.

He looked at the bedroom door.

—Would you mind if I lay down for a bit.

—No, I said.—Fire away.

She was asleep, five steps and a wall away. She'd come to the house fresh off the plane, a few hours before. I'd told her my soldiering days were over. This man's accent would tell her I'd lied. That, and the fact that he was carrying himself like a bad actor. When it came to carrying bullets bad actors always did it better than the good ones.

Saoirse hadn't stayed with me before. She had her own place, a flat or something, that her Uncle Ivan had given her years before. But she'd had an extra room built onto the back of my house, along with the jacks and everything else. That was where she was now, asleep, inhaling the new paint.

—Go on ahead, I said.

—Right, he said.—Right.

I heard him sit down on my bed. I heard no gasps as he escaped from the jacket.

I sat, and accepted that they were going to meet. I didn't care. I closed my eyes and listened for significant noise from outside. Screeching brakes, or fat breath climbing over the back wall. I even listened out for helicopter blades.

He'd come on his own, despite the new wound locked into the sleeve. He wouldn't have gone to bed without warning whoever was waiting for him outside.

He was alone.

He slept for three hours. I heard him wake and groan. The bed creaked as he put his shoes back on. He looked no better when he came back into the kitchen.

I listened for creaks from the other bed. But she was still asleep. There was still a chance he might be gone before she woke. I'd take his message and show him the door.

He held himself like he was trying to get as far from the wounded shoulder as he could – as if he could stop owning it. He was trying to hide, and he was frightened.

—What happened you? I asked.

—Ach, some rogue shot at me.

—He didn't miss.

—Aye. He didn't.

—A cop?

—Some loyalist scut trying to make a name for himself. Came up beside me on a wee Honda.

—Alone?

—Aye.

I didn't believe him.

—And you were alone?

—Aye, he said.—On my way down to the shop.

He was fitting himself into the ordinary life, going for a bottle of milk and a packet of Tayto. The bullet was one fact, a straightforward event in the life of a militant republican, there to be believed – I could stick my finger in the hole. The other fact, the one he was trying to create, was a different hole. The fact that he could be left alone, to walk the streets and be shot, to get across the border two days later, one-armed; the fact that he wouldn't be missed; the fact that he wasn't hiding from his own people, and that this was regular business – I wasn't going to stick my finger in that one. The man was lying.

He looked at the front door.

—This is delicate, he said.

He was talking more than he wanted to; he was killing the pain with confession.

—Only a few people know I'm here, he said.—And my wife.

—You're married.

—Aye. She helped me over the wall.

He was definitely giving me more than he wanted to; I could see it on his face. He was close to crying, sentimental; he wanted to sing the ballad of his missis. But he snorted, and shoved back the moment.

—No one knows you're here, I said.

—Not true.

—Listen, I said.—I don't trust this. You're sneaking around like a fuckin' tout.

Only the shoulder was keeping him back.

—There's only one tout in this room, he said.

—So, why am I still alive?

—You're useful.

—A messenger boy.

—No, he said.—Your time's coming.

—I'm eighty-four, for fuck sake. I'm not immortal.

—You will be.

—No, I said.—I won't.

He grabbed me with his good hand and pulled me to his chest.

—You will, he said.

His roar took all the room and everything in it. Like a bull being cut into parts – it was much more than that. And he was falling on top of me.

I was grabbed by Saoirse. She'd whacked his shoulder – I was catching up – and she was pulling me out from under him.

He was on the floor and he wasn't moving – except his mouth; he was trying to swallow the roar, gobbling it back before it went too far and gave him away.

—What's happening here?

Saoirse examined my jumper, felt the sleeves, made sure I was still in there.

—Who is that man?

She stopped patting my jumper – a present from her. It was navy, with a deer's head on it.

—You told me you were finished with them, she said.—I think he's injured.

—He's been shot, I told her.

She got down beside him. I cursed the fucker; he was taking her attention.

—I don't see blood.

—It happened a few days ago, I told her.

—You old fool.

And the man on the floor laughed. Or tried to. He was still in agony but bringing it under control. She still knelt, but well back from him.

—Why don't you leave him alone? she said.—He's an old man.

—Ach, he said.—We're old friends. That right, Henry?

—That's right.

He was sitting now. He already looked like a man who didn't need help.

—I was just going, he said.

—That would be nice, she said.

He turned his head slowly. He looked at her but he spoke to me.

—We're willing to talk, Henry. Will you remember that?

—Yeah, I said.—You're willing to talk.

—Aye, he said.—No matter what's being said and done.

—Fair enough.

—What is this? Saoirse asked.

She was furious, upset. She tried to stand up quickly, to get there before he did. But – I saw it – her moves were stiff.

—I'm away, he said.

If the house was bugged, he'd just delivered the message himself. But I wasn't sure he knew that. He walked out without letting us see his face. He left the door open.

—You promised me, she said, when she knew he'd gone.

—It's nothing, I said.

—You're as bad as she was.

She went into the new room and came back out quickly with her case.

—Will I call a taxi for you?

—No, thank you.

She didn't close the door either.

I turned on the radio. I lay back carefully on the bed. I closed my eyes. I drifted, but the radio stayed with me. The news came on. The big story that day was the shooting. A leading republican had been shot by a loyalist paramilitary. The gunman had fired only one bullet before making his getaway. A burnt-out Honda 50 was found in an alley off the Shankill Road.

I got up and made it to the fridge. I took out the eggs I'd bought for her.

He'd delayed the news. As the bullet dug into him, he'd seen the chance and grabbed it. They'd got him off the street and they'd washed the blood off the road before the R.U.C. or the Brits came in after the bullet's echo, looking for the body. (The kid on the Honda would have been sent there by a man who knew a man who wore a uniform.) But there was no body. There was nothing. It had been a quick decision – his. Republicans would control their own news and have a laugh at the fuckers, even as he bit on his shirt cuff to stop himself from roaring, before they got him off the street. And by hiding behind the decision, he'd been able to sneak away.

I was making it up but I knew it was true. *We're willing to talk, no matter what's being said and done.* He'd risked his life for that.

My omelette was a dry oul' thing but I ate it.

The victim's condition was said to be stable. His wounds were not life-threatening.

—Saoirse's over again, I told the woman in the bed.

It came natural now, the talking. Even though I knew I was being recorded. It didn't matter. I could talk to her and no one else.

—We had a bit of a row, I told her.—She doesn't like me being involved.

Involved – I tried hard not to sound as if I was reading one of Ford's scripts.

—You know yourself, I said.—A lad came down from Belfast with a message for me. It was a bit awkward.

I sat up – that wasn't easy. My back cried for the back of the chair.

—So, anyway, I said.—She walked out. Has she been here to see you?

—No, she hasn't, said the woman behind me – the nurse.

I looked at my wife.

I didn't have time to lean forward.

—Die, love, I said.—Will yeh?

—Did I hear you right?

—Or wake up and blink or something.

She stood behind me.

—It must be hard.

She sighed.

—What was the message, Henry?

—I want to talk to someone else.

—What was the message?

I looked behind – my neck cracked. She wasn't there; she'd gone.

—I'll only tell the top man, I told Miss O'Shea.

I stood. I used the side of the bed to help me.

—D'yeh hear me?

I bent down – that came natural. I went down to her lips. Someone had put Vaseline into the corner creases. My own lips were a lot drier than hers. I kissed her. I looked into her eye and I kissed her.

And I saw it – something. In her far ear, the one I hadn't really seen since they'd put her into the bed against the wall. The bed was on wheels. I grabbed the rail above her head, and pulled. I made sure I didn't bring the glucose down on top of her. The bed slid away easily enough. The castors squealed on the lino. I pulled the bed again. I'd enough room now. I looked at the door, before I started. There was no one there, I could hear no urgent feet.

I got around the bed. I could look down across her forehead, at the bridge of her nose, the slope that was still lovely. She was no more dead than I was, not from where I stood now. I was delighted, and annoyed; I'd let myself be ruled by the position of the chair. I'd never wandered from it. She was still there, still alive, under the bedclothes. It was like looking down from the summit of a mountain as it took over the world below and spread out and became the coast. Her feet, sticking up, Howth Head and Dun Laoghaire. This was the best thing I'd done in years.

I kept going around the bed, and I saw it. A grey plastic wire, running from the edge of the bed into the mix of tubes and wires that I'd thought were there to keep her alive. I didn't touch the wire. I pulled the bed – a few inches, enough to let me get under the glucose tube and around to the side that was against the wall. I held the rail and bent down and followed the grey wire up, off the bed, along her neck – there was a thin strip of flesh-coloured tape holding it tight and well hidden. To her ear. I bent right down now, further than had become normal.

—Ah, I groaned,—fuck —

Right into her ear.

—Sorry, love, I said.

I whispered to her, over the tiny microphone I saw sitting right behind the little mound that guarded the beautiful hole – it was still beautiful.

This was the best thing I'd done.

I kissed the lobe. I barely touched the skin, so there'd be nothing to hear back in Harcourt Street.

Then I spoke into the mic's ugly little silver head.

—You'll have to talk to me, lads, I said.

I carefully lifted the head out of the ear. It came easily – it was just sitting in there, its burrow. I took a corner of the tape; I was even more careful. I pulled it away, slowly. I watched the old skin lift with it. I felt it myself, in my back, as I bent right down so I could see exactly what needed doing. The last corner gave up, and the tape came away with the wire. I had the mic in my fingers now. I dropped it to the ground. I found it again, just at my foot. I stood on it. I'd smash it and they'd have to come and get me.

But then, as I put more of my weight on the bug under my foot, I realised: if I killed the bug, then they could kill its hiding place. I took my foot off it. I hauled it up – it was weightless – by its flex. I brought it up to my eyes. It didn't look too bad, just dusty. I rubbed it on my sleeve. Then I put it back where I'd found it.

He was standing against a car – a red Fiat Strada. He was in good shape and clearly earning more money.

—Campion went to Australia.

—Jesus, Henry, he said.—We're supposed to be the ones spying on you.

—How's he getting on?

—Grand, he said.—So I hear.

—Good.

—Sure, he's no Provos or the other mad feckers to contend with down there.

—He's a cop still?

—That was the deal.

—And you're doing alright yourself, I said.

—I'm grand. Will we go for a jaunt?

—No, I said.—No fucking around.

—You're in charge, Henry. You've the info, so you call the shots.

He patted his trouser pockets, like he was looking for his smokes. But he'd the red, slapped face of a man who'd given them up.

—What have you for us?

—Just a message, I said.

—Good.

—You haven't heard it already, no?

He shook his head once, just slightly.

I planted my arse beside his, on the bonnet of the car. The heat bit sharp, but I stayed where I was. He hadn't moved, to put space between my hip and his. We were old pals.

It had been a good day. I'd kissed my wife. I'd taken a deep breath and oxygen had rolled into corners that had been flat and stagnant for years. I was a big man today, not the ghost of one. It was all clear, in front of me; I knew what I was going to do.

—We're willing to talk, no matter what's being said and done.

—That's the lot, is it?

—That's it, I said.—Does it make sense?

—I'd say so.

I rang her Dublin number. She never answered. I rang her American number and waited for Benjamin to pick up the phone. But he didn't. Her machine and her realtor's delivery – *Hi! This is Seer-she Smart-O'Shea* – were gone. *I'm not here right now but I'm not far away!* I phoned every night but no one picked up and nothing behind the ringing clicked.

The Special Branch nurse was still up at the home. She was *Yes Henry, No Henry*, none of the old snottiness. I asked to see my wife's file and she trotted off to find it. I sat at the end of the bed this time, so I could look at my wife from between her feet. The nurse came back with the file and she left me alone while I found my daughter's, the next-of-kin's, address.

I knew the place. Kenilworth Square. I hadn't been in that part of the city since there'd been a curfew and I'd been running for my life.

I rang the bell, and waited. I rang again. Hers was the ground-floor flat; her bay window was right beside me. I leaned out and tapped the glass. It was an old lock, easily jemmied. But I rang once more, and waited.

She wasn't there. I left.

It was raining the next time. He was sitting inside his car, the window down and his elbow getting very wet. I'd just got off the bus. The car was in on the grass, behind the nursing home gate.

—You're back on the smokes.

—I'm an eejit, he said.

I nodded at the two baby seats in the back of the car, behind him.

—Is it twins you have?

—That's right.

—That would explain the smoking.

301

—Not at all, he said.—I've another four. I'm only after coming from a parent-teacher meeting. You're lucky I made it. Get in out of the rain there.

—No.

—You're the boss.

—How did it go?

—The meeting?

—Yeah.

—Great, he said.—The eldest. She's college material. So they're saying, her teachers.

—That's good.

—Great school. I've a message for you.

—Okay.

—I gave your one to my people and they're keen that you get this one back to your lad.

—What is it?

—We're listening.

—She's not in her flat, I said.

I was sitting in my old spot, so I could hold Miss O'Shea's hand.

—I've been out three times and she hasn't answered. Or her phone. It just rings out. And something about the curtains. They haven't been touched, they're hanging the exact same way every time I've been there.

I squeezed the hand.

—She could be gone back to America but she's not answering that one either. Or her husband. Or her answering machine. Or the fuckin' dogs.

I put her hand back up on the bed.

—I know what it is, though.

I stood.

—She doesn't want to be found. It's in the fuckin' blood.

—We're listening?

—That's what he told me, I said.—We're listening. I remember every word.

We were in the supermarket, H. Williams, staring down at the rashers. I was there for the rashers; he was the one who'd come

302

up and stood beside me. He was out of the jacket now, in a tight, black T-shirt. The angry, mad stiffness was out of his body. We stood shoulder to shoulder, two clueless men sent out to do the shopping.

—Traditional or maple-cured? I asked.

—We always go for the traditional at home, he said.

—Same here, I said.—I once hijacked pigs for Ireland, did I ever tell you?

—Is that right?

—Yeah. Me and the man who signed the order to have me shot.

—Tough times.

—Good rashers. So, am I going to say anything back to them?

—Aye. You are.

I leaned down for the rashers; the effort nearly sent me falling in beside them. I managed it, though. I had the pack in my basket and started to walk away. He was right up beside me, my body-guard. I came to a crossroads in the aisles and I knew something, immediately.

—You're not on your own this time.

There were two of them, like brothers, two days' worth of unshaven face each. The one to the left wanted shampoo and the other, to my right, was reading the ingredients on a can of Bachelor's peas. I didn't think I'd seen them before but I knew exactly who and what they were.

He grabbed my arm but let go quickly when I stopped.

—Why would I be on my own? he asked.

—I just spotted the lads, I said.—I didn't see them the last time.

—They were there, alright.

—Grand.

I knew why he was being stupid. He was worried about the last time he'd met me; he wasn't sure of what he'd said. The two strong men were there to assure me: he was on official business.

—This is what I want you to bring back to them, he said.

—Fire away.

—A change of direction is on the cards if the right conditions can be met. Is that too long?

—No, I said.

—Don't put it onto paper.

—Don't worry, I said.

I'd be writing it down when I got home. I knew my limits – I did in my hole.

—But I'll tell you, I said.—I don't like the sound of it.

I didn't know why I was saying it.

He smiled – he was already the politician – a well-cooked mix of reassurance and threat.

Standing up for my wife – it felt like that, and right. I spoke loud enough to spook him.

—You're selling us down the river, I said.—Aren't you?

His smile swerved towards threat. He knew I was powerless. Long before I did.

—How's that daughter of yours? he said.—Have you seen her lately, hey?

Everything else fell away.

—No, I said.

—Give the message back to me, before I leave you alone.

The words were clear, carved, unforgettable.

—A change of direction is on the cards if the right conditions can be met.

—Good man.

I still searched for her. In case I hadn't heard him. In case I had. In case I died if I stayed still.

A taxi to Kingsbridge.

A train to Roscommon.

A taxi.

Old Missis O'Shea's house had been gone the last time I'd been there. This time even the gate was gone, and the posts that had held it. I couldn't see a way into the field. The road was tarmacked now, solid where it hadn't been before. I got back into the taxi.

—The politician, I said.—Reynolds.

—Ivan Reynolds?

—Yeah. D'you know where he lives?

—Nowhere. Since he died, like. Is that news to you?

—No.

—And the son isn't called Ivan.

—He has a son?

—Four of the bucks.

—And none called Ivan, no?

304

—Only one of them.

—You just told me the son isn't called Ivan.

—The son that matters, said the driver.—The one that took the seat when the dad left it vacant.

The house was gone but the place hadn't changed.

—Is there a widow? I asked.—Straight answer.

—There is.

—Can you take me to her?

He started the car. I rolled down the window and listened for other engines starting. But there was nothing.

—D'you know her name?

—Peggy.

—Thanks.

—Auntie Peggy.

—For fuck sake.

He drove on roads I didn't recognise. There was new country laid on top of the country I'd known. I gave up trying to find myself in it.

—Does she still live in the house? I asked.

—She does, said the driver.—But she's frail enough.

—Does she live alone?

—People come in and out.

He turned off the road, over a cattle grid, through trees, and up to a house that got bigger and more familiar as we drew nearer. I wished Ivan was there with me, so I could thump his back and congratulate him. It was the old Fitzgalway house, rebuilt. Ivan had burnt it to the ground in 1920. But there it was in front of me, turrets and all.

I'd made Ivan and his men dig two graves in the lawn in front of the house, one for Fitzgalway and the other for his horse, two clear messages, invitations to get out of the country.

I got out of the taxi – unfolding myself wasn't too hard.

I knew exactly where I was. I'd declared the Republic here, more than sixty years before.

There were steps. There was a knocker.

The driver stayed in the car.

I could have gone round to the back. That was where the widow was going to be, in the kitchen. But I lifted the knocker and watched flakes of rust fall from under it. I let go, and it stayed in midair, unwilling, unable to drop. I pushed it back down to its home.

The door opened slowly. A young one looked out and up, at me.

—What? she said.

She wasn't Saoirse, and it took me a while to accept that fact. It was just a kid at the door.

—I'm looking for Saoirse, I said.

—She's not here, said the child.

—Do you know Saoirse? I asked.

—Yes, I do.

—Has she been here recently?

—No, said the kid.—I don't think.

—Is your granny in?

—Yes.

—Can I see her to say hello?

The door moved, and the mother was standing behind the girl. I looked for Saoirse in her as well, but she was just a good-looking woman.

—Can I help you? she said.

I could see she saw no harm in me. She waved at the taxi.

—My name's Henry Smart, I said.

It meant nothing.

—I'm Saoirse's father.

—Oh, she said.—Of course. You'd better come in.

—Thanks.

I sat in the kitchen and knew I'd find nothing. The mother and girl were lovely, Ivan's youngest daughter and grandchild. The widow sat in an armchair, beside a bellows wheel that wasn't used any more. She stared out from deep in her head and, now and again, she saw me. I tried to see her at my wedding, one of the young ones who'd danced around the table. But there was nothing in her face; she'd already said goodbye to her memories.

—It'd be three weeks, at least, said the daughter, whose name, she told me, was Nuala.—Isn't that right, Mammy?

Mammy wasn't answering.

—How was she? I asked.

—Grand, said Nuala.

—She gave me fifty p, said the kid.

—Is that right?

—Yes.

She was scrounging for another fifty. I'd give her a quid before I left, and she'd always remember me.

—Shush, pet, said her mother.—Are you worried? she asked me.

—I am, a bit. She'd normally contact me when —

—But I have to say, she told me.—She's never mentioned you.

—Has she not?

—Not to me, she said.—I don't mean to be hurtful. Did Saoirse ever talk about Mister Smart, Mammy?

Still no word from Ivan's widow. There was something about the way she held her hands; she'd been gorgeous once.

I remembered something.

—I was at the funeral, I said.

—The funeral?

—Your father's, I said.—I was there with Saoirse.

—Oh, yes, said Nuala.—I think I remember seeing you. But there were thousands around that day. You know yourself.

—Yeah, I said, although I'd no memory of the day.

—Does she visit you a lot? I asked.

—Oh yes, all the time, said Nuala.—When she isn't busy with her politics.

—Politics?

—Ah sure, the H-Blocks and all that crack. You know yourself.

I nodded.

—But even then, she'd stay the few days. Catch up with us all, you know.

I nodded again.

I didn't want to hear any more. I thought I was going to be sick – but I remembered the money for the kid. I handed over the folding punt.

—Say thank you, Jessica, said her mother.

—Thank you very much.

—You're grand.

The widow spoke as I passed her. The words were cracked but definitely there.

—There was a man called Henry Smart, she said.

—Is that right? I said.

—He had an eye for the girls.

—Go 'way.

—And he went and married Nuala O'Shea.

I'd just heard my wife's name for the first time. That, or she'd confused my wife with her youngest daughter.

—That's right, Mammy, said the daughter.

★   ★   ★

307

—Nuala.

I sat where I could see her eye. I'd catch her.

—Nuala, I said.

Not a twitch, or a hint of one.

—I know your name, Nuala.

Nothing.

—You said in Chicago that your real name was too complicated for the Yanks. What's complicated about fuckin' Nuala?

Nothing.

—Did you know? I asked.—About Saoirse?

Nothing at all.

—Did you arrange it between yis? I asked.—You'd pretend to be dead and she'd be the dog lover.

It made no sense – nothing made sense – and there was nothing behind it. But it gave me something to say.

—Nuala.

I took her hand from under the sheet. I kissed the liver spots, one at a time.

—I'll have to get used to it, I suppose.

I was talking to her and no one else. The bug from her ear was dangling outside, below the window ledge. I'd haul it back in a minute and park it in her ear. But, for now, it was the pair of us, under the sods in Roscommon, in the Oklahoma dust, on the road, riding the rails, riding the bike, together.

—I love you.

I looked at the creases that met right under her eye. I looked for the one that had once pulled up her smile. But nothing happened, she stayed absolutely still.

It didn't matter.

I passed on more messages, each one as bland and harmless as the last. *Are the conditions affordable?* I waited for the question that would feel like the real one, the question that would rattle history. For a while, in late '85, they came fast, like the rush before Christmas – *Can you bring your people along with this? Will deniability be shared?* I reminded myself I was probably juggling with war and peace, and that people would continue to breathe and cope because each question bred another question. I even had to remind myself that my daughter might be gagged and strapped to a chair somewhere, in a damp house built on the dark side of a mountain, alive for only as long as I kept running with the messages.

Then they stopped, the replies and counter-replies – the negotiations stopped.

I wasn't needed any more, or the last question I'd carried – I couldn't remember it – had been the wrong one. There'd been no slowing down – the shooting and bombing, the headlines. There was no ceasefire, or intensification. A mortar bomb sent into an R.U.C. barracks wall; a Saracen driven over a kid who'd fallen asleep on the street after his first pints; a body found wrapped in black plastic after the wind took the top off some sand dunes – an informer, buried seven years before. They left a ham and a big chicken on the step, and a small net of sprouts, two days before Christmas. And a card: *Tiocfaidh ár Lá – Beannachtaí na Nollag.* I phoned Chicago on Christmas Day but no one answered.

I sat beside the duck pond for hours, in January and February of 1986, froze the bollix off myself, but no one sat beside me. Except a nun from the convent up the road who took my hand out of my jacket pocket and asked me if I knew what hypothermia was.

—Yeah, I lied.

—You know what it means?

—I'm grand.

—It'll creep up on you if you're not wrapped up, she said.

—Won't be the first thing to creep up on me, I told her.

She smiled. (I looked up *hypothermia* on my way home. The library was full – the unemployed staying out of the cold. There was a whole family at one table, living a quieter version of their home life.)

—I'll leave you to it, she said.

I didn't answer.

I gave up on the pond when kids on the mitch started throwing stones at the ice just in front of my feet. They looked like they were still in primary school. They smoked and spat and didn't feel the cold.

I sat at home. I went up to Howth. I phoned Chicago. I phoned Roscommon.

—No sign of her, Mister Smart; sorry.

—Okay.

—You must be worried.

—I am.

—Have you let the Guards know?

—I have, yeah.

—She'll be grand.

—I know.

—Bye, so.

The bug was back in Miss O'Shea's ear but there was no one listening. I was yesterday's man. They were meeting face to face. Or the last message I'd handed over had been final, wrong one. The struggle went on; the long war got longer. The man with the beard might have been caught and dealt with; he'd been disappeared into a hole in the woods somewhere, wrapped in his own black plastic. There was no leak or announcement. Nothing had happened. I listened for news of dead republicans.

The phone rang, once.

I picked it up.

—She's grand.

A man's voice, a Dublin accent. The phone was dead before I could say anything.

They still needed me. They were holding her, or she was staying away. Because there was more I'd have to do.

I waited. I had no choice.

There were the bombings, the kneecappings, the horrors that bored most men and women south of the border. It was business as usual. It was *Northern* Ireland.

I sat with Miss O'Shea. I looked at her and I never saw a Nuala. The name had changed nothing. She was still up on the crossbar, snug and wild between my legs – or dead in the bed with a bug in her ear.

The Special Branch nurse was gone. Her replacement wasn't double-jobbing, as far as I could make out. She was only a nurse, although the wire still led to Miss O'Shea's ear and no one seemed to have touched it.

—I'm tired, I said.

I was sitting at the end of the bed, between Dun Laoghaire and Howth.

—Life-tired, I told her.—Not just ordinary tired.

I waited.

—I wish it would stop.

And I meant it. Whatever I'd been dreaming of, my place in history, hauling my whole life onto the back of the republican truck: there was nothing left.

I phoned Chicago every Sunday. I phoned Roscommon.

—Is that Mister Smart?

—Yeah. Hello.

—No word here, Mister Smart.

—Thanks.

—She'll be grand.

—I know.

It didn't matter.

I was tired.

—It's the right time, I told Miss O'Shea.—There's nothing left.

I'd lie beside my wife and turn off the glucose.

But I couldn't. It was sentimental shite; I didn't want to die.
I wanted to see Saoirse and I didn't want to leave my wife alone.
I was curious when I could concentrate. I was angry. Angry enough
to stay awake. Angry enough to sit all night, in the dark, facing
the door.

Anger kept me alive. Anger kept me awake.

But he was there before I knew it. He was standing over me;
I knew it was him. The shock and the cold hauled me up from
the dead.

—You shouldn't be falling asleep in this cold, he said.

His breath licked my face.

—You should be in your bed.

—I wasn't asleep.

—No, he said.—Right enough.

He stepped away.

—I'm turning the light on, he said.

—Alright.

He was smiling when the light screamed across the room. He
was looking well. He had a grey scarf, and an overcoat that had
never seen a ditch.

—Where's my daughter?

—She's fine.

—Where is she?

He was still smiling.

—She's where she wants to be, he said.

—I want to see her.

—Aye.

Still smiling.

—And you will.

—When?

—Christ, Henry, you've central heating and all in here now. Why aren't you using it?

—When?

He waited till he was ready, when he knew I was going to hear him.

—It's all mapped out, he said.

He walked to the sink.

—I'll wet the tea, he said.—Then I've some things to tell you.

He turned off the tap and plugged in the kettle. I watched him bend a bit, to listen for the whisper of the kettle as it got to work. He turned away and looked at me.

—All set.

—Where is she?

—I'll say it once. She's safe.

—Where is she?

—Jesus, Henry, you know the score. If I say she's safe, she's safe. You'll be having tea, hey?

—No.

—Fine. I'll make some for the boys, then we can chat.

He wasn't alone. There'd be a driver outside, and another man. Two trusted men, willing to die. He moved now like a man who was protected. The stiffness was out of him. A born leader, he knew how much sugar his men took.

—D'you have a tray?

—No, I said.

—I'm betting you do, he said.—But alright.

He opened the front door and went back to the counter for two mugs.

He was back quickly. He pushed the door shut.

—Right.

He went to the counter and picked up his own mug. Then he came back to me and pulled out a chair.

—Are you ready for action, Henry?

I was all set to hug him – but only for a second.

—What action?

He'd turned on the heat but I was still stiff – solid; even talk felt like something that could break me.

—Right, he said.—Here's what. We need to resurrect you.

—Another commemoration?

—Aye.

—No.

312

—Aye.

He stared at me.

—That war's over, Henry.

I hadn't heard the morning's news but I knew he was lying.

—The country's been united?

—Aye.

—You're talking through your hole.

He picked up his mug. I expected him to swing it at me, to let it break against my head.

—I can see why you might say that, right enough.

He drank, and put the mug back on the table.

—It wouldn't be most people's analysis, he said.

He still held onto the mug.

—It'll take a while for the news to settle, he said.—Especially as there won't be any news. Not for a long while yet.

He picked up the mug, but he didn't drink.

—The armed struggle will continue, he said.—But the struggle is actually over.

—Look it, son. I heard this shite before.

—I can see why you might think that as well, he said.—But you're wrong.

He knocked back the last of his tea.

—Listen now, he said.—What's the war been about?

He'd caught me; I didn't know – I knew, but I couldn't think.

—I'll tell you, he said.—It's about what being Irish means.

—I don't get you.

—The armed struggle has been about ownership of the definition of Irishness. It has never been about territory. Republicans do not want to send unionists back to Scotland. Some among us think we do but I'm telling you now, we don't. You understand that.

—Yeah.

—Aye, he said.—It's a small island but there's room for us all. There was water in his eyes.

—There's room for us all, he said.—Now.

—Why the war then?

—I told you, Henry. The copyright. The brand. Who owns Irishness, hey?

He was looking for an answer.

—All of us.

—No, he said.—Not at all. We do.

—We?

—Aye. We. Us. *Sinn Féin*.

He smiled.

—We've battered all other definitions into submission.

The smile was off him now.

—There'll be talks, he said.—Dublin will talk to London. London will talk to unionism, and Dublin will talk to nationalism. They'll all agree to talk to republicanism. In secret, mind. None of this will ever have happened, until it's over. The armed struggle will continue. We've some right fireworks coming in from Libya. We'll have our own Tet Offensive. D'you mind that one, Henry?

I nodded.

—Our people will think it's Tet, he said.—But it won't be. It'll be a bargaining ploy, that's all. There'll be talk about respect for other traditions on the island. But —

He picked up the mug.

—There's only one tradition that matters now. There's only one oppressed people. Only one war.

He looked into the mug and shrugged.

—And only one victor. We've won.

He put the mug back down.

—There's only one Ireland.

He smiled.

—You ask a Yank what an Irishman is, what'll he tell you?

—I don't know.

—You do, right enough. The man he'll describe will be you or me. Republican, Catholic, oppressed by Britain, fond of a jar, game for a laugh, prone to violence. But only for political reasons. He'll fight to the death. For freedom. He's a great lad. I'm right?

—Probably.

—Aye. All over the world, the same story. Republican, Catholic, downtrodden but fighting. That's us, Henry. All of us.

—What about the Prods and them?

—Not Irish, he said.

—Just like that?

—Aye, he said.—There is no other definition. We should have a drink to celebrate.

—There's nothing in the house.

—Too early anyway. I'm not much of a drinker.

He stood up. He clapped his hands and shook the house.

314

—But we'll have more tea.

—Fuck tea.

—Hey!

I looked at him.

—Republican, Catholic, tea-drinking Irishman. You don't have a choice.

The smile was huge again, a sudden gash across his face.

He got the kettle going and found two clean mugs and teabags.

—You don't drink tea but you've a house full of teabags.

—My daughter.

—Aye. Of course.

—Where is she?

He didn't answer. He wasn't going to.

—We actually had it won years ago, he said.

He brought the mugs to the table. He put one beside me.

—There you go.

He sat down.

—I'm going to tell you a wee story. Drink your tea.

—I don't drink tea.

—The story, he said.—D'you want to hear it?

—Okay.

—Right. D'you mind a man called John Ford?

—I do, yeah.

—You knew him.

—I did, yeah.

—You knew him well. You had long chats, great debate and analysis. There was talk of a film.

—Yeah.

—Your story.

—Yeah.

—*The Quiet Man*. One man's story. The struggle, the fight and ultimate betrayal. The failure of the revolution.

He waited.

—Yeah.

—We couldn't have that, he said.

I was such a fuckin' eejit.

—There's sugar in your tea, Henry, he said.—Two spoons. You look like you might want it.

I picked up the mug. It was heavy and masked the shakes. I sipped.

It wasn't too bad.

—You weren't fuckin' born, I said.

—I was, in actual fact, he said.—I was just a wee fella. But it's not about me. I took up the flame when my time came. And I'll be passing it on. Eventually.

I took more of the tea.

—He was a good man, Ford, he said.—Well liked by our people beyond. And he let us read the script. An early draft, like. It was dynamite. There's a man I know read it. He said it was great. He cried when he read it, he'd tell you that himself. It was exactly as it had happened. But —

He smiled.

—It would have been the last nail in the coffin of republicanism. A bit like a film about the Apaches. The end of a way of life and no one left to bring it back. And no Apaches starring in it.

—What happened?

—You know what happened.

—I don't.

—Aye. You do. He made *The Quiet Man*.

—Why?

—To show a place worth fighting for.

He said it quietly, like he was telling me something true.

—Something beautiful that was going to be destroyed.

—For fuck sake.

—Aye, he said.

It made sense, but not complete sense.

—De Valera's Ireland, he said.—Comely maidens and the rest of it. Maureen O'Hara. They don't come comelier than her.

—Did she know?

—Not at all, he said.—No one knew. Just Mister Ford and our people.

—He never told me.

—He was no informer.

—The cunt.

—I can see why you might say that, right enough.

—The fuckin' cunt.

—Aye.

—It was only a fuckin' film.

—That's true, he said.—But it turned out well. Better than we could have hoped for. Have you seen it, hey?

—I have, yeah.

—It's beautiful. Isn't it? Gorgeous.

316

—It's shite.

—Aye. But it's beautiful.

—Yeah.

—It's beautiful and funny and carefree, he said.—It's Ireland.

—No, it isn't.

—Oh, it is. As far as millions of people were concerned. And they travelled here to see it with their own eyes. And we tried to live up to it. Certainly, you people down here in the Free State did. Bord Fáilte and the rest of it. Ireland was *The Quiet Man*. Not Dublin or Belfast, or the slums or the queues for the boat out. Or the true story of Henry Smart. That'll be a different day's work. A different film altogether.

I drank some more of the tea – I had to do something.

—So, he said.—*The Quiet Man*, Henry. It's the story of Ireland. Catholics and Protestants side by side, in harmony. Fishing and horse racing. It's every German's idea of Paradise. And it's sexy as well.

He blushed – he actually did. The blood crept up out of his beard. He got in behind his mug for a few seconds.

—I still don't get it, I said.

—Heaven on earth, he said.—The Ireland your generation fought for, Henry. And the Brits went and destroyed it.

—What?

—That's what people saw. Bloody Sunday, the hunger strikes. Heaven destroyed. All because the Brits wouldn't pack up and leave.

—You planned it?

—Aye.

—No.

—We did, aye. It's not the whole picture, mind. But fundamentally that was the plan.

—Fuckin' hell.

—Maureen O'Hara versus Margaret Thatcher. Which one of those girls would you be up for, Henry?

I smiled – I couldn't help it.

—We were always winning, he said.—Do you understand?

—Yeah, I said.—I do.

—You're impressed?

—No.

—Ah, well. But you should be pleased.

—De Valera's Ireland?

—Any Ireland we want, he said.—We hold the copyright. We can do what we like with it. In time.

—Time?

—Aye. These talks coming up. No one knows about them yet. Including most of the people who'll be talking. They'll never talk to terrorists. And they mean it sincerely. Not the Brits, mind. They've always talked to us. I mean loyalism. But they'll talk, even Paisley, and that will be that. Over. They'll talk, so they'll surrender. They can wear their sashes and march all year and no one will care.

—You have it all mapped out.

—Aye.

—For fuck sake.

—It won't be overnight, mind. We have a deadline. You can guess what it is, Henry.

—Yeah, I said.—I can.

—Well?

—2016.

—Aye.

The day was well on. We'd been sitting there for hours. My tea was cold but he was right; I needed the sugar. I held my head right back – heard the crack – so I could catch the sludge from the bottom of the mug.

—So, I said.—There'll be a 32-County Republic by 2016.

—Aye, he said.—But not *by*. In.

—It's thirty years away.

—Aye.

—And you're saying you've won.

—We have, aye.

—So —

—Why the wait?

—Yeah.

—Well, we've won but no one knows. Our analysis would be considered mad, especially within republicanism. There'd be trouble if it was broadcast today or tomorrow. It'll need time. There's a lot to do. Your work's not finished yet, Henry.

—And what else?

—We wouldn't want the Declaration in any other year.

—Even if you don't live?

—I told you, he said.—It's not about me. I'll die happy knowing it's coming.

—Well, I won't be there, anyway.

—You never know.

He stood up.

—Your country needs you again, Henry. Up you get.

Did I have a choice? I still don't know. But I stood up and I got my coat and hat.

—Will I bring the leg?

—Aye, do.

That was March 1986.

He took me to a commemoration in a cemetery just north of the border. We stood at the grave of a kid who'd been shot three years before. I was keeping my daughter alive. That was what held me. The chance that they'd kill her if I refused, kill her and call her an informer, put the cardboard sign around her neck.

But no. It was freezing but I loved being there. I was back. I stood as firm as I could manage beside the man who delivered the oration. *We stand for an Ireland free, united, socialist and Gaelic.* I'd seen him before in the hunger strike days. A man who looked cheerful and dangerous. I'd see a lot more of him during the next months, through Easter Week and the marching season. He smelt of Old Spice and gun oil. He shook my hand – he shook everyone's hand. He held mine firm, and I loved it.

No. I hated standing there, propped up by the boys, and looking back out at the adoring, stupid eyes of the men hidden in their balaclavas.

—We didn't wear masks in my day.

—Right enough, Henry. Men were men.

—Fuckin' sure.

They laughed because I'd made them laugh. We were comrades. Rebels, revolutionaries.

Bollix.

There were the men who made the small crowds – the crowds were almost always small – the civilians, the sympathisers, and their sons, and their grandsons in buggies. And the women, bitter and cold, carrying their dead sons and husbands on their backs; hard-faced and magnificent. And their daughters in black coats, girls who'd been away to university, who'd tasted life beyond the parish, who'd been happily felt up by hands that weren't always Catholic; home now, teachers – guilty, angry, lost, whistled at by soldiers, winked at by men who'd grown up with their fathers. And little boys and girls, their daddies in the graves they stood on. All holding out for their united Ireland. Listening out for skids and slammed doors, or headlines that would tell them that the man or girl they loved wouldn't be coming home for tea. Who sacrificed their lives for the better life they'd never get. I watched them listen to the cheerful, dangerous man, the man they loved and called by his first name, as he fed them the shite they'd grown up needing. To a dozen in North Kerry, to a hundred in Parnell Square, to three hundred in Bodenstown, to two thousand in Milltown. The message was consistent. The armed struggle would continue until the Republic was a fact. I saw them looking and believing. They were keeping their dead alive. And I knew that, by being there, facing them, in my trenchcoat – it was new but battered, to look like it had been worn through a mist of blood and brick dust – with the famous leg, my piece of the true cross, I knew that I was lying and destroying them. I was part of a conspiracy that would have me killed if I revealed it, would have me killed if it was ever revealed. But I saw them look and I looked straight back.

I didn't see Dinny Archer.

—Is he dead?

—Not yet.

—Where is he?

—We're keeping him away. Encouraging him to stay out of the cold.

—Why?

—He wouldn't accept our analysis of the current situation.

—Have you told him?

—No.

The cheerful, dangerous man – I liked him. I knew I'd have died for him if we'd known each other seventy years before.

—You're Denis Archer now, Henry, he told me.—You're our link to the First Dáil.

The time had come.

—I wasn't there, I told him – just him. I spoke very quietly.

—We know that, he said, quietly too.—Don't worry. We've always known that. But so have you. There's no harm done.

—It's all a fuckin' con job, I said.

—Cop yourself on, he said.—You need a fuckin' pint.

Six months of gravesides. They were leading me to something.

Taking me across the country, to the places in the south where guns and men were hidden, but especially to the mad spots in the north. The Republican clubs and the G.A.A. clubs, towns that meant nothing to me as the car charged through. North of the border, the key men never travelled with me. I was in the car with my son – that was the story – any one of seven men. Trusted men who could have been touts.

—Talk about nothing, I was told.—And never answer a question if they ask one. They're good lads and torture wouldn't shake them. But other things might.

This was the cheerful man again.

—The gee, Henry, he said.—It's downed manys the good Irishman.

He slapped my shoulder.

—Am I right?

—Yeah.

I crossed the border more times in those months than I'd ever done before, even during the hunger strikes. No car I was in was ever stopped at a checkpoint. I slept in houses that were never raided. I'd get out of a car, alone, and there'd be a key man – there were five key men, five men who *knew* – beside me. We'd walk together to the grave. We'd stand together, in the rain, and then, as the year went on, the high heat of midday. They ran me ragged. I loved it.

—The war's over, I told her.

There was something. Far less than a flicker. But something moved, or threatened to. At her eye, right under her skin. Something tiny buried in there, tested a wing, pressed against her skin.

—The war's over, I said.—No fourth green field.

It moved again. Bent the wing.

—Yeah, I said.—It's over.

Nothing this time. Her face was the same, the red mask it had been for years. But I'd just seen the life beneath it.

—After all that, I said.—All for nothing.

The thing jumped again.

—So there you go. It's over.

I heard it. The mouth moved – I saw it.

—No!

Almost silent, but a roar.

321

I laughed.

—You're in there.

I held her hand.

—You are.

I felt it. I looked down at my hand and saw her fingers squeeze or try to squeeze.

The cruelty was gone. I quickly told her a different truth.

—The war's over, I said.—They've gone.

The wings fluttered, the fingers shifted.

—The British are getting onto the boats in Belfast, I said.—You should see it.

She'd heard me.

And she died.

Strange that I knew it, but I did. Nothing went slack, no shock passed across her, she didn't bare her teeth or howl. She was just gone. Dead.

I sat there for a good long while. I still held the hand.

The good news – my lie – had killed her. Released her. There was no new serenity on the face. I knew she was dead but no one else did. The eye was still open. She was as stiff and as livid as ever.

—We're free, I told her now.

A simple lie.

I walked in front of the men who carried her to the republican plot in Glasnevin. I walked past old and new republicans, and young women who were claiming the women of 1916 as their own, the women who'd been hidden, no streets or train stations named after them, the names forgotten, except on the side of a swimming baths or the odd block of flats. They stood as we buried their new discovery, one of their dead heroines who'd been living all along.

There were as many women as men but my daughter wasn't one of them. The funeral had brought her mother back. She was Our Lady of the Machine-Gun again. Her place in the story was safe.

—We're here today, here in this hallowed place, to celebrate a life that was dedicated to one ideal. An Ireland free. She almost saw it. The struggle will continue.

I spoke the words. They were cracked and difficult. I saw faces around me trying to catch their meaning.

—Nuala O'Shea will not be disappointed.

322

I saw hands join, then the applause that lasted minutes. Women queued to shake my hand.

—That was beautiful, thank you.

The struggle will continue. I told the lie, to make up for the lie that I'd told her. And I'd called her Nuala. Calling her *Miss* would have caused a riot, even in a graveyard. These young women owned her now, not me.

There was one of them now, in front of me. A skinny young one, with hair like Stan Laurel's, dyed pink.

—I'll be calling her Nuala Smart in my thesis. Is that okay?

I nodded.

—Grand.

There was jostling, pushing, and another woman was there. I spoke first.

—Saoirse.

—I know what you're doing.

—Do you?

—Yes, she said.—I do.

—You don't approve.

—I do not.

—Then why have you been hiding?

That much was clear. She was standing in front of me, so she hadn't been gagged and locked away.

—Why aren't you shouting about it? I asked.

We'd been given the room to speak. The crowd was still there but we had an island beside the open grave.

—I can't, she said.

—Why not?

—You know.

—I don't.

She stared right at me; I saw the water in her eyes.

—They said they'd kill you if I talk.

She was gone. Lifted – gone. Nowhere in the crowd.

PART FOUR

12

The car stopped beside another car. I watched a back door of the other car open, and the man with the beard climbed out.

He got in beside me.

—Henry, *a chara*. How are you?

—Grand.

—We need to have a wee chat.

We were going to the Mansion House. Back to the birthplace of our religion.

—There's no need to be nervous, he said.—You'll be with friends.

He'd been there himself. He'd just come away. It wasn't going well. Decades of anger, north–south resentment – the smart money was on a split.

—That's one thing I always promised myself, he said.

We were back on a main road, flying past an empty industrial estate.

—I would never allow another split in republicanism.

He was silent for a long time.

—Your input will shift this, Henry, he said.—Don't let me down.

Two minutes from the Mansion House.

—You'll be asked a question, he said.—You'll give the answer.

—Will Dinny Archer be there?

—No, he said.—Denis isn't well.

He looked at me.

—It's time the dead handed over to the living, he said.—What do you think?

I nodded.

—Right enough, he said.

We were there.

—A simple question and a simple answer, he said.—If we don't get the result —

He didn't finish; he didn't need to.

The passenger doors were open and a hard, smiling man helped me out of the car.

It was cold, November, and dark although it wasn't late.

I went up steps. Hands helped me along. Down a small corridor, into the Round Room. The applause was there before I was. I walked straight into it. I could feel it against my skin as I walked between the ranks of standing men and women.

I was doing the right thing.

More steps, to a stage. I got up them on my own. I pushed back a helping hand. The cheerful man was there, and other men and women I'd seen before or hadn't seen.

I walked over to a microphone. I knew I was doing it right.

I stood there.

The applause died. Some of the men and women sat, then all of them sat.

The cheerful man looked dangerous, stern. He took the place in front of the microphone.

—The delegates here at the Árd Fheis have made it plain that they welcome Volunteer Henry Smart.

More applause, but this time it didn't stay. There was a crackle in the air now, a sudden chill in the heat and cigarette smoke.

—We've been debating this issue for five hours, *a cháirde*. Henry Smart is no stranger to this great room. I don't need to remind you all of his position in republicanism. Henry and Denis Archer were in this room when the Republic was declared.

I listened carefully to every word – I *looked* at every word.

—Denis, unfortunately, isn't well enough to be here with us today. We send him our fraternal greetings and wish him a speedy and full recovery.

Hands behind me clapped.

—But we're blessed, said the cheerful man.—Because we do have Henry Smart here.

He turned to me.

—Henry, he said.—*A chara*. As you know, the motion before the delegates today is that Sinn Féin should drop its longstanding and consistent opposition to running candidates in the elections to the Free State parliament, the so-called Dáil.

I was still there, still alive.

—Henry, are you in agreement with this motion?

He stepped back and I took his place. I looked over the room and every person in it. I made sure they all knew I was talking to them.

—Yeah, I said.—I am.

I didn't stay for the vote. I didn't have to.

I'd done the right thing.

I knew it then. I know it now.

The war raged on but the end had started. They voted to run candidates in the south – to recognise the southern state. The wedge had been driven in by me. The Armalite and the ballot box – you know the rest of the story. It was an old story before it became the news.

The war went on, because it had to – the pressure had to be maintained. They tore up Enniskillen, they made human bombs out of terrified husbands, they kneecapped men because they didn't like them. They smuggled diesel, they shifted heroin. They killed children in Warrington and shopkeepers in London. There were diehard millionaires who had to be appeased. There were mad fuckers, clowns who thought the dead deserved more than the living; they had to be brought along or bumped off. The splits had to be dealt with and corralled. Good suits had to be bought, bad hands had to be shaken.

I thought I'd die. I'm well past old. But I'm still here. I can walk if I'm picked up out of the bed. My daughter is almost ninety but she can do that, when she wants to. I can go as far as the front door. I can sit on a warm day.

They think they have me. They call – they check. There are six years to go, to 2016. They think I'll be there, on the podium with them, declaring the next and final republic.

But I won't be. I'm going to die. Tonight. I have to die before my daughter.

But I think that every night. I close my eyes.

This is the last time. The last time I'll let myself be picked up off the bed. She'll understand. She's tired too.

I'll close my eyes, finally, tonight. It's early afternoon, a nice day. I've seven hours left, maybe eight. I've lived a life. I'm a hundred and eight. I'm Henry Smart.

To the authors of the following books, thank you:

Garry Wills, *John Wayne's America*; Gerald Peary (ed.), *John Ford Interviews*; Joseph McBride, *Searching for John Ford*; Harry Carey Jr, *Company of Heroes*; Lindsay Anderson, *About John Ford*; Dan Ford, *Pappy: The Life of John Ford*; Maureen O'Hara, *Tis Herself*; Robert Parrish, *Growing Up in Hollywood* (1976); Scott Eyman/Paul Duncan, *John Ford: The Complete Films*; Maurice Walsh, *The Quiet Man*; Des MacHale, *The Complete Guide to the Quiet Man*; Des MacHale, *Picture the Quiet Man*; Luke Gibbons, *The Quiet Man*; Gerry McNee, *In the Footsteps of 'The Quiet Man'*; Don Mullan, *The Dublin and Monaghan Bombings*; Derek Lundy, *Men that God Made Mad*; Ed Moloney, *A Secret History of the IRA*; Richard English, *Armed Struggle*; Kevin Toolis, *Rebel Hearts*; Henry McDonald, *Gunsmoke and Mirrors*; Danny Morrison, *Then the Walls Came Down*; Eamon Collins, *Killing Rage*; Martin Dillon, *The Trigger Men*; Slavoj Žižek, *Violence*.